LIFE SUPPORT

Secret Operations

A House Divided

by Joseph L. Kellogg

Joseph L. Kellogg is an author and chemist living in Alabama with his wife and two corgis.

You can see more of his stories at www.JosephLKellogg.com

Cover art by www.100covers.com

This story is a work of fiction. Any resemblance to real persons or events are purely coincidental.

ISBN: 979-8-9854727-2-1

To Julie

PART ONE

SECRET OPERATIONS

Chapter One

Father Tanner pulled back the torn flap of sun-beaten skin and probed into the wound with his forceps. Deep red blood oozed from the injury, washing over the dried blood that coated the nearby skin which was mottled with sand and dust. The nurse on the other side of the table suctioned away the blood with a plastic tube stained with years of repeated use. A curtain hung to Tanner's side, shielding the patient's face from view, but he still heard the patient's moans of pain through gritted teeth. Tanner threw up a quick prayer for forgiveness for the pain he was causing as he operated; a stick clamped between the teeth was a poor substitute for anesthetic, but it was all they had at this point.

"It looks like the shrapnel nicked an artery," Tanner said, "but it's holding it closed for now. Get the clamp ready, Ghenni."

The masked nurse grabbed an instrument from the table, tensed in anticipation of the next command. Tanner gripped the offending piece of metal, and carefully coaxed it out of its place. More blood squirted out of the artery, staining the patient's pant leg and spattering on the battered metal operating table. Tanner tossed the shard into a dish of water.

"Clamp," he said, keeping his eyes on the patient as he held his hand out. Ghenni passed it to him, and Tanner placed it on the artery to stop the flow of blood as he continued in his work. With quick, practiced movements he ran a thread through the vessel's ruptured wall, slowly pulling the hole closed. After a few more stitches, he re-examined his work, admiring the small amount of order he was able to bring to the chaos of mangled flesh. He removed the clamp, and the artery surged with blood again, but the stitches held under the pressure. After closing his eyes for a quick prayer of thanksgiving, Tanner sutured the wound, backed by a chorus of pained whimpers.

As Ghenni began cleaning the patient, rinsing the instruments, and loading them into the autoclave for the next surgery, Father Tanner turned his attention to the piece of shrapnel. A quick shake rinsed the thick liquid off, dyeing the water red. Then he pulled the shard of metal out and wiped it off with a dirty cloth. It was thin, with twisted, jagged edges from the terrible force of the explosion that ripped it apart. Inscrutable etching marked its surface; Tanner scrubbed it until he could make out the minuscule writing: a serial number in Arabic numerals. With a sigh, he pulled off his surgical mask and trudged back toward his office.

Father Tanner's slow footsteps in the hallway were drowned out by the dull roar of crying children, shouting parents, and patients moaning with pain and nausea. The last of the battle casualties were stabilized, but that left dozens of non-emergency cases backed up. Twisted limbs, grotesque tumors, and deformed faces all waiting for him, for a second chance at a normal life. They came from hundreds of miles away, from remote villages without so much as an herbalist, or from other cities where all the doctors were conscripted into the endless war with the Consortium. But they would have to wait a while longer. Without anesthetics, he couldn't risk any "elective" surgeries. He sank against the wall, just out sight of the open waiting room door, letting the chaotic noise was over him as he pulled off his bifocals, rubbed his eyes, and ran his fingers through his close-cropped, graying hair.

He tried to remind himself that all this pain and suffering was just a symptom. The outward groans of a world that was cursed and broken. The mangled bodies were the result of mangled souls, fighting their fellow man for farmland and water rights. Children were born into a fallen, sinful world with twisted bodies, then abandoned by parents who saw them only as burdens. Father Tanner's primary goal here wasn't to bring physical healing, but spiritual. That kind of healing didn't require expensive equipment or drugs, it only required the simple truth of God. But that goal seemed to be falling further and further into the background as the physical maladies piled up in the clinic. He was barely treading water in the operating room, and after fourteen straight hours of surgery, he was still farther behind than the day before. With more supplies, he could run two operating tables at the same time, but the latest shipment was late. Again.

The slap of hurried footsteps on the stone floor snapped him out of his brooding, and he quickly stood resolutely upright. Ghenni hustled briskly around the corner, his surgical mask gone, showing the *glia* that dangled like seaweed from his bulldog-like face.

"Any news of the shipment?" Father Tanner asked.

"Not yet," Ghenni said, "and we're running out of time. We've been running without proper anesthesia for a week, and we're almost out of antibiotics. We'll probably be without those within two of your weeks."

"What about other drugs?"

"Our supply with those is holding out for now, for the little difference it is. My people are killing each other too fast for anyone to get sick."

"Apparently not fast enough for somebody," replied Father Tanner. He fished in the pocket of his lab coat for the piece of shrapnel and showed it to Ghenni. "You see the serial number?"

Ghenni took the piece from his hand to peer closer. "This is English numbers?"

Tanner nodded. "Someone is supplying them with Earth weapons. Perhaps a grenade of some sort, by the looks of it."

"Is this some sort of espionage with your Consortium?" Ghenni's face flashed with anger briefly. His planet had been been dragged into the space age when they were conscripted a few decades ago into a massive totalitarian alliance of multiple alien species that spanned half of known space. Even though their conflict with Earth's own alliance of planets had been imposed on them from outside, Ghenni was young enough to have been raised by Brotherhood propaganda.

"Not *my* Consortium; I'm not much more welcome there than on your planet. But no, the CIP has much more efficient ways to carry out their business." Tanner plunged his hands back into his coat pockets, so Ghenni wouldn't see him clenching his fists. "If I were a gambling man, I'd wager it was a smuggler or independent arms dealer, willing to equip warring clans to wipe each other out, just to line his own pockets."

Ghenni snarled. "I pray Mennas chokes him of his own purse strings."

Father Tanner grunted. "I don't think he needs help from your gods. He will be judged, in this life or the next."

"What do we do in the meantime?"

Tanner pinched his nose as he considered the problem for a moment. "There's a woman who lives nearby; she's an herbalist. I'll have her take Andrew out and see if they can find some traditional medicines to fill in the gaps. I'm going to go into town and see if I can find some proper supplies."

"Good luck," Ghenni said, glancing out the window at the bright Trenthan sun and gusts of sandy wind. "You're going to need it."

As the first traces of atmosphere began to register on the control panel in front of Damien, two yellow lights on the far end flickered and winked out into darkness. The pile of plastic dishes, encrusted with days-old traces of reconstituted protein, shimmied down the last few inches of the console as it vibrated, then fell to the floor of the cockpit with a clatter. He added the inertial buffers to his mental list of things that needed replacing once he landed. When he reached over to activate the landing controls, a few of the lights remained dim.

"Uh, Eve?" he asked, flicking the switch back and forth. "The fine control thrusters..."

"Yeah, I see it down here," she replied, her voice filtering through the intercom. "I told you that scrap dealer looked shady."

"Great," Damien said, engaging the engines to slow the ship's descent. "You can lecture me on shopping later. Right now I need you to fix those thrusters before we try to land."

"You're kidding, right? I can't fix those in the next few minutes; it would probably take a spacewalk just to diagnose the problem. You're going to have to abort the reentry and go into orbit."

Damien watched the dishes vibrate across the floor, dragged toward the rear door by the slightly out-of-calibration artificial gravity. Then he glanced back at the rapidly expanding planet on the viewscreen. "Yeah, about that... I don't think the inertial buffers are up to a course change that sharp. Even if the hull stayed intact, we'd be splattered all over the ceiling, and the maid's not due until Thursday. We're pretty committed at this point."

"Brilliant," Eve growled. "So what's your plan?"

"I'm thinking, I'm thinking..."

Damien ran through the options in his head. He could still slow down just fine with the primary thrusters, but they didn't have the kind of precision he needed to guide the *Malika* down for a gentle landing. He could go for a water landing somewhere; they'd *survive*, but there was no way he could get her out again, and life without his ship just wasn't worth thinking about. That left the repulsors. They were made to deflect micrometeorites, but a planet was just a big one of those, right?

"Repulsors are still online, yeah?"

"You're not serious," Eve said. It was more of a statement than a question.

"Yeah, yeah, yeah. It's gonna be a little rough, alright?"

"Can you at least promise you'll get us down in one piece?" Eve asked.

"Right, one piece. Two pieces, max."

In the main viewing window, Damien saw the landscape slowly opening before him. Clouds whiffed by into the periphery of his view, and in the center was the bustling city of Calchassa, now just a splotch on the pale brown plains surrounding it. Green patches of farmland and scraggly forest dotted the scene, gradually slipping out of view as he made his approach.

He keyed some buttons on his control panel, and an icon popped up in the corner of the viewing window, blinking yellow, then blue.

"Calchassa Spaceport Authority," Damien said into the radio, "this is the BCS *Malika*, requesting a landing space." The ship continued to shake as it was buffeted by the rapidly thickening atmosphere, and a loud crash sounded behind him as a rifle fell from its rack and clattered against the inside of the gun cabinet. After a few long moments, the icon on the screen expanded into a set of coordinates, and Damien ported them to his navigation controls with a swipe of his finger.

Individual streets were now visible, and the activity of ships buzzing around was clearly centered on a wide-open space on the edge of the city. Damien continued to slow the ship, giving it quick, measured bursts on the remaining thrusters to guide it into the proper landing site. Eventually, he could make out individual humanoid figures on the spaceport's packed-dirt floor, along with the white chalk outlines that parceled it out into landing spaces.

By now, the *Malika* had slowed to a crawl, and Damien tried to keep her as steady as possible, but she swayed up, down, and side-to-side as he made repeated over-corrections with the primary thrusters. Soon he was low enough to make out individual faces, and out of the corner of his eye he saw the crowd of other travelers and attendants all stopping to watch the spectacle of his clumsy landing. Crews of the ships in adjacent spaces waved their arms to warn him away, and he gave one of them a friendly wave back through the viewing window. *Malika* lurched to the side as he pushed it into his assigned space, and the crowd recoiled. Finally, he switched over to the remaining fine control thrusters. The only ones left were on the back of the ship, and he kept the repulsors running on the front end. As the back eased gently down, the front dropped freely, slowed by the smallest bursts Damien could manage on the primary thrusters. Finally the repulsor field meet the ground, and alarms wailed in time with the flashing red light on his panel.

"Come on, baby," he muttered, "I know you've got it in you."

When the back end was settled, Damien flicked off the repulsors. The alarms went silent, but his stomach lurched as the cockpit fell. It shuddered briefly as the landing leg hit the ground, and Damien realized he was holding his breath. He released it, and the ship immediately dropped again as the leg buckled beneath the weight. A puff of dust kicked up in front of the cockpit, and the metal hull settled and cooled with a few muffled clangs and pops. The crowd outside dissipated within moments; in a spaceport frequented by criminals, it was best not to get caught gawking too much.

Damien shook his head, slapped his face a few times, and let out a whoop of triumph. Then he sank back into the battered leather captain's chair. That was a close one, even for him. After catching his breath, he got up and briefly considered cleaning before disembarking. His dishes were scattered across the metal floor and onto the tattered rug. Something was starting to smell, too. Some old laundry was draped over the empty co-captain's chair, and a lot of the labels on the instrument panel were fading and peeling. But all that could wait until after he had a job. He heard footsteps in the hallway behind him, so he jumped up to his feet and kicked the used dishes off to the side. Just as the path from his chair to the door was clear, it slid open with a *thunk*.

"That wasn't so bad, was it?" he asked.

"No," Eve said as she slathered her face with greasy sunscreen. "You probably only took about ten years off the service life of the hull. And dear God, it smells like something died in here, and it looks like it went out with a fight. Maybe we should bump the maid up to twice a week." Her dark hair was tucked up under a wide-brimmed hat to guard against the harsh Trenthan sun.

"I'll try to find room in the budget," Damien said as he flicked a series of switches on the control panel. Indicator lights went out, and the whine of the engine gradually lessened as the flight systems powered down. Then he climbed against the new incline of the cockpit to the back wall, grabbed his belt and holster off of a hook next to the gun cabinet, and fastened it around his worn khaki pants. "But for now, I guess you'll be wanting some money to get started on repairs."

"I'd like to get paid myself for once too."

"Aw, and here I thought you stuck around because you liked me." He fished around in his pockets, produced a rolled-up wad of paper currency, and peeled off a few bills for himself before handing it over. "Don't spend it all in one place."

Eve flipped through it, then stuffed it in her pocket with a grunt. "This isn't going to fix everything on this piece of junk, you know. And it won't even *start* to fix the inter-stellar drive."

"Yeah, I know." Damien pushed past her to the exterior door around the corner. He pressed a button and the lock disengaged with a *ka-chunk*, followed by the hiss of equalizing pressures, allowing him to swing the door down and unfold it into a ramp. "I'll find work soon enough."

"Work that doesn't require an IS drive?" she asked, following him down the ramp. Eve leaned to the left to counter the forward tilt of the ship.

"Sure," Damien replied. He slipped on sunglasses as he stepped out into the blinding glare of the beating sun. His ancestors from too many generations ago to care about had come from Africa, so he waved away the sunscreen when Eve offered it to him. By this point the crowd had completely forgotten about the dramatic landing and were going about their own business. People of a variety of species bustled about the landing area; some were humanoid, others less so, and a few were concealed in bulky environment suits to protect them from the—to them—corrosive oxygen atmosphere. But most of them were Trenthans; basically human-looking, but with a droopy face kind of like a dog in an old cartoon he'd half-forgotten, which was partly obscured by their *glia*: thin, limp growths dangling from their chins and cheeks. He'd read that they were actually sexual organs, but thankfully he'd never learned details beyond that.

One of the Trenthans scurried up near the ship and planted his feet in front of Damien, giving a slight nod. He held a small electronic ledger in the crook of one arm, its screen scratched by sand, and stylus in the other hand. He gave Damien an expectant look, his hand with the stylus poised over the ledger to begin taking down information, but didn't say anything. Damien pulled a couple of bills from his pocket, careful to conceal the larger bundle, and passed them to the attendant, who slipped them discretely into his own pocket with a practiced motion.

"No questions asked, right?" Damien said.

The Trenthan nodded emphatically a few times before scampering off back toward a control tower on the outer wall. Likely, he hadn't understood a word of what Damien said, but cash had a way of transcending language barriers. The intent was clear enough: any human on Trenth would want to keep his presence officially secret, in case some goody two-shoes decided that the reward on a Consortium species was worth stopping the flow of black-market goods to Calchassa. The people here barely scraped by; most of their resources were taken at gunpoint by the Brotherhood of Allied Planets to wage a drawn-out cold war against the Consortium. The local authorities were willing to turn a blind eye to foreign smugglers like Damien as long as they kept cheap goods flowing, but if any Brotherhood brass decided to drop by, they'd be lining up to collect the reward before the G-Men did it themselves. A Consortium species in Brotherhood territory was automatically considered a spy, no trial required, and would be treated as such, regardless of his actual business there.

Damien took a step over one of the half-buried cables that ran across the ground, and surveyed the ships around him. They weren't quite as exotic as the people. Most of them were utilitarian in design, little more than jumbo-sized shipping crates with a couple of drive modules strapped on. A few spaces down, he saw a ship that could have been *Malika*'s twin: a bulky cargo hold with dual drive mods in back, a two-story living area in the middle, and a trapezoidal cockpit on the front. But this other one was a lot shinier, and more of the assorted sensors and other equipment were still attached. He glanced back at his own ship, wishing he had known her when she was still that young.

"Damien!"

He snapped out of his envious reverie, and looked back at Eve, who stood several paces back, examining the side of the ship.

"Yeah?"

"It's not going to take me long to burn through this cash you gave me. That landing leg alone with probably be a few hundred. Quit daydreaming, and start looking for work."

"Right, right," Damien muttered, trudging off toward the exit of the spaceport.

"Oh, and good luck," Eve called out as a gust of wind blew a dust cloud between them. "You're going to need it."

Chapter Two

Andrew Cho peered intently at the leaf in his hand, then took a sniff. It had a musky smell, but still held the dusty odor of the dry soil that it had grown in. Nothing else really stood out about it, but the Trenthan woman in front of him nodded excitedly as she pointed at it. Her face was withered, *glia* thin with age, and burned dark by a long life in the sun. She and her aluminum walking cane made a comical silhouette against the bright sky as she mimed vomiting onto the ground.

"Vomiting, yes," he said in English. "Is it an emetic, uh..." He trailed off, searching for the right Trenthan word for something that caused vomiting, but he kept drawing a blank. His church missions training crash course had assured him that he would pick up the language quickly once immersed, but he didn't have the knack for it. Not like Father Tanner; that man breathed languages, and his work behind the pulpit or as a counselor seemed just as effortless as his work at the operating table. No wonder he was Acting Director. Andrew, on the other hand, had spent six years studying at university and earned his Ph.D. in Pharmacology, and now he was playing charades on an alien planet with an elderly woman that he was supposed to be at war with.

Andrew steadied himself against the gnarled tree they had plucked the leaf from, glad for the oasis of meager shade in the hot, dusty countryside. Finally he gave up on finding the right word, and started trying to piece together the concept from the small, broken words he did know, supplemented by some pantomime of his own.

Finally, he said something along the lines of "stop food return journey," and pretended to eat the leaf then rub his stomach in satisfaction. At this, the old medicine woman bobbed her head excitedly and thumped her cane on the ground. "An *anti*-emetic then," he muttered. He sighed, then reached up and plucked a few more handfuls of leaves from the lowest-hanging branches of the tree. People were dying, but without the resources from that supply shipment, there wasn't much he could do about it. Unless they were dying of an upset stomach.

He shoved the medicinal plants into a bag slung over his shoulder, and brushed the dust from the knees of his cotton slacks. Taking a deep breath to steel himself against the sunlight, Andrew stepped out of the shade and began trudging back toward the mission.

Damien wandered the narrow paths of the Calchassa bazaar, jostled by Trenthans in brightly-colored wrapped garments, trying to find his bearings. All the vendors' stalls changed every time he visited, but the strings of animal carcasses, bins of vegetables, and racks of garish fabric all blended into each other anyway. Every so often the glint of metal or polished plastic caught Damien's eye: black market electronics from a dozen planets hidden sloppily behind counters. Hairy quadrupeds filed by, their short legs shuffling quickly while their elongated necks swayed from side to side. Their backs were laden with packages, and they smelled even worse than Damien's cockpit. The streets weren't labeled, at least not in any language he could read, and dried mud and clay started to all look the same after a while. The only landmark he could navigate by was the cluster of sleek high-tech skyscrapers that jutted above the skyline in the Brotherhood district, a sharp contrast to the ancient, dirty city they'd chosen as the planetary capitol.

He felt the surreptitious glances directed at him as the dirty, noisy crowds parted to let him past, but nobody dared do anything. They knew who he was, and a lot of them had bought from him in the past. A good smuggler was worth a lot more than the price on his head; anything worth buying was either appropriated for the war effort, or taxed out of any normal citizen's price range. On the other hand, nobody was going to stick their neck out in the open air to offer directions.

Down a long alley, he spotted a tall figure in a pale robe and hood. Its face was hidden, and that made Damien nervous. It could be a Brotherhood agent; he could think of one or two other humanoid species that could live unprotected on Trenth, and a couple more that could wear suits light enough to hide under that robe. He ducked into a different alley and tried to find his way again. There he spotted a stain on a wall that he recognized as matching a head he had smashed into it several years before. It was worn down by sand and bleached by the sun, but he was definitely on the right track.

The narrower streets and taller buildings here choked out the sunlight, and the bustling hordes thinned down to a slow trickle. No matter the planet, crime bosses love the shadows. The shouts of marketplace haggling and the smell of cooking meat got weaker, and Damien slowly realized where he was. Behind him, he caught another glimpse of the hooded figure crossing the alleyway, this time closer. He slid into a doorway and waited. He swore as quietly as he could; it was just his luck to get stranded on Trenth right as the Brotherhood goons decided to drop in.

He peeked out from the doorway, and only shadows crossed the alleyway now; it was empty again. He made a rough figure-eight through the mostly deserted corridors to throw the robe off his trail, in case it really was following him. When he finally reached his destination, he gave the stout wooden door a carefully timed series of knocks. The sun was completely obscured now by the tall buildings and multitude of awnings over the narrow alley, and Damien glanced nervously both ways while he waited. There was no sign of the market crowds now, except for the occasional shopper who hurried past without looking up. People knew better than to get caught loitering around Boss Galessi's place for no good reason. A few moments later, a panel slid open in the door, and he saw the scarred face of another Trenthan.

"Damien Rogers. I'm here to see Galessi about a job."

The man grunted, and the crossbar scraped against the other side of the door. As it opened to reveal two burly guards, shirtless and snarling, Damien begrudgingly unfastened his gun belt and handed it over. He wasn't really worried about his safety. After all, Galessi wasn't the double-crossing type; you didn't get far in this business with a reputation for screwing people over. He just felt a little naked when he had to go unarmed. A handful of small high windows lit the room dimly, and the beams of light filtered lazily through the smoke of the local incense that stung Damien's nose. A pair of stools flanked the door, and a few battered lockers sat on the far end. The clanking of dishes drifted in from a room on the right, set to a background of buzzing and whining music.

A pair of silk curtains to the left parted, and a strange figure walked out. It stood short for a humanoid, only about five feet tall, but with an extra set of arms. The bulky gray environment suit it wore obscured any further detail. A small blast of hot air from a cooling unit hit Damien's face as the creature brushed by him and out the door with quick, waddling steps. Luckily he couldn't see through the tinted UV-proof visor; Lippilligin faces gave Damien the willies.

With the visitor gone, the two guards gestured for Damien to go in. He brushed past their muscled torsos and ducked under the silk curtain as they held it to the side. The room was small, but luxurious, by local standards at least. Rich tapestries hung from the walls, and the wisps of incense smoke drifted among fronds of potted plants. A rather fat Trenthan man sat on a pile of sumptuous pillows in the middle of the room, with a low table set over his legs, where he peered intently at some papers. He looked up at Damien and smiled.

"Damien!" he cried out in English, but with a thick Trenthan accent. "I haven't seen you in years."

"Even more by my calendar," Damien replied.

"What can I do for you?" Galessi gestured to some unoccupied pillows beside him. Damien sat down, glad to get below the cloud of incense, and felt the material of the pillows between his fingers. It was good stuff, and probably cost a fortune to get his hands on. That's the kind of cargo Damien liked to carry: a big payout, and he could roll around in it whenever he got bored.

"Same as usual; I'm looking for work."

"There's always work for a reliable pilot like you."

"That's what I was hoping to hear," Damien said with a smile.

"Let's see," Galessi said, flipping through the papers in front of him. "I have some... 'medicinal' plant products I've been trying to get to the Tiklin system. Always good money there. I was about to give the job to a local kid, but I could be persuaded to give it to you instead, as a favor to an old friend."

"I'd love to take it on, but that's a bit out of my normal route. What kind of cut am I looking at?"

"You'd get three thousand now, and another seven thousand on completion. I assume that's satisfactory?"

"Hmm..." Damien muttered, scratching his chin. "Coming back just for the other seven would represent a lot of lost time and fuel. If you save me the return trip, I'll cut you a break and do it for nine."

Galessi snorted derisively. "You know I can't offer the whole payment up front like that. You intended to come in here and insult my intelligence?"

"No, of course not. I just thought we were friends, and past all that petty distrust. You'd be saving me time, and I'd be saving you money. It's a win for everybody."

"Why are you so hungry for cash, Damien?" Galessi peered at him, and Damien willed himself to meet his gaze without looking away. "Are you in some kind of trouble I don't know about?"

"No trouble, Galessi. Just a few minor repairs on *Malika* to get her in tip-top shape. If you can pay up front, I can afford to let Eve give her a full tune-up, and I could probably shave a whole day off the trip."

"Nine thousand in repairs is far from minor," Galessi said, setting his papers down and looking coolly back at Damien. "Can I really trust your ship to make it all the way to Tiklin?"

"Aw, come on now," Damien replied, leaning back on the pillows. "Now you're insulting my ship. I could go as low as eight-five, but you're practically robbing me."

"Far be it from me to *steal*," Galessi said with a grin. "I'm afraid I'll have to look elsewhere, for a captain who isn't looking for charity, and willing to run by my rules."

"It's not charity; think of it as an investment. You help me out now, and you'll be keeping one of your best contractors in the air, where I can bring us both wealth for years to come."

"As much as I love making dreams come true, I'm a businessman first. I can't front nine thousand for every operator who comes in here with a sob story about a broken-down ship. I make an exception for you, and everybody starts to think I'm an easy mark."

"OK," Damien said, leaning forward and clasping his hands together. "Forget Tiklin. I can ship anything you want planet-side with the standard before/after split."

"Oh, so it's your IS drive that needs repairing? You're in worse shape than I thought. You couldn't survive on what I pay to ship domestic. I can get kids with sticks to do it for two meals a day and a rag to sleep under. We don't have any heat on Trenth to worry about."

"So that's it then? You're going to let one of your best business associates go hungry?"

"I could always hire you as muscle, but it would take you years to save up enough to get an IS drive up and running."

"Well," said Damien, standing up and brushing himself off. "I guess I'll take my skills elsewhere."

"Good luck with that," Galessi said. "I doubt you'll find a softer touch around here."

"Thanks for your time." Damien parted the curtain to leave the room.

"Damien," Galessi said, catching him in the doorway. "Have a drink, on me. It's the least I could do. And let me know when you get that hunk of metal off the ground, so I can help you for real." He gestured toward one of the guards, who handed Damien back his gun belt and the handful of bullets from the pistols.

"You're a generous man," Damien said as he fastened the belt around his waist. "I don't know what I'd do without you."

"Starve, most likely."

Father Tanner tossed back the hood of his robe, now that he was in the shade of the back alleys. He knocked loudly on the heavy wooden door in front of him, and glanced at the piles of trash and broken-down appliances that spotted the edges of the buildings. A panel in the door slid open, revealing a pair of dull eyes.

"What do you want?" a voice asked.

"I'm Father Tanner from the mission," he replied. "I'm looking to buy some supplies."

The eyes disappeared and the panel closed again. A couple of muffled voices talked back and forth for a few moments, until eventually the door swung open and two Trenthan thugs ushered him in. When the door closed behind him, they quickly patted him down for weapons, then ushered him through the silk curtain to Galessi's office. He sat up from his reclining position as Tanner walked in, and waved for him to sit down.

"Father Tanner," he said in his own language, "what brings you to the shady part of town? Considering a change of careers?"

Tanner sat on a single pillow, crossing his legs under him, a comfortable distance from Galessi's obese figure. "Not quite yet," he replied in the alien tongue. "God willing, I still have some doctoring to do."

"Then why are you coming to see me? Are you having trouble at the mission?"

"I'm afraid so. We're using supplies faster than anticipated, and our stores won't last much longer at this rate."

"You're due for another shipment from your sponsors on Earth, aren't you?"

"They seem to be late," Father Tanner said, "no doubt dodging the border patrol. You haven't heard anything, have you?"

Galessi grunted in laughter. "I don't waste my resources tracking shipments from other operators. And even if I did, information costs money. Was that all you wanted?" He grinned slightly, as if he already knew the answer.

Tanner took a deep breath. "I need more medicine to hold us over until the shipment arrives. Mostly anesthetic and antibiotics, but I have a full list with specific names."

Galessi leaned back thoughtfully. "I think I know where I might find some."

"From the military? I don't want to steal from the poor somewhere else."

"Scruples cost extra, but it could be arranged. What can you afford?"

"I can repay you in supplies when our shipment arrives," Tanner said, "plus interest from the financial support we receive."

"You want a loan?" Galessi asked, reeling in disbelief. "Does everybody think I'm a chump today? I just had one of my smugglers ask for a loan to fix his IS drive, and now you; I can't operate on credit."

Tanner leaned forward and lowered his voice, locking eyes with Galessi. "I could stop charging you and your men for medical treatment."

"As much as I would appreciate getting the same deal as the *shellep* herders you treat, I don't deal in favors. They have a way of disappearing from the ledger when the heat comes by."

"Is there anything else you'd take in payment?"

"If you don't have cash or goods on hand to trade, there's nothing I can do for you. Unlike the Emmanuelites, I don't run a charity here."

Tanner gritted his teeth and counted to ten in his head. "Very well," he finally replied, standing up slowly. "Thank you for your time."

"And Father," Galessi said as Tanner turned to leave, "use the front door. People see a priest going out the back, and they're liable to think I'm getting soft."

Damien smacked his lips at the bitter, watered-down flavor of the Trenthan fruit juice. He wished it were something harder, but ethanol would kill any Brotherhood species that could survive on Trenth, so stocking it was a dead giveaway that the bar was expecting less-than-legal company. The wall in front of him was covered with shelves filled with Trenthan glycol drinks, but it was poison to Damien, and he didn't have a death wish. Not yet, anyway.

A handful of other customers sat scattered around the room, but they mainly stayed as far away from Damien as possible, just in case. They ate at polished wooden tables, stained with years of spilled drinks and food, and chatted amiably as they took shelter from the harsh mid-day sun. A set of relatively modern speakers piped in some warbling music, which sounded like a flock of geese either fighting or mating with a swarm of bees. Galessi was one of the few proprietors around that could afford equipment that nice, but Damien wished he wasn't; it gave him a headache.

The door behind him swung open with a creak, and he turned to see the robed figure from the alleyways enter. Instinctively Damien jumped up, and his hand flew to the cool metal of his pistol. But before he could draw, he realized that the man's hood was down, and his frail face was thoroughly human.

"Alright, I surrender," the man said flatly, freezing in place. "What do you want?"

"Sorry," Damien said, relaxing and sitting back down. "I recognized your robe from the alleys. I thought I was being trailed by Brotherhood heat."

"I suppose I was following you a bit. I don't get to see many other humans in this part of space."

"I know the feeling. Have a drink?"

"I suppose it couldn't hurt. Just a water, please." The man sat on the stool next to Damien, and he couldn't see the outline of a weapon anywhere beneath the robe, but that didn't mean much. Damien called out the order in Trenthan tongue, and the man looked impressed. "You speak Trenthan? I'm surprised; it's a tricky one."

"Bits and pieces," Damien said. "I make a point of knowing how to order a drink wherever I travel. The name's Damien Rogers." He held out his hand, but the man stared at it for a moment before shaking it.

"Sorry," he said, "I haven't shaken hands with anyone in a while. I'm Father Tanner."

"Father?" Damien asked as the bartender plopped a cold mug on the counter. "I wouldn't think a priest would be one for high treason. What brings you to enemy territory?"

"I run a medical mission on the outskirts of town. We started it a couple of years ago."

"You're not worried about someone going after the price on your head, turning you in as a spy?"

"Not when we're the only proper medical care within several hundred miles. There's only one hospital in Calchassa, and that's reserved for highly-placed Brotherhood officials. Trenth is too poor to run their own medical colleges; the cities had barely industrialized when the Brotherhood gunships showed up, and most of the planet is still agrarian. I may have a price on my head, but I provide a service that's worth breaking the rules for. You'd be surprised how many doors will open to you when you're holding a doctor's bag."

"Fair enough," Damien replied, taking a swig from his glass.

"What about you?" Tanner asked. "What business takes you all the way out here?"

"Let's call it shipping," Damien said with a smirk.

"We're all criminals here, so I can only assume you mean smuggling."

"Oh, is there a legal kind? I think I'd forgotten."

"Do you specialize in anything in particular?" Tanner asked.

"Oh, this and that. Are you looking for something?"

"I'm in the market for some medical supplies."

"I'm afraid I can't help you there," Damien replied. "I won't be getting anything new until I can scrounge up some money to fix my IS drive."

"What about weapons?"

Damien leaned back and looked Tanner up and down. He didn't look like a fighting man, and the priest bit didn't help the image either. "Are you expecting trouble? Because I've done some security work before, and I'm looking for work that'll keep me in the area; the weather's good for my sinuses, after all."

"It never hurts to be prepared. You probably don't keep up with local news, but with the expansion of the iron mines, a lot of the water sources have been diverted to Brotherhood operations and away from the farms. People are getting desperate out there. Some have even taken shots at Brotherhood-controlled land, and there's no telling what repercussions that might bring."

"Yeah, tell me about it. Anyway, I've got a dry hold right now. But I've done some gun-running in the past, and for a price I might be able to point you in the right direction. What kind of weapons are you in the market for?"

"What about grenades?"

Damien saw the priest's face flushing; something had him worked up, especially if he was asking for heavier ordnance, and not just small arms.

"Hey, I like your style. I off-loaded some frags last time I was here, and some of my contacts might-"

Tanner's fist lashed out without warning and struck Damien across the face. The impact nearly sent him tumbling from his seat, and warmth blossomed in his face as blood welled to the site of the blow.

"It was you, wasn't it?" Tanner snarled. "I've been cleaning up your messes ever since I got here. I spent half my antibiotics patching up bullet holes from weapons you sold!"

The two bouncers by the back door rushed forward and grabbed Tanner by the arms, half lifting him from his chair. Damien waved them off. The toughs dropped the priest unceremoniously back into his chair.

"You know, Pops," he said curtly, "considering you're giving medical aid to an enemy planet that supplies iron for ships built to attack Earth, I don't see that you've got a lot of room for moral outrage. It might have been me, or it might have been one of a hundred others who would gladly take my place if I weren't around." Tanner seemed to deflate a bit, and straightened the sleeves of his robe.

Damien pulled a coin out of his pocket and slammed it down on the counter. "That's for your drink. And you might want to talk to one of your doctor friends about getting that plank out of your eye."

Chapter Three

Father Tanner trudged into the mission late that afternoon, ready to get out of the hot, heavy robe, but found Andrew already in the hallway, moving to intercept him. Andrew was a short, sturdily build man with close-cropped black hair, and he held a dingy sheet of paper in his hand, covered with neatly typed writing. The low sun beamed through the windows, illuminating golden shapes on the earthen wall.

"We have good news and bad news," Andrew said, stopping a few feet in front of Tanner.

Tanner sighed, pulled off his glasses, and rubbed his temples. "The bad news first, I suppose."

Andrew took a deep breath; he looked hesitant to speak, almost as if he were ashamed of the news. "Word got back that the ship with our supplies got caught by Brotherhood patrols. It, uh, looks like we're not getting any help from Earth any time soon."

Father Tanner grimaced and clenched his teeth. He tried to count to ten in his head, but when he reached three, he lashed out and struck the wall. The grit of the dried mud scraped his hand, and the pain helped to snap him back into the present moment.

Andrew paused, watching, before continuing. "With any luck," he said, "the Brotherhood will be lenient, since they were only carrying medical supplies, right?"

"I'm not sure we can hope for as much from the Consortium, if they ever get back home," Tanner replied. "Did you have any luck with that herbalist? Anything we can use?"

"There's a little bit, but it's all palliative. Anti-emetics, mild analgesics, things like that. Nothing that's going to save lives."

"Please tell me that wasn't the good news."

"No, it wasn't. The good news is that there was a distress signal sent out a few hours ago. It seems there was a mining official doing an inspection tour of the larger mines here on Trenth. They had an explosion, and he was hurt pretty badly. They patched him up as best they could, but he's not getting better; he needs more specialized medical attention."

"You have a strange idea of what qualifies as good news," Father Tanner said. "If he's a Brotherhood official, can't they find a Brotherhood doctor to treat him?"

"That's where it gets interesting; he's a Hountan. There's nobody on the whole planet who's qualified to treat an ammonia-based life form. He's not stable enough to risk inter-stellar travel, so they put out a call looking for passing ships that might have a doctor on board who can help. Now, you said you worked on Hountans during the active hostilities, right?"

"I did, but it's been quite a while," Tanner said as he walked toward his office. "Besides, they'd turn us in for certain; it would be suicide."

"Well, we don't have to tell them we're human, do we?" Andrew asked, following. "They're ammonia-based; we'd have to be in suits the whole time anyway. We could pass ourselves off as Trenthans, and they'd never know the difference."

"That's an awful lot of trouble and risk to go to for one more patient." Tanner pulled off his robe and stripped down to the simple cotton shirt beneath. "We have plenty of work here to keep us busy without going out looking for more."

"Ah, but here's the twist: they're offering a reward."

Tanner froze. "How much?"

"Forty thousand."

"That is good news. Forty thousand could probably replace all our vital equipment, and keep us stocked with drugs for at least a year."

"Right. And we already have some environment suits with surgical-grade gloves; they're old, but they'll do the job, won't they?"

"Where is the patient?"

Andrew cringed. "That's the other problem. They're keeping him in orbit in case his condition takes a turn for the worse, and they have to risk IS travel at a moment's notice. So I guess we need a ship. But you know some people in town, so I thought you might have an idea of who is desperate enough to risk harboring spies."

Father Tanner thought for a moment. "I think I know just the person."

Damien ducked his opponent's punch and responded with a quick jab to the gut. He went for a left cross, but the Trenthan in front of him twisted out of the way and delivered a knee to Damien's side. Adrenaline kept the pain at bay, but the force knocked him to his hands and knees. Stinging drops of sweat bounced off his face and into his eyes. The bright spotlights of the arena obscured his view of the crowds around him, but he heard them either cheering him on or clapping in disapproval. Mostly the latter. He got one foot back under him, and wiped the blood from the swollen, seeping wound on his forehead.

His opponent paced back and forth, waiting for Damien to stand up. His bare torso was lean, but deceptively strong. His *glia* were pulled back and tied off in pigtails on either side of his face, revealing more of his droopy cheeks. He bounced up and down as he walked, keeping on his toes and snarling at Damien with dull, uneven teeth.

The other boxer charged before Damien had gotten completely to his feet. He swung two meaty fists straight to Damien's torso. Damien dodged the first one, but the second hit like a sledgehammer, knocking the breath out of him. He grabbed the Trenthan's arm and pulled him close, trying to wrestle him down to the ground. The crowd cheered, and the referee started counting loudly, but the Trenthan twisted out of Damien's grip. The buzzer sounded. Damien's opponent sneered, and defiantly flicked his *glia* in Damien's direction as he sauntered back to his corner.

Damien slumped into the stool along one side of the ring. He reached into a bucket next to his seat and splashed ice water onto his face, counting the cuts on his face by the separate stings. Across from him, his opponent glared with a lazy eye and crooked, flat nose as an assistant administered a salve with bowed head and nervous movements, while muttering unctuous assurances to the combatant. On the other side of the slack chain links that circled the ring, the audience murmured loudly to themselves as they waited for the next round to start. Most of them looked even poorer than he was. They held greasy snacks hawked by a vendor in the back, and jostled each other with boisterous laughs, jeering at the human. However a few wore nicer clothing, and Damien thought he spied Galessi in a private box in the back.

"I was told I could find you here."

Damien turned around. The priest from earlier stood next to the ring. He seemed out of place with his calm composure and soft, human face, compared to the raucous crowd all around him.

"The registration table's in the back," Damien said, "but I don't think you'll get in any lucky sucker punches around here."

"I need to talk to you," Tanner said.

"I'm kind of busy here, if you didn't notice." He spat a mouthful of blood onto the floor of the ring."

"It's about a job."

Damien paused. "Alright, I'm interested. Make yourself useful though."

Tanner climbed up onto the mat next to Damien, picked up a piece of ice from the bucket, and rubbed it on the swollen parts of Damien's face. "You said you're looking for work, and you need something that doesn't require an IS drive, correct?"

"I said part of that; not sure where you got the rest."

"I pieced it together from something Galessi told me. Apparently you annoyed him, and he needed to vent."

"I'll have to have a talk with him about discretion," Damien said. "So what's the job?"

"We need a ship to take us into orbit," Tanner replied.

"A lot of heathens in the upper atmosphere, are there?"

"I'm meeting with another ship."

"Yeah? Who?"

"Just a minor government official."

"The Brotherhood?" Damien asked. "What business would they have with the likes of you?"

"He's a patient that needs treatment. He's not stable enough to risk a landing, so I have to go meet him."

"Are you insane, Pops?"

"It's possible," Tanner replied. "They're offering forty thousand; of course, half of that would be yours. That would be enough to fix your IS drive, wouldn't it?"

Damien mulled it over for a few seconds, but just for show. "You know," he said, "I'm starting to feel a little crazy myself."

"I thought you might."

"But I have to win this purse just to get off the ground. You'd better start praying."

Damien got up, and steadied himself on the chains. His opponent was standing up too, and the referee approached to begin the next round.

"His kidney's a couple of inches lower than ours," Tanner said. "And he's leaving his right side open too, so take advantage of it. I'll meet you outside."

Eve tightened the last bolt of the access panel, and climbed down the step ladder, steadying herself against the *Malika* with one hand. Her eyelids were about to collapse of their own accord; it had already been afternoon by the ship's clock when they landed, but morning by local time, and she had to take advantage of all the daylight she could. She wiped the grease from her face and slowly dialed back the knob on the lift, easing the ship down onto its new landing leg. The new piece was relatively clean and shiny compared to the pockmarks and grime covering the rest of the ship, but it would only take a few months for it to accumulate enough wear to match.

A handful of floodlights on towers along the perimeter of the landing area cast criss-crossing half shadows from every ship, providing just enough light to work in. The area was mostly deserted, and above her Eve saw only occasional ships gliding across the starry sky, their beacon lights tracing lazy orbits above her head.

She locked up her toolbox and wheeled it up the ramp back into the ship. She'd haggled until her throat was sore, trying to squeeze as much as she could from the meager bundle of cash Damien had given her. Then she worked on the ship until her knuckles were raw and smeared with grease and blood. It had been a long day. She debated in her mind whether she should take a hot shower, or go straight to collapsing on her bunk, but before she got all the way inside, Damien's voice called out behind her.

"Don't close up just yet," he said. Eve turned around and saw him walking toward her with a thin man, who wore a pale robe and a full head of salt-and-pepper hair. "We've got a job."

"What happened to you?" Eve asked. Damien's face was bruised, swollen, and bleeding slightly, although small white bandages held closed the worst injuries.

"I won," Damien replied, tossing a stack of well-worn and stained bills at her. "Take that money and use it to get us ready for outer orbit and ship-to-ship docking tomorrow morning."

"The morning?" Eve groaned, incredulous. "What's so important that it can't wait?"

"It could be a matter of life and death," the older man said.

"And money," Damien added, passing Eve on the ramp. "Don't forget the money. You haven't taken apart the radio, have you?"

"No, it should be fine." She turned back to the other man. "Are you the client, then?"

"Not really. More like a partner in crime." He offered his hand. "Father Tanner."

"Eve Romano," she answered, shaking his hand absentmindedly. "Father? As in a priest?"

"Yes, I run a clinic and mission on the outskirts of town."

"And the captain actually agreed to work with you? I guess our situation is worst than I thought."

"Perhaps so," Tanner replied. "Well, it was nice to meet you, Ms. Romano. If you'll excuse me, I'll leave you to your work while I get the rest of my team."

The lump on the bed stirred slightly as Father Tanner flicked on the light in the small room in the back of the clinic. The cramped room held half-empty crates of medical supplies and a couple of shabby chairs for visitors, and the bed took up what little space was left. A drawn curtain on one side kept the dark out, and the only sound was a faint beeping from a heart monitor.

Tanner examined the monitor, moving his head up and down to read around a crack in the plastic display screen. A soft groan came from the bed behind him.

"It's the middle of the night. Shouldn't you be sleeping?"

Tanner turned to the man in the bed. "No rest for the weary, I'm afraid."

The man in the bed was Trenthan, his *glia* withered to the thickness of spaghetti, and his face rough and drooping with age. A thin plastic tube trailed from under the coarse blanket and up to an IV bag hanging from the same rack as the heart monitor.

"Father Nellin, how are you feeling?" Tanner asked.

"You just woke me up; how do you think I'm feeling?" Nellin tried to glare at Father Tanner, but quickly broke into a smile. "To tell the truth, I haven't been sleeping well. I can feel it too much in my leg."

"Well, I'm going to do something about that," Tanner said. "If all goes well in the next day or two, I should have enough money to keep the clinic running for a couple of years. I'll be able to get the drugs you need, plus something for that pain."

"Don't worry about me," Nellin replied. "It won't be too long before this pain is just a fading memory."

"Don't talk like that. I couldn't run this mission without you."

"Please," Nellin said with a chuckle, "you already are. You have been ever since I got sick. I'm not doing anyone any good just hanging on here. I'm ready to go home."

"You *are* still doing good here. You're my friend, and without you around, who am I supposed to unload all of my frustrations on?"

"The walls seem to be doing the job quite nicely."

"Don't tell me you heard that, Father?"

Nellin laughed, which set off a brief coughing fit before he spoke again. "Just guessing, actually, but it seems I had the right of it. Just try to get control of that temper; we wouldn't want you to damage those surgeon's hands of yours, would we?"

"I'll try," said Tanner. "I have to go now and look after another patient. Don't go anywhere until I get back, OK?"

"Are you sure?" Nellin asked, coughing. "I was considering on taking a trip, maybe to the coast."

"You know what I mean."

"Alright, alright, I'll see what I can do."

"Try to get some rest while I'm gone."

Father Tanner turned to leave, flipping the light switch off again and plunging the room back into darkness. The only light came from the open door and the faint glow of the moon through the thin curtains. As he passed through the doorway, he heard Nellin muttering a prayer quietly behind him.

Andrew wheeled two large crates on a dolly across the smooth, dusty surface of the spaceport, leaving crooked parallel trails on the bare dirt up to the entrance ramp.

"Excuse me," he said to the pair of unfamiliar legs on the other side of a large access panel that hung open. A woman stepped out from behind it, wearing faded, greasy coveralls. Her long black hair was clamped against her shoulders by a bundle of cables draped around her neck. She held a screwdriver in one hand, a multimeter in the other, and a pair of wire cutters dangled by one handle from her mouth. She took it out and waited for a question.

"Oh, hi," Andrew said, smiling awkwardly and clearing his throat. "Uh, do you know where I can put my things in the ship?"

"The captain should be in there," she said. "He can show you where the spare quarters are."

"Oh, thanks." Andrew climbed up the ramp into the ship, and a rhythmic thump punctuated the squeaking of the dolly wheels as they rolled over the seams between metal plates. The inside of the ship was dimly lit and rather cramped. On the left, he saw an empty captain's chair, along with the night sky through the viewing window of the cockpit. To the right a long corridor stretched out with doors on either side. "Hello?"

A man stepped out from behind the wall of the cockpit, presumably the ship's captain, though he didn't dress the part. He was dark-skinned, bald, and wore khaki cargo pants and a matching vest over an undershirt which probably used to be white. He held a stick of dried meat in one hand, tore off a piece with his teeth and chewed it casually while he spoke. "Hey, I'm Damien, *Malika*'s captain. What do you need?"

"Sorry, where can I put this stuff?" Andrew asked, gesturing to the crates.

"What is it?"

"Lab equipment. Mostly just a lot of pharmacology kits and chemicals in case we need to synthesize something on the fly. Oh, by the way, I'm Dr. Cho." He held out his hand for Damien to shake.

"Yeah, I'm not calling you doctor. You got a first name?"

"Oh. It's Andrew."

"Drew? Andy?"

"Just Andrew, actually."

"Alright Andrew," Damien replied, "that's going in the cargo hold with all the other medical stuff. All the way down, and through the big door."

"Thanks."

Andrew turned and rolled the crates down the hallway, careful to keep from bumping it against any of the walls. He passed four doors that seemed to lead to living quarters; one had "Eve" written in old, faded chalk letters, and two of the others displayed faded names smeared into illegibility. That kind of history in the ship made him nervous. Two people had been reduced to smears in the wall, and he couldn't help but wonder about the circumstances.

He kept going through the large door at the end of the hall, and it opened into a cavernous room. In the far-right corner was a walled-off section with windows and a control panel by the door, along with a computer console. That had to be the airlock, where they would be docking with the other ship. Most of the rest of the room was empty, but miscellaneous rigging equipment hung from the ceiling, and a large door took up much of the left wall. Up against the airlock, Father Tanner was securing his own containers of surgical supplies, strapping them down to prepare for takeoff.

"I see you found the place alright," Father Tanner said.

"Yeah. It's certainly not much."

"But it's more lab space than you're used to, right?"

"True, but space doesn't count for much when you don't have

equipment to put in it, does it?" Andrew said, carefully stacking his crates alongside the others.

"I guess not," Father Tanner replied.

Andrew paused. He knew he had to say something, but it took a few moments to screw up the conviction. "OK, I have to say something. I know this was my suggestion, but I'm having second thoughts. After all, we *are* at war. Are we really doing the right thing by helping a Brotherhood agent?"

"We're trying to save a life," Father Tanner replied. "I think that's always the right thing."

"But this guy isn't a farmer or rancher just trying to feed his family. He's a government official, in charge of mines that produce iron for Brotherhood fleets. By saving him, we could be helping the war effort against us."

"We preach the gospel to *every* tribe, tongue, and nation, Andrew. Not just the friendly ones." Tanner paused and considered a moment before shrugging. "Besides, he's a bureaucrat. I don't think any war effort was ever helped by an abundance of bureaucrats."

"Maybe," Andrew said with a snort. "But what if we can't pull it off? If we get caught and deported, or even killed, we'd be leaving the mission in the hands of the locals, and I'm not sure they're ready yet."

"We've been training them for over a year," Father Tanner said. "Some of them are quite gifted, and as long as they stay supplied, I'm sure they can manage without us. They still have Father Nellin for guidance as well."

"But Ghenni is the best of the local talent, and we're taking him with us."

"We need a good nurse, and a Trenthan face for the operation. Besides, he was never in line for a leadership role. Not while he's still committed to his own beliefs."

"But if they-"

Father Tanner stopped his work and placed both hands on a crate, closing his eyes and taking measured breaths. Andrew shut up.

"Look, I'm scared too, Andrew. I don't know for sure that we're doing the right thing, or what will happen. But God gave us this opportunity, and we're pursuing it with prayer and our God-given wisdom. That's the best we can ever hope for in this life, so if something happens to us, we have to be satisfied that it was God's will, and that we were faithful servants."

"You're right, I'm sorry," Andrew said. "I'll get the rest of our stuff."

"Don't be sorry for your doubts, Andrew. Let them advise you; just don't let them rule you."

Andrew nodded, then took the dolly back outside. It took the better part of an hour to finish wheeling the crates of glassware, chemicals, and medical instruments into the cargo hold and secure it for takeoff the next morning. He checked his watch, and saw through the scratched up glass face that it was only a few hours before dawn. Sleep sounded appealing, but he was curious too, and he wandered outside instead. The woman from before was still working on the ship, examining wires and tubing that gushed out of an open hatch in the side.

"Sure got cold out here, didn't it?" he said loudly. The brisk air cut through his thin shirt like it wasn't there, and he shoved his hands under his armpits to keep them warm.

The woman turned around at his voice, and smiled briefly. "I like it better like this," she said before returning to her work.

"You're Eve, right?"

"Yeah. I never got your name, though."

"I'm Andrew. I, uh, I saw your name on the door inside. That's how I knew."

"Oh, right."

"So, do you need any help out here? I've been known to do some wrench work, back home."

Eve gave him a bemused look. "I think I'm all good on the... wrench work. But you can hand me that electrical tape if you don't mind."

Andrew picked up the small roll from the top of the toolbox and handed it to her. She took it, and turned back to her work. Andrew stood behind her for a moment, patting his legs absentmindedly, before speaking again.

"So... what brings you out to Brotherhood country?"

"Same as everybody else, I suppose. There wasn't really room for me back in the Consortium."

"How come?"

"I'd rather not talk about it. Wire cutters?"

Andrew rifled through a couple of drawers, then produced them and handed them over. Eve began stripping the insulation from one of the wires.

"Sorry," Andrew said. "I didn't mean to pry."

"It's OK," Eve replied. "I can't really blame you."

Andrew nodded. "So is it just you and the captain running the ship?"

"For now. We usually have a couple of hired guns on hand, but they just got too rich, too quick."

Andrew glanced around the shabby surroundings. "That's... sarcasm, right?"

Eve answered through gritted teeth with a loop of wire hanging from her mouth. "You're quick."

"How come you're still around?" Andrew asked.

"Because I'm not in it for the money."

"Oh, so you and the captain..." He cleared his throat.

"God, no," Eve said, scrunching her face. "He has a robot for that."

"Oh."

"Yeah, it's best to knock before going into his quarters, you know?"

Andrew stuck his hands into his pockets, and scanned the mostly-deserted spaceport around him. "Well," he eventually said, "I guess I'll go and let you finish your work." He was halfway up the ramp when Eve stopped him.

"Hey," she said, finally turning to face him. "I'm sorry if I'm a little distracted right now. I'm tired, I still have work to do, and... it was really nice talking to you."

"Yeah," said Andrew, nodding, "it was nice talking to you too."

Ghenni woke up a few minutes before dawn and lit sticks of incense in a circle around him on the floor. The small space of the ship's quarters filled with the aroma more quickly than his home on the plains, and wisps of white smoke felt their way into the ventilation ducts. The earthy smell filled him with a sense of oneness with the planet. He smelled the dryness of the deserts that surrounded them, and the moisture of the oceans that abutted their shores, and the lushness of the rainforests hundreds of miles away. Crystals of salt ground under his fingers as he rubbed his small soulstone with a mixture of preservatives and spices to ask the gods for protection. With an ash-covered finger, he traced the circle of the world on the ground, feeling the grit of the charred wood between his skin and the metal floor. He placed his soulstone in the middle of it, and chanted as he slid it slowly outside the circle, signifying his upcoming departure from the terrestrial surface, directing his supplications to the god of the vacuum of space.

Muffled footsteps and voices outside his door indicated that the ship was coming to life again as he finished his chants. He extinguished the incense, packed it into his bag, and opened the door to the corridor. Captain Damien stood on the other side, his hand poised to knock, and a plume of fragrant smoke billowed out. He reeled back and fanned the pungent clouds from his face.

"Geez, Ghenni, what's on fire?"

"Incense," he replied in heavily accented English. "And it has been made extinguished."

"Why are you burning incense in my ship?"

"To ask the god in outer space to keep my spirit safe while I'm in orbit."

"God of outer space, huh? I guess you're not part of the Emmanuelite fan club you run around with, then."

"Father Tanner has been... tremendously helpful to the people of my area, but I still hold to the traditional beliefs with my people."

"And he's OK with that? He's never, oh I don't know, punched you in the face or anything?"

Ghenni paused before answering. "It's been a source of tension, but on most days he is pleasant."

"Yesterday must not have been one of those days," Damien said, gingerly feeling the wound on his lip.

"You are not Emmanuelite as well, Captain Damien?"

"It's all just fairy tales as far as I'm concerned," he replied. Down the hall, Father Tanner stepped out of his own quarters and looked at the two briefly, coughing a few times as he walked toward the cargo hold. "But if your little rituals bother Pops, they can't be all bad, eh?"

"What was it you came to see me on?" asked Ghenni.

"Right," Damien said, pulling out a clothes hanger from under his arm. On it hung a dark blue uniform, crisp with starch and glistening with a dozen small medals and pins. Down each arm ran a white stripe, with a smaller red stripe on either side of it. The sight of one of his people's uniforms sent an involuntary swell of pride to his chest, and he stood up straighter in its presence. "This is your uniform. You'll be playing the part of Captain Chinnassa of the Brotherhood Shipping Corps. You'll do all the talking on the vid screen in the cockpit. You think you can handle that?"

"I believe so, but I admit I'm not skilled in lying."

"Don't worry. You'll be using a translator, which makes lying a piece of cake, especially with a non-humanoid species. You don't really have to worry too much about non-verbal cues, so long as you don't actually say anything monumentally stupid, you should be fine."

"I'll certainly do my best."

"Glad to hear it. Now get changed, because it won't take us long to establish radio contact. We lift off in ten."

Damien left the uniform with Ghenni and walked to the cockpit. He slid into the pilot's chair and started running through all his pre-flight checks. The room seemed almost measurably brighter from the greater number of indicators glowing yellow and green today compared to the last week. Eve had really outdone herself, and deserved to stay passed out in her quarters as they lifted off. The whole cockpit seemed larger too, now that he had cleaned out all the clutter and wiped the crumbs off the panels. He should have done that months ago.

There was still a lot more work to do on the *Malika* though. Twenty thousand would probably fix up the last of the worn-out systems, on top of replacing the IS drive. There might even be enough left over to find a real, genuine Earth-cow steak, and not the stuff that passed for meat out here in Brotherhood space. The thought made his mouth water, but the moment passed as soon as he took a sip of the watered-down imitation coffee from the plastic mug on the console. As he finished checking the ship's systems, Ghenni walked into the cockpit, dressed in the long blue coat and hat of the Brotherhood Shipping Corps.

"Looking good, buddy," Damien said as he fiddled with the controls. "I'm rerouting the flight controls to my mobile, so I can still fly this thing while you're doing your talking in here."

"Very well."

Damien pressed the button for the intercom, and leaned into the microphone. "Everybody ready for takeoff?" A chorus of agreements sounded over the speaker. "Alright then. Let's make some money."

Chapter Four

An early-morning spray of water held down the dust of the landing area as the *Malika* pushed off against the surface of Trenth and lifted itself into the air. The mix of figures from dozens of other worlds shrank to dots, then out of vision entirely. The city of Calchassa receded until it reduced to a splotch on the patchy brown and green landscape. After a few minutes, the planet was merely a huge sphere rotating slowly in the windows.

"Alright," Damien said, "We're in orbit. Get on the vid screen and tell them we just dropped out of subspace on the far side of Trenth, and we're coming around turn-wise. I'm going to my quarters to steer." He tucked the rolled-up mobile computer tablet under his arm and pulled a small earpiece from his pocket, handing it to Ghenni. "I'll be listening in. If you need any help, I can nudge you along with this." He walked out the door, leaving Ghenni alone in the cockpit.

Ghenni adjusted the earpiece to fit his alien ear, and put it in. He pushed the buttons that Damien had showed him on the console, and the inside of the other ship flickered into view. The construction was not terribly different than their own, although the placement of the control consoles suggested it was built for a vastly different anatomy. Those differences were quite apparent in the two Hountans standing in the cockpit of the other ship. They were built like four-legged spiders, four or five feet across, with greenish-yellow skin. The main body was suspended in the middle, with two eyes on the front, flanked by a pair of thin arms. Another eye was set into the body on each side, between the legs. The Hountan at the view screen leaned forward to present its mouth, a circular hole in the top of its head, lined with teeth.

Ghenni was startled for a moment; he had known that the many species throughout space could be quite varied, but he had never seen one up close before. However, he quickly recovered and spoke.

"This is Captain Chinnassa of the *APS Malika*. We are responding to your request for medical aid."

"We are most grateful for your assistance," the Hountan said. His own language was a series of barks and howls that pained Ghenni's ears. Thankfully, they were mostly canceled out by the communications equipment, and replaced by computer-generated translations. "This is Captain Fanwon of the *BCS Houniik*. You said before that you have a doctor on board with experience treating Hountans?"

"Yes, he treated them during active hostilities in the war."

"Very well. We have set up an operating theater in the airlock; all medicines and other supplies are in place."

"Excellent," Ghenni said, "we are in orbit on the far side of the planet, and will be coming turn-wise. Please prepare to receive us for docking."

"In the meantime, we would like to speak with your doctor, to give him more details on the condition of the patient."

"I will patch him through on the radio."

"It would be better to talk to him on the video screen," Fanwon said, "so that he may see the damage for himself."

Ghenni stumbled for a second, not sure what to do. Of course they couldn't see Father Tanner himself, or any of the humans, since they were legally an enemy of the Brotherhood. If they wanted to see the doctor, Ghenni was the only one who could pass. "I... I will go find him and bring him to the cockpit."

"Can you not call him on the ship's intercom?"

"The intercom is not currently working. I will have him here momentarily."

Ghenni calmly reached up to the controls and cut off the video feed. Then he took off running out of the cockpit and down the corridor to the cargo hold, his boots clanging on the hard metal floor with each step. Damien was already half-way down the hall, screaming for Father Tanner.

"Pops!" he called out as he skidded to a halt. "We need one of your laboratory coats, right now."

"I have one in my quarters," Father Tanner said, walking hurriedly to the door. "What happened?"

"The Hountans want to talk to the doctor face-to-face."

Ghenni reached the door of the cargo hold just as the others were rushing out, and he turned and followed them to Father Tanner's room, where the doctor yanked open a battered rucksack. He hurriedly rooted around until he produced a white coat, still stained with faded patches of red and brown bodily fluids. He gave it to Ghenni, who quickly put it on over his uniform. While he buttoned it, Father Tanner reached up to his hat.

"You have too much decoration for a doctor," Tanner said, unpinning some of the medals. "Now hurry up and get back."

Ghenni ran back to the cockpit and paused for a moment to catch his breath as Damien ducked back into his own room. He swallowed and took two deep breaths to calm his racing heart before turning the video feed back on. "This is Doctor..."

Damien picked up on the pause, and hissed through the earpiece. "Make something up."

"...Ankassa. What is the status of the patient?"

"His condition is deteriorating. The explosion launched a metal rod that punctured his suit and entered his head, just to the left of his principal arm, and exiting on the right side, just below the mouth." The screen changed to the perspective of a handheld camera that panned around the injured Hountan, giving Ghenni a close-up view of the damage. The creature's eyes were closed, and greenish-yellow flesh was inexpertly stitched together around two large wounds, seeping with a bronze-colored fluid. It showed no sign of consciousness, its limbs drooped limply on the table.

"What treatment has he already received?"

"A doctor from the nearest city was able to repair the physical trauma, treat the sudden decompression, and stabilize body temperature. However, he had no knowledge of Hountan physiology, and could do little more than suturing. Fearing infection, we administered antibiotics from our store on the ship, but were unsure about the proper dosage. He is still not improving, but we did not want to risk giving any more medicine without further knowledge of what exactly was wrong."

There was some whispering from the earpiece, and Father Tanner's voice spoke up. "Ask what his symptoms are."

"What symptoms does he have?" Ghenni asked.

"The wounds are not healing properly, and his heart rate is fast, but weak. He is also fading in and out of consciousness."

"Was the patient on any drugs before the accident, especially circulatory medication?" Father Tanner asked. Ghenni repeated the question.

"No, he did not register any medications when we began our voyage."

"Did he or any other passengers show any symptoms prior to the accident?"

"They all had medical inspections before leaving, and all were in good health."

Father Tanner pitched in again. "Ask if he has any young children."

"Yes," Captain Fanwon said, "he has a son at home. However, I do not know what his health is like."

"That's all my questions for now," said Father Tanner, "although we'll need a complete medical history forwarded to us."

"Thank you for the information," Ghenni said. "I must prepare to receive the patient, and we will need a copy of his medical history as well. *Malika* out."

Ghenni switched off the screen and sank into the pilot's chair with relief. Damien and Father Tanner stepped in through the door.

"Nice work there, buddy," Damien said. "Hard to believe the suckers didn't notice you were playing both parts."

"Could you tell the difference between the Hountans?" asked Father Tanner.

"True enough. Anyway, I'll leave you doctors to do your thing while I try to get these ships a little better acquainted."

Ghenni and Father Tanner walked back toward the cargo hold, while Ghenni removed his lab coat. Despite the cold of the ship, he was sweating from the ordeal, and his heart was still calming down. "What are your impressions?" Ghenni asked.

"It sounds like it might just be from blood loss. I'll have to take a look at him myself, but in the meantime you and Andrew should get ready to perform a transfusion with one of the other Hountans."

"Very well."

"It looks like this may be easier than I thought," Father Tanner said, raising his hand as if to knock on something. Then he paused, furrowed his brow, and scanned the corridor.

"Is something wrong?" Ghenni asked.

"There's nothing wooden on board, is there?"

"I don't know. Do you need it for something?"

"Let's hope not."

"You guys all ready?" Damien asked over the ship's intercom. "Prepare for docking."

Ghenni, Andrew, and Father Tanner all stood by the airlock, dressed in old, but well-kept surgical suits. They were made specifically for operating on beings of radically different physiologies, with airtight seals, their own refillable air supply, and resistance to all but the harshest of chemical agents. The arms tapered down from the elbows into skin-tight gloves over the hands, to allow for precise handling of surgical instruments. Andrew started sweating, both from the heat of the air-tight suit and general nervousness. His mind told him that the Hountans wouldn't have any reason to suspect he was human, and couldn't see his face though the helmet. But the thought of being only a few feet away from actual Brotherhood government officials, who could throw him in prison for no reason other than being human, sent shivers down his spine.

The whole ship shuddered as it came into direct contact with the Hountan vessel, and they watched it through the window of the airlock. Hollow clanking sounds reverberated through the cargo hold as the two ships latched onto each other, but a few moments later, the last of the noise faded away, and Damien's voice came over the intercom again. "We're good. Get ready to go aboard."

The three of them walked into the airlock, and the door sealed tight behind them. The airlock was large and open, made for loading cargo from inhospitable planets. It filled with the loud roar of pumps sucking the oxygenated air back into the ship's reserves. When it was mostly gone, other pumps kicked in, replacing the remaining air with inert nitrogen; some pressure had to remain at all times, because the surgical suits weren't built to handle exposure to direct vacuum. When the last of the oxygen was gone, the toxic air from the Hountan ship began filling the airlock. The increasing pressure squeezed them inside their suits until the pumps shut off, at twice the pressure of Earth's atmosphere. Finally, the doors of the two airlocks opened with a hiss, as the two formerly separate environments reached complete equilibrium.

The other airlock was smaller, made to transfer only a handful of people at a time. But now it was filled wall-to-wall with medical equipment, along with the patient lying unconscious on the bed in the middle of it. A simple monitoring device, the readouts of which only Father Tanner could understand, was attached to the immobile patient, but the quick and steady blooping sound was unmistakable: the quickened heartbeat of a creature in distress.

Ghenni shivered. "Why do they must keep it so cold in here?" he asked over the suit radio.

"Hountans use ammonia as their bodily solvent, instead of water like us," explained Father Tanner. "They have to keep it at lower temperatures and higher pressures to keep from drying out."

"Don't worry," Andrew said, "these suits don't exactly breathe well. You'll get plenty warm in no time."

The other Hountan in the room advanced toward them and crouched down on his front legs. Andrew and Ghenni both instinctively took a half-step back.

"He's not going to pounce," said Father Tanner, "he's presenting his mouth so we can hear him better when he speaks. It's a greeting."

The Hountan let loose a series of barks and howls, which were drowned out and translated by the suits' communications equipment. "Greetings and thanks for your assistance. I am Captain Fanwon."

"Greetings to you, Captain," Father Tanner replied. "I am Doctor Ankassa. Has there been any change?"

"No. He's stable, but slowly weakening."

Father Tanner walked up to the patient and examined him more closely. He looked much the same as he had on the video screen before, but the two stitched wounds were covered with bandages. Andrew's heart twisted in his chest, and all his previous doubts about whether they were doing the right thing melted away; here was someone sick, maybe even dying, and it was his job to make him whole again. "His skin is discolored," Father Tanner said. He glanced up at the monitor. "Heart rate is elevated and blood pressure is low. It looks like simple blood loss."

"Should we begin a transfusion?" asked Ghenni.

"Not yet," Father Tanner said with a sigh, "I'm going to have to redo these stitches first. He's still losing blood, which explains why he's still getting weaker." He lifted the bandage over the exit wound to reveal the white cloth soaked with a copper-colored liquid.

"That's his blood?" asked Ghenni.

"It's mostly ammonia," Andrew said, "with a lot of lithium metal dissolved in it. It's at a high enough concentration that it looks and acts like liquid metal."

"That's right," Father Tanner said. "Beautiful, isn't it?"

"It's also incredibly corrosive, so don't let it sit on your gloves for too long. As sturdy as they are, the blood could start to burn through if you give it enough time."

"Very well. I'll begin redoing these sutures, and you two find a donor for the transfusion, about half a liter. I should be done by the time you get it."

"Right," said Andrew, "I'll get the equipment together, and Ghenni, why don't you get back on the other ship and get on the screen to look for a volunteer?"

"Alright," said Ghenni, turning to enter the airlock again.

"Oh, and Ghenni," Father Tanner said.

"Yes?"

"Remember to be the Captain. The doctor is in here."

When the door opened, Ghenni stepped out of the airlock and peeled off his helmet. Despite the cooler temperatures in the alien ship, the suit's insulation kept most of the heat in, and by the time he got back out it was stifling. He couldn't imagine what it must be like for the humans, who were used to even cooler temperatures than Trenthans were. The blast of cooler air from the cargo hold washed over his sweaty neck with an invigorating crispness. He strolled quickly back to his quarters, changed back into the captains' uniform, and went to the bridge. Damien was sitting at the main control console, fiddling with some knobs. He looked up.

"You need me to clear out of here?" he asked Ghenni.

"Yes, I need to speak to the other captain to make a suitable blood donor."

Damien grabbed his mobile and stood up. "So how are things going in there?"

"They seem to be going well," Ghenni replied. "It may be a matter of just a few hours."

"Glad to hear it," Damien said as he walked out the door. "This'll be the fastest money I ever made."

Ghenni straightened his hat and flicked the control to call the other ship. At first the screen only blinked a blue stand-by message, but after a few moments, the Hountan captain appeared on the screen.

"What is it I can do for you?" he asked. "Have you made any progress?"

"The patient is suffering from blood loss due to his injuries. The doctor is redoing his sutures, but he will need to receive a transfusion from another one of your crew in order to fully recover."

"Very well," the captain said. "Shall I select one of my crew for you?"

"First I will need to see the medical records of everyone on the ship, to determine which of them has a compatible blood type."

The Hountan captain paused before speaking. "What do you mean by 'blood type'?"

"It tells what proteins are present in the blood, so we can avoid any adverse reactions to the transfusion."

The captain paused again, and his forward-facing eye darted back and forth. "There is no such parameter in our medical information. All Hountans may accept blood from any other."

"I'm sorry," said Ghenni, "I was not aware of that fact. In that case, it would be best for you to choose which crew member should contribute."

"Are you sure your doctor can provide adequate care to our species?"

"Yes, I assure you that he can. As I said before, he treated Hountans in the Alliance Fleet during active hostilities."

"But he only held the rank of lieutenant," the captain pointed out. "Surely if he has been serving since then, he would have been promoted much higher by now."

Ghenni's mind raced as he searched for a plausible answer to the question. Surely the captain must have been suspicious from the start: the ship was visibly old, and a doctor capable of treating multiple species would have had more important duties than traveling with a freight ship. From the Hountan point of view, it all had to look a little too convenient.

"He has had... authority issues," Ghenni finally said, "that have prevented him from achieving higher rank."

"I see."

"If you will excuse me, I have other duties to attend to. When you have chosen a crew member, have him sent to the operating theater."

"Very well. *Houniik* out."

When the screen went blank, Ghenni chanted a quick prayer. When he finished, he got on the radio and called Father Tanner's suit.

"Father Tanner, the Hountan captain will be sending over someone with the transfusion soon."

"Great. Good work, Ghenni."

"You forgot to mention that Hountans do not have different blood types."

"Oh. I guess I did. What happened?"

"I believe the Hountan captain is suspicious. He questioned our doctor's qualifications, on the grounds that he was too low of a rank to have treated Hountans in the war."

"Alright," said Father Tanner, "let's try to keep face-to-face contact down to a minimum, so we don't do any more damage."

"And hope we have not done too much damage already."

Chapter Five

Copper-colored liquid crept up the tubing into the transparent sack as Father Tanner checked the flow of blood into the plastic bag. The unconscious patient had been pushed to one side of the room, and the quiet beeping of his monitor filled the air. The Hountan crew member donating the blood was perched on a stool, his four legs just barely touching the floor in each direction. Its eyes flicked about the room, dwelling on the patient, and then again on Tanner as he worked slow and methodically.

"You're not very talkative for a doctor," the Hountan said.

"I'm sorry," Father Tanner said. "I just have a lot of things on my mind."

"I hear working for the Shipping Corps keeps you away from family for a long time. I'm sure it's tough."

"No," said Father Tanner, "no family. It's an old friend of mine; he's sick, and I'm not sure if he'll get medical care in time."

The Hountan squinted its eyes and grunted in agreement. "Good doctors are rare these days. The military takes what it wants with no thought for the rest of us. We were lucky you came along. It would have been a tragedy if he didn't survive."

"Is he a friend of yours?"

"I wouldn't go that far," the Hountan said, "but Counhack was a good man to work for, very generous. I was eager to give back to him in any way I could."

"Loyalty like that is all too uncommon these days," Father Tanner said.

"Yes, doctors aren't the only thing in short supply in the Brotherhood. It's nice to know that there are still good people around." One of its legs scraped absentmindedly against the floor, in a gesture that Tanner knew from experience indicated deep thought.

Father Tanner removed the tube from the Hountan's arm, and wiped off the few drops of residual blood. "That should be sufficient," he said. "You can return to your quarters, but try to get some rest, and drink plenty of ammonia."

"Of course," the creature said, heaving himself off the stool. He plodded a few steps across the airlock, but before scurrying out the door, he turned slightly to better align one of his eyes to look back at Tanner. "You do the Brotherhood a great service."

Eve heaved the large tool bag over her shoulder and crossed the threshold as the tight corridor opened into the cavernous cargo hold. The strap bit into her shoulder as it swung back and forth with each step, but she didn't have far to walk. She dropped the bag in front of a large access panel on the left wall, right next to where Andrew was fiddling with a hand-held scanner of some kind. He smiled up at her.

"What's up?" he asked.

"Just trying to get this ship to run right for once in her life," Eve grumbled, unscrewing the panel from the wall.

"What's wrong with it now?"

"Wiring. I think. I won't know for sure until I get a look in there."

"Uh, anything I need to be worried about?" Andrew said with a nervous look that was probably just for show.

"Not unless we go into deep space," she said, setting the panel down on the floor and examining the wires.

"I wouldn't want to have your job," Andrew said, shaking his head. "Not on a ship like this."

"I wouldn't want you to either," Eve said with a smile. "You'd probably get us all killed."

Andrew cleared his throat awkwardly, turning back to his work in silence. Eve groaned and set down the bundle of wires she was looking through.

"I'm sorry, that was a rude thing to say. I haven't talked to another human being in a long time, and Damien and I have this kind of insulting banter thing we do. It's just how I'm used to communicating."

"Right," Andrew said, still turned away, working. "I understand."

"What are you doing?" Eve asked as she browsed through the bundle of multi-colored wires.

"I'm setting up the X-ray machine to irradiate the blood for the transfusion."

"Irradiate it?" Eve asked. "What for?"

"To sterilize it. We don't want to give him any germs along with the new blood. He's too weak to fight off an infection."

"Oh, that makes sense I guess. Are you going to irradiate yourselves, so you don't bring any of their germs in here?"

"If I brought any in with me," said Andrew, "they'll all be dead anyway. The Hountan planet has an ammonia-based biology, so any germs that make it out of the airlock would just get fried by the oxygen on contact."

"Cool," said Eve, sticking her head and torso into the wall.

"Yeah," said Andrew absentmindedly as he tried to see what she was doing. Eve let out a yelp, followed immediately by a metal clang. "Are you OK?"

"Yep," said Eve as she emerged from the panel, with a rat skewered on her screwdriver. A few drops of blood dripped down the shaft. "Better than OK. This explains a lot, actually."

"Oh. Good for you, I guess."

"Feel like breaking for a snack?" Eve asked, smiling, as she brushed her hair out of her face and thrust the dead rodent forward.

"Um..." he muttered, raising one eyebrow, "I can't say that I'm hungry right now. Not anymore."

"Suit yourself." Eve sat up and looked around her. "Do you have a... trash bag or something over there?"

"I'll take it to the incinerator," Andrew said, "I was going to get some things out of my quarters anyway."

"Thanks," Eve said as she handed the rat kebab to him.

* * *

Andrew strolled across the cargo hold to the hallway, the cold metallic clang of his boots on the floor barely registering in his mind. With a start, he found himself stopped in the middle of the hallway with Damien's hand on his chest.

"What's with the rat-on-a-stick?" he asked. "And why are you smiling like an idiot?" Damien peered at him with an expression that could have been resentment, confusion, or just a lack of sleep.

"Oh, Eve found it inside the wall. I was just getting rid of it for her."

"Right," Damien said curtly as he studied Andrew's face. After a few moments he seemed satisfied, and grunted as he pushed past Andrew. After a few steps, he turned and called back. "Hey, you know you're not going to be here for much longer."

"Yeah," Andrew said with just a tinge of remorse, "I know."

"Don't let her get attached to you. 'Cause I'm the one that's going to have to clean up your mess."

"I'll try."

"You'd better."

Father Tanner hung the bag of donated blood on the IV rack, and lifted up the patient's eyelid. The eye underneath was black, with a yellow pupil in the center. It made no attempt to constrict when the bright beam of Father Tanner's flashlight danced across it.

"He's still unconscious," he said. "We'd better hurry up; he's been out for over a day, and the longer we wait, the greater the chance of permanent brain damage."

"Yeah," pitched in Damien over the radio, "and the sooner I get my money, the better."

"Are you watching the procedure?"

"Got no flying to do. Might as well."

"Well, I should warn you that it's going to be boring," Tanner said. "About three hours of watching blood drip."

Damien sighed melodramatically. "At least it's a pretty color."

"It looks like we're all set, Father," Andrew said. "Where's the needle?"

"No needle," said Father Tanner, "we're going through the hands."

"Sounds painful," Damien said.

"The Hountans have an orifice in the hands, specifically for transferring blood," Tanner explained. "Back in less healthy times, fathers would link hands with their children to filter pathogens and toxins from their systems and take them on themselves, like a natural dialysis. In modern times, it's used only rarely, for emergencies and ceremonial occasions."

"Weird," said Damien.

"Yes, but it's also a wonderful metaphor for substitutionary atonement; I wrote a sermon on it once."

"I'm sure you did."

Father Tanner took the Hountan's hand and carefully opened it up, revealing a small opening in the palm, covered with a tough flap of skin. Peeling it back revealed a pale, thin tube nestled under the surface. Pressing on the skin around it caused the tube to poke out of its hole, and Father Tanner inserted the catheter into it. Musculature at the tip reflexively clamped down on it, and Andrew opened the flow. For several moments, no one spoke, but only watched. Eventually, the beeping from the monitor changed in tempo.

"Heart rate is decreasing back toward normal range," Andrew said with a sigh of relief, and Tanner could hear a smile through the radio. "It looks like it's working."

"Glad to hear it," Damien said.

"What are you going to use your share of the money for?" Tanner said. "If you don't mind me asking."

"I'm gonna fix up *Malika* here, get a new IS drive, maybe a hot tub..."

"I don't suppose you would consider a donation to charity, would you?"

Damien laughed. "You want me to help fund your little operation, huh?"

"I'm sure somebody in your line of work has plenty of penance to pay."

"Well, it just so happens I already contributed to your charity."

"Oh really?" asked Father Tanner. "When was that?"

"Back at Galessi's joint, when I didn't punch you back."

Tanner chuckled. "I suppose beggars can't be choosers."

The heart rate monitor picked up speed, and the patient shifted, legs weakly searching for traction on the table.

"He's waking up," Andrew said.

"Hold him down," Tanner said, "We don't want him to get spooked and pull out the catheter." He switched on the outer radio, and spoke to the patient through the translator. "It's alright," he said, "we're friends. You're receiving necessary medical attention."

The patient growled and mumbled noises that couldn't be translated, his mouth twitching and quivering, and tried to sit up. Andrew grasped his torso, and tried to gently keep him from moving. The patient began shaking slightly, and then collapsed onto the table.

"He's out again," Andrew said.

"He must still be weak," Tanner said, "He should come to, once the transfusion is over."

Andrew peered closely at the Hountan's torso. "Does his skin look discolored to you?"

"I think you're right," Tanner said. "And it's not just from hypovolemia." He picked up a hypodermic needle and inserted it slowly into the discolored patch. A pull on the plunger filled the tube with thick, deep blue fluid that swirled with thin streaks of copper.

"Well, that's not good," Andrew said.

"That's what I thought," Father Tanner said, "It's acidosis; we need to get him on lithium now."

"Right," said Andrew, running to get the supplies.

"Ghenni!" called Father Tanner over the radio.

"Yes, Father?"

"I need you to get on the radio with the Hountan captain. We need to double the pressure in this airlock."

"Why?"

"Because something in the patient's body is producing acid, and when that acid hits the blood, it turns into hydrogen gas. Those bubbles are going to give him a really bad case of the bends unless we get the pressure up."

"Very well, I'll tell them."

"This is bad news for us, isn't it?" asked Damien.

"It looks like we won't be getting our money quite so easily," Father Tanner said as he helped Andrew set up the new intravenous bag, "but there's good news too."

"What's that?"

"You're not bored right now, are you?"

The aroma of stale coffee filled the air, keeping the bitter aftertaste on Father Tanner's tongue. He sat in the ship's galley, at a table covered in tattered medical texts, their pages once slick but now smudged with ancient use. Most of them were in the Hountan script, a combination of swirls and sharp lines that were starting to give him a headache. He slipped off his glasses and slowly rubbed his eyes, until a voice spoke behind him.

"Why is there tape on the intercom?" Damien asked.

"To hold the button down, obviously," Tanner said. He took another drink from his plastic mug, and grimaced at the cheap, lukewarm coffee. There were much better drinks for keeping awake on Trenth, but Damien was apparently intent on using smuggled coffee beans that ended up spending months lying in a secret compartment next to God-only-knew-what. "Andrew's in with the patient to keep an eye on him, but I need to brainstorm with him to figure out the diagnosis."

"So you still don't know what's wrong with him?" Damien asked as he poured a cup of coffee from the stained pot on the counter to the side. He took a drink, then closed his eyes and shook his head sharply at the metallic overtones.

"Not yet," Father Tanner sighed.

"Where's Ghenni?"

"He's on the radio with the other captain, trying to do damage control."

Andrew's voice came in over the intercom. "People don't always eat well on space flights," he said. "Maybe it's a vitamin deficiency?"

"I already thought of that, and I've checked, but there aren't any vitamin deficiencies that can cause acidosis like that."

"Even when combined with severe blood loss?"

"No, I'm afraid not."

"Weird..." muttered Damien.

"What?" Father Tanner asked.

"It's just that I actually understand what you're talking about. I assumed all the medical talk would seem more, well, alien."

"Aliens aren't as different from us as you might think. Every intelligent life form still needs some kind of brain to process thought, some kind of circulatory system to deliver nutrients, and an excretory system to remove waste."

"And lungs to breathe air, I suppose?"

"Actually, Hountans don't breathe, but they do have lungs for speech. They can survive just fine without them."

"They don't breathe?"

"Well, they still exhale waste," said Father Tanner, "but they don't get their energy from oxygen. They get it from sulfur dissolved in the ammonia they drink."

"If they don't breathe, then why are we so worried about keeping the air separate?"

"Because the waste they exhale is hydrogen sulfide gas, which is toxic to us, and our oxygen is corrosive to their tissues. Not to mention, they need the pressure to keep the gases properly dissolved in their blood. Now, if you're done asking questions-"

"Hey, he did get sick right after you gave him the blood. Could that be the problem?"

Father Tanner scratched the side of his head and took a deep breath before answering. "We bombarded the donated blood with X-rays to prevent infection, and if it already had acidosis, we would have noticed the change in color. Now, would you mind leaving us alone so we can get back to work?"

"I'll shut up Pops," Damien said, leaning against the counter as he took a sip of coffee, "but I'm not leaving. I'm the captain, so I need to know what's going on around here."

"Suit yourself."

"He was on an inspection tour, right?" crackled Andrew's voice from the speaker. "Maybe he stopped on a planet where he didn't need a suit, and picked up an infection."

"It's a possibility," Father Tanner said. "I'll have Ghenni ask about their itinerary. In the meantime, I want to get an X-ray scan, and look for anything out of the ordinary."

"Alright, I'll get the scanner set up. Back up, that is."

"What kind of antibiotics do we have on hand?"

"Just some broad-spectrum stuff they had in their first-aid kits. Nothing too powerful."

"In that case, you'd better let me do the scan. As our resident chemist, I need you to get started making some more potent antibiotics, just in case."

"Are we going to get a chance to eat somewhere in there?"

The thought triggered a rumbling in Father Tanner's stomach. "We could stand to break for dinner," he said, turning toward Damien.

Damien looked down into his cup of coffee, and gave a slight grunt. "Give me half an hour," he said, "and I'll have something ready."

Andrew strolled into kitchen, still wearing his surgical suit and holding the helmet under his arm, to find everybody else sitting down to a table of empty bowls. The table was a simple, small rectangle, topped with polymer colored in a poor imitation of wood grain. Along the far corner ran a stainless steel counter, sprinkled with spilled rice and coffee grounds, along with red spots of long-dried sauces. Damien's mobile hung on the wall, and the entire span of it was acting as a video monitor, patched into the camera and vital signs monitor in the operating theater. The patient remained still, and the heartbeat weak but steady.

"Looks like I'm just in time," Andrew took a chair next to Eve and peeled off his gloves.

She recoiled as he sat down and fanned the air from her nose. "Ugh," she groaned with a chuckle, "you smell horrible!" She scooted her chair a couple of inches farther away from him.

"Sorry about that," Andrew said. "I have to keep the suit on in case there's an emergency in the airlock. I guess there's still a bit of ammonia hanging on, isn't there?"

Damien walked over from the stove holding a large, steaming black pot with pink floral oven mitts. The dish plopped down in the middle of the table with a thud, causing the table settings to rattle. He walked around behind Andrew to the last empty seat, and paused, glancing at him, before sitting down.

"What is it?" asked Ghenni.

"Rice and beans," replied Damien, pulling his chair forward and reaching out to spoon himself a bowlful.

"What kind of beans?"

"Pinto beans. You're safe, buddy."

"Father," said Andrew, holding out his hands on either side, "would you like to bless the food?"

Father Tanner looked at Andrew and raised one eyebrow. Andrew looked to Eve, who looked back at him quizzically, and then to Damien, who glared back with narrowed eyes.

"I guess we're not holding hands then," Andrew said, pulling his hands back onto his lap.

"We're not praying either," Damien said, shoving a forkful of rice into his mouth. "My cooking's gone unblessed for years, and it hasn't made anybody sick yet."

Eve cleared her throat loudly.

"Okay, one time!" Damien said. "And it wasn't my fault; that guy unloaded some sausages on me that were a *bit* past the expiration date."

"You know," Father Tanner said, "there's plenty of good food on Trenth, as well as some of the other planets in the Alliance. It would be a lot cheaper than shipping it in from Earth."

"Maybe," Damien said. "But you never know what might end up being toxic. Plus, this stuff reminds me of home."

"If you say so," Father Tanner replied. He bowed his head for a few moments, and Andrew followed suit. When they opened their eyes, Eve was filling her bowl, and Ghenni was quietly chanting while holding his soulstone. When he finished, he placed it in the bowl and spooned rice on top of it.

"Why is there a rock in your bowl?" asked Eve.

"It's my soulstone," Ghenni explained. "I'm asking the gods to provide nourishment on my soul as well as my body."

"That's interesting; is that something a lot of Trenthans do?"

"Many of my people have fallen away from our traditional rites, but I am surprised that you haven't encountered others in your dealings on Trenth."

"Well, the smuggling business doesn't attract the most devout crowd, you know. So if you're not an Emmanuelite, how did you end up working with Father Tanner?"

Ghenni paused and shifted in his seat before answering. "The

Brotherhood Fleet has... conscripted almost all the doctors to serve in the war, leaving my planet with a shortage of medical aid. I decided that it would be worthwhile to work by Father Tanner to save the lives of my people, even if it means letting him preach a foreign religion."

"What Ghenni fails to mention," Father Tanner said, "is that Emmanuelites are native to Trenth. Native to all planets, in fact."

"What Father Tanner fails to mention," Ghenni replied, "is that what he calls Emmanuelites were an obscure sect, scattered across Trenth, and generally regarded as fools."

"Sounds a lot like Earth," Damien said with a smile, "last time I was there."

"Don't you find it the least bit coincidental," Father Tanner asked, "that every known sentient race has a religion based on a man who was God incarnate, dying to absolve the people of their sins?"

"No, I don't," Damien said, "just like I don't think it's a coincidence that they all invented knives either. Any sentient beings that weren't able to think those things up never lasted long enough to become civilized."

Father Tanner nodded in approval. "The Messianic Sociology argument. I see you've done your reading."

"When you're hiding out on an asteroid for a week, waiting for the heat to move on, there's not much else to do. You can only bang sexbots so many times in a day."

Father Tanner cleared his throat and went back to eating.

"Aww, I made him blush," Damien said with a smile as he took another bite.

"What about you?" Andrew said to Eve. Her eyebrows shot up before Andrew continued. "I mean, what do you believe?"

"Oh," she said, brushing back her hair and looking into her bowl. "My grandparents were fairly strict Catholics hold-outs from the Emmanuelite Unification. I heard a lot of lectures growing up about how the aliens were demons, that kind of thing. But I haven't been to Mass since I was a girl."

"I see," said Andrew, turning back to his bowl after glancing at the watching eyes of Father Tanner and Damien. They all spent the next few minutes eating in silence.

"Well," said Father Tanner eventually, putting down his empty bowl, pushing back his chair, and standing up, "I think that's enough idle chit-chat for tonight. We have a patient to cure."

Andrew cleared his throat and stood to leave as well. "I've got the scanner ready for you to do the X-ray. As soon as you're suited up, I'll get started on the antibiotics."

"And be quick about it," Damien said as Andrew and Father Tanner left. "If you spend the night again, I'll have to wash your sheets, and the maid charges extra for that."

Chapter Six

"I have some questions for you regarding the patient's medical history," Ghenni said. He was back in the captain's uniform, which itched from being over-starched. On the video screen of the cockpit, the captain of the Hountan ship sat on his stool, wrapped in his own rust-brown uniform leggings. He twitched in agitation.

"I thought the blood transfusion was supposed to cure him."

"New symptoms have appeared," Ghenni said, "which indicate there is an underlying medical problem in addition to his injuries."

"What information do you need?" the captain asked, raising his torso slightly. Ghenni wasn't sure what to make of the body language.

"The doctor believes he may have picked up an infection. We need to know what planets he visited during the inspection tour, so that we can determine when he might have been exposed, and to what."

The Hountan's eye flicked back and forth for a moment before he responded. "That business is classified information. In any case, he was wearing a suit on all stops, so an infection is out of the question. You would do well to keep your questions to medical matters only."

"I'm terribly sorry, but I–"

"What are the other possibilities?"

Ghenni cleared his throat. "The doctor is preparing to do an X-ray scan to look for any malignant growths or other anomalies."

"You have an X-ray scanner on board?"

"Yes, we do."

"Is that normal, for a freighter?"

"The doctor likes to be prepared."

"Apparently so," said the captain. After a pause, he continued. "Let me know when you have more information." The screen clicked off abruptly.

Ghenni jogged down the corridor to the cargo hold, the clang of his boots echoing harshly in the metal corridor. When he got there, he found Andrew in the corner, wearing safety glasses and a stained white coat, tinkering with a desktop microsynthesis kit. He walked up to the airlock, and through the multiple windows he could just make out a suited figure holding the X-ray wand over the patient. The button on the intercom clicked faintly as he connected to Father Tanner's suit radio.

"Father," he said, "I spoke with the Hountan captain, and he says that they made no stops without suits."

"Alright," Father Tanner said, "I'll have the X-ray up in a few minutes, and we'll see where we go from there."

"The captain definitely suspects something," Ghenni added. "When I asked what planets they stopped at, he was very defensive, and seemed to think we were stepping out of our bounds. I don't think we can push him with any more information."

"Then we'd better hope and pray we don't need any more."

"Hey guys," Damien's nervous voice said over the intercom, "I just picked up a coded subspace transmission from the Hountan ship. It's got some heavy-duty encryption on it, so it's probably headed for a regional command center at least. It looks like somebody's checking up on us."

"What do you want me to do about it?" asked Father Tanner over his radio.

"It's only going to be a matter of hours before they find out we're not really a Brotherhood freighter," Damien said. "That means we need to get this guy patched up, seal the deal, and get out of Dodge before then. Can you handle that, Pops?"

"I haven't even diagnosed him yet. It depends on what he has, but it's going to be a tight squeeze at best."

"I'm never one to shy away from a tight squeeze."

Father Tanner sighed, and then came into *Malika*'s airlock. "I've got the scan," he said. "I'll get it uploaded and take a look as soon as I get back in there."

The airlock hissed as the gases inside were switched out and the pressures equalized. After a few minutes, Father Tanner emerged from the door and peeled off his helmet. He went up to the computer console on the cargo hold wall, and punched a few buttons to link up to the scanner. Andrew and Ghenni gathered around, and with a few more keystrokes Father Tanner brought up the X-ray scan.

"Well," said Andrew, "I guess that's the problem."

A semi-transparent picture of the Hountan patient sprawled across the screen. The light images of bones were stretched out, prostrate, and covered by the thin, ethereal shapes of flesh and organs. And right in the middle of the body was a small, opaque spot.

"What is it?" asked Ghenni.

"It's too dark and rigid to be a growth. Must be a foreign object," said Father Tanner.

"But what exactly?" asked Andrew. "And how did it get there? It's not in the digestive system or any orifice."

"At least, not any natural orifice," pointed out Father Tanner. He used a stylus to circle a couple of spots on the creature's perimeter, and marked the line between them. "It's right in the path of the wounds from the accident."

"You're right," said Andrew, "it must have gotten lodged in there from the explosion. But what kind of foreign object would cause severe acidosis? Certainly not metal shrapnel."

"Perhaps fleshy matter from another victim," said Ghenni.

"No," said Father Tanner, "that wouldn't be opaque on the X-ray like this." He paused for a few seconds. "What were they mining there?"

"Most likely iron," answered Ghenni. "It's the only significant resource we ship off-planet."

"That means hematite," said Andrew. "That's a hydrated mineral. It's been leeching water into his system."

"But water isn't an acid," said Ghenni.

"It is to them," Father Tanner said. "All of the Hountan body systems are based on ammonia, which is a potent base. Water to them would be like injecting one of us with hydrochloric acid."

"So it looks like we need to do surgery then," Andrew said.

"Yes, and we need to do it fast," said Father Tanner. "Ghenni, you'll need to stay out here in case the Hountans want to talk to you. Andrew, you'll be my nurse, but we may need an extra person to run the anesthetic."

"I bet we could get Eve to help out," Andrew said.

"I'm afraid that would be too much of a distraction."

"Come on, give me some credit as a professional."

Tanner rolled his eyes. "I meant for her; she still has repairs to do on the ship, and we need to be ready to leave at a moment's notice."

"Oh, right. I guess that leaves Damien."

Father Tanner rolled his eyes and leaned into the intercom, "Captain Rogers," he said, "we're preparing for surgery, and we could use an extra pair of hands. How would you feel about being our anesthetist today?"

"What does that mean?" Damien asked.

"It means you turn a knob when I say so."

"That doesn't sound like a lot of fun."

"It would help you get your money faster."

"Then I'm in. I'll be right down to suit up."

Half an hour later, Damien stood in the Hountan airlock, shifting awkwardly in the surgical suit as he kept his fingers poised on the valve in the IV drip, ready to turn it whenever Tanner told him to. The anesthetic kept the alien creature entirely motionless, although he had never actually become completely lucid since he was brought over. The thing creeped him out royally. The mouth seemed entirely too large for its body, and he always felt like it was about to jump up and clamp on his arm with its rings of teeth.

"So this is all I'm doing?" Damien asked. "Keeping my hand on this knob thing?"

"And waiting for instructions," Tanner added. "First, let's pray for a successful surgery."

"Sheesh. Before eating, doing surgery... Can you even go to the bathroom without praying first?"

"Yes, if I'm not expecting trouble."

Tanner and Andrew bowed their heads almost imperceptibly inside their helmets, and the priest prayed in a low voice.

"Father, we lift up this man to You, and ask that You help bring him healing in Your capacity as the Great Physician. We thank You for the gifts You have given us to carry out Your work of healing–"

"I hate just waiting around doing nothing," mumbled Damien.

Tanner cleared his throat, continuing. "And ask that the Spirit guide our hands as we minister to Your creation. By the Spirit, through the Son, to the Father. Amen." After a pause, he took a deep breath. "Scalpel." Andrew handed the instrument to him.

"So how long is this going to take, anyway?" Damien asked.

"The surgery itself should be only a few minutes," Tanner said, slicing open the sutures on the patient's abdomen. The skin peeled away in fits and starts as the sutures snapped one by one, revealing bronze-stained wet flesh underneath. "It'll take a few hours for clean-up and post-op before we can leave."

Damien sighed melodramatically, slowly rocking forward and backward.

"Endoscope," Tanner said. Andrew handed him the long, flexible tube, and Tanner inserted it into the opening. He pressed a button on his end of the tube, and an image appeared on a video screen on the wall. It looked like a dark tunnel, its sides made up of yellow and pale green tissues, laced with webs of blood vessels and wet with metallic Hountan bodily fluids. There were visible streaks of raw and torn flesh all along the path as Tanner fed the endoscope farther inside, most of them patched up with thin plastic sutures.

"That's some ugly crap in there," said Damien.

"It's beautiful in its own way," Tanner said. "Maybe not in appearance, but in design. Everything working together, automatically and in complete harmony, even down to the atomic level. It's poetic, really."

"Until it gets a pipe launched through it, that is."

"True enough."

The camera kept moving through the patient's body, and past an indistinct lump of flesh, a spot of red and brown appeared, speckled with bright blue liquid.

"That looks like it," Andrew said.

Tanner advanced the camera forward, and the piece of hematite ore came into full view. The doctor pressed another button, and four thin metal fingers slid out of the end of the tube, expanding into a claw. It reached forward and wrapped around the chunk of mineral, pulling it toward the camera as the wires retracted into the endoscope. It took a couple of tries to get a firm grip, but after just a minute or two, it latched on solidly.

"I've got it," Tanner said. "I'm pulling out."

A calm beeping came over the radio, and Damien stiffened. All the background noise faded away as his heart quickened, and the blood pounded in his ears.

"What's that?" asked Andrew.

"That," said Damien, "is very bad news."

"How bad?" asked Father Tanner.

"We just picked up an encrypted subspace signal meant for the Hountan ship. In about five minutes, they'll be coming in here after us."

"I thought we were supposed to have several hours," said Father Tanner. He hastily pulled the endoscope the rest of the way out and dropped it to the instrument table with a clatter.

"There must have been a fleet command ship nearby with its own database," Damien said, shutting off the flow of the anesthetic drip. "We need to get out of here. Close him up, Pops."

"I can't just staple him shut and hand him over," cried Tanner, hurriedly grabbing the suture kit. "He needs post-op care."

"Then it's a good thing we're not handing him over," said Damien. He pressed himself against the wall and scanned the corners of the airlock, until he found a small indentation.

"We're not taking him with us," Tanner said, "I'm not going to add kidnapping to my list of sins."

Before Damien to reply, the Hountan captain came over the radio. "You will step away from the patient immediately," he said. "You are under arrest for espionage and impersonating the officers of a Brotherhood ship."

"I'm going to need to borrow this," Damien said, ripping one of the air tanks off Father Tanner's back. He pointed the nozzle at the small indentation he had found in the corner of the wall, and opened it all the way. A white plume of condensing ammonia vapor formed in the air ahead of him as the rapidly expanding gases cooled the atmosphere. The white cloud billowed up and mushroomed across the ceiling before beginning to drift down.

"What are you doing?" screamed Tanner.

"I'm fouling the air sensor so they can't open the door."

"You'll poison the patient!"

"Then I guess you'll just have to take him into our ship! Eve, I need you to get us ready to detach. And override the air sensor fail-safe."

"Already started, captain."

Tanner clenched his fists for a moment, and then gave a quick sigh. "Grab him," he said to Andrew, "and get all the equipment you can in with him."

A piercing alarm sounded through the airlock and flashing lights bathed the room in a pulsing red glow. Andrew and Tanner hurriedly shuttled carts full of medicines and surgical instruments back into the *Malika*'s airlock, while Damien kept the leaking air tank spewing its toxic contents on the air sensor. Through the small window into the Hountan ship, he saw the spider-like creatures scurrying around the door, trying to hack into their own computers and override the fail-safe to keep the humans from escaping with their crew mate.

By the time the alarm stopped, the airlock was mostly empty, its contents thrown haphazardly into the *Malika*'s larger freight airlock chamber.

"Get into our ship!" Damien yelled. "It looks like they got the override to work. Eve, close the door now!"

Damien dropped the air cylinder and bolted for his own ship's airlock. The door slid down quickly from the ceiling, and he dropped down to the ground, letting his momentum slide him under the door. The hiss of the door behind him announced the arrival of the Hountan crew, and just before his own door closed, a hail of bullets ricocheted off the outside with curt metallic pings. Damien didn't stop his slide soon enough, and crashed into a cart, which spilled surgical instruments on top of him as it fell.

"Is everybody alright?" he muttered as he carefully stood up among the blades scattered around him.

"They shot at us," said Andrew, dumbfounded.

"What, you've never been shot at before?"

"No."

"Well, it may be fun the first time, but it loses its appeal pretty quick."

A muffled hiss filled the air as the ship detached itself and took off.

"Do you want to open fire?" asked Eve from the cockpit.

"No, let them go," Damien said. "We still need our money."

"Are you insane?" asked Tanner. "You think they're still going to pay us for our services after we kidnapped the patient?"

"No," said Damien, "I think they're going to pay us ransom. We can probably get more than forty-thousand too, so count yourself lucky."

"You can't possibly expect me to be a party to this."

"Look, you already handled the doctoring. Let me handle the business transactions."

"We're talking about a man's life!"

"I'm talking about our lives," said Damien. "We both need the money to keep going."

"Yes, but honest money," Tanner said, "not blood money."

"For crying out loud, we're not going to kill him! If he dies, we don't get anything."

"We should have just cut our losses and left without him," Tanner said.

"It just so happens that our hostage is the only thing standing between us and those 29-GM laser cannons that the other ship was packing. Or didn't you notice? As long as we have him, we're safe and we have leverage."

Tanner fumed for a moment, and kicked an ammonia tank, sending it clanging to the ground, where it rolled slowly in an arc. "What do we do now?"

"Eve's taking us to a hideout I know, and we can take stock of things once we're safe there. But for now," Damien said, reaching for the control panel, "I need to get out of this suit and change into some fresh clothes."

"Don't hit that," said Tanner, grabbing his wrist. "We can't switch atmospheres while the patient is in here."

"So... how do we get out?"

"We need to get Eve and Ghenni to set up a pressure tent at the doorway to serve as a makeshift airlock. Please tell me you have one aboard somewhere."

"Yeah, I do," said Damien.

He relayed the instructions to Ghenni on setting up the pressure tent, and within a few minutes, it began to take shape on the other side of the window. Plastic supports held up semi-transparent polymer sheets, and slowly expanded them into a general boxy shape, large enough to hold a few people tightly packed.

As Damien watched Ghenni and Eve assemble the skeleton of the device, the steady beeping of the patient's monitors quickened, and the metal framework of the examination table rattled with increasing volume. All three humans turned to look at the Hountan, who kicked his legs spasmodically and threatened to tumble to the floor.

"He's seizing!" Andrew shouted, putting his weight against the patient to keep him from shaking himself off the table.

"We need three mils of cretamiphan," said Tanner, rushing to one of the containers full of medicine.

"You wanna get that for me?" Andrew said. "I'm a little busy at the moment."

"Got it," Tanner said, turning around and jamming the syringe into the patient's leg. After a few seconds, the patient slowly relaxed and went limp, and the beeping of the monitors settled back to normal.

"I thought you said you fixed him," Damien said.

"I thought I did," said Tanner. "There must be something else wrong with him."

Damien gave a frustrated grunt. "This just got a lot trickier, didn't it?"

Chapter Seven

Half an hour later, the three emerged from the flimsy plastic pressure tent set up over the airlock door. Andrew peeled off his helmet with a sigh of relief, reveling in the blast of cool air against his sweat-dampened skin, and immediately began taking off the rest.

"Eve," Damien asked over the intercom, his helmet already under his arm, "where do we stand?"

"We've got about twenty minutes until we need to start the descent. You'd better be up here for the landing."

"Where are we going?" asked Andrew.

"I know a great little spot up north," replied Damien, stepping out of the body of the suit. "There's a cave that I hide in when the heat's on too thick. Between all the rock, and magnetic pole right next door, the ship is practically undetectable."

"You think they're going to come after us?"

"Not them specifically, but you can bet they've already sent a distress call to that Brotherhood fleet command ship. They're not equipped for this sort of thing. Within a few hours they'll have ships scouring the whole planet, not to mention the rest of the solar system, for us."

"What do we do now?"

"You two," said Damien, wagging his finger back and forth between Andrew and Father Tanner, "are going to concentrate on curing our guest. A dead hostage doesn't give us much bargaining power."

"I still don't think that we should be trading sentient lives like commodities," Father Tanner said as he pulled off his gloves.

"Yes, your opinion has already been duly noted and filed under 'I don't give a rat's ass.'"

"*But*," Father Tanner continued, "as I was going to say, for now I'm going to concentrate on doing my job, and we can re-examine the options when the patient is stable."

"Right, whatever. I'm going to go land the ship, and you two can start doctoring."

Damien sauntered out of the cargo hold, and Andrew and Father Tanner finished taking off their suits and hung them up on the wall. Sweat plastered their clothes against their skin, and Andrew was glad to feel the refreshing flow of air on each new exposed section of his body.

"Let's get Ghenni and start a differential diagnosis in a few minutes," Father Tanner said, "In the meantime, you find something to write with, and I need to visit the facilities."

"Yes, Father."

"And Andrew," Father Tanner called out as he turned to leave.

"Yes?"

"You didn't speak up when we talked about holding the patient for ransom. I'm trying to do the right thing here, but I need to know that you'll back me up. Don't you have a problem with what's going on?"

"I don't want to do it," said Andrew, shrugging, "but as long as no one gets hurt, it seems like the best option, doesn't it?"

Father Tanner pursed his lips. "I know. That's what I'm afraid of."

A few minutes later, Andrew stood by the cargo hold wall, marker in hand, while Father Tanner and Ghenni seated themselves on empty crates in the middle of the floor. A large patch of the steel wall had been scrubbed clear of grime to provide a writing surface, and it shone slightly in the diffuse lighting of the room.

"Let's get started," Father Tanner said. "What are the patient's symptoms?"

"Well, seizures, obviously," Andrew said, writing the word on the wall.

"And," said Ghenni, peering through the airlock window at the monitors, "a slight fever."

"Anything else?" asked Andrew.

"He could have any manner of pains or discomforts," Father Tanner said, "but he can't report them, and they would be masked by his physical injuries anyway, so nothing else is certain."

"That doesn't give us much to go on," Andrew said, but he marked it on the wall, followed by a question mark.

"I think we can start by assuming that this new condition is also a result of the accident. It seems much more likely than a pure coincidence."

"So what about getting impaled would cause seizures?" Andrew asked.

"The injury was several inches from the brain, so there wasn't any direct physical trauma," said Father Tanner.

"Could it be an infection?" asked Ghenni.

"No, any microbes native to the patient would have been killed when the suit was torn open, and any native to Trenth would be killed by the patient's own bodily fluids."

"I guess that leaves toxins, then," said Andrew.

Father Tanner stared at the wall and rubbed his chin in thought for several moments before nodding. "Agreed. Now the question is, what toxins would be present in the mine?"

"The mines aren't known for their... cleanliness," Ghenni said. "There could be many poisonous things there."

"Whatever it was," Father Tanner said, "it would have had to have been either on the pipe, or the chunk of ore that was lodged inside his body."

"There could have been grease of some kind with the pipe," said Ghenni.

"I don't think grease would cause such severe symptoms," Andrew said. "Hountans are still carbon-based. Simple hydrocarbons would be relatively inert."

The three sat in silence for a moment, until Andrew perked up. "What about heavy metal poisoning from the pipe itself?"

"The pipe was steel," Father Tanner said, "it wouldn't have done this. Although... what kind of explosives do they use in the mine?"

"They probably use lead azide for a primary explosive," Andrew said.

"So there could very easily have been lead dust in the air and on the shrapnel," said Father Tanner, "and lead poisoning would present with neurological symptoms."

"It definitely fits," Andrew said.

"Good. I want you to see if we have any appropriate chelating agents, Andrew, and start making one if we don't."

"I'm on it."

"Ghenni, you keep an eye on the patient, and I'm going to look at some literature and keep working on the diagnosis, just in case."

The ship lurched as it hit the planet's atmosphere, and continued shaking as the air buffeted it at hundreds of miles per hour.

"And pray that this thing holds together," muttered Father Tanner.

Clanging footsteps sounded behind Andrew while he finished dialing the settings on his synthesis unit. The apparatus was the size of a large piece of luggage, with a dozen spots for injecting reagents and a large digital display with temperature and other settings. The interior workings were largely hidden, but a few windows allowed him to see the various chemicals inside. He turned around to see Eve walking out of the corridor with a tool bag slung over her shoulder, and moved to intercept her.

"Thanks for coming," he said with a smile.

"What is it you need help with?" asked Eve.

"I was hoping you could help me with the ventilation system," he said, leading her toward his set-up. "Is there a way to have the vents in just this corner pump the air outside?"

"I should be able to set that up on the console, sure. Why do you want it?"

"Take a couple more steps over here and you'll figure it out."

Eve walked a little closer, took a sniff, and recoiled. "What is that?"

she asked, disgusted.

"It's the chelating agent I'm working on."

Eve gave him a blank look.

"It's the medicine we need for the patient."

"Right," said Eve, walking toward the console on the wall. "But why does it have to smell so bad?"

"It has a lot of thiol groups in it," Andrew said.

"I'm still waiting for the explanation."

"Have you ever smelled a skunk?"

"Oh, gotcha," she said, turning on the console. "What's all this stuff you have pulled up?"

"That's my reference material for the synthesis," Andrew replied. "I had to piece it together from articles on Hountan pharmacology, and translate it with the computer."

"Sounds complicated." Eve punched commands into the screen.

"Yeah, the translation gets a little iffy with all this jargon. I just hope I don't screw anything up."

"Me too," Eve said. "If you blow something up, I'm the one who has to patch up the holes."

Andrew chuckled and smiled broadly at the back of Eve's head. Her hair cascaded gracefully along her shoulders and back, and he couldn't help imagining what it would be like to touch it, feel it run through his fingers, and brush it behind her ear. After a moment he shook his head to snap himself out of his daydreaming. "So... what have you been up to since we landed?"

"Just general maintenance," she said, somewhat absentmindedly. "I finished about an hour ago. Well I'm never *finished*, not with this ship especially, but there's nothing else I can do without more supplies."

The roar of ventilation fans started up behind them, and Andrew tossed a cursory glance back at his workstation. "It looks like that did it," he said. "Thanks."

"You're welcome," Eve said, smiling. "I guess I'd better let you get back to work."

"Actually," he said, "once I get it going, the reaction has to run for a few hours, so I just have to babysit it. You know, watching for error messages, that kind of thing."

"OK..." said Eve awkwardly, fingering the strap on her bag.

"Do you... want to babysit with me?"

"I'm don't think watching a box of tubes is my idea of a fun Friday night," she said.

"Actually, I thought we might pull up a movie on the console, and I have some Trenthan grain puffs, which are the closest thing to popcorn I've been able to find on this planet. No butter, but hey, there's a war on, you know?"

Eve chuckled and looked down at her feet for a second, and then looked back up at Andrew. "Alright," she said, "just let me put my things back in my room."

Damien lumbered out of his quarters and locked the door behind him. He inhaled a lungful of air, fresh air piped in from outside, not recycled or filled with the waste gases of a bustling city. With all the planets he had been on, he was something of a connoisseur of air by now, and Trenth had a pristine, earthy smell that hadn't been destroyed by centuries of pre-nuclear industry. Ghenni came walking down the corridor from his own quarters, and paused and nodded to Damien.

"I was wondering where you were, Captain," he said.

"I've been getting some sleep," Damien replied, straightening his belt.

Ghenni eyed the bottle in his hand. "Is that alcohol?" he asked.

"Mostly, yeah."

"I believed that humans didn't take strong drink right after waking up."

"If you'd lived my life, you wouldn't care about the time of day so much," Damien replied, walking off.

"From being in space so much?" asked Ghenni, following him.

Damien chuckled. "Right, exactly."

They walked in silence for a few paces, and then Damien stopped. "Are you following me?"

"I was already going this way," Ghenni replied. "I intended to sit outside for a bit, at the open air."

"Great minds think alike, huh?"

Damien reached the outer door and hit the button, and the door lock released. Horizontal light bathed the door in a yellow glare as he unfolded it into a ramp to the ground below. "I guess you can pull up a rock if you want," he said, walking down the ramp to the dirt below.

The sun hung low on the horizon, and flooded the landscape with oranges, purples, and the sharp dramatic shadows of looming mountains. Some stars were just visible higher up in the sky. The land just outside the mouth of the cave was littered with pale gray rocks, and a small river wound its way between sheer rock walls, filling the air with the faint gurgling of flowing water.

"Is that sunrise or sunset, do you suppose?" Damien asked as he brushed off a rock and sat on it. A gust of wind whistled across the cave entrance, and he shivered at the thought of the sharply cold mountain breeze outside.

"It's spring in the Northern hemisphere," Ghenni replied, sitting nearby, "so that must be the sunrise. But this close to the axis, it will soon go back down."

Damien gave a thoughtful grunt, and took a drink. The alcohol burned his throat, and drowned out any other flavors that may have been jostling for attention, but he hadn't drunk for the flavor in years. They sat in silence for a few moments, before he spoke. "It's beautiful, isn't it? Things change so fast these days: planets move, and cities grow or get shelled out of existence. But here? These mountains look the same every time I come here."

"I admit I haven't done much traveling. Most Trenthans find the mountains too cold to live among. And it's too hard to grow food, so there are no tribal wars being waged above it. It's nice to see a landscape untainted by blood."

"That's what all the squabbling is about? Farmland?"

"No, water. Much of what we used for farming has been diverted for use in the mines. Now anyone who is too poor to buy food shipped in from other planets must either face an early death in the Brotherhood mines, or fight for the resources to grow their own food. Some have even started attacking Brotherhood facilities, trying to run them off."

"Idiots," Damien grunted. "The Brotherhood has hundreds of industrialized planets, any one of which could blow a city off the map without a second thought."

"That's true," said Ghenni. "But they believe that fighting upon oppression is noble, even if it's hopeless."

"Almost makes me proud to be from the Consortium," Damien said. He was quiet for a few moments, letting his mind drift back to his home. "Do you have a girl back home?"

"I am not yet of age for... sexual relations," Ghenni replied.

"'Sexual relations,'" Damien said in a high, mocking tone. "You learned English from the Father, didn't you? You can say the naughty words in front of me. And anyway, that's not a 'no.' There's somebody, isn't there?"

Ghenni's nose wrinkled with pleasure. "There is a woman that I especially enjoy spending time by," he admitted.

"Just what I thought," Damien said, tossing back another drink. "Same on every planet."

"Are you and Eve a pair?" asked Ghenni.

Damien chuckled. "No, a kick in the crotch cured me of that notion a long time ago."

"I don't understand. Your 'crotch?'"

"Oh, right," Damien said, "you guys don't have any equipment down there. You have the... uh..." He gestured to his face, "danglies. *Glia*. Imagine if someone grabbed those and gave them a good yank."

Ghenni recoiled slightly at the thought. "I see." After a pause, he continued. "So do you not have a woman somewhere?"

"Used to, but not anymore," Damien said, taking another drink.

"Did you have a disagreement?"

"No, she just... never mind. Forget I brought it up."

Neither of them spoke for a few moments. Finally, Ghenni broke the silence. "It seems that the sun is higher now, so it must be sunrise. Excuse me," he said, getting up. He walked to the mouth of the cave, and pulled his soul stone from his pocket. He held it up in front of his face, blocking out the sun, and chanted in a low voice. A couple of minutes passed, and it looked like he might even have fallen asleep standing up. Finally his arm dropped, slipped the stone back into his pocket, and Ghenni sat back down.

"How do you put up with him?" Damien asked.

"Who?"

"Tanner."

Ghenni thought for a moment. "He's a good doctor, and pleasant to be around most of the time. I do my best to avoid conversations on my beliefs."

"So he's that arrogant and self-righteous all the time?"

"I think dealing with criminals makes him worse," Ghenni noted.

"Oh, thanks a lot."

"I didn't mean to insult you."

"Nah, don't worry about it. I've been called worse."

"He likes to fix people," Ghenni continued. "Not just physically, as a doctor, but... spiritually. He thinks his beliefs will fix people."

"I wish it were that easy," Damien muttered.

"If there were no end in sight, I don't think I could tolerate it. But once I am more experienced, I will be able to find employment as a doctor elsewhere."

"Maybe you could take over the mission hospital, and kick Pops out," Damien suggested with a chuckle.

"I would enjoy the responsibility, but I am afraid Father Tanner would never leave the mission in the hands of a... pagan. He already has another Emmanuelite like him training to replace him. Unless something disastrous happens, it will be me that will leave."

"Tough break." Damien mulled it over for a moment. "Well, I suppose I should go do some captainly things. I'll leave the door open for you."

"For the record," Andrew said, as he walked slowly down the corridor with Eve, his legs swinging lackadaisically wide with each step, "I saw that ending coming long before you did. I'm kind of a movie expert."

"Oh really?" Eve said indignantly, "Then why did I have to tell what was going to happen?"

"I just thought it was so obvious, I didn't need to say anything," Andrew said. He let his hand swing a bit farther out than was natural, and felt the cool smooth skin of the back of Eve's hand against his. A single second of lingering was enough of a conformation for him, and he slipped his hand around to the other side, sliding his fingers in between hers and squeezing lightly. He felt like a teenager again, with the warm, slightly moist hand setting his heart to pounding.

"Thanks a lot for tonight," Eve said more softly as they slowly stopped in front of her room. "Most guys on Earth won't take a girl on a date until they've already slept together."

"Well, I guess I have different priorities."

Eve turned to face him, and they both stood silent for a few seconds. Andrew felt her thumb rubbing softly against his hand; he remembered now how good it felt, just to have a woman's skin against his own. As he looked into her eyes, there was no world; everything that existed rested beneath the soft canopy of dark hair. Her face no longer seemed a whole thing, but each angle and curve stood on its own, and each was flawless and inviting. He closed his eyes just before their faces met, and then their noses touched lightly. For a few brief seconds, they simply rubbed noses, reveling in the long-forgotten sensation of someone else's hot breath, until their lips collapsed onto each other in a passionate kiss.

Andrew wrapped his arms around her, holding her as tight as he could and exploring the distinctive feminine contours he hadn't ever felt since he landed on Trenth. Eve reached around him, running her fingers across his back and neck, then clutching with fierce passion. Their lips caressed each other, and nothing else mattered. Eve's tongue felt along Andrew's lips, and then slowly slipped inside his mouth. It touched Andrew's tongue, sending a shiver down both of their bodies, and they kissed with renewed vigor. Eve's hands slipped sensuously down Andrew's back, onto his hips, and then around to the front of his pants. She slowly pulled the zipper down, and Andrew pulled back with a start.

"What are you doing?" he asked.

"What do you think I'm doing?" Eve replied with a mischievous smile. "Come on inside."

"I... can't. We... we just met each other, and..." He wanted to. He wanted desperately to go with her, to follow his body where it wanted to take him. But he knew he couldn't, knew that it was wrong. As fast as it was beating with excitement, Andrew's heart weighed down by the leaden chains of conviction.

"I know we just met," Eve implored, "but I really like you, and I don't know the next time I'll meet someone human out here that isn't a total sleazeball."

"But... weren't you just complaining about guys trying to sleep with you right off the bat?"

"But now we've *been* on a date. And I definitely like you."

"I'm sorry, but... it wouldn't... I just can't."

"Forget about all your rules for a night!" Eve pleaded. "I need this. I need you."

"I-I'm sorry," Andrew said. With that, he turned away sharply, all the smells and sensations torn away from him and replaced with the cold ship. He walked quickly down the corridor to his own quarters, and closed the door behind him. Once inside, he threw himself on the bed, and screamed as loud as he could into a pillow.

"Girl trouble?" asked Father Tanner, who was sitting down on the other side of the room, leafing through a Bible.

"What are you doing here?" Andrew moaned as he turned to face him.

"I saw you and Eve in the cargo hold, and I figured however it went, you'd want to talk about it."

"She wanted to have sex with me."

"I can see that," Father Tanner said. "Your airlock's open."

Andrew looked down, and zipped up his pants. "Sorry."

"So what did you do?"

"I told her I couldn't, and then I came in here. To be alone."

"Is that all you told her?"

"Yeah, pretty much," Andrew said with a sigh.

"I can't imagine she'd take that well," Father Tanner said.

"I think she might have been starting to cry when I left."

He winced. "Ouch. But I'm still proud of you for not giving in. Sexual temptation is one of our biggest struggles as men."

"I know, but... I want to have sex; I want to get married and settle down with someone, start a family, all of that. But it doesn't look like it's going to happen any time soon. Not out here."

"Surely you didn't think this mission would be a good way to meet women. So why did you come out here?" asked Father Tanner, setting down his Bible and not-so-subtly shifting into counselor mode.

"I wanted adventure, I suppose," said Andrew. "And now that I have it, I don't want it any more."

"Did you already want a family back then?"

"I think so. But a few years didn't seem so long then. Plus, I guess I figured God might bring along someone for me, even all the way out in Brotherhood territory," Andrew said, propping himself up on one elbow. "But what if Eve was it, and I just blew my chances?"

"Would you want your future wife to be the kind of woman that throws herself at the first guy to come around? You're not even that good-looking."

Andrew chuckled and collapsed back down. "Thanks a lot."

"Besides," continued Father Tanner, "you know it wouldn't be a good idea to become involved with someone who isn't a believer. You clearly have different values; it would only end in heartache, one way or another."

"Then why didn't you stop me?"

"I would have, if I thought it was physically possible."

Andrew groaned and buried his head in his arms. "What am I supposed to do now?"

"Well, if your right hand causes you to sin..."

"I don't think we've quite gotten to *that* point," Andrew said with a chuckle.

"Are you sure?" Father Tanner replied. "I know a good surgeon. Anyway, how is the chelating agent coming?"

"It has to reflux overnight. Or morning, or whatever it is here. For several hours more, at any rate. Have you confirmed the diagnosis?"

"Not really," Father Tanner said, shaking his head. "We don't have the materials for a blood lead test, and we don't have time to synthesize them or do a fecal analysis. It's going to be faster to just run the chelation therapy and see if it helps."

"Have there been any more seizures?"

"Nothing major. Ghenni did note some twitching of the eyes."

"Alright," Andrew said. "I guess I'll get some sleep for now."

"And I should go take over for Ghenni, watching the patient," Father Tanner said, standing up. He picked up a glass of water sitting next to him, and threw it on Andrew. The ice-cold deluge bit into his chest and lap, sending a wave of goosebumps across his flesh.

"What was *that* for?" Andrew peeled the cold, wet shirt away from his skin.

Father Tanner smiled as he stopped to close the door on his way out. "Just in case."

Fluorescent lights. Rattling in the air duct. The weight of a blanket.

Andrew's senses came online one by one has he slowly faded into consciousness several hours later, incessantly poked in the back by the springs in the worn-out mattress. He heaved himself out of bed, still wearing his clothes from the day before, and brushed his teeth at the grimy sink in the corner. The polished steel mirror warped his face and obscured the wrinkles left on his face by the pillow. As he stepped out into the corridor, the brighter light stung his eyes, and the distant whir and buzz of power tools hummed in his ears. The noise grew louder as he walked down the hallway toward the cargo bay. Inside, he found a large floor panel opened, and the flickering glow of cutting torches played on the walls.

"What's going on in here?" he called, walking toward the edge of the open pit.

Damien's head popped up, covered with soot. "Just working on our end-game."

"What do you mean?"

"I'm getting the ship set up for handing off our hostage. Speaking of which, how's the bug coming?"

"I was about to check on his medicine," Andrew replied.

"Well hurry up. The sooner we hand him over to the Brotherhood, the sooner we can get out of here."

Andrew kept walking around the open pit, to the table with his synthesis kit. A brown residue covered the inside of one of the visible reaction chambers. He quickly checked the settings and saw an oxygen level warning on the display.

"No, no, no, no, *no!*" he cried.

The noise of work in the pit stopped, and Damien and Eve both raised their heads up.

"What is it?" Damien asked.

"Did one of you touch my unit?" Andrew asked angrily.

Damien raised an eyebrow. "Why? What happened?"

"It looks like one of the internal components cracked. Air got into the reaction, and now the medicine is ruined!"

"Are you sure it wasn't cracked when you started?" Damien asked.

"I leak checked it before I started it. It was fine."

"Well, spaceships can be kind of bumpy," Damien said. "I'm sure it was an accident. I certainly know enough to not mess with junk like that."

"Yeah," Eve added, "I know *I*, for one, wouldn't want to hurt someone I'm working with."

"How long will it take to make some more?" Damien asked, casting a glance back at Eve.

"I used up all the catalyst for the first batch," Andrew said. "I'll have to start practically from scratch. It'll take days, and I'm not even sure I have all the materials."

Damien rubbed his forehead in frustration. "Well, we don't exactly have that kind of time."

"So what are we supposed to do now?" Andrew asked.

Damien was silent for a few moments. "Alright, get everybody in here," he said, climbing out of the pit, "It looks like the career criminal is going to have to save the day again."

Chapter Eight

Damien's mobile screen glowed with artificial light as it lay unrolled on the floor and displayed a monochrome satellite image of a city. Everyone clustered tightly around it, sitting on the floor, but Father Tanner paced around the others with his arms crossed, looking down on it from above. His stomach twisted in his gut; this whole operation had gotten way out of hand, but there wasn't anything else they could do now. The whole task was falling apart around him, and despite his best efforts, it was harder and harder to keep faith that things would turn out well in the end.

"OK, our homemade drugs went screwy," Damien explained, "so we're going to have to do a little shopping."

"I assume," said Tanner, "that your idea of shopping doesn't involve paying."

"Not if I can help it."

"Where are we going to find Hountan medical supplies on Trenth?" asked Ghenni. "They won't be stocked with the hospitals."

"It's not exactly well-advertised," Damien said, "but every Brotherhood planet has a stash of medical supplies somewhere for every Brotherhood species, and most of the Federation species too, for emergencies like this."

"Where is it on Trenth?" asked Tanner.

"Back in good ol' Calchassa," replied Damien, zooming in on a sector of the map on his mobile. "On a backwater planet like this, there are only a handful of buildings with their permits blacked out in the city administration server. Those are mostly the 'secret' Brotherhood facilities, and there's only one of those..." Damien pointed at a street corner, "right next to the hospital."

"Won't they expect us to come there?" Andrew asked. "We could be walking into a trap."

"The last they saw of us," Tanner said, "we were already saving the patient."

"Right," said Damien. "They should think the bug is already ship-shape, and they're just waiting for the ransom demand."

"So how do we get in?" Andrew asked.

"We don't know what the inside looks like, so we'll have to play pretty fast and loose on the details. But you can see here..." Damien zoomed in farther, to the grainy aerial photo of the building in question. It was a plain-looking warehouse, long, wide, and shallow, but with fans and air ducts concentrated in one area. "Lots of ventilation and cooling equipment. So that corner is where they keep the drugs. Security will be light, relying mostly on obscurity; just cameras, keypad locks, and a couple of armed guards inside."

"And I'm sure it goes without saying," Tanner said flatly, "that we do this with no body count. No one gets hurt." He crossed his arms and paced around the circle to get a better angle to see the map.

"Relax, Pops. We don't want to draw the kind of attention a frontal assault will get us. We clear the building first, take out the cameras, go in through the back door, grab it, and get out."

"Oh, is that all?" Father Tanner asked. "Just go in the back door?"

"Come on," Damien said. "I know what I'm doing. You don't second-guess the crime, and I don't second-guess the doctoring. Crime is what I do for a living, remember?"

"How could I forget?" muttered Father Tanner.

"Andrew," Damien said, "I need you with me, since you know the shopping list. Eve's going to go into town separately to pick up some other supplies while we're in the neighborhood. That leaves Ghenni and Tanner to watch the hostage."

"The patient," corrected Father Tanner.

"Yeah, whatever. We'll put down outside of Calchassa in three hours. Make sure you're ready."

Andrew sat on the bed in his room with his knees pulled up to his chin. His heart pounded, his mouth was dry, and he prayed silently for peace, eyes closed, but it didn't come. A soft knock rattled the door, and Father Tanner poked his head in.

"Mind if I join you?" he asked.

"Go ahead," Andrew said, letting go of his legs and standing up. He quickly tossed his blanket over the pistol that sat next to him on the mattress.

"Are you sure you're OK going with Damien?" Father Tanner asked.

"I don't really have a choice, do I?" Andrew asked, pacing back and forth. "There's a life on the line." He scratched his head and ran his fingers through his hair, as if to tear out all the doubts and fears that circled in his mind.

"But how do you feel about it?"

"I'm nervous, scared. But I have to admit," Andrew replied with a guilty smile, "it's kind of exciting." Of course, he had originally thought the same thing about working in the mission field, and that wasn't exactly working out well.

"Excuse me if I don't share in your enthusiasm."

"But I can't help but wonder about the failed reaction," said Andrew, chewing on a fingernail. "We could have avoided all this if that hadn't gone bad."

"Accidents happen," said Father Tanner with a shrug.

"Well, what if it wasn't an accident?"

"You think it was deliberate?"

"I don't know. Eve's still really mad at me. You don't think she could have done it, do you?"

"I highly doubt it," Father Tanner said thoughtfully. "It would take a special kind of crazy to try to kill our meal ticket."

"Well I don't think she's crazy," Andrew said, "but she is behind enemy lines in the middle of an inter-planetary cold war. Normal people don't end up in this kind of situation."

"I suppose we can't rule it out completely," said Father Tanner. He glanced over to the bed, and pulled back the blanket. "Is that a gun?"

"Yeah," said Andrew picking it up carefully. "Damien gave it to me. 'Just in case,' he said."

"I'm sure I don't have to tell you, but if it comes down to you or someone else, even Captain Rogers..."

"I know. I'm the one who's prepared for judgment. I'll... try to remember that."

A shout echoed in from the hallway, followed by the crash of a slamming door. Andrew and Father Tanner exchanged glances and ran outside. They found the commotion in the captain's quarters, where Damien was grabbing at Ghenni and pulling him away from the bed as he shouted.

"Get your filthy xenner hands off her!"

Before they could stop him, Damien tossed Ghenni into the opposite wall, knocking a framed picture from the wall, shattering the glass on the floor. Father Tanner rushed forward and pulled Damien away, twisting him into an arm lock while Andrew ran to Ghenni and helped him up. The Trenthan's face was pale with fear.

"I'd appreciate it if you keep your hands off my people." Father Tanner said sternly. "Now explain yourself."

Damien wrenched his arm away from Tanner's grip, but didn't make any moves toward Ghenni. He just rubbed his arm absentmindedly where the priest had grabbed him. "He came into my room and tried to use my sex bot."

"I was only curious about the human... sexuality," Ghenni explained. "I promise I meant no harm or disrespect."

Andrew looked over at the bed and saw the female figure slumped awkwardly among the blankets. She had on only skimpy underwear, showing ample amounts of dark brown skin on her slightly plump figure. The overall effect was an air of playful sensuality, but the give-away was in the eyes. They couldn't hide the lifelessness of the cybernetic contraption. As Andrew studied it, the robot adjusted itself to sit up straighter. It chimed in, "What's wrong, Damey?"

"That's no ordinary sex bot, is it?" Father Tanner asked. "That voice programming is too complicated to be off-the-shelf."

"Hey, I'm not the one on trial here. Besides, what do you know about sex bots?" Damien sneered. He reached around the back of her head and flipped the switch, dropping the woman lifeless onto the bed.

"As a minister, I can assure you I know a lot more about sin than I do about righteousness," he said. "Not to mention this." Father Tanner picked up the broken frame from the nightstand. It contained a portrait of a woman, the same face as on the robot. "Your wife, I presume?"

"It's none of your damn business," Damien said. "Get out. Everybody get out!"

The *Malika* cruised through the lower atmosphere of Trenth in stealth mode. It was a common modification for smuggling ships, and made it invisible to passive scanning instruments. More intensive scans, or simple visual searches, could still see it, so stealth mode was best for hiding out in debris fields and asteroid belts, where other ships were scarce and visual identification was difficult. But being so close to a busy spaceport, Damien simply crossed his fingers and hoped that no one ran into them, literally or figuratively.

The ship settled down gently into a forest clearing several miles outside of the city. The trees around them were scraggly and thin, struggling for survival against the hot, dry climate of the area, but they worked well enough as cover. Damien powered down the ship as much as possible to avoid detection, and hoped that the Alliance had few enough ships to make a visual search impractical.

"Are you ready?" Damien asked Andrew, a bag of equipment slung over his shoulder.

"I think so," Andrew said.

Damien tossed him a khaki hooded robe as they walked down the corridor to the cargo hold. "Put that on. It should make us slightly less conspicuous." He pushed a button on the console in the hold, and a motor overhead started up. As it whined, a small two-person buggy lowered slowly from the ceiling by a winch. Another button opened the large door to the outside, flooding the cargo hold with sunlight, and Damien and Andrew both climbed into the buggy.

"Are you sure you're ready?" Andrew asked. "You know, considering..."

"I'm a lot better than you're going to be if you bring it up," Damien said as he checked the gauges on the dashboard console. Some people needed to learn to leave well enough alone.

"Alright, never mind then."

Damien started up the engine and slipped on some sunglasses. The roar and vibration of the engine beneath the driver's seat made him feel right at home again. "OK, let's go steal us some medicine."

It was a quiet ride through the outskirts of town, apart from the churning of the antiquated internal combustion engine; the sparse greenery of the trees gradually gave way to the dusty dirt roads and earthen buildings of civilization. They slowed when they got into the city limits, and kept their heads down as much as possible. Crowds filled the streets, but Damien knew they wouldn't bother him; even with a price on his head, they didn't dare. At the insistence of the hand-held computer map, Damien turned down an empty alley. The noise of the city faded between the walls of the buildings, while the engine noise reflected off the walls, and seemed even more out of place. Damien turned the buggy so it was pointing out of the alley, and parked it against the wall, blocked from sight by some piles of broken lumber.

The supply dump was barely recognizable at street level. On the satellite image, it was a simple, neat gray rectangle, but in person it was about fifty by a hundred yards of corrugated metal, battered and corroded with age. It looked like hell, but it was decent enough camouflage in the middle of the city. Only the relatively high-end cooling equipment and well-hidden security cameras hinted at the valuable contents.

A couple of blocks away stood the Brotherhood government district, all plate glass, polymer concrete, and stainless steel, a monument of space-age engineering rising out of the slums. A few of the taller buildings towered over the city, peeking above the surrounding rooftops into view and gleaming in black and silver. And on the nearest edge of that stood the government hospital, catering to only the highest local and foreign officials, as well as those who could make generous donations to the war coffers of the Brotherhood.

"Alright," Damien said, "I'm going to trip the alarm. You have the EMP gun?"

"Got it," Andrew said, brandishing the bulky plastic gun. It was full of heavy-duty capacitors that could deliver a pulse of electromagnetic energy strong enough to fry any electronics in its path. It was simpler than hacking or trying to spoof the camera feed, but it lacked subtlety; of course, subtle had never really been Damien's style.

"Stop waving it around like that," Damien said. "Go when the alarm goes off."

Damien walked down the alley toward the street and the front of the warehouse. Near the edge were a handful of high windows, which probably marked the office area. He crouched behind a broken-down washing machine and bicycle, which were rusting into oblivion in the neglected passageway, hiding himself from the gaze of curious onlookers and busybodies walking by in the sunlit thoroughfare. Through one of the windows he could just make out the metal protrusion of a sprinkler system.

"Jackpot."

He pulled a small laser from his pocket. It was compact, but held enough punch in it to start a fire after a few moments if he wanted. He aimed the laser at the sprinkler head, steadying it against his knee. The beam danced around slightly with the vibrations of his hand and knee, but soon he saw the air around it blurring with heat. Within a few seconds, the sprinkler erupted into a shower of water, and the loud shrieks of a fire alarm filled the air. Farther down the alley, Andrew quickly lifted the EMP gun, and sent an invisible pulse of electromagnetic energy hurtling toward the security cameras on the exterior wall, destroying the electronics inside.

"The cameras are out," Andrew said as Damien hurried to the dented metal door in the back.

"Now to get inside," Damien said. He reached into his bag and pulled out a long, thin rope of a gray, clay-like substance. After all, no heist was complete without a little plastic explosive. He pressed it into the seam between the door and door frame, and it oozed into all the tiny cracks and contours. Another chunk went over the electric lock and door handle. Then he placed two electrical contacts into each piece, equipped with a short-range radio antenna. "Come on, around the corner."

They both hurried around the corner from the door, leaning against the textured metal, and Damien produced a small detonator switch. Andrew clamped his arms over his head and tucked it between his legs; Damien just rolled his eyes. He flipped open the red cap and pressed the button underneath it, producing a faint beep, followed immediately by the concussive thud of a small explosion. A tap on Andrew's shoulder got his attention, and the went back around the corner to the door. White smoke drifted from the blackened and bent metal of the wall, where the door hung loosely from its hinges. A couple of solid kicks broke the last twisted bits that held it on, and the door clattered to the concrete floor inside.

Damien grabbed the EMP gun from Andrew. Pulling his hood down low, he plunged into the icy torrent of dank water from the sprinklers. It soaked through the rough fabric of the robe, piercing down to his skin in seconds. Ignoring the cold, he turned in a methodical circle, pointing the gun at each security camera in turn, discharging one of the capacitors until each of the cameras was nothing but an inert hunk of glass and metal. When he stopped, Andrew ran past him to the shelves, feet splashing in the thin layer of water that coated the floor.

Damien pulled back his hood to better survey the room. It sprawled out farther than he could see in the deluge, with rows and rows of supplies stacked to the ceiling. The nearest half of the large room was taken up with rolling shelves pressed against each other, all filled with small vials, bottles, and boxes of IV drip bags. A variety of large specialized equipment took up most of the rest of the room, while the far corner held a door to the rest of the building. Water continued to pour in torrents from the sprinkler system, soaking both of them through, and plastering their hair to their heads. That, combined with the almost freezing temperature required to keep the medicine fresh, sent a shiver down Damien's spine.

Damien let out a low whistle. "Sure is a big place."

"There are a several dozen Alliance species, some of them pretty big," Andrew said. "It takes a lot of medical supplies to be prepared for anything."

The fire alarm droned incessantly, reverberating through the large warehouse like a crying child. Damien tapped his foot impatiently as he kept his eyes on the entrances. There was still no sign of a response, but it was only a matter of time before they discovered the alarm was bogus. "Come on," he said. "What's taking so long?"

"Hountan!" cried Andrew. "I found it." He heaved the stack of shelves along their rollers, opening a gap big enough to access the contents. His eyes and hands scanned the boxes for a few moments, until he gave a cry of recognition and pulled one out to look inside. "It's not like these are in English, you know. It takes some time to translate from Trenthan."

"Just remember we don't have all day," Damien said.

"If you're so anxious, get some of these canisters of nutritive ammonia and wheel them out to the buggy. We're running low on the ship."

Damien grabbed a nearby dolly and loaded it with one of the stout metal cylinders from the bottom shelf that Andrew had indicated. They still had the polyethylene seal on the end, and an intact coat of paint, even if it was covered with the grime of wet dust. Once he had it on, he wheeled it through the blown-open doorway and into the alley. His shoes were soon covered with dirt, sticking to the wet rubber, but the disappearance of the sprinkler water and the lessening of the alarm was a welcome relief to his senses. He hoisted the canister into the back of the buggy, and turned to get another. By this time he saw a small crowd gathered outside the front of the building, watching the commotion, but they didn't pay much attention to Damien running around in the alleyway, dripping wet. He plunged back into the din and deluge, making three more trips to load the buggy with supplies. When he finished, he came back inside and found Andrew still sorting through the bin.

"Are you about ready or what?" asked Damien.

"I still haven't found the right medicine," protested Andrew. "It has to be in one of these two boxes."

"Can't we just take them all?"

"I guess so," said Andrew, pulling the fine-meshed plastic boxes from the shelf. "Put them on the dolly."

Damien helped Andrew stack the boxes on the dolly, the glass bottles clinking together and water pouring through the mesh as they went. When they finished, Damien wheeled the cart toward the door with Andrew close behind. Without warning, the flow of water and the wail of the alarm stopped, leaving only the squeak and splash of wheels filling the room. Andrew paused at the sudden change, and when he did Damien grabbed him by his shirt, slammed him face-first into the shelves, and twisted his arm behind him.

"Now let's you and me have a little chat."

Chapter Nine

"What are you doing?" cried Andrew, his voice distorted by the shelf pressed against his face.

"I warned you not to hurt her," Damien growled. "I told you I was going to have to pick up the pieces, and that's what happened. She came to me last night, *crying*." He pressed even harder to emphasize the point.

"I'm sorry," Andrew mumbled. The words were rendered almost unintelligible, and he struggled to breathe against the pressure. "She was the one who wanted to take it farther."

"What are you talking about?" Damien asked, pulling Andrew back just far enough to slam him into the wall again. The remaining water on his head continued to drip down his forehead, stinging his eyes.

"I-I had to cut it off," Andrew said. "I knew it would be worse if we slept together."

The sound of distant voices drifted in from the far room. "It looks like they've given the all-clear," Damien said. "Give me one good reason why I shouldn't leave you here for them to find."

"You need me to give the medicine."

"Somehow, I think Tanner will do just fine without you."

"Please, I... I'm sorry."

Damien released the pressure, and let Andrew step away from the wall. He rubbed his arm where he still felt the pain of Damien's grip lingering. "You're lucky I'm in a good mood," he said. "Get the meds."

Andrew grabbed the dolly and quickly wheeled it out from between the shelves and toward the door they had come in. Echoing splashes of footsteps sounded in the opposite corner, and Andrew and Damien both looked behind them. Two Trenthan guards had come through the interior door, with rifles slung over their shoulders. They readied their weapons and shouted a warning, but the two thieves quickly ducked behind the shelf nearest the door.

"I don't think we're going to have time to load the buggy before they catch up to us," Damien said, stopping and pulling out his pistol. "You load the boxes while I take care of these guys."

Andrew scanned the shelf they were hiding behind, and caught sight of the species label. "I've got a better idea," he said, grabbing a cylinder of compressed gas chained to the wall. "Lippilligins breathe chlorine, but Trenthans won't." One of the guns fired with two quick pops, and a bottle near his head exploded. The other bullet ricocheted against the metal wall with a brilliant spark as Andrew ducked reflexively. He turned the nozzle toward the space in front of the doorway, and opened the valve all the way. A thin stream of greenish-yellow gas spewed from the cylinder with a sinister hiss, expanded into an opaque cloud, and drifted slowly to the floor.

"That should hold them back for a while," Andrew said, hurriedly grabbing the cart and taking it into the alley.

"But not quite as much fun," Damien muttered. He ducked down and bolted out from behind the shelf and through the doorway. The rifles cracked behind him, sending two more bullets sailing over his head. He sprinted toward the buggy with soggy steps, and jumped into the driver's seat while Andrew tossed the boxes of medicine into the back. By the time he got into the passenger's seat, the engine had roared to life, and they took off with a lurch and a cloud of dust from the ground. The back tires spewed dirt and pebbles as they slid sideways with the sharp turn out of the alley, and two pedestrians dove out of the way to avoid being run over.

As soon as the buggy was in the street, Damien slowed down and did his best to blend into the other traffic, pulling his sopping-wet hood back over his face. A stream of other motor vehicles stretched out in front of him, while to his left was bustling throng of stubby-legged *shelleps*, carrying baskets and passengers as their long necks swayed back and forth.

"Shouldn't we be getting out of here a little faster?" asked Andrew.

"I don't think they saw our vehicle," Damien said, "so our best bet is just to blend in." As he finished, a loud report erupted behind them, and a metallic ping sounded from the metal frame behind Andrew. A *shellep* just next to them bellowed and jumped up from the sting of a ricochet.

"On the other hand, maybe not." Damien slammed down hard on the accelerator, and the buggy peeled off from the line of traffic and into a side street. The engine noise rose from a low roar to a furious whine as it worked faster to escape their pursuers. The new street was deserted, and barely wider than an alley; tall buildings on either side blocked out the harsh morning sun. The roar of the engine filled the air, blocking out the noise from the traffic behind them. As they approached another crossing alleyway, a Trenthan stepped out from it with a basket balanced on her head. Damien swerved to the side to avoid her, swinging the back of the buggy into the wall on the other side as she stumbled back and spilled the contents of her basket on the ground.

As he emerged into the larger street on the other side, Damien pressed on the horn, but its feeble, high-pitched sound did less to warn the pedestrians on the other side than the echoing noise of the engine. The buggy cut recklessly through the perpendicular line of traffic and made a sharp left turn. They drove on the right edge of the street, popping up onto the sidewalk every so often to avoid hitting another car or animal, and causing the people on foot to scatter out of the way, diving behind fruit stands and piles of merchandise.

Three more bullets whizzed by Damien's ear, and Andrew turned to look behind them.

"Uhh..." he said, "We've got some company back here."

Damien risked a glance and saw two motorbikes trailing them. The drivers wore Brotherhood uniforms, and had pistols leveled at the buggy, searching for a clean shot. "Oh, that's just great," he said. "I'm busy driving. Can you shoot them for me?"

"Are you crazy? I don't know how to use a gun; I couldn't hit them from here if they were standing still!"

Damien leaned forward, deep in concentration on the road ahead. The motorbikes behind them weaved back and forth, avoiding pedestrians that had fallen down while jumping out of the way.

"Try the EMP gun," Damien said. "It should take out the fuel injectors, and it takes a lot less precision."

Andrew grabbed the device and pointed it behind them, steadying it on the back of the seat to counter the bumpy road and evasive driving tactics. Another shot rang out, punching a hole in one of the canisters and filling the air with the pungent odor of ammonia. He pulled the trigger, and the gun crackled as the capacitor discharged, but the Trenthans stayed in close pursuit.

"Nothing happened," shouted Andrew.

"They must still be using carburetors," said Damien. "Talk about backwater planets..."

"So what do we do now?"

"You're going to have to take the wheel," said Damien, "and let me do the shooting."

"Oh God," said Andrew. "Alright, how do we switch seats?"

"We don't," replied Damien. "You just take the wheel, and I keep using the pedals. Just tell me if I need to brake."

Andrew grabbed the steering wheel cautiously, and Damien turned around in his seat, leveling his pistol on the headrest.

"Aim for the tires," Andrew said. "Don't shoot the people."

"What?"

"No body count, remember?"

"You know, you're making this *really* hard."

Damien fired several rounds at the approaching motorbikes, but the impacts were lost in the cloud of dust thrown up by the rapidly spinning wheels. The rough road, combined with the constant weaving of the buggy, threw off his aim, and it was hard to tell which way to correct. Finally, one round threw a burst of sparks as it grazed the metal frame of one of the bikes, and the next ruptured the front tire with a loud pop, throwing its rider from his seat as the bike tumbled forward and fell over.

"That's one," Damien said, reaching to his belt. "Reloading."

He pulled out another magazine, and brought it up to reload, but the buggy lurched to the side, and the sudden movement caught him off guard. His arm slammed against the door, and the magazine fell onto the quickly retreating ground. He saw the remaining motorbike behind him swerve to miss the bus lumbering out of a side street.

"Hey!" Damien yelled.

"Sorry," Andrew said.

Damien turned back around and sank back into his seat. "Alright, I'm taking over again."

Another bullet whistled as it passed just over Damien's head. He glided expertly left and right, dodging traffic and pedestrians, as they made their way toward the outskirts of town on the dusty street. With steady determination, Damien turned to the edge of the road and crashed through the wooden poles supporting the awning of a merchant, sending splinters showering into their hair. The large cloth sheet settled on Andrew's side, along with the attached upper half of the pole.

"Try tossing that awning back at him," Damien said, "but keep the pole."

Andrew pulled the billowing cloth off the buggy and threw it up, where it caught the air and blew back. Only a second later, the motorbike pulled back into view as it drove effortlessly around the cloth.

"No good," said Andrew.

"Damn. Hand me the pole then."

Damien took the pole from Andrew, and pulled into another alley. He stopped as soon as they were around the corner, and jammed the broken end of the pole against the sturdy metal framing of the buggy. As soon as he did, the bike came speeding around the corner. Without time to stop, or even slow down, the guard riding it slammed into the flat end of the pole, throwing him back a few feet as the bike continued on. The Trenthan lay on the ground behind them, not stirring, and the engine of the motorbike rumbled quietly as it lay on the ground and idled.

"It looks like that's that," said Damien coolly, as he got out of the buggy. He stuck his face in his elbow as he grabbed the leaking canister of ammonia and tossed it to the other side of the alley.

Andrew jumped out and checked for a pulse. It was steady; he must have just been knocked unconscious, but probably cracked some ribs.

Damien pushed Andrew aside and started unbuttoning his uniform jacket. "Let's strip him. This guy is going to lend us an air of legitimacy."

"How is that?"

"Because fugitives being driven around by a police officer look like they've already been caught. Cover for me while I change clothes with him."

Andrew kept a lookout as Damien dragged the unconscious and bruised Trenthan behind the buggy and swapped his clothes for the dark green of the local police. It was a bit snug around the chest, and he had a few inches of leg showing above his socks when he bent at the knee, but it was otherwise a good fit. Scratching at the unfamiliar fabric, Damien loaded the officer into the middle of the front seat, then ran over to where the motorbike lay in the dirt humming to itself.

"What are you doing now?" Andrew asked.

"You know how much an official police bike could get on the black market?"

"No, I guess I don't.

"Well, me neither," Damien said, shutting off the engine and walking it back toward the buggy, "but it's gotta be something. Help me get it up on the back."

They placed the motorbike as gently as possible on top of the boxes and canisters in the back of the buggy, and Damien took the driver's seat. He put on the Trenthan's motorcycle helmet, obscuring his smooth human face.

"Not a bad score," he said. "Now let's get out of here."

Father Tanner stood impatiently by the cargo bay door as it lumbered open to receive the buggy. The influx of sunlight and fresh air only lifted his mood a little bit. Bits of dust and sand blew in the opening, along with the dry scent of the forest.

"It's about time you got back," Tanner said as they pulled into the ship. He slammed his fist on the large button to close the door, and it slowly cut off the sunlight from outside. "I thought it was supposed to be a quick job. What took you so long?"

"We had to loop around a few times, to make sure no one was

following us," Andrew said.

"Did you get the medicine?" Tanner asked.

"Yeah," said Damien. "We got enough medicine to treat an army, along with a police motorbike, and this sweet little uniform." He closely examined the fabric he was wearing. "This is actually really comfortable. Breathable."

"Where did you get it?" Tanner asked.

"Off the guy who was wearing it before."

"You didn't kill him did you?"

"Relax," Damien said. "He should be waking up in a couple of hours outside a bar, with almost twice as many ribs as he had yesterday. You might even get to treat him at the mission when we're done."

Andrew hefted one of the metal containers from the back of the buggy and half-dragged it toward the airlock. "We got some more nutritive ammonia," he said, "along with most of the common antidotes and other bread-and-butter drugs. Should I go ahead and start the chelation therapy?"

"Are there any diagnostic materials in there?" Tanner asked, peering into a box. Glass bottles, plastic bags, and small cardboard boxes littered the bin haphazardly. "It would be best to double-check the diagnosis if we have the facilities."

"So no new symptoms then?"

"The patient is awake, but lethargic, and his speech is slurred enough that the translators can't pick anything up. He seems to be in pain too."

"What about the seizures?"

"Mostly just random twitching in the eye. Some periodic minor seizures too."

"And you think lead poisoning is still the best diagnosis? Andrew asked.

Tanner sighed. He wasn't sure of much anymore. "In theory, it could have any one of a number of neurological roots, but lead poisoning makes the most sense in the context."

"Ah, here we go," Andrew said, pulling a packet from one of the boxes. "Some blood work strips. Do we have any blood drawn?"

"No," Tanner said. "I'll get Ghenni on it." He walked over to the wall console, repeated the request through the intercom, and then returned. Damien walked slowly toward the cockpit, and when he was out of sight, Tanner turned to Andrew. "So how did it go?"

Andrew paused for a moment, and the corner of his mouth twitched like it always did when he was hiding something. "Fine, I suppose," he said, hauling the boxes to his work area.

"You two didn't kill anyone?"

"As far as I know, we just broke some bones. Maybe a *lot* of bones."

"Bones do heal," Tanner said, "so I suppose that's something we can live with."

"Is Eve back yet?" Andrew asked.

"No, I haven't heard from her."

"I hope she's alright."

"Me too," said Tanner. "At any rate, I had better get these blood work strips into Ghenni. If we do have to revise the diagnosis, I'd rather start sooner than later."

"Right," said Andrew. He gave a small yelp of satisfaction and pulled out one of the bottles of medicine. "Take this too, so we can start the chelation when you're done."

Tanner slipped on a bulky surgical suit and entered the makeshift airlock. The plastic lining stretched taut as the air was pumped out, bulging inward with the pressure and outlining the struts. The pumps switched directions, and soon the plastic relaxed as the pressure equalized with the outside. The door to the operating theater hissed slightly as it opened, and Tanner walked in to find Ghenni, unrecognizable in the suit, checking the patient's intravenous drip.

"Father, you have the medicine?" he asked.

"Yes," Tanner replied, gently setting the glass bottle on the metal table. "But first, let me see the blood sample you took."

Ghenni handed over a small glass vial, filled with the bronze blood of the Hountan. Father Tanner set it down while he plugged a small paper-like strip into the hand-held testing computer. A few button taps brought it to the right setting, and he picked up a small eyedropper and took up a few drops of the blood. The metallic fluid hit the paper and spread out, drawn by tiny channels that guided the blood toward the array of electrodes on the end. After a few seconds the computer beeped and displayed its measurement. Tanner sighed and turned to the intercom.

"Are you there, Andrew?" he said.

"Yes," Andrew replied when he reached the console. "Did you get the test results?"

"I did, and it's bad news. Lead levels are normal; in fact, all heavy metals are within acceptable limits. We're back to square one."

Eve picked her way through the narrow aisles of the hardware store, staying as quiet and unobtrusive as possible. She scanned dusty and poorly labeled collections of used circuit boards, fuses, and other parts that she needed to keep *Malika* in working order. They rattled in the plastic trays as she pulled them out, rifled through them, and pushed them in again. A Trenthan dressed in tattered and greasy work clothes crossed the aisle a few yards down with slow, scraping footsteps, watching her. She turned away and pulled her heavy hood farther forward to hide her smooth, human face. It was oppressively hot underneath, but it was the only way she could go in public with a modicum of safety. With the Brotherhood heat on the planet, searching specifically for Consortium species, the usual unspoken truce was out the window; no one wanted to be suspected of aiding a spy by looking the other way. Unfortunately, there was no other place to get the parts she needed to get the ship ready for the hostage exchange.

She dropped a handful of parts into her basket, and jumped at the sound of a hurried footstep behind her. Her nervousness was heightened by the buzzing and flickering of a fluorescent light as it sputtered through the last of its useful days. Whispering filtered over the shelf, and by peering between the bins, Eve could see a few figures standing at the counter, looking suspiciously over their shoulders as they talked in low tones. It wasn't safe here.

Eve gently set her basket down on the ground, and tip-toed toward the back door as quickly as she could. On the other side of the shelf, the quickened slap of feet on concrete outpaced her, and a burly, unkempt Trenthan appeared at the other end of the aisle with a sneer. She turned to run out the other direction, but that end was already blocked off by another customer. The first one said something to Eve, but it was just a garbled series of hums and clicks to her. But his intent was unmistakable, because now he was aiming an old, worn pistol directly at her.

"I think we need to re-evaluate our limitations on the diagnosis," Andrew said. Father Tanner sat at the table in the ship's kitchen, drinking bad coffee and discussing the patient with Andrew, while Damien paced back and forth with a small earpiece. "As far as I can tell, we've exhausted all the possible causes from the accident, so we need to look for pre-existing conditions. It *has* to be a coincidence."

"What do you suggest?" Tanner asked.

"We ruled out a vitamin deficiency before because it didn't fit with acidosis. But since we've already solved that with the water in the chunk of ore, can we rule malnutrition back in?"

"But the patient has been on a nutritive ammonia drip for the past two days or so," Tanner said. "Any symptoms stemming from malnutrition should have shown improvement by now."

"So what does that leave us with?"

Tanner thought silently for a moment with his hands clasped together in front of his mouth. He wasn't a diagnostician; he could treat trauma, basic illnesses, even deliver babies. This was supposed to have been a simple operation, just stitching him up. But now it seemed he might be out of his depth; they just didn't have the equipment, background, or time to work through a complicated diagnosis. And if they couldn't cure the patient, they didn't have anything but a few days standing between them and a Brotherhood interrogation room.

"If we open up the diagnosis to pre-existing conditions," Tanner said, "there isn't much we can do until new symptoms present themselves. All we know is that the symptoms are basically neurological. It could be any of several dozen infections, or he could have visited a front-line planet on his last stop, and been exposed to residual nerve gas. If I wanted, I'm sure I could come up with a dozen other possible diagnoses. Unfortunately, we don't have the resources to test for them."

"Then we should start him on broad-spectrum antibiotics for now, and go from there," Andrew said.

Tanner nodded. "By tomorrow, he should either be improved, or have a new symptom to go on."

"I'll take over for Ghenni, and get started on that, then."

Andrew got up and left, while Tanner stood up slowly and turned toward Damien. "Captain Ro-" he began. Damien lifted up a hand to silence him, and listened intently. After a moment, he put his hand down again.

"Sorry, what were you saying?" he asked.

"What are you listening to?" asked Tanner.

"Eve should have been back by now," he explained, leaning forward nervously, and propping himself up with both hands on the table. "I can't reach her on the radio, so I'm listening to the police chatter, just in case."

"I wanted to ask you again what happened when you were out with Andrew. I asked him, but I think he was hiding something."

"You're asking if I killed anybody?"

"Yes, that's what I'm asking."

Damien stood up straight, and gave Tanner a quizzical look. "And just what would you do about it if I did?"

"I would ask you to take the patient, my team, and myself back to the mission, so we can continue to treat him without putting anyone else in danger."

Damien threw back his head and laughed deeply. "You're a piece of work, you know that? You think that I would give up my shot at a hard-earned ransom to satisfy your little moral quibbles?"

"I can accept stealing in order to save a life, but taking one innocent life to save another is where I draw the line."

Damien leaned forward, bringing himself only inches away from Tanner's face. "Let's get one thing straight here. They're not innocent, not a single damn one of them. And neither am I, and neither is anybody, so you can stop acting so high and mighty." He straightened up and gave a crooked smile, but still kept eye contact. "But no, I didn't kill anybody. No matter how much he might have deserved it. Are you satisfied?"

Tanner peered intently into Damien's face. "I think so, ye-"

Damien held up his hand. "Waitwaitwaitwaitwait," he said quietly. He furrowed his eyebrows as tinny translated voices drifted from the earpiece. After a moment, his eyes widened, and he pursed his lips. A few seconds later, he tore the earpiece from his head and threw it on the ground.

"They got her!" he yelled. "The dirty little xenners turned her in!"

"What happened?" asked Tanner.

Damien stormed off toward the cockpit, and Tanner followed him. "The xenners at the parts shop called the Brotherhood and turned her in for the reward."

"What are you planning on doing?" Tanner asked.

Damien opened a cabinet set in the wall of the cockpit to reveal an array of pistols, automatic rifles, and submachine guns. He pulled a few of them out and started shoving every pocket full of extra ammunition. "What do you think I'm doing to do?" he sneered.

"I can't let you just go in there, guns blazing, to break her out of jail."

"Oh yeah? Then I *dare* you to try and stop me."

"This isn't the right way to go about things," Tanner protested.

"I don't have time to listen to one of your moral lectures," Damien said.

"Forget morals; if you go all by yourself, you'll be killed, and you won't be doing anybody any good. We have to take the time to think this through and plan a safer course of action."

Damien shook his head. "That's not good enough. I don't care if you don't want to be a part of it, but you sure as hell better stay out of my way."

"I'm talking about ten minutes to sit and plan," Tanner said. "Is that really so much to ask?"

Damien's hand gripped the edge of the cabinet door, knuckles white, as he leaned forward against the wall. His breaths came out long and forceful. "I can't lose her. Her and this ship are all I have left."

"You think doing something rash is going to save her?"

"God, you sound just like my CO back during the war. Real intellectual type like you." He released the cabinet door, and paced back and forth in the cockpit.

"Did he stop you from getting yourself killed too?"

Damien stopped pacing and leaned against the captain's chair, taking a few deep breaths. "The colony I was stationed at was invaded. Strike force dropped out of IS while we were on patrol on the surface, took position over the city. I wanted to go in and start helping with evacuations, but my commander was afraid we'd get overwhelmed by the ground invasion force. He told us to hold back until reinforcements arrived."

"And what happened?"

"Turns out they weren't occupying the colony. By the time our reinforcements arrived, the bastards had leveled the whole city from orbit."

"You would have died if you'd gone in," Tanner said.

"Maybe. But I might have gotten my wife out first."

Tanner sighed and nodded. "I see. And you blame yourself for her death?"

Damien turned to face Tanner, lips curled with rage. "No, I blame *them. I* could have saved her if they'd have let me. From then on, I promised myself I wouldn't let anybody order me around, especially when it comes to protecting the people I care about."

"Then let me help you," Tanner pleaded. "We can figure out a way to get her back, without getting any of us killed in the process."

"Oh, I suppose you're an expert on jailbreaks?"

"No, but I do know something about people, and getting hostile governments to do what I want."

"The clergy angle might work for starting a clinic, but I don't think anybody's going to hand over a prisoner to you just for being a man of the cloth."

"No, but surely they would hand her over to a special agent from the Brotherhood."

"Well," said Damien, "seeing as how we look pretty human, I don't think anybody is going to think this is the face of a Brotherhood agent."

Tanner smiled mischievously. "But it just so happens that I know where we can get some suits with helmets."

Chapter Ten

"Have I mentioned how hot these things are?" Damien asked. The Trenthan sun beat down on the surgical suits, emblazoned with forged Brotherhood insignia. Sidearms hung strapped to their legs, and Ghenni walked just in front of them in the pilfered police uniform. Ahead of them loomed the imposing facade of the local Brotherhood prison. The front building was made of stout concrete, and a razor-wire fence ran around the compound. Soldiers watched from several guard towers in strategic positions, and others patrolled the grounds on foot. Barely visible in the distance sat a large plasma turret nestled in the patchy trees, covered with rust and grime.

"I've lost count of how many times," Tanner replied over the radio.

They stopped in front of the main building as two guards armed with rifles blocked their path. They wore the dull red uniforms of the Brotherhood, instead of the dark green of the local security forces, and stood with the nervous military pseudo-precision of someone expecting to be reprimanded for getting sloppy.

"What is your business here?" one of the guards asked. His eyes darted back and forth between Damien's faceplate and the space straight ahead of him.

"I was asked to escort these agents to the prison," Ghenni said, "regarding the human spy."

The guard cast a quick glance at the identifying symbols on the pair's suits, and then silently stepped aside to let them in. Through the main door they entered a lobby, with bare unpainted concrete for the floors and walls, cast in the sickly yellow glow of cheap electric lights overhead. A metal fan in an upper corner lazily pushed in air from outside, framed by a ring of sunlight. Behind a metal grating on one side sat a plump Trenthan woman in a tiny office. Her desk was littered with papers, and she hurriedly stood up as the suited figures walked in.

"Well, here goes nothing," Damien said as they approached.

"I should do the talking," Tanner said.

"Are you kidding?" Damien asked. "I'm the professional criminal here."

"But I've been wheedling my way past government officials for-"

"Can I help you?" the woman asked. She clasped her hands in front of her, then switched behind, and finally back in front as she waited for an answer.

"We have come for the prisoner," Damien said through the external speaker. His words were processed and regurgitated by the suit's translator, emerging in cold, menacing tones in the local tongue.

"What prisoner is that?"

"The human prisoner," Damien replied. "Do you think we would come all the way to your planet for anything other than a Consortium spy?"

"Don't antagonize her," Tanner said on a private channel.

"I know what I'm doing," Damien said. "Belittling them makes them less likely to challenge you."

"Let me get the warden," the woman said. She picked up a telephone and punched a few numbers into it; her hand held the receiver in a white-knuckled death grip. After a few seconds she spoke in low tones that weren't picked up by the translator, then nodded in affirmation a few times until she hung up. "You three can follow me into the main office, where you can speak with the warden."

"Yes," Tanner and Damien said in unison. The woman stepped around a corner and through the door into the lobby, and Tanner, Damien, and Ghenni followed her into another room. Here the light switched from natural to fluorescent, one of the tubes flickering occasionally. Half a dozen uniformed officers pretended to do work on their antiquated computers as they gawked at the strangers.

"You're going to blow our cover," Damien said as they walked.

"No, you're going to blow it by being suspiciously rude."

"This is the Brotherhood we're talking about. Being anything but rude is suspiciously nice."

"I've never had a problem before," Father Tanner said.

"But that's because they weren't expec-"

Another voice broke in. "I'm told you are here for the human prisoner."

In front of them stood a stocky Trenthan man, dressed in a military uniform with the insignia of something roughly equivalent to a colonel. Certainly the highest-ranked official they were going to find here. He looked them over, fidgeting slightly.

"Yes," said Tanner. "We are transferring her to a Brotherhood ship for questioning."

"I have not received any orders regarding a prisoner transfer."

"It is a matter of Brotherhood security," Damien said. "We wish to keep our interrogation... off the record. I'm sure you understand."

"Yes, of course," the warden said flatly. "I will send for some guards to fetch her."

Beside him, Damien saw Ghenni's eyes darting back and forth as the warden walked away, scanning the faces of the other office workers. Something was up. With no warning, he reached down to Damien's leg and grabbed his pistol from its holster, pulling back the slide and pointing it at Tanner and Damien. Immediately, the other Trenthans in the room burst into a flurry of motion as they pulled out pistols of their own from desk drawers and ankle holsters, and aimed them at the three. The warden turned back around.

"What's going on here?" he asked.

"They are not real Brotherhood agents," Ghenni said. "They forced me to help them break their friend out of prison. They are human. Citizens of the Consortium."

"Why you little son of a..." Damien growled. The little twerp had a crooked smile on his face, glancing back at Damien and Tanner.

"Is that so?" the warden asked. He walked to a nearby desk and pulled out a hand-held device, sweeping it over the suits and examining the display. Damien's heart thumped audibly in his chest for a long few seconds as the beeping scanner examined the contents of his suit. Finally it stopped, and the room hung deathly quiet.

"He's right. Arrest them, and get them out of those suits."

Two guards stepped forward and ushered them at gunpoint through a door in the back. Damien looked back as they left, and saw Ghenni staring back at them, looking satisfied.

"Well, well, well," the warden said, leaning against the wall across from the holding cell as two guards began to strip the two captives of their suits. "Father Tanner from the mission, and Damien Rogers the smuggler. I must say, I never expected to see the two of you working together."

"I guess I'm just full of surprises," Damien said, as a guard twisted the helmet from his head.

"Oh, I'm not surprised at you," the warden said. "You don't have many standards when it comes to the company you keep. But Father Tanner here should have more scruples."

"Thanks a lot," Damien muttered.

"As I understand, this other prisoner... Eve, I believe? She is an associate of yours, Captain Rogers?"

"Yeah, so if you just bring her out, we'll be on our way."

"I am afraid that's impossible."

"Come on," Damien pleaded. "We've done this before, and you owe me. Half of the guns those guys pulled on us came from me."

Tanner chuckled at the irony, and Damien glared at him.

"What are you laughing at?" he asked. He turned back to the warden. "And Tanner here does a lot of doctoring. I'm sure you'd be glad to keep him in business."

"Yes, he fixed my son's broken leg a few years ago," the warden answered. "But I can't let you just walk out of here. Even if you had the money, you couldn't bribe me. There are powerful Brotherhood agents here on Trenth now, looking for Consortium spies. If word ever gets out that I let human prisoners go, they would have my *glia* for it."

The guards finished removing the suits, and left the room, closing the door to the cell behind them. The warden started to follow, and then stopped and turned back. "I'm sorry I can't help you this time. If it's any consolation, know that the reward on your heads will provide for my family for a long time. Someone will be along shortly to process you and put you in more... permanent accommodations."

The warden walked out, back to the front offices, and Damien sank down to the floor. "Well," he said, "this is it. By this time tomorrow, we'll be on board a Brotherhood ship, on our way to a core planet to be tortured to death. And all because your stinking little xenner friend decided to turn us in."

"I would appreciate it if you would stop using slurs like that," Tanner said. He paced back and forth in front of the bars, his arms crossed. With no airflow, his sweat-soaked shirt stuck to his skin like a warm compress. Staring at the blank walls, he prayed for safety. *Lord, you broke the apostles out of prison to do your work, and I know you can do the same here.* But in the back of his mind, he knew that divine rescue was the exception, rather than the rule.

"Oh, get over yourself. If there was ever a time for racial slurs, this is it. You think a guy's gonna help you out, and he stabs you in the back."

"Believe me," Tanner said, "I'm as surprised as you are."

"Well, maybe you shouldn't be."

"What do you mean?" asked Father Tanner.

"I know he resented you. You, always preaching to him, and he knew you'd never let him run the clinic, just because he didn't believe the same fairy tale as you."

"I always made a point of letting him know how much I respected him as a doctor. But it isn't just a clinic; it's a mission as well. I have to think not just of my patients' bodies, but of their souls as well." He paused, leaned his head against the wall, and closed his eyes. "At least I didn't physically assault him."

"Fair enough. I guess you should've let me finish him off then, huh?"

Tanner sighed, but didn't say anything. He had of course been prepared to give his life for the missions, but the imminence of such a fate revealed a lot about his character that he wasn't thrilled to admit to himself. He was scared, and felt abandoned, and he had dragged two other people into it with him.

"Let me tell you something about prison..." began Damien.

"You don't have to," Tanner said. "I've been in plenty of prisons in my time."

Damien chuckled. "I didn't peg you as the type to get yourself thrown in jail. I didn't think Emmanuelites were the criminal sort. What did you do wrong?"

"I've done plenty that's wrong, and plenty to get myself thrown in jail, but they were never the same thing."

"So what, you got arrested for traipsing around Brotherhood planets, spreading the good news of a hundred different Jesuses?" Damien cocked his head to the side and furrowed his brow. "Jesi?"

"The plural is 'Christs,'" said Father Tanner. "And yes, most of my arrests were for my missions work."

"And the rest?" Damien asked, curiously.

"I did a few years on Earth, right before becoming a missionary."

"Is that so? I didn't think Christianity was illegal on Earth. You knock off a bank to fund one of your clinics or something?"

Tanner chuckled. "Might have gotten off easier if I had. The Christianity allowed in the cities of Earth is a joke, a sanitized version carefully stripped of anything that could challenge the ideology and power of the corporations and politicians. Because I preached the Gospel, I was imprisoned for being an 'enemy of free thought.' Ironic, isn't it? What once used to be all about questioning dogmas has become its own unquestionable dogma."

"Free anything is a joke anymore," Damien said. "You're either a slave to the Brotherhood government, or you're a slave to the Consortium megacorps. People like us are probably the closest thing there is to a free man these days."

"And now we're in prison."

"Yep."

Andrew ran through all the scenarios in his mind, searching for benign reasons that the others could be taking so long to get back. His heavy breathing was amplified by his helmet, and he tried to pay more attention to the patient, if only to keep his mind off of it. He didn't want to think about the prospect of being left completely alone on a ship that wasn't his, with a patient he didn't know how to treat. But it was hard not to.

The spider-like creature on the table shifted, dropping one leg off the edge. Andrew tried to lift it back on, but the patient moved it of his own accord, and his twitching eye was trained on the doctor. It barked something weakly, and there was a lag of a couple of seconds as the translator tried to parse the slurred speech and find an accurate translation.

"Where am I?"

"You're safe," Andrew said. "I'm a doctor, and I'm here to help you."

"I remember... an explosion. What happened?"

"There was an accident in the mine you were inspecting," Andrew said. "You were hurt, but we're patching you up. Can you tell us your name?"

"My name is... is... Hounack. Where are... my crewmates? I want to see them."

"They're not here," said Andrew. "How do you feel?"

"I'm... in pain," the alien said.

"You did just have surgery. There's bound to be some soreness for a while."

"No, not there. In my eyes. I... I can't see. Why can't I see? What just happened?"

Andrew grabbed a flashlight, and passed the beam over the desperately searching eye. "You suddenly can't see anything?"

"I see... light, but nothing else. It hurts when I move it."

"It sounds like optic neuritis," Andrew said. "I think your optic nerve is swelling."

"Why... why does it hurt?"

"I don't know," said Andrew, "but I'm going to give you something to make it feel better." He rifled through the boxes of medicine, searching for an appropriate medicine. The labels were printed in both Trenthan and Hountan scripts, and it took a few moments to translate each one. Finally he found the right bottle, and after consulting the label and doing a little guesswork, injected a dose into the intravenous drip.

As he was cleaning up, he heard the intercom crackle into life. "Andrew, are you there?" It was Ghenni's voice.

"Thank God!" Andrew replied. "I was wondering what was

taking you guys so long. Is Eve alright?"

There was a pause at the other end. Eventually, Ghenni's voice came back on. "They're not with me. I'm the only person that returned."

Andrew's stomach lurched. They were the only ones here. What were they supposed to do now? Neither of them knew how to fly the ship, or had any experience with trying to hand over a hostage to the authorities. If they were lucky they might be able to save the patient's life, but their own lives were surely forfeit. It was only a matter of time before they were tracked down as well, and all five of them were shipped off to an Brotherhood interrogation facility. Andrew was OK with the idea of martyrdom in theory, but he wasn't eager to put it into practice.

"What are we going to do?" asked Ghenni.

"I'm not sure," said Andrew. "We have to get them out of there somehow."

"We already tried to break someone out once. I don't see how we would have more luck this time. We don't have any experience with criminal activity."

"No," said Andrew. "But I know someone who does."

Ghenni knocked on the door in the alleyway, humming the tune that Andrew had given him to remember the timing. He'd grown up in this city, so he knew that this was *not* the part of town that nice children wandered around in. The panel in the door slid open, revealing close-set eyes in a massive head on the other side.

"Use the front door," the face said gruffly. The panel slid shut again. Ghenni pounded on the door again until the eyes reappeared, this time wide with rage. The man on the other side made a pair of scissors from his fingers and mimed snipping off one of his *glia*. "Go away. A man could end up with a smooth face if he's not careful."

"Father Tanner sent me," said Ghenni, swallowing the lump in his throat. "I have a business opportunity for your boss."

The eyes peered out of the slot for a moment, then the panel slid closed again. Ghenni waited for a few moments, then reached up to knock again. But as he raised his hand, the lock scraped on the other side, and the door creaked open. A tall, muscular Trenthan, gun stuck indiscreetly in his belt, leaned out the doorway to check the alleyway.

It was empty. Then with a nod, he led Ghenni inside.

The air inside was smoky, filled with the scent of incense. But it wasn't the local incense that Ghenni used, but something exotic and sweeter. Something expensive. The guard led him through a doorway into Galessi's parlor, littered with sumptuous pillows and ferns. Galessi looked up from a plate of meats, wiped his fingers on a piece of bread, and set aside the small table from in front of him.

"Have a seat," he said, gesturing to some pillows across from him. Ghenni obliged, sitting down carefully and making sure that his legs were crossed in the proper respectful position. He coughed, half from the incense and half from nervousness. He stared at the plump crime lord, looking for the words that had fled from his mind upon entering. Several times he tried to speak up, but his voice wouldn't work properly. Finally, Galessi spoke up.

"So the priest is now more desperate for supplies, but he sends his lackey to negotiate for him?"

"I didn't... I work for Father Tanner, but he didn't send me."

"Then explain yourself quickly, before I take too much offense at your deception."

"He didn't send me because he can't. This is about Father Tanner, really."

"How so?"

"He was... Father Tanner was taken."

Galessi straightened up with interest, and his eyes opened wide with curiosity and shock. "Do you mean to say..."

"Father Tanner was arrested," Ghenni said.

"Roasted Menos!" cried Galessi. "I heard that someone had kidnapped a Brotherhood official, but you're telling me that it was the Father? I don't believe it."

"We were trying to give him medical treatment, but things got out of control. We had no other choice."

"Now let me guess," said Galessi. "You want my help to break him out of prison?"

"Yes," said Ghenni, "him and the people we were working with. A Captain Rogers, and his partner Eve."

"Oh, Damien Rogers is involved in this? Now it makes a lot more sense. He always had a bad habit of getting in over his head."

"I could offer you... ten thousand to get them out."

Galessi threw his head back and laughed, with a deep echo that filled the room. Then in an instant, the smile dropped from his face and he leaned forward intensely. "Get this straight kid. Half of my best smugglers had to scramble underground once the word got out that Consortium people had kidnapped that bureaucrat. I have several deadlines that I'm going to have a lot of trouble meeting as it is, and now some serious Brotherhood heat is on the way. And you want me to break into a Brotherhood prison with zero planning time, and make a personal enemy of the local administrators, all for a measly ten thousand?"

Ghenni's heart pounded, and the blood rushing in his ears seemed to drown out all the other sound. "Twe-twenty thousand. I can offer twenty thousand, but that's all we're going to get from the job, I swear."

"Is there a sign on the door saying that I offer loans?" Galessi looked at the guard, who shook his head solemnly. "'Going to get?' I'll tell you what I'll do. I'll let you walk out of here with all your fingers and bones intact, since you gave me a good laugh. But this whole kidnapping fiasco is costing me money, so the next time any of the mission crowd wants something, they'd better come with cash in hand, ready to pay a very generous gratuity."

Galessi nodded at the guard, who pulled Ghenni roughly to his feet and led him out the side door. He stumbled into the sunlight outside, and the door slammed shut behind him. His fingers dug in his pocket for his soul stone, and he pulled it out, kissing the smooth surface and asking for guidance. With Father Tanner gone, the mission could very well fall apart, even if it managed to avoid being shut down by the authorities. Andrew was next in line to run it, but it was no secret that he didn't have an administrative bone in his body. If Father Tanner died, it could throw the whole operation into chaos, and Ghenni would likely lose his salary. That meant he would have to either go to work in the iron mines, or risk getting caught up in the water wars as a farmer to help support his parents.

He walked the few blocks to where he had parked the buggy, started it up, and let it carry him at random through the bustling streets, raucous market stands, and blazing sun of Calchassa. He couldn't go back to Andrew with no help. Whatever happened, Father

Tanner had to be rescued somehow, but Ghenni had no idea how to go about it. The shouts and advertisements of the merchants, pushing their vegetables, fabrics, and household wares, passed over him with no reaction. After half an hour, the roar and shadow of a passing ship pulled his attention to the sky. The mass of steel shot out of sight in an instant, but the size of it, along with the guns bristling on the front, told him all he needed to know about it. The Brotherhood was here.

The crack of gunshots erupted around a corner, along with angry shouts. The crowd in the street parted carefully, and a large flat-bed truck lumbered out from a side street. On the back sat a score of Trenthan men of every age, scarves pulled up over their *glia* and holding automatic rifles and a couple of larger guns of some kind. As they passed, the soldiers shook their fists at the sky, shouting slogans of defiance at the crowd. Some of the people in the street joined in, but most simply got out of the way and went on with their business. The truck was driving toward the Brotherhood district's spaceport. Ghenni closed his eyes and thought for a moment, then turned the buggy around and drove after them.

Chapter Eleven

"Damien!"

Eve's voice carried down the cavernous hallway, above the murmurings and jeers of the other prisoners in the cell block. Broken sunlight streamed through the bars on the windows, half-blinding Damien at regular intervals as they walked. The other prisoners were all Trenthans, staring at the two new captives with sunken eyes as he passed, with the settled-in look of people who had resigned themselves to a life of walls and bars.

As Damien approached the end of the cell block, he made out Eve's face straining to smile back at him through the bars of the cell wall. Technically it was a smile, but it was twisted with pain and hopelessness.

"Staying out of trouble?" he asked as the guard opened the creaking door and shoved him and Father Tanner inside. When the door was closed, the two of them stuck their cuffed hands through the bars for the guard to unlock.

"You can keep those on," the guard said, his eyes gleaming. "You won't be staying here for too long. We've got some Brotherhood agents already on their way to pick you up."

"Thanks for the friendly service!" Damien shouted at him as he sauntered off. "I'll be sure to leave a generous tip!"

Tanner pulled his arms back inside, and trudged over to the worn-out bed, where he plopped down and held his head in his hands. Damien turned around and took Eve in his arms, while she buried her face in his shoulder.

"I'm so happy to see you," she said. "Well, except for you being in prison I guess."

"Yeah, same here."

"So," she whispered, pulling close to his ear. "This is part of your plan to break me out, right?"

"Uh... sure," Damien said. "Let's go with that."

"Ugh, great," Eve said, pushing him away and joining Tanner in sitting on the bed. "So there's no plan? We're just stuck here?"

"Don't worry, I'll think of something." He paused, and paced around the cell for a few moments. "Pops, you have any ideas?"

"I'm afraid not," Father Tanner said, keeping his head bowed and eyes closed. "I'm no good at scheming, but I can pray."

"Well if you don't mind, I'd like to be a little more pro-active." Damien spun around, scanning the small room. "Alright, let's list our assets. We have... three able-bodied people... an old mattress and a bed frame that's bolted to the wall and floor... a really gross toilet in the corner... two pairs of handcuffs, already in use. Anything else?" He looked expectantly at Tanner. "And if you say 'God,' I'll slap you."

"I think that just about covers it," Tanner said, opening his eyes and leaning back.

"Alright. A plan, a plan, a plan..." Damien clasped his hands behind his head, closed his eyes, and walked in small circles. They certainly didn't have time for a tunnel. They could try attacking when the guards came back to escort them away, but they didn't have weapons. And Tanner wasn't likely to be on board for that, so it would be just him and Eve against three or four guys with guns. Not exactly great odds.

From the other end of the cell block came the raucous cries and insults of dozens of prisoners, moving slowly along the length of the hallway like an ocean breaker. Finally Damien heard the scrape of footsteps on the concrete, and the Brotherhood agents strode into view.

The first looked something like a giraffe, with four long legs that

116

strode confidently down the hall with loud clomps. A long torso stretched up from the lower body, with a pair of arms somewhere in the middle, ending in a head about seven feet off the floor, with a flat, wide mouth and yellow eyes. Its body was a reddish-orange, but mostly covered in the dull red uniform of its station in the Brotherhood security forces. He couldn't remember what it was called, though; he was pretty sure it started with an "A".

The other agent, a Lippilligin, was enclosed in a bulky polymer suit, about four and a half feet tall with two legs and four arms. Its solid black face plate blocked out the ultraviolet light that could tear apart the chlorine it was breathing. The suit was emblazoned with Brotherhood insignia, and Damien winced at the realization of how shoddy their own reproductions had been; the plan probably wouldn't have worked anyway. Two Trenthan soldiers walked with them, and stood at rigid attention as they stopped at the cell.

"You will come with us," said the creature in the suit, in the mechanical tones of a translator. "You will be charged with subterfuge against the Brotherhood, and executed."

"Well," muttered Eve, "at least we're going to get a fair trial."

The Trenthan soldiers motioned her forward, and she stuck her arms through the bars to be cuffed, as the alien agents watched flatly. When she had her arms back inside the cell, they opened the door and waved automatic rifles at the prisoners, gesturing for them to step out.

"See?" said Damien as they were escorted down the hallway. "They're just walking us out. This is progress!" The cold point of a gun barrel nudged him in the back, and he shut up.

They plodded on out of the building and into the bright sun in the prison yard outside. It beat down, reflecting off the pale concrete buildings and barren dirt, and sweat prickled on Damien's skin. Towers loomed overhead, with prison guards scanning the grounds with high-powered, scoped rifles at the ready. After passing through a transfer building, where they were signed out by the agents, the three prisoners were led out of the main gate, and toward a large black van that sat idling on the pavement. In front of it sat a buggy, and behind it were a pair of police motorbikes, all of them manned by Trenthans in Brotherhood uniforms. One of the soldiers opened the back door, revealing a half-dozen other prisoners already inside, their hands in shackles. They looked dully up at the new arrivals, eyes vacant with despair.

After urging Damien, Eve, and Tanner into the back, the Lippilligin climbed in along with one of the Trenthans, shutting the door behind them. The suited figure sat watching the crowd stoically, while the Trenthan kept his rifle pointed casually at the prisoners. The giraffe creature clambered into the passenger side up front, folding his legs and neck to fit; now that Damien looked closer, he saw the cab had been modified to fit the creature's large body. The last Trenthan guard climbed into the driver's seat, and the van lurched into life.

"So," said Damien, nodding to one of their fellow captives. "What are you in for?"

He only glanced blankly up at Damien, but Tanner said something in his own language, and the prisoner answered sharply, intrigued but still sullen.

"He says they were part of a resistance group," Tanner said. "They got tired of fighting each other over the water, and chose to band together and strike at the Brotherhood operations. I cleaned up the language, of course."

"Naturally, naturally. So the Brotherhood doesn't care much if they kill each other, but once the locals start attacking them, they clamp down and start making examples."

"It seems so," said Tanner.

"Well, at least we're in good company as we get shipped off to die."

Ghenni idled the engine of the buggy as he surreptitiously watched the armed men unload from the truck in the back alley. They milled around, some of them barking orders and others following them, automatic rifles hanging casually from their shoulders. Two large rocket launchers hung in baskets as they were pulled up toward the roof of a flat earthen building by ropes.

A cold metal finger poked into his back, and someone snarled "Don't move."

Ghenni slowly raised his hands off the steering wheel and lifted them above his head. "P-please," he stammered, "don't shoot."

"Curiosity can be a dangerous thing," said the voice. "Tell me, are you spying for the Brotherhood?"

"No, I just... I wanted to see where you were going."

"What business is it of yours?"

Ghenni swallowed, and took a few deep breaths before answering. "I was hoping you might be able to help me."

"Turn around," the voice said. Ghenni carefully turned in his seat, keeping his hands up in the air. The man behind him was young, but patches of his face were marred by the scars of severe burns, and a few of his *glia* were missing from one side. He looked Ghenni up and down with a glare, then gestured for a fellow militant to pat Ghenni down. Finding nothing, he then let his rifle relax a bit. "You're Lerra's boy, aren't you?"

"Yes, my name is Ghenni. You know my parents?"

"He's a good man, your father. What is it you need?"

"My friends were arrested," Ghenni said, "and they will be taken by the Brotherhood-"

"You have friends in the Expulsion movement?"

"No, they are doctors. Humans, from the Consortium, and good people. We were treating a Br- uh, a patient, and things got out of hand and-"

The man burst into boisterous laughter. "It was the priest that took him? The bastard was actually trying to cure him, wasn't he?"

"Yes, but things didn't work out like we expected."

"I'll say. Well, since you're Merra's boy and work with the priest, I suppose you can be trusted. Call me Selen." The man extended his hands, and Ghenni clasped his over them in greeting.

"What are you planning?" Ghenni asked.

"I can't get into details. But they are not the only ones being taken off-world today. The Brotherhood is taking the opportunity to transport some of the Expulsion leaders with them. We intend to make sure they never get the chance."

"Then you're going to free the prisoners?"

"Yes," said Selen. "And if your friends are in with them, then you should count yourself lucky."

"Let me help then," Ghenni said.

"We don't have any spare guns, but hop in. If one of our brothers falls, pick up his rifle and continue on fighting." Selen raised a fist in the air and shouted, "Victory for Trenth!" The rest of the group cheered in agreement, and engines revved up in anticipation. At the wave of Selen's hand, the vehicles all lurched forward, roaring toward the space-age spires of the Brotherhood district.

"So tell me," said Damien to the Lippilligin's face plate, "what do they pay you for this job? I've thought about getting into the bounty hunting business myself on the side, but it's kind of a conflict of interest when you're a criminal yourself, you know?" The creature didn't respond. Tanner also stayed silent, head bowed in prayer

"Just give it up," groaned Eve, head in her hands. "You're not going to talk your way out of this; he's not even listening."

"Of course he's listening," Damien said. "I'll wear him down soon enough."

Eve pointed to a tiny unlit bulb on the side of the helmet. "He turned his microphone off ten minutes ago."

Damien peered at the dull bulb for show. "Yeah, I guess you're right." They rode in silence for a few more minutes, bouncing along the rough roads of the city, with only the sunlight from the windshield at the front providing illumination. The other prisoners sat morosely, murmuring quietly to each other.

A thought popped into Damien's head. "Allosan!" he cried suddenly. Some of the other prisoners looked up at him blankly, but soon ignored him again.

"What?" asked Eve.

"I just remembered what those giraffe guys are called," Damien answered gesturing toward the Brotherhood agent up front. "I've been trying to think of it since we saw him."

Eve sighed and thumped the back of her head against the wall. "Did you ever come up with an escape plan?"

"Not yet," Damien said, "but I'm still trying. I'm sure something will present-"

Before he could finish, a loud crack split the air along with the sound of breaking glass. The van lurched to the right, and Damien looked up to see a spiderweb of cracks across the windshield, splattered with specks of deep red blood. The Trenthan driver slumped to the side, motionless. The Allosan leaned its long orange body across to grab the steering wheel, and straightened the course of the van. But within seconds, a smoky trail darted from a nearby rooftop and collided with the escort buggy in front of them, exploding into a brilliant flash of light and shaking the van with concussive force. The van veered again to dodge the flaming wreckage as more gunshots erupted outside.

"What's going on?" asked Tanner, jolted out of his prayer.

"It's a rescue!" Damien shouted. "Just like I promised!" He leapt up from his seat and tackled the Lippilligin, feeling the polymer suit crumple beneath his weight. On the other side of the van, two of the Trenthan prisoners did the same for the other guard. Damien grabbed for the submachine gun in his hand, but the Lippilligin grasped it with both of his right arms, keeping it out of Damien's grip. With his left arms, the alien grabbed Damien's head by the hair, and pummeled him in the side. He held on tightly to the gun, keeping it pointed safely at the roof of the van, as forceful punches rained down on him. The gloves did little to soften the blows.

Eve jumped up beside him, grabbing the creature's arms from behind and pulling back on them as hard as she could. The punches stopped, and eventually the hand released from Damien's hair, leaving him to concentrate on the gun. It continued to waver in the air as they struggled. The alien's finger must have slipped, and the gun fired in the air, peppering the ceiling with bullet holes that let in shafts of sunlight, and deafening Damien's unprotected ears in the close confines of the van.

The van slowed to a crawl now that the driver couldn't apply the accelerator, and it shook as the front doors were jerked open roughly. Armed men with clothes over their faces grabbed the Allosan agent and dragged him outside. The alien kicked furiously but futilely at his assailants. Blinding light flooded the back of the van as the rear doors were opened, and more attackers grabbed the Lippilligin from behind, pulling him onto the dirt road.

The prisoners hurriedly filed out of the van and into the sun, where the normal crowds were conspicuously absent. Ragtag soldiers dragged the suited alien out into an open area and removed his two air tanks. Pale green vapors trailed out of the now-open ports in the respiration system, and the Lippilligin struggled to stand up. Keeping him down were two of the armed men, pinning him to the ground with their feet as one arm aimed an automatic rifle at their captive, and the other was drawn across their face to protect them from the toxic chlorine gas as it mixed with the outside air.

Damien stumbled out of the van and squinted against the light, searching for his bearings. Two wrecked motorbikes littered the ground, along with spots of blood mixed with dust. The roar of an engine pulled up beside him, and Damien's eyes adjusted to see Ghenni in the driver's seat.

"Let's go," he said. Damien obliged, and jumped in the back. Tanner and Eve saw it too, and climbed in after him. Ghenni cranked up the throttle, tearing off down the street among jubilant cries of victory and sporadic gunshots.

Father Tanner climbed out of the buggy in the cargo hold of the *Malika*, his senses still coming down from the adrenaline high. It would probably be a few hours before his heart rate and breathing were back to normal. The closing door shut out the last fiery rays of the setting sun.

"Whoo!" Damien cried, jumping over the railing and landing on the hard metal floor with a thud. "I don't know how you put that together Ghenni, but that has to be the most dramatic escape I ever made."

"I apologize for turning you in earlier," Ghenni said. "I could see they didn't believe your story. I had to make myself your enemy for to escape myself."

"Hey, all is forgiven, buddy." Damien slapped him on the back.

"You know my policy on violence, Ghenni," Tanner said in between deep breaths, as he sat on an empty crate. "Was this... *assault* all your doing?"

"Uh, hello?" asked Damien. "If he hadn't rustled up that attack, we'd be halfway to the core planets by now, ready to be executed. You're alive because of him."

"But at what cost? How many innocent people were murdered to free us?"

"Well let's see," said Damien, counting on his fingers. "Um, none. They were all working for a government that was about to kill us for something we... OK we *did* actually kidnap him, but that's not the point. They're part of a brutal regime which, you may remember, we're technically at war with. So I'm not seeing the dilemma."

"You may see them as just faceless agents of the Brotherhood," Tanner said, "but they still bear the image of God. Killing should always be an absolute last resort."

"Right, because we were almost out of there with Plan A, weren't we?"

"Father," Ghenni said meekly, taking a cautious step forward, "they were already planning the attack. I merely stumbled upon it. I couldn't have stopped it if I'd wanted to."

"Hey, you prayed for deliverance, didn't you, Father?" Damien asked smugly. "I guess God works in mysterious ways, et cetera, et cetera."

Tanner stood up and paced quickly around the room, unable to sit still as fire pulsed through his veins. "But I watched them hold a man down as he choked to death on oxygen. We could have stopped them."

"They made the smart choice," Damien said. "He only had a few hours of chlorine in those tanks, and it would have been impossible to get any kind of ransom for him in that time."

"Then they could hand him over for free, or let him walk the rest of the way to the Alliance district. They could have at least tried to show mercy, but instead they murdered him and called it virtue. Now I have to spend the rest of my life knowing that I only live because others were killed."

"If I remember right," Damien said, "that was how the whole Jesus thing worked, right?"

"Do you really want to debate theology with me right now?" Tanner snapped. All his rage just poured out, beyond his control. "Because I swear on all that's holy that I would destroy you. And I..." He stopped himself and took a few deep breaths, choking down his emotion. All his feelings—the shame, guilt and remorse for the attack, the anger at the others, and the residual despair from facing certain death—swirled inside of him in a maelstrom. "I... I need to go pray."

He turned quickly, forcing himself to not say any more, and walked as fast as he could toward his quarters. The polished metal mirror on the wall rattled as he slammed the door behind him, and he collapsed to his knees at the bedside. It felt as though swords pierced his heart, and hot tears streamed down his face as he cried out to God in the darkness.

I thought this was Your will, he prayed. *I thought this was an opportunity to save lives, but now half a dozen men are dead in our wake.* The words of God drifted into his mind, battling with his own thoughts for supremacy. *"You meant it for evil, but God meant it for good." But was I complicit in this sin?* He asked. *Perhaps I was selfish and naïve to think that I could work with this captain, to be unequally yoked in a business partnership, a criminal endeavor, with an unbeliever. Is it even right to call this "business" when we're dealing in lives?*

As he continued praying, though he heard no answer, he felt the anguish begin to drain from his heart. Replacing it was something approaching peace, not that things were right, but that the past was done. Ahead lay the future, and he prayed for guidance and clarity of thought in treating their patient. Some time in the next several minutes, without noticing, he slipped from prayer into sleep.

Ghenni walked back into the cargo hold as Andrew finished pulling off the last shoe of his surgical suit. "I suppose it's my turn to watch the patient?" he asked.

"Yeah, thanks," Andrew answered. "I really need to take a lunch break." His stomach growled, and his mouth watered at the thought of any flavor besides recycled air. As he strapped on his regular shoes, the ship lurched and the lights flickered.

"Where are we going?" Andrew asked.

"Captain Rogers is taking us back to the cave where we hid before. They will only be looking for us harder now, after what happened."

"I suppose so," Andrew said. "Hey, I'm glad you guys made it back alright."

"Thank you," Ghenni said. He paused in the middle of pulling on his own suit. "Do you think what I did was wrong, working with the militants?"

Andrew heaved a sigh. "Maybe. I don't know. There's so much wrong in the world, just swirling all around us, it's hard to tell when we're part of it, and when it's just happening nearby. But even if it was, I don't think I would have had the strength to say no." He trudged out of the cargo bay and down the corridor toward his room, fanning his sweaty shirt to get cool air flowing inside of it. As he started to go in, he saw Eve through the crack of her door sitting on her bed, knees pulled up to her chin, sobbing gently. He stopped in the doorway as his heart and mind, and, he had to admit, other parts of his body, wrestled over whether to do anything. He wanted to comfort her, but he also didn't want to hurt her more by showing up unwelcome. And part of him wondered if he thought comforting would lead to something more, but he wasn't sure if his subconscious was using that to justify going in, or justify ignoring her. Finally he walked softly up to the door, and gave a few meek knocks that made the door creak slightly as it drifted farther open.

"Hey," he said, leaning against the doorway with his hands in his pockets. "I'm glad to see you made it back alright."

"I noticed you weren't there to help." She didn't look up.

"There was nothing that I could have done. I sent Ghenni for help, but I had no idea what the plan ended up being. Besides, I had to stay here with the patient."

"Of course."

Andrew was silent for a moment as he considered what to say, and Eve sniffed and wiped her nose with her sleeve.

"Listen," he said, "I'm sorry about... how things happened the other night."

"It's fine."

"Well, even so, I wanted to apologize..."

"I don't want to talk about it right now, OK?"

"Alright," Andrew said. "I'm sorry I brought it up."

"No," said Eve, standing up and turning to face him, "it's not fine. I almost died today, and all I could think about was you. The only other humans I meet out here are scumbags and criminals, but this time, I thought I'd met someone I could trust. You're one of the few truly honest people I've met in years, so I couldn't help but care what you thought about me. As much as you were a jerk to me, I can't help thinking of you."

"It's not that I don't like you..." began Andrew.

"Then what is it?"

"I just don't think it's a good idea for us to get involved."

"Why not?"

"Because... we don't really share the same beliefs."

"Why does that matter so much to you?" Eve asked.

"When I get involved with a woman, I want it to be for life."

"But I'm not marriage material, is what you're saying?"

Andrew groaned and rubbed his eyes. "No, it's... Even if I leave the missions field, I'm still going to be in ministry of some kind. When I get married, I need to know that my wife is on-board with my mission a hundred percent."

"Oh my God," Eve cried. "I'm not talking about settling down! I just wanted someone that I could relax and be myself with. Someone I could really *trust*. You were the first person out here I met who was running *to* something, and not away. I thought you could be that person, but I guess not."

"If you don't like the people you meet out here, then why did you even start working with Damien? Why don't you just go back to Earth?"

"Because I can't!" she yelled.

"Why not?"

Eve's lip quivered, and she leaned back against the wall, closing her eyes. Andrew considered moving to sit by her, but decided it was safer by the doorway. "I have probably the worst ex-fiancé ever," she said. "A real grade-A psycho, tried to kill me a couple of times."

"You had to come all the way out to Brotherhood territory to get away from him?"

"He has a long reach," Eve said, absentmindedly stroking her ring finger. "I had to get off the grid completely. I hired Damien to take me across the border, and he gave me a job. It pays the bills, I suppose."

"It's OK," Andrew said, taking a cautious step inside. Eve's eyes snapped open, and she marched to the door, chasing Andrew out. "Don't even try to come in," she said. "It's too late for that." She slammed the door in Andrew's face, and he retreated to his own quarters and threw himself on the bed.

Chapter Twelve

An hour later, the inertial dampeners flickered as Damien began the descent toward the atmosphere. "Just FYI," he announced over the intercom, "we're coming in for a landing on the planet." A red light blipped on the console, and he tapped it to bring up a display of the warning. The alert expanded on the screen to display an image of a lumbering chunk of metal, bristling with spiny protrusions, silhouetted against the planet. An unmapped satellite lay directly in the ship's path for re-entry.

"Stupid Brotherhood black sats," Damien muttered. "Gonna put somebody's eye out one of these days." The Brotherhood had a bad habit of leaving secret satellites lying around without registering them on the orbital maps of their planets. Anyone who wasn't paying attention, or didn't have their sensors working, was liable to run into one when they came in to land. He gave the thrusters a quick burst to nudge them around the obstacle, but the controls clicked ineffectually.

"Uhh..." he said over the intercom to Eve, "why don't I have thrusters?"

"I don't know," she replied in a croaking voice, followed by a deep sniff. "I fixed them just the other day."

"Well, they're not working now, and I kind of need them."

"It's probably just a bad splice. I can have it fixed by the time you're ready to land."

"I'm going to need it a lot sooner than that," Damien said, talking louder and sitting up straighter. He tapped furiously on the button, but it still didn't respond. "We're on a collision course with a satellite."

Eve cursed, and Damien heard the jingle of hastily grabbed tools. "Can you get around it with just the main engines?"

"I'm trying, but it's not going to be enough. We're still going to sideswipe it."

"What about repulsors?"

"It's too big for that!"

"How big is it?"

"Big enough to rip *Malika* a new one."

"Then you're going to have to try something else," Eve said, "because it's going to take me two or three minutes to find and fix the issue."

"Well I've got less than a minute," Damien said. He scanned the control console, looking for anything that might offer a way out. He briefly considered using the ship's weapons to blow the satellite out of the way, but taking out a Brotherhood satellite top secret enough to be unmapped was the best way to let the investigating agents know where to find them. His eyes finally caught on the atmospheric controls. He grabbed the intercom again.

"Whoever's in the airlock had better hold on tight, *right now*. I'm about to open a window."

Ghenni pressed down firmly on the Hountan's four legs as they fought furiously against the restraints, caught up in violent spasms. The creature's circular mouth opened and closed erratically, biting at the air, and spewed forth a jumble of shrill sounds that the translator couldn't make sense of. One of its legs kicked out and struck Ghenni's stomach, but it was still too feeble to do any real damage. After a few minutes its muscles slackened, reduced to mere twitches as the patient's body sank into unconscious exhaustion. When it was finally still, Ghenni was able to relax his grip, stand up straight, and take another look at the monitors. Vital signs were returning to normal, but the seizures seemed to be getting worse.

The intercom crackled, followed by Damien's voice. "Whoever's in the airlock had better hold on tight, *right now*. I'm about to open a window."

Ghenni wondered what he meant by that, but his thoughts were interrupted immediately by the flashing red light and howling warning siren of the airlock. Shit. He realized what was about to happen just in time to grab onto the patient's table. The outer door opened with a deafening hiss, as the alien atmosphere vented into the vacuum of space. The force of the out-rushing wind picked up some of the smaller equipment, whisking it away into nothingness, where it would gradually fall toward the planet and burn up in a brief flash of fire.

The same force pulled the rolling table that the Hountan was on, dragging it toward the open door. The two ends caught on either side of the doorway, bringing the table to a jarring halt. Ghenni's momentum carried him out into the open, and pulled his left arm loose from its grip, but he held tightly to the edge of the table with his right arm, which kept him tethered to the mass of the ship, dangling over the mottled mixture of blue, green, and brown on the surface of Trenth. His stomach twisted as the artificial gravity and inertial dampeners lost their grip on him, and he transitioned from standing firmly on the ground to being swung out to the side in empty space. One of the electronic monitors missed the table, and it flew off into the void, ripping the sensors off the patient's body. Most of the other large equipment collected against the far side of the table, and in just a few seconds stasis had been reached, and everything was still again.

Ghenni tried to pull himself back in, but the shooting pain quickly informed him that the force of his sudden stop had pulled his arm out of joint. Without the inertial dampeners, the centrifugal force of the turning ship was too much, and his single arm wasn't sufficient to get back inside. His left arm searched for a handhold, but he was already hanging onto the far-left end of the table, and there was no railing left. He looked around for a solution, and it was then that he saw the satellite.

It was big, looming silent in space, with solar panels, antennae, and other instruments thrusting out in every direction. One antenna was of particular concern as it raked across the side of the ship, straight toward him. It dragged across the outer hull, leaving a dark trail behind it, but it made no sound in the vacuum of space. Ghenni only felt the vibrations that rumbled through the hull of the ship and into his arm. He did his best to twist out of the way, but he didn't have much leverage, and the large metal rod slid inexorably along and slammed against his leg. Pain shot through his body as it was tossed easily aside by the cold, unyielding machine. Once it began to subside, Ghenni noticed the rush of air down by his foot. The surgical suits were made for separating one atmosphere from another, not for holding in vital gases against the boundless void. The seals were already too weak to be safe for space-walks, and the impact had damaged the one by his foot, allowing precious air to escape. The suit's air tanks automatically began pumping more air out to compensate, but the reserves wouldn't last for more than a few minutes at this rate. Ghenni tried to pull himself back in, but the pain in his arm was still too great.

"Ghenni," Damien said over the radio, "we need to re-pressurize the airlock, but we can't do that until we close the door with you inside."

"I can't," Ghenni said. "My arm is hurt."

"Well, we're going to get you back in somehow. So just hang on. Literally, I guess."

Ghenni hung limply for a few minutes, as the air traveled quickly from his tanks, to the suit, to outer space. The red pulsing light of an air level warning on the inside of his helmet told him that the oxygen was almost exhausted. A flicker of motion caught his eye, and he looked up into the airlock to see another, bulkier suit coming slowly toward him.

"Don't worry," he heard Father Tanner say, "I'm coming for you."

He inched his way slowly toward the open door. With the door open, the artificial gravity and inertia controls were unpredictable around the doorway. Father Tanner anchored himself, and stretched out an arm toward Ghenni's hand on the table. He wrapped his fingers around Ghenni's wrist.

"I've got you," he said. "You're going to have to let go of the table and grab my hand so I can pull you in."

"Are you sure you have me?" Ghenni asked.

"I won't let anything happen to you."

Ghenni quickly released his hand from the table, and grabbed

Father Tanner's wrist firmly. Father Tanner braced himself against the doorway, and slowly pulled him inside. Ghenni floated over the immobilized patient, and quickly drifted down toward the floor as the artificial gravity got a hold of him. With a finalizing thud, Ghenni tumbled down bumping his foot on the table and landing on his shoulder with a cry of pain.

"We're in," said Father Tanner to Damien in the cockpit, "you can close the door. And we need double air pressure to treat the decompression."

"Got it," Damien said.

The outer barrier slid closed silently, cutting them off from the empty expanse outside. When it was locked in place, the pumps began filling the room with the ammonia-laden air.

"The leg of my suit is leaking," Ghenni said.

"Then we need to get that patched up before the oxygen poisons our patient," Father Tanner replied. He ran over to a cabinet that had been tossed against the wall, and searched through the drawers, eventually producing a roll of duct tape. He tore off a long strip and wrapped it tightly around the broken seal, allowing Ghenni's air tanks to finally reach an equilibrium and stop pumping the toxic oxygen into the patient's room.

"We must attend to the patient," Ghenni said, standing up. "He was without air for a great while."

"Hountan's don't require air for respiration," Father Tanner said. "They breathe just for speech, and to absorb trace nutrients. It's this frostbite I'm worried about." He examined the patient's body, which Ghenni saw was spotted with dry, discolored regions where the fluids inside the cells had frozen, tearing apart the tissue as the ammonia crystals grew.

"The coldness of space must take effect quickly."

"Space isn't cold," Father Tanner said, "it's insulating. It's the rapid expansion of the gases that cools things off." He grabbed a blanket and wrapped the patient tightly, allowing his natural body heat to begin warming the affected areas.

"Ghenni," he continued, "I need you to get some nutritive ammonia. Heat some up to body temperature to help thaw the tissue, and spike the rest with extra sulfur to help fight necrosis." As he finished wrapping the patient in blankets, he paused, tilting his head

with thought. "You said the twitching was constant now, right?"
"Yes, that's correct."

"It's stopped. Even the eyes are sitting still."

"What does that mean?"

Father Tanner paused. "It means that we still don't know what's wrong with him, but we may have just inadvertently treated him."

Chapter Thirteen

Damien passed by the open door to Tanner's quarters, stripped down to an undershirt and covered in smears of grease. Eve followed behind him with a large box of tools, her hair pulled back tightly. They both stopped, and Damien poked his head inside. Tanner sat with Andrew at a small table, poring over Hountan medical texts. Papers, charts, and diagrams spilled over the edge, and a few loose pages fell on the floor as Andrew dug through them.

"You guys might want to close the door," he said. "We're going to be kind of noisy."

"Doing what?" asked Andrew.

"Engine work, I guess you could say. On the IS drive."

"I thought it was out of commission," said Tanner.

"I think I can squeeze one last escape out of it," Damien said with a smile.

"I've been meaning to talk to you about that," Tanner said, pulling off his glasses and standing up. "There's not going to be an escape, because we're not holding him for ransom."

"Not this bit again," groaned Damien, pinching the bridge of his nose. "Look, I appreciate you talking me down from the whole assaulting-the-prison plan, I really do. When it comes to my wife, I let my emotions get the best of me. But it's a two-way street. You need to think smart about this."

"I've thought plenty about it. I can't let you put any more lives in danger for the sake of money. During the war, I had to watch people get shot and poisoned for my sake, and I'll be damned if I let that happen to anyone else, even a Brotherhood soldier."

"And you think they're going to let this whole kidnapping thing slide, just because you want to play nice all of a sudden? They're going to be coming after us either way; the only difference is that with your plan, they'll know we're weak."

"That's a chance we're going to have to take," said Tanner.

"And what about all those people at the clinic? Without this money, you won't be able to stay open. You're willing to let them die for certain, rather than risk someone *possibly* getting hurt here?"

"There has to be another way."

"There is no other way!" Damien cried. "I'm the captain of this ship, and as long as I'm in charge, mine is the only way you've got to choose from."

Tanner sighed. "That's what I realized too," he said. He reached into his robe, and Damien saw the glint of metal tucked underneath. Instinctively he reached for his pistol, and in half a second of lightning motion, they both looked down the barrel of the other's gun. Andrew backed up against the wall, his eyes rapidly passing from Damien to Tanner and back again. Eve retreated around the corner, peeking half of her head into the doorway to see.

"Pops," Damien said, straining to keep his voice calm, "I'm surprised at you." He scanned the Father's body language, looking for any twitch that would betray an intent to pull the trigger. His own heart was pounding, and the gun quickly grew slippery with sweat in his hand. Facing down a fellow criminal was one thing—they were predictable—but a stand-off with a preacher scared him.

"You drew your gun awfully fast for a surprised man," Tanner answered.

"Reflex. I wasn't surprised until I thought about it."

"Now," Tanner said, "I ask that you please put down your weapon and drop us off somewhere safe with the patient."

"Half the Brotherhood is combing the planet looking for us. This ship is the safest place for you."

"I'm not going to argue with you anymore!" shouted Tanner. "We're going to do this my way."

"Oh, surprise, surprise! Who would have guessed that the priest would want to control everything? But as a doctor, you should realize that if you shoot me, I'll still have enough time to shoot you back before I bleed out. But somehow I doubt-"

"Would you all just stop it, please?" yelled Eve from the hallway. "We have an entire inter-planetary government breathing down our necks. We should be working together, but we're at each other's throats instead. Are you really going to start killing each other over an argument about whose plan is the safest?"

"We're attacking each other instead of protecting each other," mumbled Tanner. He fidgeted with the gun in his hand, and furrowed his eyebrows. Damien saw the wheels turning in his head as Tanner thought about something else entirely.

"Yes... that's right," Eve said hesitantly.

"That's it." Tanner lowered his gun. "Come on, Andrew; I have an idea." He started to push past Damien, who pushed him back.

"Where do you think you're going with that?" he asked.

"Oh, this," Father Tanner said, looking at the gun in his hand. He tossed it on the bed. "It's not loaded. Come on."

He slid past Damien and Eve, and Andrew followed sheepishly behind. "Excuse me," he said.

"What just happened?" Damien asked.

"I'm not sure," Eve said. "Kind of looked like an epiphany."

Tanner pressed the button on the intercom near the airlock.

"Ghenni," he said. "Is the patient awake?"

"Yes," Ghenni replied, "but he isn't coherent."

"I need to ask him a question. I'm switching to your external speakers."

Tanner pressed a few more buttons on the intercom, and sloppily growled some question in the Hountan language. The patient moved slightly, its rear legs struggling to lift its weight off the cold metal table. It gave a few weak barks before lowering itself slowly back down. Father Tanner nodded, and switched the intercom back to Ghenni's suit.

"I think I've got the diagnosis. I'll need to come in to take a sample of cerebral fluid to confirm."

"Can we treat him?" Ghenni asked.

"If we're not too late."

Tanner hurriedly put on a suit and tapped his foot impatiently as he waited for the pressure tent to finish swapping out the gases. Finally it let him inside the airlock, and he swabbed a spot on the patient's head.

"What are you doing?" he asked.

"Please stay still," Tanner said. "Andrew tells me your name is Counhack, right? Well Counhack, I won't lie. This is going to hurt, but I need a sample from the fluid around your brain. That will help us know what's making you sick."

The alien creature groaned slightly, and collapsed back onto the table. His legs tensed and pulled inward as Tanner pierced his skin with a needle. A pull on the plunger filled the syringe with another bronze-colored fluid, but of a lighter tone than blood. He quickly took the needle out and let Ghenni tend to the patient as he set up the diagnostic equipment.

Once the test was running, Tanner turned to the console on the wall and punched buttons until a video feed popped up on the screen. On the other end was a brightly lit room full of stacks of medical and theological texts, and an outdated medical certificate framed on the wall. A Trenthan man wearing ragged scrubs sat in front of the screen, and looked up when the feed turned on.

"This is Nateth speaking," the man said. "Who is this? I can't see through your helmet."

"It's me, Father Tanner. I see you've settled into my office quite nicely."

"Father," replied Nateth, his face beaming. "We haven't heard from you since you left. We were starting to get worried."

"Things got complicated, I'm afraid. How is the mission doing?"

"About the same as when you left," Nateth answered, smiling weakly. "We've had to turn away a lot of people who have been waiting for surgery for months. Without the drugs, there's not much we can do here."

"I know," Tanner said. "I just... Can I speak with Father Nellin?"

The pained smile dropped from Nateth's face. "I'm sorry Father, but he's not doing well. He's in and out of consciousness, and even when awake, he's in too much pain to carry on a conversation. I wouldn't expect him to live much longer."

Tanner sighed, a handful of tears slowly falling down his face. He couldn't wipe them away, but at least Nateth couldn't see him crying through the helmet either. "I'm afraid I need his guidance now more than ever."

"What's troubling you, Father?"

"To finish this job I took on, and get the money for it, I'll be putting people's lives at risk. I don't think I should do that. I don't think I *can* do that."

"Yes, we've all heard about the kidnapping," Nateth said. "I figured you were part of that somehow. But surely you have control over whether you harm others or not."

"Myself, yes," said Tanner. "But I'm not sure about everyone I'm working with."

"But look at the timing. In our darkest hour of need, an opportunity arises, one that you were precisely qualified for. I don't think you can deny that God was moving behind these events. Wouldn't giving up be an insult to Providence?"

"Perhaps..."

"Even if things go bad," Nateth said, "thankfully we serve a God who is always ready to forgive."

"Thank you," Tanner said, trying to keep his voice from cracking. "I think I needed to hear that. I should get back to my patient."

"I'll be praying for you."

Damien crawled out of the pit in the middle of the cargo hold, covered with grime and sweat. He grabbed a hook that hung on a cable over his head, suspended from a pulley, and attached it to the harness that held the inter-stellar drive. Then he strolled over to a winch that sat anchored to the wall, and switched it on. The motor worked noisily, almost drowned out by the groaning metal casing of the ship's heart as it was lifted from rest, yawning like a waking giant. It crept up, inch by inch, revealing itself almost sensuously. It looked like an amalgam of scrap metal, with occasional flashes of reflected blue light from the powerful spark within it. Wires and tubing still connected it to the bottom of the pit, but they stretched far enough for the drive to be lifted entirely out, and the floor put most of the way back in place for it to rest on.

As Damien reached up to unhook the cable from the harness, he noticed Tanner, who sat at the makeshift workstation in the corner. He got up hurriedly and gave Andrew some instructions, which he rushed to carry out.

"Good news, Pops?" he asked as he walked towards him, wiping off his hands with a rag.

"Yes, very good news," Tanner said. "I've just confirmed the diagnosis, and we should be able to help our patient."

"You don't say. So what was the problem?"

"It was an autoimmune disease," Tanner said, leading Damien over to the workstation, "similar to multiple sclerosis in humans. The body's own immune system begins attacking the brain, causing inflammation and a host of neurological symptoms. So when he was exposed to the cold when the airlock depressurized-"

"It made the swelling go down."

"Exactly. He'll have to stay on immunosuppressants for the rest of his life, but it should be manageable."

"So how did he get something like this in the first place?" Damien asked.

"Look here," Tanner said, pointing to the microscope. Damien looked in the eyepiece, and saw a pink-stained background of round cells, with a few scraggly deformed cells mixed in. "See those diseased-looking cells? They don't belong to our patient. They're not microbes, but brain cells from another person; it's called 'microchimerism.'"

"So these came from some other unlucky guy in the mine explosion?" Damien asked as he stood up straight again.

"No, any Trenthan cells would have been completely torn apart by his ammonia-based blood. These come from another Hountan. Specifically, his son."

"How did his son's cells get there?"

"I believe I mentioned before how the Hountans can filter their children's blood to cleanse it of toxins and pathogens..."

"Yeah, I remember that, but didn't you say they didn't do that anymore? All these new-fangled drugs and so forth."

"It's no longer necessary, true, but as it turns out, our patient belongs to a minor religion that performs ritual cleansing ceremonies before major events."

"Like an extended tour through space?"

"That's right. These foreign cells got lodged in his brain tissue and, along with the trauma suffered in the explosion, triggered an overzealous immune response."

"Well," said Damien, slapping Tanner on the back, "it sounds like good news all around, then."

"Not quite," said Father Tanner with a sigh. "As you can imagine, Hountan brain cells don't normally just flake off like this. His son is suffering from a degenerative brain disease. Ten-to-one he'll be dead before his father gets back home."

"Then we'll just have to do our best to get him home safely."

Tanner paused for a moment. "I've been thinking about that."

Damien tensed. "Are you gonna pull another gun on me?"

"No, I'm sorry about that. I overreacted."

"A bit."

"It's usually hard enough just to do the right thing, but I've never had this much trouble simply figuring out what the right thing is. Honestly, I've prayed and prayed, but I still don't know for sure what the best course of action is. But... I've decided to trust you."

Damien raised one eyebrow. "Why the sudden change of heart?"

"I found out a little bit ago that an old friend of mine, one of the first people I met on Trenth, is getting sicker. He needs drugs, and without the money from this... job, he'll die. And I believe God has placed you in our path, so I'm choosing to trust that it was for a purpose."

"Don't worry," Damien said as he turned to walk away, "you'll get your money." He walked a few steps away, and then turned around with a quizzical look on his face. "How did you find out?"

"Oh, I called the mission on the console to check in. I hope you don't mind."

Damien's heart stopped. "Are you insane?" he yelled.

"I thought you had it secured," Tanner said, his eyes wide in frightened confusion.

"For day-to-day stuff, yeah, but we've got some serious heat on our tails. They know you're involved, and they're bound to be watching the mission. It's only a matter of hours until they hack my encryption and trace that call back here."

"I'm sorry," Tanner said. "What should we do?"

Damien sighed and rubbed his forehead thoughtfully. "The IS drive is pretty much ready. We'll need to send out a ransom demand and get this cargo hold cleared out; it's going to be open to space. I'll also need to override some safety protocols in the controls. In the meantime, I have something for you to do."

"What is it?"

"Just a little, shall we say, *elective surgery* on our patient."

Chapter Fourteen

Andrew injected the patient's IV bag with a round of immunosuppressants, spiked with a mild sedative to make the transfer easier, and the yellow liquid slowly absorbed into the lustrous ammonia solution, where its own color was overwhelmed by the metallic sheen. The patient was unconscious for the moment, but they couldn't take a chance with him causing trouble during the exchange.

"Just don't wake up," Andrew said. "You're going to be going home soon."

The radio crackled in Andrew's ear. "We have the Brotherhood ships in sight," Damien said. "You'd better get up here."

Andrew quickly packed up the last of the loose supplies, leaving the room stripped bare except for the Hountan sprawled on the table, and stepped out of the airlock into the small pressure tent. The door closed behind him, the atmosphere vented, and he stepped out into the cargo hold. To his right, the large bay doors were raised, replaced by a field of black vacuum speckled with stars. The artificial gravity was still turned on, but a cord hung between the airlock door and the door leading to the rest of the ship, just in case. Andrew followed it to a second make-shift airlock, and in a few minutes was in the corridor, taking off his suit as he walked toward the cockpit.

Everyone else was there waiting, and Damien was half-dressed in his own space suit. Out the cockpit window, three specks moved slowly toward them. A magnified inset showed that the specks were three ships: one was the Hountan ship they had first taken the patient from, while the other two were standard Brotherhood patrol ships. They looked almost like cats, the rear drive modules resembling haunches poised as if about to pounce. The ships were small, but with enough firepower to blow the *Malika* out of existence without a second thought.

Eve sat in the captain's chair, and she turned around when a tone sounded on the controls. "The Hountan ship will be docking with us in about five minutes," she said.

"Great," Damien replied as Father Tanner helped him put the helmet on his suit. When it was secured, he turned to the shelf behind him, and picked up a submachine gun in one hand, and a detonator switch in the other. "Let's rock-and-roll."

Father Tanner closed his eyes and muttered a quick prayer. "Godspeed, I suppose."

A few minutes later, Damien crouched in the airlock, shielding himself the best that he could behind the Hountan patient, who was strapped down to the operating table. The room echoed with the ominous clangs and thumps of the enemy ship making airtight contact with his own. The noises ceased, but the outer airlock door stayed closed for a few gut-wrenching moments. Damien's hands grew sweaty inside his gloves, and he did his best to keep his grip on the gun, and keep the button pressed on the device in his other hand.

Eventually, the door slid open with a hiss of equalizing pressure to reveal a handful of soldiers, all with guns trained on Damien. There were three on each side of the doors; two of them were humanoid shapes in stream-lined, transenvironmental combat suits, likely local Trenthan forces, while the other four were Hountans, clad in military uniforms and each holding a small rifle in its two hands. At least one of them was bound to be a good enough shot to easily hit Damien without endangering the patient, but they were waiting on the order to fire from their commander.

"Alright," Damien said. His voice was translated into Hountan and broadcast from the external speakers in his suit, and the barks and howls drifted back into his suit, muffled and unintelligible. "Listen up you fascist knuckleheads. I bet you can guess what this baby is. While we were poking around inside your guy here, we took the liberty of implanting some explosives. I have the detonator right here, and it's on a dead-man's trigger, so if you shoot me, your friend here will be going home in a dustbin. And in case you were thinking of anything tricky, the signal is being relayed through my ship, so if you touch her, it's the same story."

The soldiers glanced at each other, in what Damien hoped was nervousness. They continued to stand still, keeping their guns pointed at Damien, and since there had been no answer, he continued. "I think one hundred thousand was our agreed-upon price. Do you have the money?"

There was some movement on the other side of the doorway, and after a few moments, one of the soldiers slid a bag across the floor to Damien, who quickly pulled it behind the table with him. He rifled through the contents, a mix of Trenthan paper currency and more universal gold and silver ingots, while keeping one eye on the soldiers. It seemed real, and there were no obvious marks. He put down his gun, and pulled a small tool off his belt, giving the money a quick scan to make sure it wasn't implanted with any electronic or radioactive tracers. After he was satisfied, he picked his gun back up, stood up straight, and kicked the bag of money into the corner.

"So far so good," Damien said. "Now I'm going to hand over the hostage, and we can all go home happy and nobody gets hurt." He unlocked the wheels on the table, and slowly edged forward, keeping the patient between himself and the soldiers. As he reached the boundary between the ships, he gave the table one last push to put it within reach of the soldiers, who quickly grabbed it and pulled it inside their ship and out of sight. Damien kept the detonator lifted high in the air, and the submachine gun pointed at the soldiers as he backed up and hit the intercom button with his elbow to talk to the cockpit.

"OK, it looks good, you can go ahead and-"

He was cut short by a sharp pain in his stomach. He looked down, and saw a large dart sticking out of his suit. He tried to pull it out, but noticed that he wasn't moving; his muscles had locked in place, but his head felt like it was twisting and turning in every direction at once. "Somebody's getting hurt," he muttered through clenched teeth before the room tumbled around and turned on its side.

The grainy image of Damien on the cockpit's video screen collapsed rigidly, and a swarm of soldiers poured out into the airlock, pulling him back into their own ship as they set to work on the control panels.

"They shot him!" cried Andrew. "Is he dead?" If they shot Damien that easily, Andrew could only imagine what they would do to the rest of them.

"No," said Father Tanner, turning away angrily, "they wouldn't have taken him inside their ship if he was dead. It was a tranquilizer dart. Hopefully self-sealing, if they don't want him to choke on the Hountan air." He stomped his foot with surprising force, which reverberated loudly in the metal floor. "I should have expected that."

"So what do we do now?" Andrew asked, pointing at the video feed of the airlock, which crawled with enemy soldiers. "They're coming for us already." He swallowed, but his mouth felt like a desert. He desperately needed a drink of water, but he couldn't tear his gaze away from the screen.

"They won't do anything too drastic for a while," said Eve, "not while they're still worrying about us setting off those explosives. They have to make sure we have hope, or else we might set them off."

"Not to mention," said Father Tanner, "they only have two Trenthans, and Hountans are nearly worthless in a fight when they're wearing suits. They have to hack into the computer to re-pressurize the cargo hold before coming after us."

"How long will that take?" asked Ghenni.

"No more than fifteen minutes," said Eve. "Maybe less."

"What are we going to do about it?"

"I don't know," Eve said, clutching her forehead in her hands.

A few tense moments of silence passed before Andrew spoke up again. "Maybe we should just get ourselves out of here. Damien wouldn't want us all to die for his sake, if we could avoid it."

"Are you crazy?" Eve shouted. "We're not leaving him behind! If Damien were here, he probably would have shot you just for suggesting it."

"Well, I don't see that we have another choice. We can't exactly shoot our way through to get him back. Do you have any ideas that will save him without getting us killed?"

Eve's head sunk for a few moments, but then she broke the silence weakly. "Father, if there's anyone here with enough good karma to get us a miracle, it's you. If you could pray..."

"Regardless of the mixed-up theology of that last statement, I'd be happy too. Andrew?"

Andrew concentrated on his breathing, trying to clamp down on the fear that radiated out from his chest. Finally he clenched his fists and walked resolutely to the gun cabinet. "You can do that Father. The hallway is a defensible area, right?" He opened the door and grabbed two rifles, handing one to Ghenni. "We'll have to try to hold the ship."

Chapter Fifteen

Damien never quite blacked out. The corridors of the Hountan ship twisted and bulged around him as he was carried deeper inside. Vomit roiled up in his stomach, but he was too groggy to even hope he wouldn't throw up. He was vaguely aware of being strapped down to a table, and after a few moments, the room around him settled down, and he slowly became cognizant again.

He flexed his fingers as the effects of the paralytic wore off. The bulkiness of the suit made it hard to feel anything, but he could tell the detonator was gone. He took stock of the situation around him: he was on a low table, low enough to be reached by Hountans, and surrounded by vials of drugs and disturbingly large needles. He could see the helmet of one of the Trenthan guards in the window of the door, and once he could turn his head, he saw the Hountan patient that had spent the last several days in his own ship.

"It looks like the tables got turned," Damien muttered. The same phrase was broadcast in the Hountan language from his external speakers, and the patient turned slightly to focus two of his eyes on Damien. "Just a couple of hours ago, we were holding you hostage in our medical bay. Or retro-fitted airlock, as the case may be." There was no reply, but the patient's eyes darted back and forth a few times, watching Damien carefully.

After a few moments, Damien broke the silence again. "Don't they have an actual brig to keep me in?"

"Ours was the only Hountan ship in the area," the patient said, his voice translated into mechanical tones by Damien's suit. "You will probably be transferred to a patrol ship, then tortured for information."

"Well, I'm glad to know you guys have a plan," Damien said.

There was another silence for a few moments, before the Hountan spoke again. "I was told that you claimed to have implanted explosives inside of me," he said, tracing the stitches that ran along his body with one of his hands. "But I don't feel anything. You were bluffing, weren't you?"

Damien sighed. "Yeah, but you've gotta promise me you won't tell anyone else. Or I might end up in some real trouble."

"It was risky, making a bluff like that. Why did you do it?"

"Well, some of my crew are sticklers about hurting innocent people. Go figure."

"Such people are hard to find in times of war. Myself, I just want to forget that our leaders are fighting, and go home to my family."

"Me too," said Damien. "I hope that you get to go home sooner rather than later."

"Why do you say that?" the Hountan asked.

"I guess the doc didn't tell you, but it looks like you caught your disease from your son. The doc figures he might not last until you get back."

The Hountan's legs tensed, and his eyes closed briefly. "Do you have any family?"

"Not anymore. I used to be married, but she died in an orbital bombing."

"It almost seems as though the first things we lose are those we were trying to protect."

"I'll drink to that," Damien said.

"You're not really spies or saboteurs as they claim, are you? After all, you saved my life."

"Well, I wasn't the one doing the saving, but we really were just trying to make an honest buck. Honest-ish, anyway."

"I wish things were different," said the Hountan, "so I could thank you all personally."

"Well, I imagine they're long gone by now."

"I haven't heard their ship disengage."

"Really?" asked Damien, trying to sit up, forgetting the restraints. "They must be counting on me escaping or something. Idiots."

There was another brief pause. "If you had the opportunity," the Hountan asked, "could you escape without hurting anyone?"

Damien twisted his head to the side out of curiosity. "I might be able to do it without killing or maiming anyone. I'd certainly like to give it a shot."

The Hountan slowly lifted himself off his bed, and plodded, crab-like, over to Damien's table. The tense shaking of his limbs showed that he was straining considerably to stay up. He leaned close, and began undoing the restraints. Damien watched his hands work, labored and deliberate, as his nearest eye concentrated on the work, glancing up occasionally to look into Damien's helmet. When he finished, he dragged himself back to his own bed while Damien flexed his stiff elbows and knees. "For the people who saved my life," he said, "it is the least I can do."

"Thanks," Damien said. "You know, I never learned your name."

"You can call me Counhack."

"I'm Damien. It's nice to meet you."

The Hountan barked in the affirmative. "Now, you should get ready for me to call the guards." He reached up to the small plastic pad stuck to his side over his heart, and pulled it off. The monitor beside his bed let out a low electronic whoop as it failed to detect a heartbeat, and in a few seconds the door opened.

The suited Trenthan guard rushed in, and a Hountan in a nurse's uniform scurried behind him. Damien lay pressed down against the table, hoping they wouldn't notice the restraints missing from his arms and legs. They didn't, running right past him to check on the patient. Damien jumped up and rushed at the guard, punching him in the back, turning him around, and slamming the back of his helmet into the wall. He slumped down to the floor, unconscious. Damien quickly slipped his leg under the Hountan nurse and pushed up with his shin, sending him toppling to the ground, where Damien delivered a single quick punch to his torso, just under the main eyes. He didn't move.

With both unconscious, Damien quickly stripped the guard of his sidearm, and liberated a couple of grenades from his belt. He pulled the pin from a flashbang and tossed it into the hallway, turning his face away and turning off the external microphone until he heard the blast go off. His suit's helmet didn't completely deaden the loud concussion, and Damien's ears were left ringing. He reached down and scooped the doctor up with one arm, holding him in front of him, and in the other arm he held the pistol to the guard's head. Dragging the unconscious Trenthan along, Damien stepped out into the hallway.

For what seemed like the hundredth time, Andrew wiped his sweaty hands off on his pants, trying to dry them enough to keep a solid grip on the rifle. He gazed down the long corridor from behind the partially closed cockpit door, concentrating intently on the cargo bay door, which he expected to open any second, filled with hostile soldiers. Sweat tickled his eyebrows, and he wiped off his face with already-grungy sleeves.

"Did you see that?" asked Eve.

"See what?" Andrew asked, getting to his feet.

"There was a flash of light from the other ship," she said. Andrew came up behind her and looked over her shoulder at the monitor. The soldiers that were standing guard in the airlock turned to look at the door, and rushed back into their own ship.

"What's going on?" Andrew asked.

"I'm not sure," Eve said, furiously flicking switches on the control panel, "but I think Damien's making a break for it."

"What are you doing?"

"The only thing we can do: give him an end-game."

Damien inched along the wall of the alien ship, holding the unconscious guard as a shield, and alternately waving his gun at the other soldiers and pointing it at his hostage's head. He had left the corridor and was entering a large open staging area; the entrance to the airlock was about fifty feet away, and beyond that, his ship. Half a dozen soldiers lined the opposite walls, guns trained on him.

"Alright," he said, "we can do this without getting anyone hurt. I'm going to need that money again."

One of the soldiers slid the bag of money, which had been taken back aboard, across the floor. Damien kicked it to his side, and pushed it along with his feet as he slowly moved closer to the door. When he had only twenty or thirty feet to go, a pair of Trenthan soldiers came down the corridor toward him and stopped several yards away. They both dropped to their knees to aim their rifles at him. There was a barely perceptible ripple of motion, a twitching of the heads, among the soldiers, letting Damien know that they were receiving orders over their radios. Two of them stood up and advanced slowly.

"You will release your captive and give yourself up," one of them ordered, "or we will use deadly force."

"You'd shoot at me and risk hitting your own man?"

"Yes."

"Oh. Uh, OK..."

Damien glanced back and forth, weighing his options. None of them looked good. If he made a break for it, they could easily just follow him into the airlock and shoot him dead. In fact, all the scenarios in his mind ended with him being shot dead. He could try shooting back indiscriminately, but he had promised not to hurt anyone. Maybe the priest had rubbed off on him, because he decided to stick to his word on that. Before he had made up his mind, the ship reverberated with the deep sound of large metal mechanisms relaxing. Everyone in the room froze for a second as they realized what was happening: the ships were disengaging from each other.

Damien sprang into action, throwing the unconscious guard toward the soldiers, scooping up the money bag, and sprinting for the airlock. Bullets struck the wall by his head as the soldiers opened fire. Sirens wailed as the ship reacted automatically to the exposure of the airlock to space. Damien sprayed some covering fire behind him as he dove into the airlock, the door sliding closed just behind him to protect the rest of the ship from vacuum. As it did, the *Malika* pushed itself off, the air from both airlocks escaping rapidly and pushing the ships farther apart. Damien noticed the hiss of escaping gas; one of the bullets had grazed his suit, and he was losing atmosphere. He had several yards of open space to cross between the ships. The Hountan ship was bound to close the outer airlock door any second. With a quick running start, Damien launched himself as fast and as far as he could toward the *Malika*.

His stomach turned as his body transitioned from the artificial gravity of the enemy ship to the weightlessness of space. Artificial gravity clung tenaciously to his legs behind him like grasping fingers, slowing him more than expected. When he was free, the leak in the leg of his suit acted as a thruster, slowly turning him around so that he was drifting back-first toward his own ship. The open airlock of his own ship hung tantalizingly close, but still several feet out of reach. Damien's mind raced, desperately searching for a way to not end up drifting in space.

He suddenly remembered the gun in his hand, held it at arm's length, and fired a shot. The momentum of the blast not only propelled him backward, but sent him spinning, without gravity or anything else to keep him steady. He spread his arms and legs to increase his moment of inertia and slow his spin. When the enemy ship spun into view again, he fired another shot from his other arm, partially canceling out his angular momentum. He crossed his fingers, hoping that the open door was behind him, placed the gun over his stomach, as close as possible to his center of gravity, and unloaded the rest of the clip.

The bullets left the gun, pushing him backward with equal momentum, and his back crashed into the side of his ship. The handle to an access panel caught the air tanks on his back, and twisted him around violently as he drifted down the length of the ship, away from the airlock. He quickly reached up and grabbed the handle, pulling himself toward the open door. When he got within arm's reach, he slipped his fingers around the doorway and pulled himself the rest of the way in, the familiar pull of gravity welcoming him back. As soon as his legs cleared the doorway, he barked into the radio. "I'm in! Close the door and go!"

The outer door of the airlock closed, and Damien got to his feet, looking out the window. Gun emplacements twitched on the enemy patrol ships, ready to detonate the *Malika* as soon as she got to a safe distance from the Hountan ship. Within seconds, a blue glow lit up the wall in front of him, and Damien turned to see the inter-stellar drive humming and pulsing. With one large jerk, the fabric of space twisted around them, throwing Damien to the floor, and then everything stopped.

Damien stood and looked back into the cargo bay. Where the IS drive had stood only moments before, there was just a large hole in the floor, trailing cables and hoses that spewed coolant into the vacuum.

"Let's hope they fall for it," he muttered to himself.

When the airlock and cargo bay had re-pressurized, Damien carried the bag of money up to the cockpit where everyone else waited.

"Somebody ask for a ransom?" he asked, plopping the sack on the floor in the middle of the room.

"I'm so glad you made it back alright," Eve said, burying her face in his shoulder.

"How did you pull it off?" Tanner asked.

"As it turns out, we had an inside man. Apparently saving somebody's life can make them do crazy things to help you out. Go figure."

"So with the help of one bedridden minor government official, you were able to escape a ship full of hostile soldiers with barely a scratch to show for it?"

"Got lucky, I guess," Damien said.

"Some might even go so far as to call it a miracle," Tanner said, giving half a smile to Eve.

"Oh no," Damien said, the smile dropping from his face. "You had him pray for me, didn't you? Eve, how could you? There'll be no living with him after this."

"How long will that be, anyway?" asked Andrew.

"Not sure," said Damien. He peered at the controls behind Eve. "How far did we end up going?"

"We're about halfway between Trenth and the next planet out," Eve said, looking back at the control panel. "It should take about four days to get back on sublights."

"All that from a split second of IS drive," Damien mused. "Crazy."

"How did you know how far the drive would take us before ripping free and heading out the door?" Andrew asked. "What if we'd ended up months away?"

"Instincts," Damien replied. "IS mechanics is more of an art than a science."

"No," said Andrew, "I'm pretty sure it's all science."

"Are you sure we won't be followed?" asked Ghenni.

"Nah," Damien said. "They'll follow the trail out a few billion miles, find where the drive fell apart, and assume we went with it. A crash at those speeds wouldn't leave enough debris to quantify. Now that they have their guy back, ten-to-one they'll cancel the special price on our heads, and we can all go back to business as usual, in relative safety."

"And what if you're wrong?" Tanner asked. "What if it's no longer safe for us on Trenth?"

"Then I'd be happy to take you wherever you need to go. For a reasonable fee, of course."

"So should we go ahead and split up the money?" asked Andrew.

"Sure," said Damien, "but before you put it away, how about a friendly game of poker?"

"I think we're taking enough of your money as it is," Tanner said. "And I think I need to take a long overdue rest in my quarters.

Damien bent down to a cabinet next to the piloting controls, pulled out a bottle of whiskey and four clear plastic tumblers, and began pouring. "Does your particular brand of faith keep you from partaking in a celebratory drink, Pops?"

Tanner slowly turned around and walked toward Damien, taking one of the filled glasses. "Alcohol does, of course, have many medicinal properties." He gave a lop-sided grin and took a sip.

"I thought so," said Damien, raising his own glass. "Cheers."

Epilogue

Tanner shoved his clothes into a wooden crate by the fistful; he could worry about folding later, along with picking out the splinters. Raised voices echoed down the hallway from the front door, chattering angrily in Trenthan. A hand grasped his shoulder from behind, and he whipped around, ready to throw a punch, but it was only Andrew.

"Are you ready?" he asked in a hurried whisper. "The buggy's out in the back. I've got the engine running."

"This is the last of it," Tanner said, hauling the crate up onto his shoulder. "Did all the staff get evacuated?"

"Yeah. Brother Nateth is going to lay low for a while before trying to open back up."

Tanner sighed. With Father Nellin passed away and the two of them fleeing, Nateth had been promoted to head surgeon and Acting Director. He didn't have more than a nurse's education and a few children's sermons under his belt, but all the more glory to God in the end, then.

Father Tanner and Andrew tip-toed out of the room, but someone shouted at them from down the hall. The figure stood silhouetted against the open door, but he saw the outline of a rifle being lowered into a firing position. The two doctors skittered around the corner toward the back door just as a pair of bullets *thwacked* into the mud wall with a puff of dust.

In the shade behind the mission, the buggy sat idling, loaded with clothes, personal effects, and medical supplies. Andrew hopped into the driver's seat, while Tanner tossed the crate into the back with the others, then jumped into the passenger side. The engine roared to life as they took off driving into the open plain, but it was soon drowned out by a louder roar of thrusters overhead. The *Malika* passed them, then lowered down toward the ground, and twisted in the air to present them with the open cargo bay door. Eve gripped the corner of the wall with one hand while waving them in with the other. The buggy shook as it drove over the threshold into the ship, and the door began closing behind them as the ship rose into the air.

"You're cutting it awfully close," Eve said.

"Oh, you know how it is when you're packing," Tanner replied.

The intercom crackled into life. "Everybody secure?" Damien asked. Everyone answered back in the affirmative, including Ghenni who jogged over from the front half of the ship.

"I'm sorry you got dragged into this, Ghenni," Tanner said. "I know it's not easy abandoning your home."

"Yeah," said Damien, "sorry about that. I thought it would blow over a little cleaner. Are your parents going to safe?"

"I believe so," Ghenni said, clutching his soulstone. "I don't think the Brotherhood will still to harass them once they know I have left. And I have always dreamed of visiting other planets."

"Sorry you got caught up in all this too," Andrew said to Eve.

"Thanks," she said with a slight smile. "But what's one more person to be on the run from, right?"

Andrew smiled back, then froze. "But you got an IS drive, right? It's installed and everything?"

"It took quite a bit of palm-greasing," Damien replied over the intercom, "and cost about double what it should have, but I got one. It didn't leave much for supplies, though."

"So where are we headed?" Tanner asked.

"I've been networking with some contacts nearby. I have some leads on some smuggling work that we can check out. And the three of you can get off at any stop you want, but I wouldn't mind having a doctor around. You might even be able to earn a little cash on the side.

What do you say?"
  "I say... this should be interesting."

PART TWO

A HOUSE DIVIDED

Chapter One

"Yesukaesuh daedabhayeo eereushidwe akhago eumlanhan sedaega pyojeogeul goohana sunjija yonaeui pyojeog bakkeneun boil pyojeogee eobneunira."

Eve looked up from the table at the sound of Andrew's words. She had some piece of machinery half-disassembled and spread out on a tattered floral towel streaked with grime on the galley table in front of her, and an open toolbox on the seat next to her. Her dark hair was pulled back into a ponytail, and grease marred her fingernails. Andrew couldn't make heads or tails of what she was working on, but he knew it was important for the ship, and very, very broken. Father Tanner for his part just looked up from his own Bible and over his glasses, and raised an eyebrow. Even on their second day of interstellar travel, his shirt was still tucked into well-ironed slacks.

"Sorry, were you talking to me?" she asked. "Because I don't speak... whatever that language was."

"Korean, yeah, sorry," Andrew said, pushing the book away from him and rubbing his eyes. Lost in his reading, he hadn't noticed how tired they were. "I didn't realize that was out loud."

"Is the Bible better in the original Korean, then?" Eve asked with a smile.

Andrew chuckled and set the book down. "No, but my mom would kill me if I get home and my Korean is too rusty. Just don't get much chance to use it out here in space, you know?"

"Fair enough," grunted Eve through clenched teeth as she strained to loosen a screw on the gadget in front of her. It finally popped, and she let go of the breath she was holding. "I haven't spoken Italian since my grandmom's funeral."

As she finished speaking, the ship around them shuddered, and a stark silence settled in the room, suddenly missing the whine of the engine that had faded into the background. Andrew didn't know much about spaceship mechanics, but it didn't seem like a good thing. He and Father Tanner traded glances at each other, the older priest furrowing his brow in confusion.

"Is that serious?" Tanner asked. He took off his glasses and his crows' feet wrinkled with tentative concern. Eve's eyes, squinting in concentration, darted from side to side as she listened to the sounds of the ship.

"That wasn't a controlled shut-off..." she muttered. She leaped to her feet and ran to the intercom by the door, tools clattering to the floor in her hurry. It buzzed into life just before her hand hit the button, and the captain's voice addressed the others.

"We hit a gravity trap!" Damien shouted over the speaker. "Kicked us out of hyperspace. Eve, secure the cargo, make sure all the secret compartments are closed and hidden."

Eve ran off, and Father Tanner stepped up to the intercom, tucking his glasses into his shirt pocket. "A trap? Set by whom?"

"I don't know yet; I think we had a voltage spike when we dropped out; half my instruments are down. We're near border space, so it could be Consortium, could be Brotherhood, could be something else."

"What should Andrew and I do?"

"Come to the cockpit and grab a couple of rifles," Damien replied.

Tanner glanced back at Andrew and sighed. "There is a war on, you know."

The two of them ran for the ladder up to the main level, and climbed out in the hallway next to the cockpit. In the other direction, the drab metal passage stretched out, flanked by sparsely decorated doors to their private quarters, until it reached the cargo hold with its mix of wooden crates and metal shipping containers loaded with valuable contraband. Andrew turned into the open door to the cockpit. Ghenni, their alien nurse from back on Trenth, was already inside, unlocking the gun cabinet on the near wall. Above his droopy cheeks and their dangling fleshy growths, his eyes were wide with concern. A deck of playing cards had been scattered across the floor, along with a plate of artificial protein nuggets and a splatter of sauce on the bare metal floor. It certainly wasn't the *worst* mess Andrew had found in there.

Damien Rogers, the dark-skinned captain, stood in front of the console, in baggy cargo pants and a baggy flannel shirt, banging on dimmed out switches and swearing under his breath. "I got nothing here," Damien muttered. He pressed on the intercom button again. "Eve, forget the cargo, check the electrical. I need instruments up here." He turned to face the others. "If they don't blow us to pieces in the next five minutes, they're going to try to board. Of course external comms are down, so I can't ask which. Get your rifles. Well, *my* rifles. You can borrow them."

Ghenni handed Andrew a semi-automatic rifle of some kind. Andrew didn't know the actual name, but Damien had trained him in at least its basic use. They'd even set up a firing range in the cargo hold once. He wasn't a great shot, but he could at least hit the target. Of course, that target had never been another person.

"We never had to do this back at the clinic," Ghenni said in halting, broken English. His *glia*, dozens of strands of growths that dangled from his saggy, bulldog-like cheeks, had been tied into a kind of pigtails, in preparation for battle. He took one of the rifles from the gun rack and slammed in a magazine. He handled the gun with more confidence, having guarded livestock from predators, both wild and civilized, on his home planet of Trenth back before he had joined the clinic as a nurse.

"To everything there is a season, Ghenni," Father Tanner said. He picked out a lighter bolt-action hunting rifle for himself and checked the chamber.

"Proverbs?" Ghenni whispered to Andrew.

"Ecclesiastes," Andrew replied.

Eve's voice crackled over the intercom. "I don't see any damage to the circuits, but I can try to reroute anyway. Check it now."

The console screen flashed colored lights in sequence, and emitted a horrible screeching noise. "Yeah, it's booting up," Damien said.

"Well, some of it anyway." His attention to the instruments was interrupted by a loud *ka-thunk* of metal on metal carrying through the hull of the ship.

"They're docking," he said, pausing as he listened carefully to the nuances of the sound of connecting ships. Then he sprang back into frenzied action. "We're getting boarded. Everybody to battle stations! Just like we practiced!"

"Once," Andrew muttered as he took off toward the cargo hold. "We practiced it once."

They jogged down the hallway, past the cramped side room bearing Andrew's name scrawled with a grease pencil. The passage ahead opened up into the cavernous cargo hold, laden with a hodge-podge of boxes and crates from a half dozen planets, labeled with a half dozen alien languages he didn't understand.

"Fan out, take cover," Damien said as they reached the hold. "They'll take a few minutes to blow the door, but when they do-"

The captain was cut off by the hiss of the cargo bay door opening on its own. "Son of a bitch," he said, his voice quiet with amazement. "They hacked us."

Before they could all get to cover behind crates, a pair of metal objects bounced into the hold, lying inert for a brief second as they rolled to a stop.

"Flashbangs!" Eve shouted.

Then they detonated.

Without time to react, Andrew's eyes blazed with phosphoric light, blinding him to anything else. The concussive blast deafened him, leaving no sound except high-pitched ringing. He thought he vaguely saw humanoid figures flood in the door, followed by a sharp prick in his stomach. His fingers felt around and brushed the soft feathers of a tranquilizer dart embedded in his torso. He didn't have time to do anything else before the rest of his senses left him, and he collapsed.

Father Tanner woke slowly from the effects of the tranquilizer. He wasn't as young as he once was, and his body wasn't used to the effects of drugs like that, so he was surprised to see he was the first awake. He took stock of the situation. They were in an unfamiliar room, so it wasn't the *Malika*; he surmised they'd been taken to another ship. The room looked like a rather large personal quarters, but stripped of all the furniture and decorations that weren't bolted down. Eve was lying on an empty metal bedframe protruding from the wall, next to a small table and pair of stools. It seemed to be a civilian ship quarters, converted into a brig, which suggested they weren't captured by military forces of either side. He scanned the others of the crew, sprawled out uncomfortably on the cold metal floor without so much as a blanket. The others seemed to be peacefully unconscious, but Ghenni breathed in shallow and raspy breaths.

Tanner shuffled over to where he laid and checked his pulse. It was weak, and his skin was cold and clammy.

"Ghenni. Ghenni, can you hear me?" No response. He jumped to his feet and fiddled with the door controls, but unsurprisingly, they were disabled, the buttons remaining dark. He pounded once on the heavy metal door in frustration, then more as he tried to get someone's attention. "Help! I need help in here!"

Turning his focus back to Ghenni, Tanner dropped to his knees on the hard metal floor, pinched the Trenthan's nose, and began breathing air into his lungs. He counted to five between each breath, checking his pulse periodically, but saw no improvement. The doctor tossed out a quick prayer as he worked: *Lord, just let him hold on. Don't let him leave me yet.*

After what seemed like hours, the door to the room slid open, and a hulking Trenthan man stood on the other side. He stood at least six feet tall, and thick muscles moved beneath his thin shirt. The *glia* on his face were equally thick and robust.

"What was in those tranquilizers?" shouted Tanner in the Trenthan language. Another breath.

The Trenthan man seemed surprised to hear his own tongue from a human, but then he shrugged. "Ship was tagged as human. We used human darts." The words repeated themselves in English, coming from a translator unit on his collar.

Another breath. "But Ghenni here is a Trenthan, see?" Another breath. "He's having some kind of reaction to it."

"You a doctor?"

Another breath. "Yes, and I need my supplies. Bring me my doctor bag. Green duffel, with a red cross on it." Another breath.

"Might be a trick. Can't do that."

Another breath. Tanner struggled to catch his own breath between the mouth-to-mouth and the conversation. "That wasn't a request! If you don't get me my supplies, he'll die!" Another breath.

The man sighed. "What do you need from the bag?"

"A manual resuscitator. Face mask with a blue bulb and a bag attached." Another breath. "And the vial of-" He sighed, realizing the futility of giving him a drug name that he couldn't read. "Just bring me all the medicine from inside. And don't break the vials!"

The door closed, and Tanner had no choice but to continue the artificial respiration, unsure if his begging had any effect. The others began to stir from their drug-induced slumber, and as soon as Andrew was awake, Tanner waved him over.

"Take over mouth-to-mouth please," he said, slumping against the wall and panting to recover his own breath. Andrew groggily nodded and filled his place, breathing air into Ghenni's lungs.

"What's going on?" Damien asked groggily.

"Ghenni had a bad reaction to the tranquilizer," Tanner said in between breaths. "I *think* they're bringing my supplies, but I'm not sure."

At that, the door opened again, and the same Trenthan man reappeared. This time he had a pistol out, but behind him was a human woman, short, blond, and wearing a raggedy blue jumpsuit. She looked nervously back and forth between the Trenthan and the crew of the *Malika*. In one hand she carried Tanner's medical bag.

"Thank you," Tanner said. "Give it here, quickly."

"Sorry," the woman said in English. "I can only bring what you need, in case you've got weapons hidden in here."

Tanner rolled his eyes. "Fine, fine, the resuscitation bag, please. You know what that is?"

"Yes, OK," she said. She rifled through the bag, and quickly produced the tool and tossed it to Tanner. He caught it and quickly set to placing it over Ghenni's mouth. He handed it to Andrew and let him resume respirating him with the bag instead of mouth-to-mouth.

"Good, thank you. Tell me, do *you* know what was used in those tranquilizer darts? Was it rigocyl?"

"I-I think so," the woman said.

"Alright then, I need a hypodermic needle with um...

cozalipham?" He glanced back at Andrew, who had much more training in pharmacology than he had.

"Right," Andrew said. "Cozalipham. Two cc's of it."

The woman dug through the bag and found the vial. She seemed to know her way around a syringe, and she had the right amount ready in a few seconds.

"Everybody else against the back wall," the Trenthan shouted, gesturing with his pistol. Damien and Eve complied, sliding along the floor to sit against the wall. "You come get it. And no tricks."

Tanner got up and approached the two cautiously. He took the syringe from the woman's hand and looked her in the eye. "Thank you," he said, nodding to her as he choked back his anger and frustration. He took the needle back to Ghenni and slowly injected it into the vein in his arm. "That should counteract the reaction to the sedative. He should be fine within a half hour. Again, thank you." He set the syringe down on the floor and gently slid it across to the doorway. The alien thug stopped it with his boot.

"So you've got two doctors, huh?" the Trenthan asked.

"Yes," Tanner replied. "We're missionaries. Our calling is to treat the sick and injured."

"Yep," Damien said with a smile. "Missionaries. All five of us. So maybe spare yourself the divine judgment and let us all go." Eve elbowed him in the ribs.

The Trenthan man grunted, then shut the door again.

"What do you think they're going to do with us?" Eve asked. "Do you think they'll kill us?"

"They could have killed us already," Damien said. "They want something from us first."

"What could they want?" Andrew said as he squeezed the bulb on the mask again. "They've probably already stripped the *Malika* for parts and left her adrift in space."

"No, they're towing her," Damien said. His gaze drifted around the small room absently.

"How could you know that?" Father Tanner asked.

"He's right," Eve said. "I hear it now, those pings and creaks. We're still docked together. And the IS drive is running rough; must have expanded the field to cover both ships."

"That doesn't explain what they need us for," Andrew said.

"I would say command codes," Damien replied, "but they already hacked our door. I'm guessing they're pretty well in the system by now. If these pirates are worth their salt, they know we've got secret compartments they haven't found. They want to know where the choicest cargo is."

"So-" Andrew began before Damien interrupted him.

"So they've probably bugged the room, and you shouldn't mention how valuable or where the cargo is, you understand?"

"Right."

The next few minutes passed in relative silence, as Tanner focused on his breathing to clear his head. Finally the door lurched open again. The Trenthan man stood there alone now, holding his pistol pointing at the floor. "The two doctors, come with me."

"I have a patient," Tanner said. "I can't leave him."

"Not a request," the man said. "You're only squeezing a bag. One of them can do it."

Father Tanner sighed. "Eve, can you take over please? Steady, even squeezes, five seconds apart. Understand?"

"Yeah," Eve said, sliding herself across the floor and taking the bag from Andrew. "I'll take care of him." Andrew handed the bag off to her and got up. The Trenthan made no move to search them for weapons; no doubt they had been thoroughly searched while unconscious. What a pleasant thought.

Their captor led them out into the hallway, and the door slid shut behind them. This ship seemed more spartan than their own; no plastic flowers hanging over the door to Eve's quarters, or strings of lights illuminating the ladder to the kitchen. The ship had an air of solemnity to it. Tanner and Andrew were led down the hall and into a cargo hold. Tanner recognized a lot of their own cargo inside; the pirate ship was larger, however, so it left quite a bit of extra room. Inside, a space had been cleared as a sort of meeting hall, with a large metal crate serving as a table and covered with printouts of astronomical charts and ledgers.

Standing near the table was another Trenthan, this one a woman, though hardly feminine. Her figure was short, but sturdy, and it was only from years of experience that Father Tanner could detect the slightly longer and more delicate structure of the *glia* on her face. A heavy gun belt hung on her hips. Next to her stood a pale human man, at least a full head taller than Tanner, with a lean frame and a long ponytail of prematurely silver hair. He wore a similar jumpsuit to the human woman, but in a red and gray color scheme.

"These are the doctors," the Trenthan man said, shoving the two of them forward. He spoke in a dialect of the Trenthan language that Tanner was familiar with: it was a sort of pidgin formed by a blending of the local language with Koljan, the Brotherhood *lingua franca*, and marked him as coming from a cosmopolitan background. Relatively speaking, that is, for a species that had been dragged into the space age within living memory.

"That's quite some luck," the woman said, "finding two doctors out here like that." Her accent was thick and rural. They may have been the same species, but they clearly came from entirely different worlds.

"Is someone sick?" Father Tanner asked in Trenthan.

The woman glared at him and swore. "You speak our tongue? Have you spent time on Trenth?"

"I ran a clinic and mission there for some years," he replied. "I would be happy to provide medical aid if required. That is what we were called to."

"Ah, so you're religious, then?" the woman asked. "Gemman prophets? Maybe I should have spaced you after all."

"Emmanuelites," Tanner replied. "Servants of the triune God of all people. I am Father Tanner, and my associate is Andrew Cho."

"Even better," the woman said, rolling her eyes. "I am Bellig. You've already met Tenik, of course." She gestured at the human, who stood stoically with his arms crossed. "And this is Carter."

Andrew reached out to shake their hands, but the Trenthans remained still. Carter unfolded his arms just enough for a cursory shake. "P-pleasure."

"Bellig," Tenik said. "They're doctors. We can't pass up an opportunity like this. They could-"

"I'm aware of what they could do," Bellig said, cutting him off sharply. "They could also betray us. We cannot afford to give them the kind of access that would require."

"I ag-gree," Carter said. "Too dangerous."

"Then you would let him die?" Tenik leaned forward, resting his clenched fists on the table.

"Who is dying?" Andrew asked, haltingly. His Trenthan wasn't as fluent as Tanner's. "We took oaths to help people. We would not betray you."

Tenik pointed forcefully at the others. "He would risk everything for any one of us. You know that. You betray him if you don't do the same."

Carter raised an eyebrow at Bellig. She pursed her lips for a moment before grunting a reply. "Bind their hands. It won't hurt to let them have a look."

Chapter Two

Damien's hand was getting tired. His forearm burned from squeezing the plastic bulb over and over for... however long it had been. Felt like forever. "Your turn again," he said to Eve.

"No way," she replied, slumped against the wall. She shook her arm out as if to emphasize her own fatigue. "You barely started."

"Says you."

Ghenni stirred under the mask. His face turned away, and a hand reached up to rub his eyes.

"Hey there, buddy," Damien said. "We were worried about you." He reached out and helped Ghenni to sit up and slide over to the wall for support. The alien nurse was his favorite among the crew of doctors, if only because they were fellow heathens in Tanner's eyes.

"What happened?" Ghenni muttered. His breath was still shallow, and he squinted against the fluorescent light in the ceiling.

"The short version? We've been hijacked by pirates. You had a bad reaction to a tranquilizer, but Pops fixed you up."

"Where is the Father and Andrew?"

The pirates seemed really interested in the fact that they were doctors," Eve said. "Maybe they've got somebody sick on board."

"That's my bet," Damien said. "Could be good leverage to get us out of here in one piece. You know what a shrewd negotiator Tanner is." Damien rolled his eyes and sighed. "Yep, probably doomed."

The door to the hallway ground open again, and the human woman stood in the doorway, this time accompanied by a human man, tall and lean with a silver ponytail and a scowl. The woman started forward, but the man grabbed her by the shoulder and kept her inside.

"C-careful Amber," he said. "They're still our p-prisoners."

"Right, sorry," the blond woman said. "It's just... I haven't seen any other humans in a long time." She waved weakly. "Hi."

"Hello yourself," Damien said, waving back from across the room. "I'm Damien, this is Eve. The non-human here is Ghenni."

"Oh, I'm Amber," she replied. "And this is Carter. I guess... welcome to the ship, the *Kuupon Luk*."

"Thanks," Damien snapped. "Your hospitality has been overwhelming so far."

"Sorry about that, but I'm kind of low on the totem pole around here. And Carter is... very concerned about security."

"Still curious though," he said, shrugging.

"I can tell," Damien said. "So what exactly is our situation here. What is it you want from us?"

"Fine," Carter said, straightening up and crossing his arms. "Right to the p-point, then. We want to m-make sure we don't miss any cargo. The g-good stuff. Tell us where it's hidden."

"And in exchange, we get... what? Spaced?"

"We're landing on a habitable planet," Amber said. "Pretty primitive, but we'll leave you with some basic supplies and a time-locked distress beacon. After three days, you can start calling for help."

"Help from who?" Eve asked. "Whose space is this planet in?"

Amber took a deep breath and gave a half-hearted smile. "True, it's Brotherhood space. But not by much. You'd be rolling the dice, but it's what we can offer. Like I said, I'm not the one making these decisions." Rolling the dice indeed. Since Earth was part of the Consortium, if they got found by the Brotherhood first, any humans be treated as enemy combatants or spies. They weren't big on the distinction between civilian and military crafts, and with nothing to pay bribes with, they were only good for bounties.

"You don't make the decisions," Damien said, "but you're the one they sent. Because they were hoping we'd be more open to dealing with fellow humans. And after they isolated us from each other, of course."

Carter shrugged and flashed Damien a smile. "True enough. You know the g-game."

"Yeah, so," Damien said, standing up. Carter tensed, but Damien held up his hands and kept his distance. "I'm gonna need some kind of show of goodwill, and some assurances. How do I know you'll keep your word?"

"We'll land, and let you see the p-place," Carter said. "We'll stage the supplies for you, even."

"And if we refuse?" Eve asked.

Carter reached into his waistband behind him, retrieved a large pistol, and worked the slide to chamber a round. "Then we don't need you anymore."

"Alright, alright, I get it," Damien said. "My money or my life. Can I take some time to think about it?"

"Of course," Amber said. "Like I told you, you can see the planet first. We should be landing in an hour or two. Think about it, OK? I'd hate to kill the first humans I've seen in years. We have to stick together, you know?"

"Oh, I feel the love for sure," Damien said, clutching melodramatically at his heart.

Carter gestured for Amber to step back, and he closed the door, leaving Damien, Eve, and Ghenni alone again.

"Do you think you are to trust them?" Ghenni asked.

"I think the terms they offered are just lousy enough to be genuine," Damien said. "But no, of course I don't trust them."

"So what's the plan?" Eve asked.

"For now, let's hope the docs manage to earn a favor or two."

Bellig stopped at the door at the end of the hallway. On a faded and dog-eared strip of plastic, a flowing, looping script labeled it in some language unfamiliar to Father Tanner. Elaborate controls and environmental readouts flanked the doorway, more than a simple door lock, which indicated some kind of complicated environmental systems inside. Again, they were in an unfamiliar language, so Tanner could only guess at the kind of ecosystem the captain's species required.

Bellig turned to Father Tanner and Andrew and sized them up for a moment before speaking. "You understand," she said, "that this is my captain. If you threaten him, you threaten the ship and everyone on it. I won't hesitate to kill you."

"I never doubted it," Tanner said.

"What's wrong with him?" Andrew asked.

Tenik sighed. "You should just see for yourself."

He pressed a button for the door, which slid into the walls with a whisper. On the other side, Tanner saw a wall of water. It was the largest aquarium he'd seen outside of a zoo, and it took up the entire room except for a four-foot walkway running along the front wall. Inside, knee-high vegetation swayed in the flow of the circulation system, bubbles sticking to blue and purple fronds surrounding an aerator in the corner.

"Where is he?" Andrew asked. "I don't see-"

A dark shape slammed into the glass mere inches from his face, sending the two doctors jumping back in surprise. A creature perhaps four feet long darted back and forth through the water, tentacles trailing behind it. It resembled something like a cuttlefish or squid, with half its length made up of several tentacles, following a dark gray conical body with wide-set eyes and bright blue markings running down its length.

"The captain is a Tuudolian?" Andrew asked, incredulous. "Interesting. I've never met one in person."

"It's been a while for me," said Tanner. Of course he had studied them briefly in medical school. They lived entirely underwater, completely unable to breathe normal air. That tended to slow down the discovery of metalworking and electricity, but they were quick learners, and took to space travel quite quickly once they were introduced to it.

Tanner studied the creature for a while, then turned to Bellig. "What's his name?"

"Lopuul," she said. "*Captain* Lopuul."

"Of course." Tanner reached for the button of the intercom system on the wall. "Captain? My name is Father Tanner. I'm a doctor, and I'm here to help you." He heard his words translated through the intercom into a muffled series of chirps and gurgles.

The creature drew back, then slammed into the tank wall again. It shrieked in rage, shouting in its language. The words came through the intercom in Trenthan: "What have I to do with you, servant of the Holy One?"

Tanner froze. He'd certainly earned some ire from time to time, but nothing quite like this. And how did the creature recognize him as a minister? He glanced down at his clothing. He was wearing slacks and a casual shirt, not his priestly garments. He did, however, have a crucifix hanging from his neck. He lifted it from his chest and held it out. "You know this symbol?"

"The God-killer," Lopuul hissed. "You wear our triumph as your trophy. Your god died in pain and humiliation, and now burns for eternity!"

The captain's tentacles beat on the glass with muffled thuds, before he darted away, back into the vegetation and out of sight. Tenik and Bellig ushered them back out into the hallway.

"As you can see," Bellig said once the door was closed, "he is very agitated."

"Looks like it's getting worse, too," Tenik added. "I've never seen him react so aggressively before."

"That's an understatement," Andrew said. "I swear I could feel spittle through the glass." He chuckled slightly, but Tanner shot him a look. What he suspected was no laughing matter.

"How have his symptoms presented until now?" Father Tanner asked.

"A lot of ranting," Bellig replied. "Religious gibberish, that kind of thing. Claiming to be someone else, lunging at people, pounding on the glass. Sometimes even trying to hurt himself."

"How long have these symptoms been present?"

"Three...?" Bellig suggested hesitantly.

"Yes, three Standard Days," Tenik confirmed.

"Was it a sudden onset, or did symptoms appear over time?"

"Quite sudden," Tenik said. "He was fine one day, then when I woke up, I discovered our course had been changed. When I went to ask about it, he was in a full-blown episode. We had to disable the ship's controls in his quarters; he tried to navigate us into a star."

"Besides the psychosis," Tanner asked, "what symptoms have there been? Any physical ailments?"

"Hard to say," Bellig said. "He will not discuss it, and he's too agitated for us to check him ourselves."

"The environmental monitors report no changes inside the tank," Tenik added, scanning the control panels by the door. "I believe he's still eating and evacuating, since the filtration system is within normal parameters. But I haven't witnessed either."

"Any change in his nutrition?" Andrew asked. "The sourcing of his food, or anything like that?"

Bellig shook her head. "Our last resupply was over a month ago. This didn't occur until weeks afterward."

"What about shore leave?" Tanner asked. "Has he traveled anywhere outside this controlled environment where he might have contracted a pathogen, or encountered something toxic in the environment?"

"No," Tenik replied. "There are only three Tuudolian planets in this quadrant: the homeworld and two colonies. We haven't visited them in several months."

"So do you think you can cure him?" Bellig asked. She folded her arms, seemingly confident the answer was "no."

Tanner glanced at Andrew, his eyes wide. He'd seen these types of symptoms a couple of times before, out among the old-fashioned idol worshipers on Trenth. "I think we may be exactly who you need to help him."

The door to the cell slid open several minutes later, and the two Trenthan crewmates reappeared with Tanner and Andrew in tow. The pirates roughly shoved the two doctors back in, then followed them in themselves.

"Still alive?" Damien asked. He hadn't *really* been worried. At least, not much. But Tanner could be stubborn as a mule sometimes, so you never knew what kind of trouble he'd get into.

"Believe it or not," Tanner replied. He turned to his nurse with a smile. "Ghenni, glad to see you're up and about now. We were worried for a minute."

"I am feeling better," Ghenni said, waving weakly from where he sat on the floor. His breathing was steadier, but he still hunched over from fatigue. "Still not on one hundred percent."

"What's the situation?" Eve asked. She sat on the other stool across from Damien, slumped against the wall.

"We made a deal," Andrew said. "Well, we've got an outline of a deal. Still hammering out the details."

"And of course you came to me," Damien said, "because as captain of the *Malika* and her crew, I'm in charge of all negotiations, right?"

"Actually it was their idea," Andrew said, gesturing with his head to the pirate crew behind him.

"You gonna keep jabbering or listen to our offer?" Bellig said through her translator.

"Alright, shoot. Figuratively speaking, of course."

"Your doctors are going to help treat our captain for a medical issue. If, and only if, they can cure him, we let you go with all your personal supplies, and half your cargo."

"'Let us go,' hmm?" Damien said, scratching his chin. "Awfully vague. How exactly do you envision that going down?"

"We're going to land on an obscure planet," Bellig replied. She counted off the points in her offer on her fingers, as if she were giving a lecture. "If and when you finish the job, we leave you on the planet with personal belongings, food and water for a week, and the promised cargo. Along with that, a time-locked distress beacon, set to not broadcast until three days after we leave."

"That's better than what Carter offered us before," Eve said, sitting up straighter. "But he also told us this is Brotherhood space. If they pick us up, we're as good as dead."

"That's why we're leaving you half the cargo," Bellig said. "You can barter for passage. Plus, this planet is quite near border space. You might get lucky and catch the attention of an unusually brave Consortium ship."

"Here's my counter-offer," Damien said, steepling his fingers and leaning forward. "You drop us off on a more civilized planet, walking distance from a city with a spaceport. A spaceport where you've parked the *Malika*. But we only take the cargo we can carry."

"No good," Bellig said, nodding her head. "Our ship's been tagged all to hell lately. We need something clean. Keeping your ship is a deal-breaker for us."

"Kind of a deal-breaker for me too," Damien said. "We could let your captain die."

"I'd take my captain's chances with his condition over your chances stepping out of the airlock."

Damien looked over his shoulder back at Eve. "This lady's good." He turned back to Bellig. "Alright, how about we go back to your plan, but we keep 75 percent of our cargo? And we want a show of good faith."

Bellig tilted her head in thought for a moment, and Damien wasn't sure if she was considering the offer, or just trying to parse the translation. Finally she spoke again. "It's a deal. As a show of good faith, we'll let you roam free outside once we land. You won't need cuffs or an escort unless you're inside the *Kuupon Luk*."

Damien exchanged a glance with Eve. "That seems... strangely generous. What is this planet, anyway?"

"You wouldn't have heard of it," Tenik replied. "Strategically unimportant, no intelligent natives. Very scenic, though."

"You're not afraid we'll run off?" Eve asked.

Bellig shrugged. "You can if you want. Won't get far. At least, not in one piece. Too many dangerous predators."

"Oh," Damien said, "that'll be fun once you take off with all the ships. I don't suppose you'll be leaving any weapons with us?"

"We'll drop some small arms once we've taken off. If you're lucky, they won't land in the sea."

"Well, who can say no to generosity like that? You've got yourself a deal."

Chapter Three

Even in the small, barren room where the crew was detained, Eve could feel the stages of descent as they approached the planet. The vibrations were different, slower as they were dampened by the thickening of the atmosphere, and the groans of the worn ship creaked in duller tones than she was used to on the *Malika*, but it was still familiar. A little bit of inertia leaked through the dampeners as they rapidly decelerated on the approach, followed by the asynchronous rhythm of stabilizing thrusters righting the ship into the correct orientation for landing. Finally, it gave one last deep shudder as the landing struts made contact with the ground.

"I'd have landed it smoother," Damien muttered. The two of them had been left alone in the room while the doctors and Ghenni examined the new patient. Damien sat on the floor, leaning against the wall directly opposite from the door, while Eve laid down on the bare metal bed frame.

Eve snorted. "If your inertial dampeners ever worked right, maybe."

"And whose job is that?" Damien asked with a smug grin.

"Can't fix it without money," Eve said. "And whose job is *that*?"

"Hey now, I thought we were a team."

Their bickering was interrupted by a blast of fresh air from the vents up in the ceiling. It wasn't that canned air that got recirculated on the ship a million times over; they must have started piping it in from outside. This had a slight tang in it, a mix of sea salt and the musk of heavy vegetation.

"Ooh, that's nice," Damien said, breathing deeply. "Are we on the beach?"

"Smells like it," Eve said. "Think I can grab my swimsuit from my quarters?"

"Better grab the sunscreen too. You've been in space so long, you'll look like a lobster within the hour."

"No fair you took both our shares of melanin," Eve said.

Damien ran a hand over his bare, dark brown head as he took in a deep breath. "I *have* been blessed. But now I've got myself thinking of lobster. You think the fishing is any good here?"

Before Eve could answer, the door slid open. Bellig stood there with a heavy automatic rifle and wearing a wide-brimmed hat. "You ready?" she asked.

"Always and forever," Damien said, jumping to his feet. Eve stood up next to him.

"This way," Bellig said, gesturing with her head.

It was hard to guess, but Eve figured it had probably been six or eight hours since they'd been captured, and they hadn't even been let out of that room to go to the bathroom. She debated in her head whether to ask to use the facilities, or just wade out into the water.

They walked past several closed doors. Eve recognized the writing on a couple of them as Trenthan, but she didn't know enough to read them. A couple of others had Amber and Carter's names on them. On one door, she didn't recognize the script at all, but it was written with a series of horizontal squiggles and straight diagonal cross-marks. Maybe Father Tanner would recognize it; he spoke languages she'd never even heard of.

They reached the cargo hold, which was packed full of boxes and crates, some of which she recognized as their own cargo, already transferred over. Bastards. Full as it was, it couldn't obscure the bright yellow sunshine pouring through the open door on the far side. She couldn't help but get a little giddy; even though they were still captive, it had been a while since she'd had any proper shore leave. Ever since they'd picked up the mission crew, any time outside the ship was spent literally *on* the outside of the ship, crawling around and fixing the things that she couldn't reach in transit. This was practically going to be a vacation.

They rounded the corner around the last stack of boxes, and the warm sun washed over Eve's skin. She squinted against the sun, and as her eyes acclimated to the brightness, she saw the beach. A thick line of vegetation formed a solid dark green wall about two hundred feet ahead of her. Flowers and fruits of every color speckled the trees and bushes, hanging from branches that swayed gently in the wind. Behind her, she heard crashing waves. She stepped around the edge of the ship and saw sparking blue waves stretching across a vast, empty horizon.

"It's beautiful," she said, half whispering in awe.

"We should have gotten captured by pirates ages ago," Damien said.

Beside the pirate ship was the *Malika*, little more than a cargo hold with dual drive modules in back, with two stories of living area and a trapezoidal cockpit in front. She looked to be in good condition, or at least as good as she was before. The cargo hold door was already hanging open, and it was quite obviously emptier than it had been. By contrast the pirate ship *Kuupon Luk*, whose name was painted in faded and indecipherable letters along the hull, was only a single level, making it longer and narrower around the body. It wasn't a design she was familiar with; maybe older, or a converted military model.

Eve turned to Bellig. "You said we can go anywhere out here? Can we swim? Is the fruit safe to eat?"

Bellig shrugged. "Feel free. Don't know how safe any of it is, though."

Damien sidled up to her and spoke in a low voice. "I want to get a feel for how long our leash is out here. Also I'm hungry. Let's saunter on over to the tree line and pick some fruit."

Eve went with him, her feet sinking into the pale brown sand as it filled her shoes. She stopped for a moment and pulled her shoes and socks off of her feet, feeling the sand between her toes instead. It was deliciously warm. She sighed and kept walking.

They reached the trees in a minute or two. In contrast to the beach, the inside of the jungle was dark, the sun blocked out almost completely by the canopy. Vines wound their way up trunks with deep brown bark, and sudden shaking of branches revealed the movements of small animals among the leaves.

One particular fruit caught Eve's eye: a big juicy orb, about fist sized and slightly oblong, colored red with streaks of orange radiating from the stem. She plucked a couple, and felt a slight give to it that told her it would be nice and juicy. Damien had zeroed in on some berries growing on a bush. He took a delicate bite, then spat it back out.

"Bitter," he said. "Could be toxic. I wouldn't risk anything that's not sweet." He glanced back over his shoulder. "Weird. She doesn't seem to care that we're all the way out here. We could easily run into the trees and disappear before she had a chance to react."

"We'd be abandoning the others though."

"Right, I mean I'm not going to *do* it. I'm just saying."

Eve sank her fingernail into the fruit she'd picked; pale yellow juice oozed out. She licked it cautiously, but it was sharp and sweet, like some kind of citrus. She sucked the rest of the juice from the cut, then took a small bite. The flesh inside practically melted on her tongue.

"Oh, this one is good," she said, swallowing the pulp. "Even the skin is sweet."

Damien grabbed one and took a hungry bite, sending juice dribbling down his chin. "Wow, you weren't kidding. I haven't tasted fresh fruit like this is a long time."

Eve went for another bite, but something stopped her. Something was wrong. Some long-buried primal instinct told her they were being watched. She looked deeper into the trees. The jungle was quieter now than when they'd first walked up. No little twitches in the branches, and some chittering that she hadn't even noticed had suddenly stopped. She scanned the foliage, looking for signs of trouble. She noticed a couple of spots of light, which she probably could have dismissed as just small specks of sunlight through breaks in the leaves, but they were a little too round and regular. And then they blinked.

"Back. Up. Slowly."

Damien looked up from his fruit. "Huh?"

Eve was already stepping back, away from the trees. "There's something out there."

Damien cocked back his arm with the half-eaten fruit as if to throw it. "Man, this is why I hate nature."

The eyes disappeared, and a vague dark shape moved against the vegetation behind it, black against dark green, imperceptible if it weren't for the rapid movement. The snap of a twig off to her side made Eve whip her head around. There wasn't just one; they were being flanked.

"Run!"

Eve turned around and bolted back to the ship. The soft sand gave way beneath her feet, sapping most of the energy of each step. Within just a few yards, her calves burned with the effort. Damien pulled slowly ahead of her with his shoes still on, and he waved his arms in the air over his head.

"Predator!"

Eve heard heavy breathing and rapid footsteps, and prayed it was her own. The safety of the ship, even the enemy ship, seemed despairingly far away, and each step brought it only infinitesimally closer. The distant figure of Bellig looked in their direction and raised her rifle. Whether she was aiming at the creature behind them or at the charging captives, she didn't know and didn't quite care. Eve just kept running, her legs and lungs on fire with the effort. After a few seconds, a muzzle flash erupted from Bellig's rifle, followed in a split second by the crack of a gunshot. Eve slid to a sharp halt in the sand, torn between the fear of a monster behind her and a warning shot from the pirate in front. She looked behind her and saw nothing but the tree line. She placed her hands on her head and walked slowly the rest of the way to the pirate ship.

"Damned thing got away," Bellig said when they got within earshot. "Told you the predators would keep you from straying too far."

"Thanks for the warning," Damien panted. He slumped down, hands on his knees as he recovered. "Well, that worked up quite a sweat. Who's ready for a swim?"

The fluorescent light struggled for a second, then flickered on and illuminated the dingy medical facility.

"Voila," Amber said, gesturing inside. "My office."

Father Tanner scanned the room. It bore only a passing resemblance to any proper operating theater. Of course, that made him feel right at home. A single reclining dentist-style chair took up the center of the room, the faux leather cracked, brittle, and showing yellow stuffing at a couple of the seams. Grimy cabinets lined two of the walls, and a dull yellow refrigerator hummed away in one corner, with a handwritten label saying "Samples Only! No Food!"

"How much medical training do you have?" Andrew asked. He and Ghenni followed Tanner into the room and poked around at surgical instruments and medicines left out on the counter. Carter lingered in the doorway, leaning against the wall as casually as he could while holding an automatic rifle.

"Formal training? I'm a veterinarian. Most of my work here is just first aid, though, so it's mostly transferable knowledge. Bullet wounds, pulling teeth, that kind of thing."

"How does a vet end up working for a pirate crew?" Father Tanner asked.

Amber shrugged. "Didn't have much choice. Captain Lopuul is the one that picked us up, and we didn't have any other place to go. It's a living, I guess."

"Picked you up?" Andrew asked. "From where, like a shipwreck?"

She sighed. "Not really. Me and Carter are crybabies."

"Crybabies?" Ghenni asked, his face twisted with confusion. "Whining children?"

"It's a slang term," Tanner said. "They were cryogenically frozen." He glanced back at Carter in the doorway and lowered his voice. "I noticed Carter's speech impediment; it's a common side effect of the freeze-thaw cycle. You were on one of the big colony ships, weren't you?"

"Yeah," said Amber. "If I understand the date conversion right, we launched about 130 years ago.

"Really?" said Andrew, his eyes wide with shock. "That must have been first gen. Pre-First-Contact, pre-IS-drive, pre-everything."

"Pre-functional cryogenic technology, even," she said with a morbid chuckle. "Carter and I were the only ones who survived the thawing, and I'm the only one who came out without any damage. Back then they just herded us onto ships and launched us at a planet somewhere. I'll never understand why they did it without even knowing it would work."

"Profits," Andrew said. "Investors were threatening to pull out of the colonizing corps unless they showed a proof-of-concept. So they gathered up a bunch of hopefuls, took their money, and launched them into space, not caring whether they made it anywhere or not."

"Is that so?" Amber asked.

"I saw a documentary about it," Andrew said.

"I learned about this as well," Ghenni said. "As an example of the callous exploitation of the Consortium culture."

"Yes," Father Tanner said, "I'm sure it was a highlight of the Brotherhood propaganda reels. I'd have to say I agree with them on that one."

Amber cleared her throat to cut off the thread of conversation. "Well," she said, "as much as I love to talk politics, shall we get on with the tour? I'd like to get the captain taken care of."

"Right," said Andrew. "What do you have in the way of Tuudolian supplies?"

Amber opened up the refrigerator and hauled out a plastic caddy of bottles. She heaved it up on the counter with a rattle. "We hit a Tuudolian freighter a few months ago and raided the infirmary. A lot of the stuff we ended up selling off, but we kept some basic medicines and diagnostic materials. Just the things we decided were better to have on hand than trade for pennies."

"Of course," Father Tanner said. He sifted through the bottles and plastic testing kits. The supplies were disappointing, to say the least. "It's a starting point, at least. We can eliminate some basic diagnoses before moving on to the more difficult conditions."

"You have experience with Tuudolians?" Amber asked. "That's impressive."

"It's marginal. As part of my surgical rotation in medical school, I was assigned to a couple of Tuudolian defectors to the Consortium. I learned some basic anatomy, enough for trauma surgery or removing basic tumors. Andrew?"

"Textbooks only," Andrew said. "Tuudolians are a flagship example of the PN_{OP} macro type."

"Meaning?" Amber asked.

"Our bodies are carbon-based, right? All of our macromolecules, things like DNA, fats, proteins, and so on are all based on long chains of carbon atoms. But Tuudolians are based on polyphosphazene, long chains of alternating phosphorous and nitrogen atoms. They breath in oxygen like us, but instead of breathing out carbon dioxide, they excrete phosphoric acid."

"That explains the smell, I guess," Amber said. "But that stuff's way over my head."

"We can start with some diagnostics then," Tanner said. "But we should have a plan in place for when it doesn't work."

"When?" Amber asked. "Not if?"

"We're looking at an advanced psychosis here," Tanner said. "There's essentially three options. One, it could be a purely physical cause, like a brain tumor which could quite easily be inoperable. Two, it could be chemical in nature, in which case we'd probably need some rather specific drugs that I doubt are included here. We have a desktop pharmaceutical synthesizer, but we need the raw materials and programming, and I don't know where we'd get them."

"I don't know about raw materials," Amber said, "but for programming, would that kind of thing be part of a Brotherhood database?"

"On a large enough ship or outpost, crewed by Tuudolians, yes. Do you have one?"

"No, but I might be able to get you access. You haven't met Neekol yet, have you?"

Tanner looked at Andrew, who shook his head. "Haven't heard the name yet, no."

Amber snorted. "Not surprised. He doesn't leave his room much. I'll have to introduce you. But you mentioned a third possibility. What's that?"

Father Tanner sighed. He didn't even want to bring it up, but he feared that was the direction this was headed in. "The cause could be spiritual. The captain reacted... very negatively to my crucifix necklace. Most Tuudolians wouldn't even recognize the cross; their Emmanuelite symbol, if I remember right, is a sun occluded by an eight-pointed star. Their incarnation of Christ was executed by being tied above water on a rock to suffocate and dry out."

"So what does that mean?" Amber asked.

"It means it might be a case of demonic possession," Andrew

added.

"You think the captain might be given to spirits?" Ghenni asked.

"Not spirits," Father Tanner said. "Demons. If that's the case, we would have to perform an exorcism, and it would be very risky to carry out with just Andrew and myself."

"Demon possession, like they do in the movies?" Amber asked. "Head spinning, and all that? I thought it was all made up."

"The movies embellish quite a bit, but yes, it's very real. I've seen it a couple of times personally."

Amber shook her head. "I've never believed in that. Of course, before I launched on that ship, I didn't believe in aliens either, so what do I know? Still, it seems kind of out there."

"We'll pray it won't come to that," Father Tanner said. "It's my duty to eliminate any medical causes before resorting to that anyway."

"Speaking of," Andrew said, "we should get started."

"I agree," Tanner replied. "I think Ghenni and I can administer the diagnostic kits ourselves, so perhaps you should meet this Neekol and see if you can get the information we need." Andrew nodded.

"Alright, follow me," Amber said. "And don't mind the smell."

Chapter Four

Andrew knocked on the hallway door. It had some kind of writing on it in a language that he didn't recognize, with a mix of squiggles and straight marks intersecting at different angles. All he could say was that it wasn't the same as the captain's quarters. He heard some kind of bass-heavy electronic music thumping away on the other side, so he knocked harder.

"Hello?"

After a brief pause, the music suddenly stopped. A moment later, the door opened a crack. The inside was dark, save for the harsh blue glow of a computer screen somewhere outside of view, while a slightly rank smell drifted through the gap.

"Yes?"

A red feathered head with a red-and-yellow-streaked beak leaned over into the gap on a long neck, and scanned Andrew up and down with quick, jerky movements. A round avian body soon toddled over to get under the head and straighten the neck as it regarded him. Its body was covered with a faded black tunic, printed with what was once a colorful logo of some kind. Its head tilted diagonally with the question.

"Hi, um, I'm Andrew. You're Neekol, right?"

"That's right. What you need?" it asked in terse, halting English.

"I was told you might be able to help me get some information from a Brotherhood database?"

"Hmm. Can help. Come inside."

The bird creature stepped back and opened the door the rest of the way. It gripped the door with a three-fingered hand at the end of a feathered wing, with brown and gray at the tips. The inside of the room was an absolute mess, even compared to the way Damien kept his cockpit. Ration wrappers littered the floor, shoved haphazardly into corners right alongside piles of laundry. As he'd been warned, the smell was almost overwhelming, mixing old food, sweat, and some kind of incense.

Neekol sat down in a chair by a computer desk, then hurriedly stood back up and brushed some crumbs off of a second chair and gestured for Andrew to sit down. As he sat, Andrew spied some sort of inventory log on the computer screen. He couldn't read it of course, but he didn't doubt that Neekol was tabulating all the loot they'd collected from the *Malika*.

"So anyway," Andrew said, "Amber said that you knew your way around a computer. I'm looking for some files to help with treating the captain."

"Oh yes. Very sad. Lopuul good captain. What files?"

Andrew took a deep breath. The whole list seemed impossibly optimistic, and he almost felt ashamed to be asking for it. "I need the whole medical database for the Tuudolian species. Anatomy, biochem, psychology, everything. Also, programming for a Gargan model 343 desktop PharmaSynth unit, for Tuudolian physiology. Especially psychoactive drugs, if you have to choose." Halfway through his description, Neekol turned back to his desk and began typing notes.

When Andrew finished, Neekol turned back to him and handed him a weathered pad of paper and a crudely-sharpened pencil. "You write down. English weak."

"Yeah, no problem," Andrew said. He set to writing down the specifications. "Your English is actually pretty good. Who's teaching you?"

"Carter. Best friend on ship. Like speaking."

"You two seem like a bit of an odd pairing. You have some kind of history together?"

"I convinced captain not leave behind. My idea humans join crew.

186

He thanks me."

Andrew nodded; it was nice to know at least somebody among the pirates had a heart. "I get it. It's sort of the same for us on our ship. Us doctors are kind of a late addition to the crew. So what do you do on the ship normally?"

"Mostly mechanic," Neekol said. "Some hacking. Not much chance."

"Oh, so that was you that got our door open?"

He bobbed his head up and down. "Easier. Less damage."

"I guess so," Andrew said, handing back the pad and pencil. "So how do you plan on getting these files?"

Neekol turned back to the computer and began typing in a plain text editor. He had a file already created, which looked to be massive. "Brotherhood mothership one system away. Full database on board. Will hack."

"Not even in this solar system?" Andrew asked. "That's gotta be what, a couple of light-years away? Even with IS-signalling, that's like an hour round-trip to talk to them. How can you interact with the database like that?"

"Burst hacking," Neekol said. "Send one signal, with program. Program does work. Sends results."

"You have a computer program that hacks for you? You're talking about an AI?"

Neekol made a snorting sound that must have been a chuckle. "Not true AI. Not possible. Just limited agent."

"How long do you think it will take?"

"Must customize. Few hours. Few more for program. Ready tomorrow."

Andrew looked around for a clock. "I don't know what time it is by your reckoning. When's tomorrow?"

"Whenever done sleeping."

Ghenni cautiously entered the captain's quarters alongside Father Tanner. His mentor had told him of what happened when he and Andrew first examined him, and he felt nervous at the prospect of seeing it firsthand. A squeaking wheel announced Amber's presence behind him as she pushed the cart containing the diagnostic tools and instruments they'd need. Carter strolled along behind her, not helping, but keeping a watchful eye on the two captives with his rifle hanging low in front of him. He didn't like the feeling of being watched so closely.

The door whispered open, and the room was as Father Tanner had described it. The strange sea creature that piloted this ship moved frenetically in and out of the vegetation, but didn't speak as he'd heard described. Tanner moved to the edge of the room where a ladder ran up the wall to a door on the top of the tank.

"How do you plan to collect the samples we need?" Ghenni asked.

"I'm still working on that," Tanner said. "I didn't have to deal with hostile patients when I worked with Tuudolians before. There's a sedative among the supplies that can be simply administered into the water, rather than injected. It can't permeate the entire tank though, so we'll need to draw him over here. That's the tricky part."

"You described him being agitated before," Ghenni said. "Perhaps you could... antagonize him?"

"It's a thought..." Father Tanner said, trailing off. He fingered his crucifix necklace in thought for a moment, then climbed up the ladder and opened the hatch on top of the tank. "Hand me the sedative, Ghenni."

Ghenni grabbed the sedative from the tray, a yellowish liquid in a thick plastic syringe with a wide opening. He handed it to the doctor who wrapped the other elbow around a rung in the ladder to brace himself, and held the crucifix in that hand.

"Our Father, who art in heaven..." the priest began to pray. Though this time he didn't close his eyes, but kept them watchful, scanning the water for movement.

"...hallowed be Thy name..."

With lightning speed, the a dark shape like a torpedo darted out of the seaweed at the bottom of the tank and surged toward the opening. Before the priest could utter another word, it launched itself half out of the water, twisting at the last moment to lash out with one of its tentacles. Taking him by surprise, the rubbery appendage grappled Tanner's arm holding the syringe and slammed it against the edge of the tank. Tanner yelped in pain, and the syringe threatened to tumble from his hand into the water. He managed to recover his grasp on it, but it had twisted in his hand, and he no longer had the proper grip to press on the plunger. Ghenni rushed forward and grabbed at the tentacles, trying to wrest his friend from the squid's embrace.

"Ghenni," Tanner said through gritted teeth as he strained against the creature's grip, "take the syringe!"

Ghenni climbed up the ladder as far as he could, pressing himself against the doctor as he reached for the instrument in his hand. The slick, wet appendages of the patient rubbed against his face, and he mentally shivered at the grotesque touch. Behind him, he heard Carter shifting, and a glance over his shoulder showed him that the pirate was on alert, his rifle gripped tightly, watching the struggle. Ghenni hoped he didn't misread the situation and decide they were hurting the captain.

Lopuul didn't seem focused on the syringe at all, and reaching as far as his arm could, Ghenni was just able to take it from Tanner's hand. He turned it to point into the water, and injected the entire dose straight into the tank. The sedative billowed in a sickly yellow cloud surrounding the squid-like alien, who still struggled against the doctor's arm. After several seconds, its grip slackened, and Tanner peeled the tentacle from his arm. He held onto it, not letting the patient slip completely underwater.

"Well, I suppose that worked, more or less," he said, panting. "We need a blood sample. Can I have the needle, please?"

Amber scanned the tray, picking up a few instruments and putting them back down as she searched. "Dammit. Sorry. People are always moving my stuff. I'll go get it." She hustled out the door, leaving Ghenni and Father Tanner alone in the room.

"Take your time," the priest muttered.

"Why does he behave like that?" Ghenni asked. "Why did he react so strongly to your prayer?" He certainly knew that some people didn't like the Emmanuelites, but had never seen them thrown into a rage merely at the sight of one like that.

"Well, there's two possibilities," Tanner said. He adjusted his stance on the ladder as Ghenni climbed back down. Ghenni spotted his eyes darting over to where Carter watched them intently, and he lowered his voice. "Either he truly is demon possessed, and the spirit detests God and those who serve Him, or he's suffering some kind of medical psychosis fixated on that same idea. We need to figure out which."

"I heard stories of possession by spirits," Ghenni said. "When I was a child, I heard that superstitious people, who lived far in the wilderness, practiced spirit rituals, channeling the ghosts of the dead to ask for guidance."

"If you ever get back to Trenth, or anywhere else they practice things like that, promise me you'll stay away. There's no such thing as ghosts, or benevolent spirits. There is only the Holy Spirit of God, and demonic powers. They hate God, and those who bear His image: every species possessing a soul. Anything they offer to help you is a trick to gain control over you. Remember that."

"You've said the same of my gods."

"And I stand by that. If they exist, they are demonic in nature, and every time you pray to them, you run the risk of inviting that power in to destroy you. Watch Lopuul carefully, because that could be you some day."

Ghenni nodded. The Emmanuelites were strange in their teachings, but had otherwise been steadfast friends and worthy teachers. He could bear the slights against his beliefs for the knowledge he gained by working with them. Although associating with them had resulted in having to flee his home, he hoped to one day return; it was difficult to say if he was better off with them than without so far. But what was done was done.

Amber re-entered the room, carefully holding a syringe with a needle tip pointing down. Tanner acknowledged her, then heaved the captain's limp body out of the tank, sloshing foul-smelling water across the floor. "Ghenni, if you'll do the honors," he said, straining to lower the squid-like creature down to his reach. "You should be able to find a good vein on the abdomen, right above each tentacle."

"No," Carter said. "Amber uses-s the needle."

"Fine, fine," Tanner grumbled. "Just hurry up; he's heavier than he looks."

Amber stepped past Ghenni and up the ladder a bit, and palpated the rubbery flesh. She found the vein and carefully plunged the needle in; soon she was drawing thick, red blood into the syringe.

"Red, just like us," Ghenni mused. He hadn't seen many aliens, but the last one they operated on had corrosive, metallic blood. He hadn't known what color to expect.

"Most species that breath oxygen will use iron to bind it in the blood," Tanner said, heaving the patient back into the tank with a splash. "That's what gives it the color." The doctor descended the ladder, shaking the water from his hands onto the floor. "Is there a shower where I can clean up? It's a bit stinky and acidic in there."

"No problem," Amber said. "You can use my room when we're finished."

Tanner paused, then wiped his hands on his sweater. "Right, when we're finished. Let's start on the test kits." He cracked the seal on one of the plastic packages on the tray, revealing a spiderweb of channels that drew the blood into a multitude of testing chambers. From what the Father had described, the poison in the blood would produce a color in one of the chambers if it was present. The construction of the kit seemed cheap, yet it was still beyond the resources they had had at the clinic on Trenth. Amber inserted the needle into the opening port, squirting a few drops to the fill line.

"What is this one testing for?" Amber asked.

"This one is for heavy metals," Ghenni said.

Tanner nodded. "That's probably our best bet for psychosis. Next is a phosphazene contaminant kit, for things like pesticides. I've got a bacterial test kit, and viral too, but I don't know that those are indicated by the symptoms."

Father Tanner and Ghenni continued opening up the plastic packages and inserting the blood to each test kit in series. Once they were all activated, Tanner wiped his hands again and tapped his foot impatiently.

"It'll be a few minutes before the results come in." He turned to Carter and gestured at his wet clothes. "May I rinse off *now*?" Ghenni could feel the strain on the doctor's composure about to crack.

Carter sighed and rolled his eyes. "Are you g-good with him by yourself for a minute?" he asked Amber

"Sure, sure," Amber said. "It's the second door on the left."

Tanner stomped off into the hallway, holding his hands in front of him, while Carter followed back a few steps.

"A little touchy, isn't he?" Amber asked once he'd left. She arranged the tools on the cart and started wheeling it back into the hallway, gesturing for Ghenni to follow.

"He has a temper," Ghenni said.

"He ever hit anybody? I had a boyfriend like that."

"Captain Rogers once, I believe. He usually leaves the room when he is tempted."

"So how did you end up on a crew full of humans, anyway?" She asked.

"The Father and Andrew ran a mission and clinic upon my home planet. I apprenticed to them as a nurse, so I could learn for service of my people as a doctor one day. Unfortunately, I was forced to be fleeing my home after we... got tangled up with a patient."

"Tangled up how?"

"We had to pretend to be a Brotherhood ship. That is why we hired Captain Rogers and Eve. The deception did not last. We had need to run away."

"Ah, gotcha." They arrived back in the infirmary, and Amber put away the instruments, and lined up the test kits on the counter. She squirted the remainder of the blood into the sink and casually cleaned out the syringe. Just as she finished, Tanner entered the infirmary, stripped down to his undershirt, with his hair mussed and his damp sweater wadded into a ball. He unfurled it and laid it across the exam chair in the middle of the room to dry. Carter lingered in the hallway, leaning against the opposite wall.

"Any results yet?" he asked.

Ghenni grabbed the first of the test kits and examined the digital readout on the side. "We have a result, but I cannot read it."

Tanner strode over and looked at the readout himself, then sighed. He turned to Amber. "Do you read Tuudolian, by any chance?"

"No, but I have a translator."

She opened up a drawer and produced a small pocket translator unit, a dark gray box no larger than the palm of her hand, and fiddled with the settings on a screen for a minute. She activated a camera and held it above the test kit; the text on the display changed to English on the screen.

"Scandium, normal levels. Titanium, normal levels... Looks normal across the board to me." She held out the translator unit to Tanner. "Feel free to look yourself." Tanner took the translator from her and methodically scrolled through the results on each test kit.

"Negative, negative, negative," he said, slamming down the last kit on the counter. Ghenni flinched at the outburst. "Can't say it's not what I expected, but it takes us back to square one."

Chapter Five

Damien woke up with Bellig standing over him. The sun had been shining when he first slumped up against the side of the pirate's ship, but now he was in shadow. Once he blinked the sleep away from his eyes, he realized it wasn't Bellig blocking the sun, but the tree line. Dusk wasn't far off.

"You're gonna want to come in for the night," Bellig said. "Those things get bolder in the dark."

"Ugh, my clock's all mixed up," Damien said, standing and brushing the sand from his pants. "I'll be up all night."

The Trenthan woman escorted him back into the ship and then into the stripped-down quarters where he'd woken up after their initial capture. The rest of his crew were already there, and apparently while he slept, their captors had brought over some pillows and blankets. Not much comfort on the cold metal floor, but it was something.

"Hope you all used the toilet," Bellig said. "We're locking you in for the night." Without waiting for an answer, she shut the door behind Damien, and he heard the faint beeping of the door controls on the other side.

"How'd it go with the captain?" Damien asked to Tanner.

The doctor sighed. "No diagnosis yet. We've eliminated some

possibilities, but it only gets us marginally closer to helping him."

"What's the next step then?"

"I've asked for some more supplies from our ship," Tanner said. "Specifically the X-ray scanner. We might be able to identify a tumor or something like that, which I pray will be operable."

"Yeah, you do that," Damien replied. He kept his voice low in case anyone was listening in, and leaned in conspiratorially. "As far as back-up plans, we can't make a run for the jungle. Too dangerous."

"We almost got eaten by something," Eve said. "Damien tried to leave me behind."

"Hey, I didn't try to leave you behind," Damien replied, putting up his hands defensively. "I *did* leave you behind, because you're out of shape and slow. And anyway, that means if Pops can't save the captain, our only other option is to take the *Malika* back by force somehow."

"I don't like our odds," Andrew said. "We're evenly matched for numbers, but most of us aren't trained fighters, and we don't have any weapons."

"I've been working on that," Damien said, fishing in his pocket. He produced a small seashell, a radiant blue piece of beach detritus with yellow spots. "This baby's pretty sharp. Maybe we break it in two and then get some sticks from the jungle to make some spears."

"Yeah, great plan," Eve said with a sneer. "We'll laboriously craft primitive weapons while the people with guns watch us."

"I admit, it's not a complete strategy yet, but it's something. The key is going to be getting one or two to take our side. Amber and Carter are human; you think we could turn their sympathies?"

"Hard to say," Andrew said. "Seemed like her feelings about the crew were mixed. Kind of rescued, kind of abducted. I don't think she's much of a fighter either. What about Carter? He seems tough."

"I've been watching the crew dynamic out there on the beach," Damien said.

"He was napping," Eve interrupted.

"Only part of the time. Before that, Carter was working pretty closely with Bellig and Tenik on transferring the cargo. I get the sense he's pretty thoroughly bought-in. Maybe he likes the work. Didn't seem to want to talk with me much."

"That might just be you," Father Tanner said with a smirk.

Damien snorted. "Well, you all should try to feel him out. See where exactly his sympathies lie. The way he carries himself, my guess is he's a career soldier. We want him on our side."

"Alright," Andrew said. "I'll try to talk to him. But I talked with Neekol the mechanic, and he said the two of them were best friends."

"Neekol? Which one of them was that?"

"Don't think you've met him. Some kind of bird species. He's the guy who hacked your door."

"Oh yeah? Might want to have a word with him..."

"It sounds like we all have tasks for tomorrow," Father Tanner said, shooting Damien a glance. "Let's not get distracted with petty vengeance."

"Right. Petty." Damien grabbed a pillow and blanket and laid against the back wall, facing the door. He needed to be well-rested. He had to be ready.

Father Tanner woke the next morning, or whatever time of day it was, with a stiff back. He was too old to be sleeping on hard metal floors like that. As usual, he was awake before anyone else, and he would normally take advantage of the fact by studying the scriptures with some privacy, but he had neither at his disposal right now. He settled on mentally reciting a few chapters, and his mind, perhaps inevitably, went to Legion.

And they came over unto the other side of the sea, into the country of the Gadarenes. And when he was come out of the ship, immediately there met him out of the tombs a man with an unclean spirit, who had his dwelling among the tombs; and no man could bind him, no, not with chains. Because that he had been often bound with fetters and chains, and the chains had been plucked asunder by him, and the fetters broken in pieces: neither could any man tame him.

Tanner's recitation was interrupted by a knock on the door. He opened his eyes and glanced around the room; the others seemed to be stirring now, so it seemed he wouldn't get any privacy after all. The door slid open, and Tanner stood to meet Tenik. He had a plastic bin at his feet that Tanner recognized as containing some of his medical supplies.

"I brought the stuff you wanted," Tenik said, nudging the bin closer with his foot.

"The X-ray scanner is in there?"

"I guess so. That's the white thing, right?"

Tanner approached and began sorting through the supplies. The X-ray scanner was indeed there; it was a horseshoe shaped contraption that tapered into flat panels at both ends: the generator and the detector. Also included was a collection of surgical tools wrapped in a leather bundle. Unfurling it, he could see that someone had removed the scalpels; he'd have to see someone about that if they got to the point of performing surgery.

Andrew staggered up beside him, rubbing the sleep from his eyes and cracking his neck. "Any chance we get breakfast before we get started?" Tenik grunted, then shut the door on them again. "Guess not."

Tanner flipped the power switch on the scanner, but nothing happened. He toggled it a few times, but it remained dead. "Was this working the last time you saw it?" he asked.

"Yeah, I put it away myself," Andrew said. "Maybe the battery's dead."

Tanner popped off the plastic panel and examined the battery. Nothing seemed obviously wrong with it. He pulled out the battery and gave it a few whacks against the heel of his palm.

"Something wrong?" Eve said, poking her head over David's shoulder.

"The thing won't start up," Andrew said.

"Give it here," Eve said, stepping forward. Tanner handed it to her, and she looked it over for a moment, testing and pulling at some of the connections.

"Well there's your problem," she finally said. "There's a break in the wire there; the battery contact isn't even attached anymore."

"Can you fix it?" Tanner asked.

"If I can get my hands on a soldering gun, sure. But..." she leaned in before continuing in a low voice. "I can't say for sure, but this doesn't look like an accident. Look at the scratches behind it. Someone was trying to pry it off with a knife or screwdriver or something."

"Why would someone sabotage us?" Andrew asked. "We're trying to help."

"We're trying to help the *captain*," Tanner said. "But if someone wants the captain out of the way, they obviously wouldn't like that."

"Great," Andrew said. "So not only are we prisoners, and trying to treat a violently psychotic patient, but someone is actively working against us. Just great."

Eve startled out of her nap when the light came on in the infirmary. She'd been reclining in the exam chair in the middle of the room, trying to catch a little better sleep than what she'd gotten on the floor of the cell. Amber strode into the room, holding a soldering gun in the air triumphantly, and muttering something to Carter in the hallway that made him nod and saunter off somewhere. Apparently he'd been watching her sleep the whole time. Ugh.

"I got it," Amber said. "I had to sneak into Neekol's quarters to find it. Luckily he's a pretty heavy sleeper."

"Thanks," Eve said, squinting at the light and climbing out of the chair. "You're a lifesaver." She stepped over to the counter where the X-ray scanner laid, and began warming up the soldering gun.

"So," said Amber, "what's your story, anyway? I mean, the missionaries I get, they're doing their thing out here. Your captain—Damien, right?—he's the independent entrepreneur type. But I can't get a read on you."

"I don't like to get into it," Eve said. "But long story short, I'm on the run. Had to hide from somebody with a long reach." She held the tip of the soldering gun close to her palm, to feel if it was warm enough. Satisfied, she pulled the lamp on the counter down to a better angle and set to work on the electronics.

"Woof. That's quite the reach to send you all the way to enemy territory. Although I guess none of us can really go back home."

"Guess not," Eve said.

"So what's your situation, you know, man-wise?" Amber leaned in conspiratorially.

Eve set down her soldering gun. Looked like she wasn't getting out of girl talk. "So are you interested in me, or one of them?"

Amber snickered, then sighed. "Don't worry. It's been a few years, but I'm not *that* desperate yet."

"So you and Carter aren't... anything?"

"*He's* not anything, as far as I can tell. I don't know if he was always like that, or if it was damage from the cryo sleep. Trust me, that's not happening. Tenik's not really an option either."

"I always wondered about that with Trenthans," Eve said. She gestured at her face, imitating the dangling growths that Ghenni and the others had. "I know they use their faces, with the *glia*, for... you know. So what's... down there?"

"Nothing that does me any good, that's for sure." She sighed wistfully and leaned on the counter. "Although I don't complain when he takes his shirt off..."

Eve chuckled, then picked the soldering gun back up. "I guess Ghenni's off the table then, too."

"What about the others?"

"Well, Tanner and Andrew are religious enough they might as well be celibate."

"Damien, then? He's the one I had my eye on. You two aren't together, are you?"

"Not like that," Eve said. "He's not my type, plus he was widowed before we met, and I don't think he's moved on enough for anything serious."

"Well I'm not talking about *serious*," Amber said. "You'll all be on your way soon, right?"

"That's the hope," Eve said. She blew on the bead of solder to make sure it was solidified. "You think your crew will keep their word? I'd hate to get spaced after all this trouble we went to for your captain."

"Truthfully?" Amber looked over her shoulder to make sure no one was listening from the doorway. "I'd watch out for Bellig. I wouldn't put it past her trying to cheat you out of your arrangement. That's a lot of money to leave on the table once your end of the deal is over."

"So you don't trust her?"

"I trust she'll do what's best for our crew. But that's no reason for *you* to trust her."

"So you're loyal to her? Never thought of leaving?"

"I don't have a choice in the matter. I don't have a home to go to, and I couldn't leave even if I did."

"Come with us then," Eve said. She studied Amber's face for a reaction, in case she knew of a double-cross on the way. "When it's all finished, and we part ways, I mean."

Amber shook her head, but Eve didn't catch any sign of duplicity. "I'm the only one with any medical training. I don't think they'd let me go without a fight."

"From what you said, it sounds like might be a fight regardless. It's just a matter of what side you're on." Eve closed up the scanner and tested the power switch. The status lights came on bright and clear. "Looks like we're good to go. I'll let the Father know."

"Alright. And I'll think about it."

Chapter Six

Andrew wheeled the cart back into the captain's quarters, this time carrying the X-ray scanner on it. Carter nodded in acknowledgment as he watched the proceedings with casual interest. Once inside, Andrew spotted Lopuul darting frenetically back and forth, his eyes tracking Father Tanner as they regarded each other through the glass. Ghenni stood to the side, watching the pair stand off.

"How do you want to-" Andrew began before Lopuul interrupted him with an outburst of blasphemy. Ghenni held out a hand, warning him to stay back.

"Slave of the Holy One, have you come to torment me?" the captain shrieked, turning his attention briefly to Andrew. "You bring your men to bind me?"

"Not to bind you, but to cast you out," Tanner replied boldly. "What is your name?"

"My name is ancient," Lopuul replied, "and cannot be spoken by human tongues. Without it, you have no power to cast me out."

"Not my power, but the power of the living God," Tanner said. He folded his arms behind his back, and silently snapped his fingers, catching Andrew's attention. He then mimed the pressing of a plunger. Andrew glanced over and spotted the syringe of sedative in Ghenni's hand. Ghenni was focused on the conversation, so Andrew slowly took it from him and crept toward the ladder, trying not to draw attention to himself.

"You think your God will grant you His power?" Lopuul asked with a chuckle. "I see your heart; I know your sin. No God would bless a soul so black."

Andrew crossed behind Tanner and put his hands slowly on the ladder, careful not to make a sound.

"You claim to worship God," the creature continued, "but only worship your own wrath. You bring knives to cut and destroy, and think you heal."

The captain started to turn its attention to Andrew, but Tanner jumped in to distract him. "You lie!" he shouted. "You serve the prince of darkness, who seeks to steal, kill, and destroy. Your hatred of the light has twisted your mind. When the final judgment comes, you will spend eternity writhing endlessly in your own wickedness."

Andrew was halfway up the ladder, and reaching up, he could just point the syringe over the edge of the tank. He pressed the plunger as quickly as he could, squirting the yellowish fluid into the water, where it began to drift toward Lopuul.

"And you will be there with me," the captain cackled. "The prince has promised me your soul to torment, as you seek to torment me. Then I will be the captor, and… you…"

The creature's wrath slackened as the sedative took hold, and his words soon became unintelligible to the translator. After a few more seconds, he was still.

"Well, he's not moving," Andrew said.

"Good work," Tanner said. "He was already active when I came in, so I decided we would need to distract him to administer the sedative. Let's grab him." Andrew spotted a waver in his mentor's voice, and sweat on his forehead. Perhaps it was more than just idle banter.

"How long can he survive outside of the water?" Ghenni asked.

"Under sedation?" Tanner said. "I wouldn't want to risk longer than three minutes. That should be enough time to get a scan of the head."

Andrew grabbed the next tool, a telescoping pole with a net on the end, like a large pool skimmer. Actually, that's probably what it was *supposed* to be for, but today they were using it to scoop out the captain. He handed it to Tanner, who angled it into the water and maneuvered the net under the creature. As he drew the net toward himself, Lopuul thrashed suddenly, tugging on the pole. Father Tanner managed to keep his grip, and the captain soon wore himself out, settling back into unconsciousness as the sedative strengthened its grip on him.

As Tanner pulled Lopuul out, black fluid trailed behind him. It billowed in the water and turned it brackish, clouding the tank.

"Was that ink?" Andrew asked.

"Tuudolians may look like squid," Tanner grunted as he pulled the captain from the water with a splash, "but they aren't. They don't have ink."

The smell hit Andrew with almost physical force. He staggered back as the black trail spattered against the bare metal floor, and Tanner's face scrunched up with disgust. "Oh, nevermind," Andrew said. "It's poop. He had diarrhea. And now he's dripping poop all over the floor. Great."

Tanner heaved Lopuul on top of the wheeled cart, his tentacles spilling over the edge and nearly reaching the floor. "You're right. We'll worry about that later. Get the scanner."

Andrew flipped the switch and activated the scanner, which came to life with a faint whine. Ghenni lifted the patient's head from the cart enough for Andrew to slip the detector under it. "Okay, steady. Hold him still for a few seconds." The whining intensified for a moment, then came to a sudden halt with a thump. They repeated the process at a few different angles to make sure they got a complete picture.

"That was pretty intense back there," Andrew said as they worked.

"Just keeping him busy," Tanner replied.

"You seemed a little shaken. Are you sure you're okay?"

Tanner paused before answering. "What he said about wrath caught me off guard. You know that is my weakness."

"Definitely not a secret," Andrew replied, shaking his head. "But do you think he was really in your head?"

"Hard to tell. I've been involved in a couple of exorcisms in the past, but never as the lead, and I was never addressed directly. I don't know what it feels like, but that was… definitely not pleasant."

Andrew nodded, and decided to let the matter drop. The scanner grabbed its last image, and he shut off the power. "Got it. Let's put him back."

Tanner and Ghenni carried him to the ladder and climbed up carefully with their legs, with the captain dangling between them. With a count of three and a grunt of effort, they tossed him back into the water.

"The filtration system should be able to cycle out the fouled water," Tanner said.

"This is a new symptom, yes?" Ghenni asked. "The diarrhea?"

"Yes," Tanner said. "It inclines me to think the cause is more likely chemical or pathological than physical like a tumor."

"Does this rule out possession?" Andrew asked. He looked around for somewhere to wipe his hands, but they didn't have any rags handy. He settled on the lower legs of his pants, and promised himself he'd wash them as soon as he could.

"I don't think so," Tanner replied, shaking his head." Expelling bodily fluids is not unheard of in cases of demon possession. Either as a way of trying to repel those who would cast it out, or as a form of self-torture."

"Well, I'll need to take the scanner to Neekol's computer to get the readout," Andrew said. "Hopefully we do find something there."

"Yes, we can only hope. First though, we should clean up. I think we all got splashed a little."

"Hey," Andrew said with a chuckle. "I just thought: somebody is going to have to swab the poop deck." He gestured at the floor beneath them, splattered with black, foul-smelling water at their feet. "Because it's a pirate ship, right?"

Tanner sighed. "Andrew…"

Andrew glanced out the open door where Carter watched with a chuckle, and his heart sank. "You're going to make us clean it up, aren't you?"

"Yeah," he said, moving from his spot for the first time, his face beaming. "I'll go g-get the mop. Have fun."

* * *

Damien lunged into the surf, his bare hands scrabbling at the loose sand, feeling around for the crustacean that he swore had been right there a second ago. The silt clouded the water, obscuring his view of the ocean floor for a few moments. By the time it settled, the creature was gone.

"Son of a bitch," he muttered. The mid-morning sun glared off the surface of the water into his eyes, and he raised the shirt from where it was tied around his waist to wipe the sweat from his forehead.

"You should count yourself lucky."

Damien turned around to find Amber leaning against the ship watching him with a smug grin. "You're after one of those lobster things, right? Let me tell you, they pinch like the devil and taste like ass."

"Worse than canned protein rations?" Damien asked.

"Believe it or not."

Damien brushed his wet, sandy hands off on his pants. "Well, I'm glad I only spent two hours on it then."

"At least you looked good doing it," Amber replied with a smile.

"Just comes naturally. Did you need something?"

Amber got up off the side of the ship and meandered a little closer. "Actually yeah. We've been doing an inventory of our new cargo."

"My cargo, you mean." He untied his shirt and shook the wrinkles out before putting it back on.

"*The* cargo, OK? Anyway, I just had some questions about some of the items, and I was hoping you could come look it over with me."

Damien let out a melodramatic sigh. "It pains me on a deep spiritual level, but you *do* call the shots around here."

"Oh, it'll be pretty painless," Amber said with a chuckle, gesturing for him to follow her back inside. "Just come on to my quarters. There's one particular package I'm interested in, and I'm… hoping you can fill me in." She glanced over her shoulder at him with a mischievous smile.

Damien stopped in the sand as she walked on. "Whoa, whoa, whoa. I see what this is now. You're a pirate, so you're after my booty, right?"

"Ah, a fellow wordplay enthusiast. Now I'm even more intrigued."

Damien sighed and held up his hands disarmingly. "Listen, babe,

I'm flattered that you want to use me as a mindless sex object, really I am, but this whole situation is a little weird." He held up two fingers close together. "To be honest, also a *liiittle* emasculating. You seem great, but I just don't think I'm interested."

Amber slumped her shoulders and pinched the bridge of her nose. "Ugh, I was afraid you'd say that. Eve told me you were still hung up."

Damien rolled his eyes. He wasn't an angry person by nature, but he could feel it welling up. "Well, I'm glad my tragic love life has brought you two some entertainment," Damien snapped. Something in the back of his brain warned him not to burn bridges with someone he was hoping might mutiny on his behalf, but he mouth was running on its own at this point. "Yeah, I guess I am still a little hung up on my *dead wife*. Sorry if that inconveniences you."

Amber threw her hands in the air dismissively. "Yeah, sure, I'm sorry, I guess I'm being selfish. I just don't know how many humans are left out there, you know?"

"In Brotherhood territory?" Damien asked derisively. "Not a ton. You might want to get out from behind enemy lines if you're trying to meet people."

"Still, with what happened to Earth..."

Damien's anger froze, his heart pounding. Had something happened recently? How out of the loop were they? "Wait, what happened to Earth?"

"You didn't hear?" Amber said. "It got hit. Bad. The surface is all but uninhabitable now."

The sound of Damien's rushing blood seemed to drown out the ocean. He shook his head, trying to reassure himself it was a mistake. "No, no, that can't be right. I would have heard that. There's not even active hostilities right now. When did this happen?"

"Years ago, before the war went cold."

OK, now he was less concerned, and more confused. "That's... But I was on Earth just three years ago. Still perfectly intact. Who told you it was destroyed?"

Amber tossed back her head with a grunt and kicked the sand in frustration. "Lopuul, that son of a bitch. That's what he told me and Carter when they first thawed us out. He said we didn't have a home to go back to."

"Bastard," Damien muttered. He knew this was his opening to undermine her loyalty, but he choked back his instinct to take the opening immediately. He needed to finesse his way in. "So that's the kind of guy you take orders from?"

"God, I feel like an *idiot*." She slammed her fist on the side of the ship to emphasize the point. "I was just so scared when I woke up, I didn't think to question what he was telling me. By the time I'd gotten my bearings, I'd been believing it for a few months, and it just stuck."

"So what are you going to do about it?" Damien asked.

Amber rubbed at her temples and sighed heavily. "I don't know. I mean he lied to manipulate me, but he's always taken care of me too. I've been with this crew for years; they're the only family I have."

"But a family that lies to you."

"I get why he did it, though. It's not like he had the resources to get me back to Earth."

"And that makes it OK?" Damien asked. He didn't want to let up the pressure.

Amber thought silently for a moment, then snorted. "Maybe it was kind of a mercy too, you know? It's been decades since I left Earth. All my friends and family are dead. It's just as much an alien planet as any other now."

"I think being the same species counts for a lot," Damien said, shrugging, "but hey, what the hell do I know?"

"Maybe." Amber turned to go back inside. "Anyway, I'm officially out of the mood now, so I'll be inside if anybody needs me."

Ghenni felt the warmth of the sun wash over him as he stepped out onto the beach. It was the first chance he'd had to go outside since they landed, and he wished he'd taken advantage of it earlier. The sand and heat reminded him of home, although it was more humid than he was used to. But when he turned around, he lost his breath for a moment. The ocean glittered like jewels under the sun, and he had to squint against the piercing lights that danced on the waves.

He had never seen the ocean before. Or at least, not at ground level. He grew up in desert scrub-land, too poor to travel to the shore hundreds of miles away. Ghenni breathed in the salty air, reveling in the unfamiliar smells.

His reverie was broken by Amber brushing swiftly past him, bumping him with an apology muttered under her breath. Captain Rogers followed close behind.

"You're soaking wet," Damien said, looking him over. "What have you been doing?"

"You don't want to know," Andrew said, coming up behind him.

"We had to mop up a… spill," Ghenni said. To speak of what they had to wash off was too humiliating. "Then we had to clean up ourselves. We came here to dry in the air."

"Well, you've got the weather for it," Damien said. "How's it going with the squid?"

"We have not diagnosed him," Ghenni said. "The X-ray was not helpful."

Damien glanced around, but with Amber back inside, none of the pirates seemed to be around. Although for all they knew, they were being monitored on camera. "Well, I might be making progress on my end," he said.

"Is that why Amber went inside in such a huff?" Andrew asked.

"Get this," Damien said. "Her and Carter thought that Earth had been wiped out. The captain lied to them to get them to join the crew."

"Do you think she might defect?" Ghenni asked.

"Maybe, maybe," Damien mused, stroking his chin. "She's pretty confused right now. I think it's going to take a delicate touch."

"Glad *you're* on the job then," Andrew said.

"I'm choosing to ignore the tone, and listen to the words," Damien said. "Anyway, I'm gonna hang out inside for a while. I want to keep an ear out for a change in atmosphere now that Amber knows she was manipulated. We need to find the fault lines in the crew and exploit them."

"You're not worried she will feel manipulated by you?" Ghenni asked. He wasn't experienced with women, but he knew they could pick up on things you wouldn't expect.

"As long as we're safe and sound and out of here, I don't care *what* the hell she feels about me after. Anyway, have fun sunbathing." Damien slapped the side of the ship as he went back into the cargo hold, leaving Andrew and Ghenni alone on the beach.

"Come on," Andrew said. "Let's walk around. If we're going to be out here, I want to at least check out the vegetation. Maybe get something fresh to eat."

"Perhaps we should not," Ghenni said. "Captain Rogers and Eve told us they spotted a dangerous animal." Ghenni was no stranger to wildlife, but he knew enough not to intrude on a predator unarmed.

"Good point. Let's at least get a *little* closer though. Or rather a little farther from our shadows." Andrew pointed to a small ridge in the sand ahead, about halfway between the ships and the treeline. "That's as good a spot as any. Let's just not fall asleep."

Ghenni trudged through the thick, loose sand toward the dune that Andrew had pointed out. The ships receded behind them, and the treeline resolved into individual plants. Some of them bore colorful fruits, but there was no telling what dangers lay inside.

As they walked, Ghenni stripped off the wet outer shirt, down to his white undershirt, and felt the sun on the bare skin of his arms. That feeling was far too rare, now that he spent so much time on the ship. When they reached the ridge, he spread the shirt out on the ground, facing the trees in case anything came out after them, and laid down. The slope was deep enough that they could have hidden behind it from the ship, but there was no point; they were safer with the pirates than in the alien jungle.

"This is the life, isn't it Ghenni?" Andrew sighed, reclining with his eyes closed. "I don't know about you, but I needed this."

Ghenni couldn't get comfortable. His head swiveled, unsure where to look. Staring at the trees made him nervous, but turning his back to them was just as bad. He gave up on lying down, and merely sat up, shivering as a breeze chilled his bare, wet skin.

"Something is not right," he said.

"What is it?" Andrew asked, sitting up. "You see something?"

"No, I-" Ghenni froze. There, just a few feet away, the sand shifted. It was small, just a lump in the contour of the beach that sank no more than half an inch. But it moved. Ghenni scrambled to his feet just as the ground opened up beneath him. A great claw covered in mottled green chitin erupted from the sand and grasped at his ankle. The razor-sharp carapace sliced into his flesh, sending searing pain shooting through his leg. He yelped in agony, and managed to pull his leg free of the pincer grip before it closed for good.

A crab-like creature rose from where they had been sitting, sand sloughing off of its shell. It shook itself, and the remaining sand seemed to melt with the vibration, cascading down to the ground. It measured perhaps ten feet across, with four evenly spaced eyes along its front quadrant. A dozen legs lifted up out of the sand and carried it toward Ghenni and Andrew.

"Help!" Andrew shouted, and Ghenni joined in. He hoped it was loud enough for someone to hear from the ship. A few moments later, his hope was answered by the crack of a rifle, followed immediately by the thwack of something striking the shell. The creature paused and twisted slightly, making Ghenni suspect it had eyes behind it as well, tracking the gunman in the distance.

Ghenni took advantage of the brief distraction and ran for the treeline, limping on his injured foot. The sand that scattered with every step stung in his fresh wound. Andrew followed along beside him, but he could feel shudders in the sand as the creature's feet impacted the sand behind him.

Another crack rang out as they fled, but it didn't have an obvious effect, and Ghenni didn't dare to look over his shoulder to check. It certainly didn't slow the pace of the footsteps. He wasn't sure if it was gaining ground on them or not; it certainly didn't have much to gain before catching up with them.

"Get to the trees!" Andrew yelled. "It can't follow us there!"

Ghenni chose not to worry about dangerous creatures *in* the trees. They couldn't be worse than the one chasing them, could they?

They were about twenty feet from the treeline when Ghenni heard a high-pitched whine behind him. It sounded mechanical, but he couldn't place the sound. When they were about ten feet from the trees, the whining raised in pitch until it culminated in an explosion. Ghenni launched into the air, searing heat blasting him forward and leaving his arms and legs wheeling through nothingness. He slammed into the ground between two trees, his fall broken by a clump of ferns. He struggled to breath, the wind knocked out of him by the impact. Andrew lay still next to him, his hair matted with blood where his head had impacted a tree.

Ghenni dragged himself over closer to Andrew and checked his pulse. It was weak, but still there. Looking back the way they'd come, pieces of the crab creature littered the ground around a smoking crater. But two more of the beasts had risen from the sand and scurried toward the trees where Ghenni and Andrew laid. Ghenni struggled to his feet, and dragged Andrew deeper into the trees where he hoped the crab things were too bulky to follow. Branches and thorns tore at his clothes as he forced his way past.

A pair of explosions sounded near the crabs, which Ghenni now realized must have been some kind of ship-mounted cannon. Those shots missed, sending plumes of sand into the air, where it filtered through the leaves like rain, gently pattering as it fell. They landed disturbingly close to the two of them, leaving Ghenni wondering if whoever was manning the cannon knew or cared that they were in the line of fire. Ghenni kept retreating, until the sunlight of the beach was crowded out by the vegetation, and the ships were blocked completely from view. One of the two new crabs exploded, sending bits of chitin flying into the jungle, cutting open several new wounds on Ghenni's skin with their broken edges.

The last of the crabs squeezed into the jungle, smaller trees bending beneath its massive weight, or cleaved from their stumps by the giant claws. The crack of snapping wood punctuated the air like gunshots, and the clatter of the crab's pincers slashed through the leaves and vines, drawing ever closer to Ghenni. He pulled Andrew as far as he could until they reached a stand of thick trees, where fallen logs blocked the path. He simply didn't have the strength to pull Andrew's dead weight up over the log, and there was no time to go around. The crab drew ever nearer, and none of the trees between them were sturdy enough to withstand the onslaught. It was mere feet away now, its eyes visible, flitting back and forth as it studied its prey. Ghenni clutched at his heart and prayed.

With one last explosion of plasma, the final creature erupted into bits, along with a few of the surrounding trees. The last thing Ghenni saw was a large piece of shell, hurtling flat toward his face.

Chapter Seven

"What the hell was that?" Damien shouted. He ran for the cockpit, and found Bellig guarding the open door. She blocked him from entering, but Damien saw Tenik sitting in the co-pilot chair with a HUD headpiece pulled down over his head. He grasped controls in both hands, whose movements synced with the sound of the ship's cannons discharging.

"Crab hunting," she said, non-chalantly.

"With *plasma cannons?*"

"Big crabs," Bellig replied.

"Is everything alright?" Father Tanner came running up, his hair disheveled and carrying a towel.

"Andrew and Ghenni were out there," Damien said.

Bellig sighed and addressed Tanner in a condescending tone. "Yes, they were the ones being attacked by the crabs. Carter ran outside when the sensors tagged them, but his rifle wasn't doing the job, so Tenik hopped on the external cannons."

"Well are they OK?" Damien asked.

Bellig turned to Tenik. "You still see them?"

Tenik slipped off the headset. "I don't see them anymore."

"Son of a bitch." Damien wheeled around and sprinted outside. He passed through the cargo hold and out onto the burning sand. Ahead a smoking crater smoldered on a ridge near the treeline, and he bolted toward it. As he approached, burning bits of chitin and intestines littered the beach. Among them he spotted a bright blue piece of cloth. He grabbed it and recognized it immediately.

"That's Ghenni's shirt," Tanner said, jogging up behind him.

Damien examined the fabric; "It's half-burned, and there's blood on it."

"So what, it got blasted right off of him?"

"I don't know! Maybe he wasn't wearing it."

"But he had to be nearby," Tanner said. "Do you see any... did they get away?"

Damien cupped his hands and called out in every direction. "Ghenni! Andrew!" His shouts drew no response. Even the birds and animals were silent in the wake of the explosion. Damien threw the shirt on the ground and let loose a string of curses.

"They might have escaped into the jungle," Tanner said. "We have to go after them."

Footsteps announced the arrival of someone behind them. "The doctor's not setting foot in there," Tenik said, jogging up alongside Tanner with his rifle at rest. "With those two gone, he's the only one who has a chance at curing the captain. And we're not risking *our* lives out there in the jungle."

"What the hell made you land on a planet this dangerous, anyway?" Damien snapped.

Tenik shrugged. "Rather deal with wildlife than patrols."

"So can *I* go after them? Or would you shoot me first?" Damien wasn't about to let any of his crew, even the missionaries, die out in the wilderness if he could help it.

"I won't stop you," Tenik said. "But this much fresh crab meat is going to draw the scavengers." He gestured with his head toward the trees.

Leaves rustling in the absence of wind, and quick furtive movements in the shadows of the trees, indicated the presence of some new animal. Maybe it was the same ones he encountered with Eve, but he couldn't get a good look. He caught glimpses of something, definitely quadruped, like a wolf or big cat, darting between trees, just out of reach of the daylight. Most disturbing was the sound of snarling and snapping jaws. They were already feeding.

"I need a rifle," Damien said, matter-of-factly. He held out a hand expectantly.

Tenik snorted. "Not happening. You'll just have to wait until they finish eating. Unless you'd like to take them on bare-handed?"

Damien balled his fists, his fingernails biting into his palm. Adrenaline ran rampant through his veins, but his options for action were all closed off. There was being heroic, and then there was being stupid. He didn't stand a chance against a whole pack of those things. And, perhaps mercifully, there was no sign of them being on the hunt for live pray. If Ghenni and Andrew were alive, they were probably safe. For now.

"How long until they finish?" Damien asked.

"They like to play with their food," Tenik said. "Could be hours."

Damien took a few deep breaths to try to calm down. It didn't help much.

"Pops, you'd better get back to work. I'd hate to abuse these people's hospitality. I'll go in after the two of them as soon as I can."

Tanner trudged back into the ship, his footsteps heavy. *Father God,* he prayed silently, *I commend Andrew and Ghenni to you. Protect them if they still live, and accept their souls with grace if they don't.* The words caught in his mind, and his stomach churned. Both of them had been his responsibility, and now they may have both been killed. His spirit was torn: he could not have possibly predicted an attack like that, but he was the reason they had been out there in the first place. The reason they were on the run, the reason they were captured. They would likely still be alive if not for his mission.

His thoughts were interrupted by Neekol standing in his path in the corridor. His head cocked to the side in curiosity as he regarded the morose doctor. In his hands he held a mobile computer tablet.

"Can I help you?" Tanner asked.

"No. Help you." The bird creature extended his wings, offering the tablet to him. "Database downloaded. On tablet, easy read. Would have given to Andrew. Sorry about it."

"Thank you," Tanner said, taking the tablet from him. "And thank you for the… sympathy. I pray that it's premature."

"Hope so too. Andrew nice." Neekol regarded Tanner up and down, then scanned the room, his head turning with quick, jerky motions. "Well. Back to work."

Neekol scurried off back into his room, and Tanner wasn't sure if that was a polite excuse to end the conversation, or an admonition for himself. In any case, there was nothing for him to do except to try to find the diagnosis that would allow him to treat the captain. Everything else was in God's hands at this point.

He sat down in the chair in the infirmary, and scanned through the database. Unfortunately, it wasn't well organized. Tanner wasn't sure if the hacking process had merely scraped the data from a more usable format, or if it was intended only for doctors with a strong background knowledge of Tuudolian physiology who knew what they were looking for. Either way, there were several textbooks-worth of information to sift through. Tanner leaned back in the chair and sighed. He was going to be there for a while.

Damien paced at the cargo bay doors. His hands itched to hold *some* kind of weapon, even just a nice, heavy stick. Vibrant colors of sunset bathed the sand dunes, but he was in no mood to enjoy the view. The howls and yips of the jungle beasts drifted to his ears every few minutes, confirming that the area was still not safe to investigate. Damien assumed it wasn't likely to become more safe after sunset, either. Were the days shorter here? He didn't have a good sense of how long he'd been watching and waiting, but it had to have been hours. His legs ached, and somewhere in the background his stomach growled as well.

As if on cue, Eve appeared from the winding pathway through the cargo hold, holding a tray of reheated food.

"Thought you might want something to eat," she said. She extended the dish out to him, complete with a plastic spoon. "We're not allowed forks, apparently, so it's more stew. Or something resembling it, anyway."

"Thanks," Damien said, taking the food. He took a few absent-minded bites, not registering any flavor except salt. "How's the doc doing?"

"He's reading, taking a lot of notes," Eve said. "He made it *very* clear there's nothing I can do to help him, so…"

"Not much you can do out here either."

"Still feeding, huh? A lot of meat out there."

"Slow eaters too." Damien paused with the spoon halfway to his mouth, then put it back in the dish and set it on the ground. Suddenly he had no appetite.

Eve went silent for a moment, and kicked the sand half-heartedly with her foot. "I think it's time to pack it in for the night," she finally said. "There's nothing either of us can do for them tonight, and you'll need your rest for tomorrow."

"Those are my people out there," Damien said. "Part of my crew. I can't abandon them."

"You're not abandoning them by waiting inside instead of outside. Look, if they're still alive at this point, they must have found some hiding place or something to wait it out. A few more hours won't make a difference one way or another."

"You're right. I just hate not being able to do anything. If we weren't prisoners, I'd have charged out there right off the bat. I need my ship back."

"I know what you mean. Unfortunately we're even worse off than before, being down two guys."

Damien glanced around to make sure nobody was listening. Carter had taken up a perch on the roof to watch for stray wildlife, but he didn't think he could hear well from where they stood. "Yeah. We'd need half of them to defect to have a decent shot of any kind of a coup."

"Well, I think Amber could be talked into it, but I'm not sure how good she'd be in a fight."

"Agreed. You'd think Carter would be our next best bet on account of being human, but he may *actually* be a robot. The man barely talks. You got any kind of read on him?"

Eve shook her head. "Not yet. But Andrew told me, you know, before, that Neekol called him his best friend. If we turn Carter, maybe we get Neekol too. You think I should try my feminine wiles on him?"

Damien rubbed his chin, as if in deep thought. "No, we need him on our side, not just barfing his guts out." Eve punched him in the arm.

"Well, I doubt it would work anyway. Amber thinks there's..." She mouthed the last word silently. "...*damage*."

Damien's eyebrows shot up involuntarily, but he dismissed the idea. "Eh, women will reach for anything when a guy turns them down. Did I tell you that Amber made a play for me?"

"She said she was going to. I told her it wouldn't work, but, well, you know."

"Yeah, you told her a lot of things, apparently. Thanks for spreading my life story around," Damien said half-jokingly.

Eve threw up her hands defensively. "Hey, I was trying to warn her off."

"I *am* pretty damn irresistible."

Eve sighed. "What about Tenik and Bellig? You think either of them could be turned?"

"Hard to tell. I'm not great at reading Trenthan body language, but Bellig is acting captain, so I don't like our odds there. Tenik is probably going to side with his fellow Trenthan. We'll have to feel him out very carefully."

"That might be a job for you," Eve said. "Let me have a crack at Carter, see if I can figure out what makes him tick."

"Alright, just... be careful."

Chapter Eight

When Andrew woke, the first thing he noticed was the pain. His body ached all over, and spots of wet, moist clothing told him that he'd been bloodied up quite a bit. As he struggled to get up, he realized why; thorny underbrush scraped and pulled at his skin when he attempted to stand up. He quickly gave up on that and took some more time to examine his situation.

Ghenni was still passed out next to him, scratched up just as much as he was. Andrew checked his leg wound, but it seemed to be clotted up with sand enough that it wasn't bleeding much anymore. Andrew checked his pulse. Still alive. That was something, at least. Scanning the vegetation around him, Andrew saw the issue. It looked like a thick thorn bush had grown up around the base of the tree they were slumped against. He and Ghenni had either been catapulted through it by the explosion, or over the top, and fell down when they collided with the tree. Touching his tender side, Andrew guessed that they had indeed struck the tree. It didn't feel broken, but pulling up his shirt, the last bits of twilight showed deep blue and purple bruising covering one side of his torso.

The thorns had the two of them completely hemmed in. It was a good thing, too, because the sounds of Andrew stirring had apparently drawn the attention of a pair of the jungle predators. They stalked the perimeter of the thorns, snarling with canine snouts, while muscles rippled under striped, hairless, green and brown flesh. Andrew searched for something to use as a weapon, but came up with nothing except a stick. It was maybe the length of his forearm, and seemed quite old and rotten; he'd be lucky if it withstood a single swing at one of the creatures. As Andrew considered his options, Ghenni groaned and sat up, clutching at his head.

"Hey, careful, no sudden moves," Andrew said.

Ghenni slowly looked around, groggily surveying the situation for himself. "Why aren't they attacking?" he asked.

"I'm guessing they don't want to deal with the thorns," Andrew said. He spun around to track the circling predators, trying to keep them from getting behind him, but he couldn't see them as they circled around the tree. "They know we have to come out eventually."

"We can't take them in a fight," Ghenni said. He nonetheless picked up a fist-sized rock and sought an effective grip to wield it. "Do you think anyone is coming to rescue us?"

"It's midday already," Andrew said. "We were unconscious for hours. If they were going to rescue us, they would have done it already. They probably think we escaped into the woods."

"So we're on our own then," Ghenni said flatly. "Do you think you can climb the tree?"

Andrew hazarded a glance at the trunk. The bark was smooth, but branches started just a bit out of Andrew's reach. He had never been that athletic, but he figured under ideal circumstances it wouldn't have been that difficult to pull himself up. While heavily bruised and scratched, not to mention recently unconscious? That was a bit more uncertain.

"Maybe. You?"

"I climbed trees like this many times when I was the boy," Ghenni said. "However, that was long time ago."

The two animals continued to circle the pair, snarling and snapping their jaws in an effort to intimidate the two of them. It was definitely working on Andrew, at least. The creatures pawed at the bushes, swatting gingerly at the bush to feel for openings that perhaps weren't as dense, or that could be torn aside.

"I don't think we have much of a choice at this point," Andrew said. "I don't know when they'll decide to risk it. You care to go first?"

"Very well."

Ghenni sized up the branch as he stretched in preparation for the jump. He winced as he twisted to the right. Andrew kept his eyes on the animals; they paused in their circling, waiting to see what their prey was up to. Ghenni jumped up and grasped the lowest sturdy branch, thrashing his legs to free them from the brambles that had caught at his ankles. After a moment, he got his feet clear and laboriously pulled himself up into the branches.

The animals snarled at this change of events, snapping and growling in frustration. They resumed circling the tree, quickening their pace as their prey threatened to evade their reach. As soon as Ghenni was clear from the lower branch, Andrew threw his stick at the nearest animal and quickly jumped up to grab at the limb above him. His hands slipped on the smooth bark, and he fell back down, feeling the sharp thorns pierce his arm where he landed on the bush. He quickly scrambled back to his feet, and by the time he did, the animals had closed in. They reared back, as if to prepare for a pounce. Andrew jumped again, and this time his hands clasped the branch firmly and his legs clawed at the tree, propelling him up.

He heard the roar from the alien beast as it launched itself across the bush, and he pulled his legs up a split-second too late. Searing pain slashed through his calf as the beast's claws raked across his leg, but it failed to get a good grip on him. The animal bounced off the tree and landed half in the brambles, yelping in pain and frustration as it quickly thrashed its way back out. Andrew heaved himself up onto the branch, then quickly hustled up a couple more branches just to be safe.

Andrew took a closer look at his leg wound once he felt more secure. It wasn't too deep, so he was more worried about infection than blood loss. Ghenni's ankle wound from the crab things looked more severe; the climb had shaken loose the sand and gotten the blood pumping again, and it trickled down his leg at a pace that made Andrew uncomfortable.

"We'd better wrap that," Andrew said, gesturing at it. He tore a strip from his freshly-shredded pants and tied it tight around his friend's wound. Ghenni winced, but bore it without complaint. Not much, but he figured it would be enough to keep the bleeding in check for the time being.

Next he surveyed the trees around them. The leaves were broad and deep, dark green, with streaks of red along the veins. This one didn't seem to bear any fruit, or at least not this time of year, but now that he had a better view, he could see the ground littered with some kind of seed pods. A few of them still clung to the branches, but on examination, they were rock hard. Andrew's stomach growled, but it didn't seem like he would be getting anything to eat up here.

"What now?" Ghenni asked. He sat straddling a large branch with his back to the trunk, picking thorns out from his lower legs. "We can't go back down."

"They might give up eventually," Andrew said. "How far are we from the treeline?"

"Too far. Perhaps in the morning, they will be gone."

"Would it even be safe to go back? If they think we tried to escape, they might not be too welcoming."

"We cannot simply stay up here for eternity," Ghenni replied.

"Well, the forest is pretty thick here, at least where it wasn't blown to smithereens. We could climb tree to tree." Andrew scanned the trees around him, trying to plot a route that might take them around the blasted area back to the treeline, where hopefully the rest of them could spot them and come help. There were a number of trees like they one they were trapped in, and some of the branches seemed to be within jumping distance of each other. It would be risky, but...

"Andrew, we may not be safe in here after all," Ghenni said. He pointed a bit farther up the trunk. "Something has clawed up here in the tree. Some other predator stalks the treetops."

Andrew looked up, and saw a spiraling gouge cut in the bark and deep into the wood. It didn't look like something an animal might do. In fact, something about it conjured up a memory of something Andrew had seen in a textbook long ago.

"That's no animal, Ghenni. This looks like rubber tapping. This planet may not be as uninhabited as they led us to believe."

"Rubber tapping?"

"Cutting strips in the bark to cause the trees to secrete resins. This looks like it's been healed for a while, but that means there's people nearby who have harvested these trees. They probably harvested it up here to keep out of reach of the animals, which means there must be a traversable path to wherever they live. "

"If there are people here, maybe they can help us."

"If they live deep in the jungle, they may be pretty primitive. But maybe we can barter with them. Trade the supplies from the pirate ship. It's worth a shot."

"If they don't kill us on sight, that is."

"Well, there's always that risk, I guess," Andrew said. "But I think I'd rather take my chances with that than trust the pirates."

"Agreed."

"Let's get moving then. We don't know how much time we have."

Father Tanner woke up with a start. There wasn't a clock in the infirmary, and he'd barely been outside, so he had no idea what time it was. His internal clock wasn't synced with local time, so it didn't matter much anyway. He wiped some drool off of the screen of the tablet, which was still open to where he'd been studying it when he fell asleep.

"Finally awake, huh?" Eve asked from behind him. Tanner turned around to see her standing in the doorway.

"I didn't even realize I'd fallen asleep," Tanner said, sitting up. He rubbed the sleep from his eyes and tried to find his place in the textbook. "What are you doing over here?"

"I've been 'assigned' to you," Eve said. "Tenik wanted me to be your assistant, since… well, you might need a hand in here."

"I wish simple manpower were the issue. I'm trying to learn years worth of internal medicine and psychiatry in hours, and even if I diagnose the problem, I probably don't have the medicine or equipment to treat it."

Eve paused for a moment. "Maybe I can get you some coffee?"

"There's coffee?" Tanner asked, spirits suddenly lifted. "Where is it?"

"I dunno. Probably several light-years away," Eve grumbled. "Sorry, I was being facetious. So how is the patient looking?"

Tanner grunted in frustration and counted to five before allowing himself to speak. "Mercifully, at least he's not getting any worse, as far as I can tell. That may be the only thing we have going for us right now."

"Any closer to a diagnosis?"

"We've screened him for every chemical contaminant we have the equipment for," Tanner said, "as well as an X-ray scan. That would really only pick up foreign objects though; it doesn't resolve images of soft tissue well, and Tuudolians don't have rigid bones, just fleshy cartilage. My next plan was to screen the blood sample we took for signs of parasites under the microscope."

"How will you know if you've found it?" Eve asked.

"That's what I was studying when I fell asleep," Tanner said, gesturing at the tablet. "There's images of some common parasites that can present with neurological symptoms. You *could* actually help me set up the microscope." He pointed at his boxes of medical supplies stacked in the corner. "If it hasn't been broken in shipping, that is."

Tanner and Eve rifled through the boxes until they found the battered microscope. It was painted beige at some point, but some parts were stained darker, and other parts stripped of paint altogether. Some kind of serial number had been scratched off, and some warning labels in an unfamiliar language were faded almost into illegibility. Tanner had had to leave behind most of his equipment for the mission when they fled, but had managed to pick up this unit at an underground market on a rainy planet he didn't know the name of. The dropper and slides took some more time to find, but he emerged triumphant from the third box.

Eve studied the contents of the boxes for a few more moments as Tanner retrieved the blood sample from the small refrigerator.

"There's no scalpels in there," Tanner said.

"How did you know that's what I was looking for?" Eve said, backing away with a sheepish grin.

Tanner kept his focus on setting up the microscope as he spoke. "I know Damien is going to look for a way to fight our way out. That's his temperament. He'd need weapons to do that, and you're obviously going to try to back him up."

"That obvious, huh?"

"Under slightly different circumstances, that's what I'd be doing too. They've loosened our leash a bit now that the numbers are tilted in their favor, what with Carter standing guard on the roof. But they already tossed those supplies for anything pointy. I have to ask permission even to use a syringe."

"Well, what about chemicals?" Eve asked.

"I have highly refined pharmaceuticals," Tanner said. "Nothing with the raw chemical volatility to make a bomb, if that's what you're thinking. *Maybe* a stink bomb, if we're lucky."

"Poisons? Laxatives, even? Come on, work with me."

Tanner put down the microscope slide a little too forcefully and took a deep breath. "I'm not going to help you attack them. God, in His providence, saw fit to cross our paths with a band of pirates with a problem that I may be uniquely equipped to address. I'm going to play this out and trust in His will on the matter."

"But you said yourself you don't know anything about treating this species," Eve said. "How are you uniquely equipped for this?"

Tanner pursed his lips and stayed silent. He didn't want to share his demonic possession theory at the moment; Eve wasn't a believer in the supernatural, so it would only serve to destroy any confidence she had in him. "Where I lack," he finally said, "God will provide."

With his slide prepared, Tanner flicked on the light for the microscope and peered inside. The bulk of the cells within the view were saddle-shaped; Tanner switched between the microscope and the reference pictures on the tablet a few times before he was satisfied that the oxygen-bearing blood cells were normal. A few spindly specimens were leukocytes, along with small dots of platelets. Tanner scanned the slide intently, looking for any other cells that didn't belong. Nothing. He backed out on the magnification, looking for larger multicellular parasites. Still nothing. No sign of infection.

Tanner pulled the slide back out from the microscope. He stared at it for a brief second as frustration bubbled up in his chest. The answer had to be somewhere, and he prayed that the problem was medical. If it were spiritual, then that was a battle he was not prepared to enter into alone. Without Andrew. He clutched the slide in his hand until the glass edges bit into the skin of his palm. With a burst of rage he hurled it at the wall. It didn't even give a satisfying sound, but rather just a tinkle of glass as it tumbled from the wall to the counter.

"You OK?" Eve asked.

Tanner removed his glasses and rubbed at the bridge of his nose. "Just back to square one."

"Come on, what else can we test?" Eve asked. He could tell from her tone she was trying to cheer him up. It wasn't working.

"The blood was a long shot. A parasite causing neurological

symptoms would be much more likely found in the cerebrospinal fluid. But getting a sample would be risky with what we have on hand. I'd give my right arm for a proper MRI."

"Well, what would it take to get one?"

"An MRI machine, of course. Which would only be found in a well-stocked hospital. We didn't even have one at the clinic on Trenth."

"We couldn't build one?"

Tanner chuckled. "It requires a very powerful, and very precisely controlled magnet."

Eve folded her arms smugly. "And we have one."

"We do?"

"Yeah, the Inter-Stellar drive. It's got a big-ass electromagnet at the core. And I *guarantee* you that the spatial mechanics involved in FTL travel require much more precise control than a brain scan."

"OK, but there's also an RF receiver component. Not to mention all the computer programming to actually interpret the signals and convert it to an image."

"We've got spare parts for the comms systems," Eve said. "I could probably jury-rig any radio equipment required if I have the technical specs. And if Neekol got you that medical database, maybe he can get his hands on the programming we need. Let him put his hacking skills to good use. Worth a shot."

The idea was a stretch, a big one, but it did give him hope. Although his cynicism reminded him of a potential problem. "That's a lot of moving parts," Tanner said. He glanced back over his shoulder to make sure no one was evesdropping. "If that X-ray scanner was sabotaged after all, the saboteur might try something here too."

"Well, we're going to need the other crew's full participation to access *Malika*'s systems to set it up. There's no way we can run the OpSec we'd need to keep one of them from sabotaging it."

"True. But keep in mind that you'll be critical in pulling this off. Which may make you a target."

Eve sighed. "What else is new?"

Tanner chuckled. After all, she'd had a target on her back for a while; it's why she was running around with them in a war zone. "Well, we certainly have our work cut out for us. You know, you're not a bad assistant after all."

"Yeah, just remember you said that next time I'm up for a raise. Now let's go talk to Neekol."

Even expecting the smell, Eve was still a bit taken aback. Most alien species had their distinctive odor, but Neekol's room was stronger than most. Although that may have been a matter of hygiene. Men were disgusting left on their own, and Neekol was no exception. His quarters looked more like a college dorm room than it had any right to.

"Come," said Neekol, gesturing her inside. "You need files?"

"Yeah," Eve said, scanning the room for somewhere to sit. She decided not to risk it. "We need to do an MRI scan. We're looking for technical specs and a software interface to interpret it."

She spent a few minutes explaining the plan to him, and Neekol took extensive hand-written notes, bobbing his head up and down as he contemplated the task. Finally, he had everything he needed.

"Plan approved?" he asked.

"What, with Bellig?" Eve replied. "Hadn't brought it up with her yet. I figured it would be better to figure out if it was feasible first, before getting everyone's hopes up."

Neekol nodded. "False hope hurts morale."

"Better to lie to people than get their hopes up for nothing, right? Especially if you need the extra hands around."

Neekol hung his head and turned his face away slightly from Eve. "Best not hurt friends. Hard though."

"Andrew was telling me... well, he told me that you and Carter were best friends on the ship. He doesn't seem like the friendly sort. What do you two even have in common?"

Neekol turned his head around to look at Eve. He was silent for a moment before he spoke. "Sad story. Not mine to tell. Lost everything."

Well, not quite everything, Eve thought. *Not Earth.* "He had family on that ship, didn't he?"

"Like said, not my story. But my story same."

"A lot of people have that same story," Eve said. "What's your version?"

Neekol turned his head back to the computer and began typing.

"Long ago. First chapter. Not good read again."

Eve nodded and stood up. "Well, thanks for the help. Let me know if you need anything else.

Neekol kept working.

Chapter Nine

Ghenni leaped from the branch, arced through the air, and slammed into the branch on the next tree. His hands scrambled to find purchase on the slick bark, and he soon had both arms wrapped around the thick limb. The one below it was near enough that once he'd regained his balance, he could just drop down a few inches and hurry to hold on to the trunk.

"You OK?" Andrew asked. Ghenni nodded, panting.

Travel through the treetops was slow. They were able to find the tapping scars in the bark of some of the trees, and when their path took them across other species, they found that the natives had left scratches to mark the path. However, the path was intended for a people more nimble than they were, especially in their tired, injured, and half-concussed state.

The sun was at its highest now, but this deep into the jungle, it was only evidenced by occasional shafts of piercing sunlight and the oppressive, sticky heat. Sporadic animal calls in the distance, and the rustle of leaves and shrubs on the ground reminded them that they weren't alone. A shrill cry of *ah-ah-ah-ah-ah* sounded from behind them.

"I do not think that be a bird," Ghenni said. He shimmied down a limb, testing the flex beneath his feet to see how far he could go before jumping to the next tree.

"What makes you say that?" Andrew asked, leaning against the trunk behind him.

"It comes from in front, then behind, back and forth. If it is one creature or many, it is circling us."

"Could just be a mating call or something," Andrew said. He didn't seem confident, though. Andrew had been raised in the city, but Ghenni knew from his childhood what it was to be stalked in the wilderness by a predator. He could *feel* it.

"No," Ghenni said, pausing on the branch. "This follows us. Always ahead and behind, we never pass it. It's waiting for a chance."

"Let's be extra sure we don't fall then, OK?"

Ghenni nodded, then took the next leap. This was an easier jump; the tree had branches galore, which grew thick with vines. If he slipped, Ghenni wasn't sure he'd hit the ground before getting caught in the tangle of growth. But he didn't, and landed easily on the branch. This would be a good place to climb back up higher, to put some more distance between them and the ground.

Andrew landed behind him once Ghenni was safely nestled in the bundle of vines along the trunk, and the limb shuddered with the impact. Ghenni felt a slight sting across his scalp; the insects had been thick through the night, but none of them had seemed to be biters or stingers until now. He raised his hand to swat it away, and felt a branch just above his head.

"Uh, Ghenni?" Andrew looked at him with wide eyes. Ghenni stepped back and looked at the branch. It wasn't there just a moment ago. And it had feathers near the end, and a pale stone tip lodged into the trunk. An arrow.

"Move!"

Ghenni scrambled up the vines as quickly as he could as more calls of *ah-ah-ah-ah-ah* resounded through the forest in every direction. His hands slipped on the damp vines, so he dug his fingernails as best he could. Sticky blue resin seeped out where he tore the flesh, but he hoisted himself up to the next branch up.

More arrows *thwacked* against the tree, some striking the trunk and branches, while others deflected off of the soft vines and clattered down to the ground. Ghenni's arms burned as he furiously grabbed whatever handholds presented themselves to pull himself up higher, out of range of the archers on the ground. Andrew followed close behind.

As Ghenni heaved himself onto the next level of branches, bent over one at the waist, he heard a yelp of pain from below. He looked back down and saw Andrew clutching at the vines with one hand, and with the other grabbing at an arrow lodged in his calf.

"Take my hand!" Ghenni yelled. Laying down, he reached as low as he could to pull Andrew up. Andrew took his outstretched hand and tried to pull himself up with the other as Ghenni assisted. Andrew pushed off with his one good leg, but a small rivulet of blood trickled down the injured one from the embedded arrow.

Ghenni's arms burned from the effort; he had little strength left after traveling all night. But with a prayer to Mennas, he lifted with all his might and brought Andrew up to the branch with him. As he did, he felt it shudder with the impact of something else. Looking down the branch, he saw a figure, perhaps five feet tall and covered in deep blue scales. It stood on the end of the branch, wielding a long club studded with jagged stones that looked like they could tear flesh as easily as any blade, and ten times as messy. Looking farther up, the man had gills along his neck, and symmetrical protrusions on his face that had the rough appearance of coral, culminating in two horn-like spires four inches long.

He pointed his club at Andrew and barked out words that sounded harsh, but fluid. "*Eeneun byuleseo on gushinga?*"

"We... we come in peace," Ghenni said.

Andrew pulled his leg in close, clutching at the arrow wound, but his face was more confused than pained. To Ghenni's surprise, he replied in what sounded like the same language. "*Neo, nae eoneo hana. Dareun eengan ana?*"

The one with the club turned to a pair of similar people who nimbly lowered themselves from branches above. "*Eedeul Jun Ha hante dereego ga. Geueui saramdeureun yeogiseo bohoreul badeulkeoya.*"

"You speak their language?" Ghenni asked Andrew, without taking his eyes off of the alien man.

"No," Andrew said. "Somehow, they speak mine. That's Korean. I'm not sure how, but I guess God has provided. We're going with them." He turned to address the aliens. "*Wooreeneun neohuideulgwa pyeonghwarobgae galgae. Woorineun akuineun eobseo.*"

"If you say so."

The cargo hold of the *Malika* filled with the whine of a heavy-duty winch, as it strained with the effort of lifting the Inter-Stellar drive out of the pit in the floor. The huge piece of machinery hung by chains from the hook, swaying in a slow rhythm as it rose in the air. A dozen massive silver-colored coils protruded from its surface at regular intervals, and a 2-foot cylinder lay horizontally in the core, with pale blue light glinting out from the seams. Countless hoses and cables still connected it to an array of ports down in the pit. Eve gave it a quick once-over to check for damage or wear as it came into view

"You might want to back up, Carter," Damien said, glancing back at their guard. "Hate for your gun to get caught by the magnetic field."

Carter took a single step backward, his rifle at a low ready. "Do I need to empty my p-pockets?" he asked sarcastically.

"If you don't, any loose change we have to pry off of the drive gets added to the coffee fund."

Carter huffed and took a second step back. It wasn't much, but Eve knew the magnetic field was contained enough not to reach that far; Damien just wanted to keep prying eyes away from him as he worked in the pit. He hopped down, and the top of the pit came about chest high on him.

The winch *thunked* to a stop, just as a couple of the cables had begun to be pulled taut. The blue light inside the drive shut off.

"Ready to flush the drive core!" Eve called out from a few feet away. She sat on a small crate with a computing tablet propped up on a larger crate in front of her like a desk. A data cable snaked along the floor to a socket on the wall near the exit to the front of the ship. From here she had a complete feed of all the diagnostic and calibration data for the drive, and it gave her the green light to proceed.

"Flushing!" Damien called back. Eve looked over casually, to see if she could spot what he was up to down there. This was a smugglers' ship, and there were compartments everywhere, including inside the drive chamber. It was small, and they didn't store metal cargo there, but it held a few packets of gemstones of dubious pedigree to serve as emergency cash supplies. More importantly, they kept a couple of weapons stashed there: a ceramic combat knife, and plastic gun with Teflon-jacketed ceramic bullets. It wasn't terribly accurate, and wouldn't survive past a single use of the nine-round magazine it was equipped with, but it was made for concealment, and it was the best weapon they had access to at the moment.

Gases hissed as the fuel and coolant drained back into the bowels of the ship. After several long moments, green lights lit up on the computer display.

"Flushing complete!" Eve shouted. Damien climbed up the step ladder back out of the pit and adjusted his pants. Eve hurried over to help Damien with the next step. In a professional shop, they'd either be in orbit and shut off the artificial gravity, or they'd have an anti-grav sled. In this case, they'd just have to be *extra* careful.

Damien twisted the large handle to disengage the drive core. It slid slowly out of the socket, and Eve moved to catch the handles on the back end as they emerged. The core wasn't heavy; even when full, the fuel was gaseous, and the components inside had a lot of empty space. The trouble was that that empty space was *very* carefully calibrated. Eve didn't know what kind of warranty a drive like this would come with from the factory, but if Damien hadn't bought this drive third-hand fresh off the back of a truck, they would have just voided it for sure.

Carrying the drive core between them, Damien and Eve lowered it gently onto a pile of shipping foam, then tied it down to the floor with ratchet straps. Damien gave the strap a tug. "That's not going anywhere," he said.

"Did everything go OK down there?" Eve asked, glancing over at Carter on the other side of the pit. Carter took a few paces to the side to keep them in view on the other side of the dangling drive.

"Yeah, I love working on the drive. Just got shivers running up my leg, you know?" Eve glanced down at his pant leg and could barely make out the outline of the concealed pistol. Not noticeable at all if you didn't know what to look for. "What do you need for this scan?" he asked.

Eve sighed and rubbed at her temples. "Neekol got us the MRI specs. I've got to calibrate the drive's magnets to the right field configuration. Then I need to jury-rig the RF coils, calibrate the positioning, and Neekol will work out the interface with the imaging software."

"Anything I can do?" Damien asked.

"You've seen me calibrate the magnets enough times, right? If you can handle that, I might take a run at Carter, see if we can get anything out of him."

"Specs are loaded already? Go for it. What's your play? Seduction?"

Eve shook her head. "If that were an option, I would have caught him looking by now. Men aren't as subtle as they think they are. Just gonna see if I can get him talking."

Eve meandered over toward Carter as Damien took a seat at her computer. The drive started whirring as the magnets fired up, but Carter's grip on his weapon didn't seem to be affected. Eve briefly considered the idea of trying to jump him now. She might be able to maneuver him closer to the drive when they turned it back on, maybe cost him his weapon. Damien couldn't draw on him fast enough, but he was no slouch in a fist-fight, if he could neutralize the rifle. On the other hand, Tenik was manning the guard post on top of the pirate ship, while Tanner was inside with Bellig, Amber, and Neekol. There was no way even the two of them could take out Tenik without firing the rifle, which would leave the three leftover pirates plenty of warning to take Tanner hostage and dig in. She didn't like those odds.

"Hey Carter," she said when she got closer. She kept her hands shoved in her pockets to seem as casual as possible. "It seems like a shame we haven't had a chance for a real conversation."

"Don't f-fraternize with the enemy," he said. Without a subject to the sentence, Eve wasn't sure if it was a statement or a command.

"I think 'enemy' is a bit of a stretch. After all, we're both human. Not a lot of us out here in Brotherhood space. That's gotta count for something. You were on one of the old colony ships, right?"

Carter sighed. He kept his gaze alternating between Damien and Eve, avoiding eye contact as he maintained stone-faced impassivity. "Don't like to t-talk about it."

"Fine, fine," Eve said. She drummed her fingers on her leg for a moment before continuing. "You seem like a military guy to me, right? Damien is too, you know. Where did you serve?"

Carter shifted his stance and pursed his lips. "You're trying to f-figure out what makes me tick, right? Well, let m-me tell you. I do my job. I like my job. Maybe you think that b-because we're both human, I might not shoot you if I get the order. But you'd b-be wrong. I signed up for the Merchant Space Marine because I like to use my g-gun, and I like money. You know what happens if you step out of line?"

Eve backed up instinctively. "Well, I guess then you'd get to use your gun, and you'd keep all of our money?"

"B-bingo."

"Fair enough," Eve said, throwing up her hands in surrender. "Message received." She strode back over to where Damien worked, nibbling on a pencil. "The man's a robot. No sentimentality at all. No way he's helping us."

"Then you'd better take over," Damien muttered, staring at the screen. "Because this is gonna have to work if we're going to get out of here."

Chapter Ten

The scaled aliens surrounded Andrew and Ghenni as they marched through the jungle in the early afternoon. There seemed to be safety in numbers, as they weren't accosted by any predators during the trip. Andrew noticed that when the aliens spoke among themselves, they used some other language of their own, comprised mostly of subvocalizations and hums; he imagined it was developed to be as intelligible as possible underwater. Unfortunately, Andrew's musings on xenolinguistics were interrupted by a half-buried stone that turned his foot. He stumbled and barely caught himself before sprawling on the ground. His leg wound, crudely wrapped in a strip torn from his shirt, blazed with fresh fire at the sudden jolt.

"How much further?" he asked in Korean.

"Soon," the leader said, looking back at him.

After several more minutes, the jungle grew steadily brighter. At first, Andrew thought it was the sun rising, but soon he saw breaks up ahead in the foliage, and the trees opened up into a large clearing. The transition was so sudden, Andrew guessed the clearing was artificial. At the center stood a concrete bunker, covered in vines and grime, with broken light fixtures at each corner. Surrounding it, perhaps a dozen thatch huts and a handful of large fires littered the area haphazardly. More of the aliens puttered around the village, cooking fish and other small animals on spits over the fires, filling the clearing with a mouth-watering scent. Others weaved nets and baskets or chased laughing children in circles.

A chorus of whispers and stares erupted as the villagers spotted Andrew and Ghenni emerging into the circle, and some of the aliens darted away to spread the word about the strangers. One of their escorts ran ahead to the bunker and disappeared inside. As they reached the structure, he reappeared, followed closely by a human. He was an Asian man, his graying hair roughly cut short, and sporting a thick beard. He wore the tattered remains of a Consortium military uniform, patched with scraps of discolored cloth. When he spotted Andrew, he froze for a second, then rushed forward and grabbed him in a bear hug.

"Welcome," he said. "I haven't seen another human in so long, I thought I would die here alone!"

"Thank you," Andrew said. It was all he could think to say.

"Is this your friend?" the man asked, pulling away and looking at Ghenni. He hurriedly ran a sleeve across his watering eyes. "Or are one of you a captive of the other?"

"A friend and colleague," Andrew said. "Do you speak English? I would like to include him in the conversation."

"Of course, of course," the man said, switching to lightly accented English. "You must be American. Where are my manners? My name is Park Jun-Ha. Most Americans end up calling me Junior."

"I'm Andrew Cho, and this is Ghenni."

"You must be parched." The man barked an order in another language, and a pair of natives went scurrying off into one of the huts. "I'm sorry to be forward, but do you have a ship? I would love nothing more than to get off of this god-forsaken rock." He glanced around at the alien soldiers surrounding them. "Don't worry about offending them. They don't speak English."

"Well," Andrew said, wincing, "Yes and no. It's kind of a long story."

"We have been attacked by pirates," Ghenni said. "Then held captive on the beach, some miles away."

Jun-Ha sighed. "Well, it is better than I'd hoped for this morning. Since you travel together, does that mean the war is over?"

"Just how out-of-date are you?" Andrew asked.

"Well, I lost contact with my chain of command in standard year 2237. I haven't kept up with the timekeeping here very well."

"That's been fifteen Earth years then," Andrew said. He let out a deep breath. "A lot's changed. The Consortium and Brotherhood have been officially in a cease-fire for the last five years or so, but still very much at war. This planet is in Brotherhood space, but near the border."

"But you two travel together?"

"We're medical missionaries. Well, I am anyway. Ghenni here is our nurse. We were chased into the jungle by giant crabs, but the rest of our crew is still with the pirates. Our ship's been impounded until we cure their captain who's fallen ill."

"What kind of defenses?" Jun-Ha asked. He smoothed his beard and looked intently at Andrew, waiting for details. As he did, the aliens re-emerged from the tent with stone bowls full of water.

"I'm sorry, we can get back to that, but first... are we prisoners?" He gestured around him to the aliens who still stood guard with weapons out, then took one of the offered bowls and drained it in one gulp as Jun-Ha answered.

"Ah, forgive me for my rudeness. I must have forgotten my manners after all these years. You're injured too. I don't have much in the way of medical supplies, but I have managed to brew some crude alcohol to disinfect that wound. Come, let's go somewhere to sit more comfortably." Jun-Ha shouted an order in a crude approximation of the aliens' language, and the alien warriors bowed from the waist before departing. "Join me inside."

Andrew and Ghenni followed Jun-Ha into the bunker. He picked up a battered electric lamp from the floor and carried it with him to light the way down a set of stairs set in the concrete corridor. The compound had a musty, damp smell to it, no doubt due to a non-functioning ventilation system. A few side rooms were labeled in Korean, with faded colored lines tracing paths along the floor. The torchlight cast shadows against the walls of the cabinets and electronic equipment that packed the pathways. Judging by the gear, this had been some kind of comms outpost.

The old soldier finally led them into a meeting room on the second basement level, and gestured for his visitors to seat themselves at a large hardwood conference table. A tattered map hung with one drooping corner from the wall, while a large portion of the room was filled with metal crates. Jun-Ha flipped on a light, evidently still running on some sort of generator, then rummaged through one of the crates and produced an old wine bottle.

"Do not get your hopes up," he said. "I drank the wine long ago and reused the bottle. This is more like rum, brewed from a local fruit. Potent stuff, better suited for stripping paint than drinking, but it should do a fine job of disinfecting that arrow wound."

"Soap would be better," Andrew said, sitting down and pulling up a second chair to prop up his leg. "Alcohol can slow down the healing process." He unwrapped the makeshift bandage, and examined the wound on his calf closely for the first time. The cloth was soaked through with blood, but fresh bleeding was minimal. The arrow hadn't penetrated deeply, but he'd been marched through the jungle since then, so the muscle had been torn further, and his sweat had left the wound with a rank stench. All in all, it looked better than he guessed from the pain. "And tweezers if you have them."

Jun-Ha produced a large combat knife and wiped it off on his pant leg. "Best I can do."

Andrew tore off a fresh bandage from his already tattered pants and soaked it with the liquor, then set about cleaning around his wound with it. "So what's your story?" Andrew asked. "This looks like a Consortium outpost, so what happened?"

Jun-Ha sat down and propped his feet up on the table. "I was a lieutenant in the 205th SigInt Brigade, of the Joseon Colonies Defense Force. We established an outpost on this island to maintain a signal relay. It was Consortium space at the time, but close to the front, so it was crucial for battlefield communications and broadcasting propaganda to Brotherhood planets."

"I thought we were in Brotherhood territory," Ghenni said. He sat down next to Andrew and used the knife to pick out bits of debris as they spoke.

"The battle lines shifted quickly, a few months after we were established. We were cut off from supply lines and ordered to go dark until the area was reclaimed, to avoid detection. That never happened."

"They never mounted a rescue mission?" Andrew asked.

Jun-Ha leaned back and chuckled. "They did! Unfortunately, I had gone into the jungle to forage for food when they arrived. No notice, and they were detected as soon as they dropped out of IS so couldn't stay long enough to go find me. Someone had scrawled in the sand out there on the beach, 'will return,' but this time, they didn't."

"Did the natives live with you this whole time?" Ghenni asked.

"No, this island was uninhabited when we arrived. The people here, I call them the Badasal, are aquatic nomads. They follow the migratory patterns of the fish they hunt for food. They showed up about a year after I was abandoned, and were intrigued by the construction of the bunker, and the small bit of agriculture I'd developed. Concept was entirely foreign to them. So together we've worked out how to survive here on this island."

Andrew cinched up the new, clean bandage on his wound, but before he could ask any more questions, the faint strains of a horn blowing from the surface interrupted him. Jun-Ha sighed, then stood up.

"I don't suppose either of you know how to shoot?" he asked as he strode briskly toward the hall.

"Those jungle beasts are attacking?" Ghenni asked.

Jun-Ha paused in the doorway. "Worse. We're at war."

Father Tanner climbed the ladder to administer the sedative one more time, in preparation for the brain scan. It was getting to be almost routine at this point. He noted the level of the medicine in its canister as he did. They seemed to be using it faster than he expected, so they couldn't afford too many more diagnostic sessions like this; they had to save some for any potential surgery.

"What are you going to do to draw him over?" Amber asked. She stood in the doorway, sipping on a mug of some kind of tea. The scent of burnt artificial grounds mixed with the musty, acrid odor of the water tank to form an unpleasant combination that put Tanner off of lunch for the day.

"Same thing as usual, I suppose," he said. He produced the crucifix necklace from under his shirt and began praying.

"Our Father, who art in heaven, hallowed be Thy name..."

Tanner paused. As yet there was no sign of movement within the tank, though he couldn't see to the other side.

"Thy kingdom come, Thy will be done, on Earth as it is in heaven."

Still nothing. Tanner listened intently for any indication of where Lopuul might be within the tank.

"Something wrong?" Amber asked.

Tanner held out a hand to shush her. He thought he heard something bubbling on the other end of the room. As he reached for the control panel to adjust the volume of the microphones, a warning flashed on the screen in bright red letters.

"What's wrong?" Amber asked, setting her cup down on the floor.

"Medical alarm," Father Tanner said. "Sensors are picking up blood in the tank."

"Oh God, what's happening?"

"I'll have to go check." He stripped off his outer shirt and climbed the rest of the way up the ladder, then jumped into the tank. Some of the tepid water splashed into his mouth, foul with acid and foreign biological matter. A few powerful strokes carried him to the other end of the tank where he saw the thrashing shape of Lopuul, surrounded by a rapidly-expanding cloud of red fluid. The squid creature lashed at its own body with some implement that Tanner couldn't identify, tearing roughly at the flesh of its torso.

The doctor dove down into the water, grasping at the captain's tentacles to stop whatever weapon it held. Lopuul slashed it at Tanner, and he felt rough stone rake across his arm, drawing some of his own blood to add to the mess. The acid in the water burned in the wound, but Tanner tried again, grappling with the alien's tentacles and finally finding a grip on the one with the weapon, which seemed to be some kind of coral implement. Sharp, but not well-suited for combat.

As he held on to the offending limb in a death grip, the other tentacles slammed into his torso, threatening to drive what little remaining air he had out of his lungs. Tuudolians lived their whole lives underwater, and even as a trained boxer against manic convulsions, Tanner didn't stand a chance in a straight fight. He kicked off from the bottom of the tank and broke his head above the surface. Fresh air surged into his lungs, and he used it all to shout, "Sedative!"

The captain pulled Tanner back under as soon as he got the word out, and one of the loose tentacles grabbed the piece of coral from the grappled one, and lashed out at Tanner again. He turned his face just in time for the weapon to graze his cheek instead of gouging an eye. Tanner kicked again, trying to maneuver Lopuul closer to the tank entrance, where he hoped Amber was deploying the sedative. Another blow came at his torso, but Tanner managed to catch the tentacle before it made contact.

He turtled up, drawing his arms in close as he grappled the creature, protecting his lungs from any more blows. The two of them struggled for what seemed like an eternity. Tanner's lungs felt ready to burst as he struggled to get back above the surface for air. More cuts and scratches across his body lit up with stinging pain, and blunt impacts promised to become bruises later.

At some point, Tanner noticed a sickly sweet taste to the water that made it into his mouth, and he thought he could detect a yellowish tinge. Lopuul's motions slowed in the water until he finally stopped moving on his own. Tanner took the opportunity to push to the surface and catch his breath with a gasp.

"Are you OK?" Amber asked, reaching out to him. "You look torn to shreds."

"I've had to wrestle patients before," Tanner said, letting her pull him to the edge of the tank, "but not like this." Tanner carried the unconscious captain with him, and pried the piece of coral from his clutching tentacle. As he hung onto the edge of the tank, he examined it. It wasn't just a decorative object; it was carved in the shape of a horrific creature, similar to a skate or ray, but with a wide maw of sinister-looking teeth.

"Do you know what this is?" Tanner asked.

Amber took the sculpture from him and turned it over. "I haven't seen it before, but I think I've heard Lopuul describe it before. I think he calls it 'Lord of the Depths,' or something like that. I guess he prays to it."

"So he's not only self-mutilating," Tanner muttered, "but performing it ritually with a carved idol."

"Does that mean something?" Amber asked. "Like, for his diagnosis?"

"I'm afraid it just might," Tanner said. "Remember when I mentioned it might be a case of demonic possession?"

"Right, even I can see how this would fit," Amber said. "Not that

I'm saying I believe in it, though. And I wouldn't go mentioning it to Bellig or Tenik. They're not exactly open-minded about that kind of stuff."

"I'm not surprised," Tanner said. He heaved himself out of the tank with a slosh of water. The clang of footsteps announced the arrival of Bellig, carrying a rifle.

"What's going on in here?" she barked. "Is the captain OK?"

"We're fine," Amber said. "He was... having a seizure or something. The doctor had to jump in and save him."

Bellig grunted, but scanned the room for signs of trouble. "Thanks, then."

"No problem," Tanner said, wincing with pain as he stepped down from the ladder.

"Have you gotten closer to figuring out what's wrong with him?" Bellig asked.

He glanced at Amber, who met his eyes and shook her head discretely. "No, not yet," he finally said. "Is the MRI ready?"

"Almost," Bellig said. "You should get cleaned up."

"Somebody order calamari?" Damien shouted as he and Carter walked into the cargo hold, carrying a rolling cart between the two of them and setting it down on the floor. Tanner jumped to his feet, waving Amber away from putting another bandage on his cut-up face, and moved to meet him. Damien had to admire the doctor's tenacity; he wasn't going to let a few lacerations slow him down.

Almost the whole of both crews were assembled inside the cargo hold of the *Malika*. Bellig and Tenik stood guard, Bellig with a rifle at a low ready, and Tenik standing with arms crossed, but with a large pistol and combat knife holstered on his belt. Neekol was huddled up next to Eve, both of them studying the computer screen intently. There in the center of the hold was the IS drive, stripped of its core but humming with powerful electromagnets, hanging by plasteel chains and stabilized by ratchet straps held taut against hooks in the floor.

"We need to transfer him to the board," Tanner said. Amber followed behind him and grabbed a thick, flat piece of plastic from where it leaned against the wall. It had been cut to fit inside the drive, so they could slide the captain in place. Damien and Carter lifted the unconscious alien and let her slide it underneath, then they took hold of the board and brought it closer to the drive

"Stop!" Eve shouted, leaping to her feet. Damien and Carter both froze in place. "I'm picking up a fluctuation in the magnetic field. Did you guys get rid of all of the metal on you?"

Damien's mind raced. He couldn't think of anything metal in his pockets, but if he had to strip down to find it, he *did* have that ceramic gun. That would be embarrassing to reveal here in front of everyone, to say the least.

"Carter," he said, doing his best to keep his voice level. "You got any hidden weapons, or a cold, robot heart you forgot about?"

Carter swore under his breath. "L-let's back up," he said. The two of them withdrew from the drive and set the captain back down. Then Carter dug inside his pants and produced a small hidden blade from inside his waistband. "Sorry, forgot. Didn't r-realize you could pick that up."

"There's not telling what kind of damage it could have done to the drive if it got pulled in," Eve said. "Not to mention the captain."

Once they were clear, Damien and Carter tried again. After a nod of approval from Eve watching the computer, they inserted the board along with the patient inside the drive. It was a tight squeeze, and Lopuul's rubbery flesh brushed along the edges of the cavity, but he made it in with only the tips of his tentacles hanging out.

"Start the scan!" Tanner called out.

"So what's the plan if you don't find anything?" Damien muttered under his breath. He glanced over at the Trenthans standing guard.

"If there's nothing on the scan, we only have one procedure left to try," Tanner said. "And it's risky."

"You think Carter's little indiscretion with that knife was deliberate? Eve said you were worried about sabotage."

"What do you think he would have done?" Tanner asked. "Stab him?"

"Well maybe he thought the knife would get pulled inside and stab him accidentally or something. I don't know how his mind works."

"It's possible, I guess. I'd prefer to focus on the diagnosis.

"Sounds par for the course. But if you don't find the problem, I need you to stall for time."

"What for?"

"I think I can flip Amber. I just need time to get one of the Trenthans on our side. I think that would tip the balance in our favor."

Tanner started to answer, but the hum of the magnets winding up drowned him out. Loud thumps reverberated through the cargo hold as the scan began. He hustled over to the computer to watch the results over Eve's shoulder and Damien ambled after him, followed by their heavily-armed shadows.

"Get anything yet?"

"Yeah," Eve said, "looks like we're getting some images. No idea what I'm looking at, though."

"We're still at the top of the head," Tanner said. "Haven't hit the brain tissue yet. The scan will proceed down the body, so we should see something useful soon."

"What exactly will this detect?" Bellig asked.

"Any abnormalities in the tissues, like tumors or things like that," Tanner replied.

Bellig stared thoughtfully at the screen. "What could have caused a tumor?"

"Usually a cancer," Tanner said.

"And what would have caused that?"

"Any number of things. Random genetic mutations can be caused by chemical contamination, infection, radiation, and so on." Bellig started to speak again, but Tanner held up a hand to cut her off. "Hold on, we're getting into the brain tissue,"

Damien had seen enough MRI images in his time to at least recognize he was looking at a brain, even if he didn't know what exactly to look for *in* the brain. The image on the screen morphed and mutated as the two-dimensional images progressed down the length of the captain's brain. Suddenly Tanner sat up and pointed at the screen.

"Pause the image there," he said. Eve hit a button and the scan froze in place on a single slice on the brain. Damien wasn't sure what captured the doctor's interest, but Tanner pointed at a particular spot near the edge. "There. It's a mass of some kind. It looks like it's growing out of the brain tissue and pressing on the skull cartilage."

"You think that's the issue?" Eve asked.

"It would be quite the coincidence if it wasn't. Pressure on the brain like that could cause all manner of neurological issues like what we've seen."

"How can you treat it?" Tenik asked.

"Surgery is probably the best option, especially since this tumor doesn't seem to be relatively small. Radiation is tricky, especially for Tuudolians; they aren't as tolerant of radiation as you and I are, since they're made to live underwater."

"Brain surgery," Tenik muttered. "Great."

"A tumor?" Bellig asked. "Can you tell what caused it?"

"Not from this," Tanner replied, shaking his head. "Like I said, it could be radiation, disease, carcinogenic chemicals..."

"I thought you said you already tested for chemicals," Bellig said. "And disease."

"Some, but not everything, and I was mostly concerned with toxins that would produce psychosis directly. Carcinogens creating a brain tumor is another story."

"Do we even have the equipment to deal with that?" Bellig asked.

"Surgery would require a long time out of the water," Tanner said. "We'd need an artificial respirator to keep him alive on the operating table for long enough."

"So where do we get this artificial respirator?" Tenik asked. "Can we make one?"

Tanner shook his head. "A diagnostic machine is one thing. Lifesaving equipment? I wouldn't want to risk it."

"Better to risk it than leave him to die for certain," Bellig said.

"Unless we could find one," Tanner said.

Tenik rubbed at his scalp in frustration. "And where would we find one?"

"Well, you're pirates, aren't you?" So steal one. Any Tuudolian planet or large ship should have one available."

"You want us to raid a Brotherhood planet?" Bellig looked at the doctor in disbelief.

Tanner shrugged. "It's your captain. I'm just telling you what you need to do to save him."

"It's too much," Bellig said, nodding her head. "Too much of a risk for a slim chance of saving him."

"He'd do the same for any of us," Tenik said. "You know he would."

Bellig pursed her lips. "Not in front of them," she finally said. She turned to Tanner. "Give us a chance to discuss it. We'll let you know what we decide."

Chapter Eleven

Ghenni and Andrew hustled back up the steps as Jun-Ha led the way with the lit lamp. The two of them lagged behind on account of their injuries, but they eventually emerged back into the sunlight. Jun-Ha barked an order in Korean, and a nearby Badasal carrying a short spear reported back.

"What's happening?" Ghenni asked.

"One of our sentries spotted a scout in the distance," Jun-Ha said. "Probably never intended to make landfall, but it could be probing our defenses and readiness. Come with me." He gestured for the two of them to follow him, and set off at a brisk stride toward one of the larger huts

"Who would attack you?" Ghenni asked.

"The Badasal are organized into tribes. From what I gather, they got in occasional skirmishes in the past, fighting over the best fishing waters, that kind of thing. But ever since I settled here, it threw the power balance out of whack. I don't know if it was us developing agriculture, or being on the receiving end of my laser rifle, but all the tribes seem fairly united against us at this point."

Jun-Ha stepped into the hut and the others followed. A handful of woven grass mats covered the floor as a sleeping area, and numerous seashells and other trinkets hung from the thatch walls. Jun-Ha went to a pile of animal pelts on the far end, and tossed the top skin off; underneath was a metal crate with Korean writing on it.

"You have laser rifles?" Andrew asked.

"Yeah, but don't get too excited." Jun-Ha opened the lid of the crate to reveal its cargo: a trio of battered, white plastic rifle-like contraptions, yellowed with age and stained with use. A couple of spare batteries lay haphazardly in with them. "They're great when you have dependable supply lines and repair facilities, but I'd kill for a good old-fashioned JP-208 and a box of bullets. I've got these three laser rifles I've managed to keep in working order, but the focus arrays are under 50 percent efficiency on all of them, and I don't have enough energy reserves to properly train anyone else. We've been relying on earthwork fortifications and proper military tactics to make up for the numbers disadvantage."

"Great," Andrew muttered to Ghenni. "Like we needed to get caught up in another war."

"If you help us," Ghenni said to Jun-Ha, "we could take back our own ship. We could get you home."

"Oh, I intend to, and I appreciate it. But not yet. I can't abandon my tribe right before an attack. And *technically*, I still have standing orders to protect this outpost. I can't be splitting my forces between two fronts. My men are stretched thin protecting this village as it is." Jun-Ha reached into the crate and pulled out one of the laser rifles, thrusting it out to the two newcomers. "Which brings me back to my previous question: can either of you shoot?"

Ghenni looked at Andrew, who shook his head. "I have fired a rifle, but never a laser."

"That's beside the point," Andrew said. "I'm a missionary. I'm not going to get dragged into taking sides in someone else's war, just based on your say-so. No offense, but we *have* just met."

Jun-Ha stroked his beard and nodded his head sagely. "That's fair. But on the other hand, if our defenses are overrun, I would not expect the enemy to respect your neutrality as well as I do. You may be forced to fight out of necessity."

Ghenni sighed with resignation and held out his hands. "You'll need to show me how to operate it."

Tenik gave Damien a gentle shove into the ship galley, where the rest of the crew had gathered. All the cooking implements and tableware had been put away, but the stains of old food and grease splatter still speckled the walls. Bellig sat at the head of the table, scowling, flanked by Carter and Neekol; the former stood leaning against the table with his hand on his sidearm, while the latter tapped away at a computer tablet, glancing up to see that everyone was assembled before putting it down. Damien insinuated himself between Eve and Father Tanner, barely able to fit around the small table.

Once everyone had found a spot, Bellig cleared her throat and spoke up. "You've all heard by now about the findings of the brain scan on our captain. I know we all want him to recover quickly, so as second-in-command, I'm approving our next raid, with the primary goal of acquiring an artificial respirator to allow the doctor to perform brain surgery." Damien nudged Tanner with a smile.

"Go team, right?"

Bellig ignored the interruption. "We'll be splitting up for this job. Tenik will take the lead, assisted by Neekol. The doctor will accompany them to make sure they get the right equipment. They will take the captured ship-"

"Oh, hell no," Damien said, standing bolt upright. "Nobody touches those controls but me." Carter glared at Damien, then pulled a huge pistol from its holster and set it casually on the table, pointing at Damien. He slumped back down and muttered, "She has a name, you know."

"As I was saying," Bellig resumed pointedly, staring daggers at Damien, "Tenik will pilot the ship, and Neekol will handle any technical issues that might arise. For instance, booby traps or hidden protocols in the piloting controls. But I'm sure anything like that would have been disabled already, correct?"

"Never touch the stuff," Damien said. "I'd probably use it on myself accidentally."

"The target is on the planet of Tiluug. It's a Tuudolian colony planet, about 95 percent water, primarily used for fishing and mineral extraction."

"Bumpkins," Carter pitched in with a grunt, which is what passed for a chuckle with him. "Should b-be an easy target."

"There's a small spaceport on one of the few permanently dry islands, designated Tiluug-Gemmel-2. That's the target. There's enough infrastructure and sprawl there that they should have the equipment we need, but small enough for us to get past security." Bellig nodded at Neekol, who angled his tablet and hit a button to project an image on the bare table. A satellite picture in shades of green displayed the tiny landmass, with a small clump of gray metal and concrete buildings on one shore, dominated by a landing pad with a handful of small ships.

"Uh, not that I doubt your capability," Damien said, "but this is still a Brotherhood military outpost. Isn't a three-man—or two-man-one-priest—crew a little light to hit a facility like this?"

Neekol piped up, and his bird-like head snapped to face Damien. "Have stolen ID codes. Not burned yet. Pretend to be Brotherhood."

"I should go too then," Damien said. "Deception is more my thing." He thought he saw Eve twitch out of the corner of his eye, but he ignored it. "And I know the *Malika*'s controls, and all her little idiosyncrasies. You need me on this."

"I'm sure you'd love a chance to get the jump on me," Tenik said with a chuckle. "I think you need to stay here with more supervision."

"Agreed," Bellig said. "Anymore questions, or suggestions from *my* crew?"

"Any s-secondary objectives?" Carter asked.

"We could use more Tuudolian food and supplies," Bellig said. She turned to Tenik. "If you can get anything along those lines, go ahead, but not at the expense of the primary objective."

"If I may," Tanner said, raising his hand, "what is our cover going to be?"

"It's a cargo ship," Tenik said, "so we'll be posing as a small courier freighter. The doctor will be a captured prisoner of war, near enough to true. We're there to pick up the supplies to deliver to a battlecruiser."

"With no paper trail?" Damien asked.

"Part of the cover is that the cruiser is on a classified mission," Bellig said. "That's why they didn't requisition the supplies directly, and the commander isn't showing up in person."

"Will introduce virus," Neekol said. "Part of landing protocol handshake. Will fake clearance."

"It's not the worst plan I've heard," Damien muttered to Eve.

"I've definitely heard worse over the years," Eve agreed. Damien stuck out his tongue at her.

"If there's nothing else," Bellig said, "we leave as soon as we put the *Malika*'s IS drive back together. Let's get going."

The crews broke up and filtered out of the galley, off to make preparations for the trip. Damien sidled up to Eve and muttered under his breath, "They left all the tough ones with us. But a single edge counts more now."

"Just don't do anything that'll get us killed," Eve said. "At least, not any more of us."

Chapter Twelve

Andrew squeezed the trigger on his rifle, and the fruit in the targeting reticle sizzled and blackened within half a second. From the stories he'd heard, a laser rifle should have been able to punch through basic ballistic armor with no trouble, but this would have to do. After all, they weren't squaring off against modern infantry; the lasers should do to their flesh exactly what they did to the fruit. Andrew tried not to think about it. Another red globe on the tree disintegrated into ash as Ghenni fired a practice shot next to him.

"Good, good," Jun-Ha said, standing over them where they lay prone in the sandy clearing. "I think we'd better save the rest of the power for actual battle. You seem to have the hang of it well enough." He shifted into speaking Korean, and addressed one of the Badasal warriors who approached at a brisk pace. "What do you think, Goom?" He was a full head taller than Jun-Ha, with an impressively-muscled physique and prominent horn-like protrusions on his head. Andrew thought he was the one who spoke to him when they were first captured, but he couldn't be sure.

"They wield your sorcery with great skill," the blue alien replied in surprisingly passable Korean.

"I agree," Jun-Ha said. He turned back to Andew and Ghenni. "This is Geumyoil, or just Goom for short. He's my lieutenant here, and my most trusted adviser."

"Lord," Goom said, "two more scouts were seen moments ago. I expect an attack at nightfall."

"Unfortunate," Jun-Ha said, his face darkening. "Send word to the women to prepare dinner early. I want everyone fed and into position before nightfall."

"Very good, my lord," Goom replied. He gave a crisp salute and jogged back toward the village.

"You sure they'll wait until dark?" Andrew asked.

"Can't be sure, but the Badasal prefer to infiltrate and sneak attack when possible. Not enough of the bunker lighting is still working to offer much illumination anymore. Barely cuts through the foliage. But let's go take a tour of the defenses before dinner."

Andrew and Ghenni slung the rifles over their shoulders while Jun-Ha led them out to the beach. The sun already passed behind the trees, but out here where the jungle opened up, daylight still prevailed. About a dozen Badasal warriors, blue scales speckled with sand, huddled in a water-filled half-moon trench behind a berm of sand, chipping at flint and seashells. Propped up against the berm were dozens of javelins, and long, heavy clubs embedded with jagged bits of rock and coral.

"These are just your basic earthworks," Jun-Ha said. "Looks more or less like a regular sand dune if you're coming from the ocean. Now, can you spot the snipers?"

Andrew scanned the trees behind them, but didn't see anything. "You got me," he said.

Jun-Ha grinned mischievously, then grabbed a piece of dark driftwood and tossed it a few feet down the beach. "Snipers!" he called out. "Hit that wood, please." A few seconds later, two arrows flew from a tree on each side of the trench, embedding themselves in the sand right next to it.

"Pretty good, yes?" he said. "We've got camouflaged blinds from here to the village. Javelins and bows. Archery is a relatively new concept for the Badasal, and I've been helping them develop it, so we have the advantage in a long-range shoot-out, although those javelins are quite deadly at medium range."

"Impressive," Ghenni said. "I think I see them now, but would be surprised."

Jun-Ha led the back toward the village, pointing out more sniper nests hidden in the trees around them. The final line of defense was the bunker itself, with a heavy steel door and small window slits, whose plastic panes had been knocked or broken out.

"Those windows are too narrow to effectively enter. Very defensible, and we can still fire out." He led them further inside and gave them a better tour of the weapon stockpiles and other supplies. It was getting late into the afternoon by the time they finished preparing, and the tribe gathered around a number of fires within the village to eat a dinner of fish and some kind of root vegetable.

"Missionaries, then?" Jun-Ha asked as he tore off bits of flaky white flesh and popped them in his mouth. "Where were you on your way to?"

"I guess you could say we're between assignments at the moment," Andrew said. "My mentor and I used to run a free clinic on the planet of Trenth. A dusty, primitive planet with a spaceport slapped on. Eventually it got too hard to keep under the Brotherhood's radar, and we had to leave. We've been wandering around since then, on a smuggler's ship."

"Hmph," Jun-Ha grunted. "I don't go in much for religion, but if anybody needs some civilizing, it's these Badasal. He nodded over at a trio on the edge of the treeline who were involved in some kind of heated argument, complete with a lot of shoving. "Brutish, selfish people. If I hadn't been fortified in this bunker with my laser when they arrived, they'd have killed me as soon as look at me."

"Why are you concerned for them, then?" Ghenni asked.

Jun-Ha shrugged. "Feel responsible, I suppose. I've put them on the first steps to some kind of real civilization instead of barbarism. If I let it all fall apart, what do I have to show for the last fifteen years?"

"Surviving here seems like its own accomplishment," Ghenni said.

"Not dying is the easy part," Jun-Ha said. "At least until it's out of your control. But to look back at your life and realize it didn't count for anything? Now that's a hard thing to do."

"What do you plan to do when you get back home?" Andrew asked. "Did you have a family?"

The old soldier shook his head. "Career man, I'm afraid. Always thought I'd have time later. For all intents and purposes, these are my children here. As for what I'll do, I haven't decided if I'll be lauded as a hero, or shuffled into obscurity to cover up somebody's screw up. I'm guessing I either end up with a promotion and some cushy desk job, or else an honorable discharge and a future of scrubbing toilets."

A piercing scream interrupted the conversation. Andrew snapped his head to look, where one of the arguing trio lay impaled with a javelin, and the other two ran for a nearby hut. Jun-Ha shouted a command as a hail of javelins flew from the trees, catching a half-dozen of the Badasal unawares as they searched for the source of the disturbance. The others sprang into action, taking up weapons and running for defensive positions.

Andrew picked up his rifle from where it leaned against the log he sat on and sprang to his feet. He and Ghenni had been sitting in the center of the clearing, out of range of the volleys so far, but a horde of other Badasal surged from the trees with crude clubs and spears. Jun-Ha fired his rifle into the line of enemy tribesmen, sending one after another to the ground, clutching at grievous burn wounds.

"They've outflanked us!" Jun-Ha shouted over the cries of pain and battle. "Fall back to the bunker!" He repeated the command in Korean for the Badasal fighters, and they began to coalesce into a somewhat organized defense, forming a contracting hemisphere around the door to the concrete building. Goom took up a central position in the formation, looming over the other warriors with his impressive height. He batted aside a javelin aimed directly at him, and swung his club at a charging warrior. Even as the enemy moved to block it, the powerful weapon crashed through and landed square in the attacker's chest, sending him sprawling to the ground, as good as dead.

Andrew slipped inside and took up a position at the window with his rifle. He hesitated to fire at the attacking aliens, but as he watched the carnage, he heard shrieks of children and wailing of women among the battle cries. One young woman, carrying a small child in her arms, ran toward the door until a javelin struck her in the back. She tumbled to the ground, the child spilling out in front of her, and the attacking warrior strode purposefully toward them, drawing one of the jagged clubs. He reached with an open hand to grab the child, and Andrew had seen enough. He raised his rifle and sent a searing beam of energy at the monstrous attacker, burning a char-black hole into his side and toppling him instantly.

"Cover me!" he shouted at Ghenni. He pushed past the retreating villagers back out into the open and toward the child, who wailed uncomprehendingly at the scene around him. None of the other fleeing aliens even cast a glance at the orphaned child; after all, it wasn't theirs. Andrew limped toward him, scanning the battle with his rifle for any other immediate threats. A stray javelin stabbed into the sand mere feet from him, and he snapped the rifle up and fired at the attacker; the enemy managed to get out of the line of fire and retreated back into the cover of the treeline. When he reached the child, Andrew slung the rifle over his shoulder and scooped him up, running as fast as his injuries permitted back to the bunker as shouts followed close behind.

He was one of the last to get inside, and Jun-Ha slammed the door shut mere moments after him. The clang of stone spearheads resounded on the metal door. He pulled Ghenni and a couple of the archers back from the windows, then threw a large red switch on the back wall. Metals shutters on the windows shot closed, and a klaxon resounded through the lower levels a few times before going silent.

"We should be safe in here for now. I've put us in lock-down mode."

"Good," Andrew said. "How bad did we get hit?"

Jun-Ha looked around the cramped lobby of the bunker. The whole place reeked of blood and urine. "Worse than it should have been. I don't know how they got around the jungle sentries, but I can only assume they were killed. The women and children have retreated to the lower levels already, but we've lost a good half of our fighting force."

Andrew surveyed the scene in front of him. Perhaps two dozen fighting men still stood in ready condition, and perhaps ten more had survivable wounds. A handful had been dragged inside, peppered with arrows or bleeding from ragged gashes in their flesh. Evidently their scales didn't provide sufficient armor to protect from such a vicious attack. Goom paced by the shuttered windows, ears trained on every sound from outside.

"They plan to wait us out," he said after a moment.

"Send someone for the medical supplies," Andrew said, "and Ghenni and I will do what we can to treat the wounded." He looked at Ghenni, who nodded in agreement.

"Thank you," Jun-Ha said, and passed the order on.

"So we are under siege?" Ghenni asked.

"Is there a plan?" Andrew asked.

"A plan?" Jun-Ha repeated. "The plan is to survive."

Father Tanner followed Tenik's prodding onto the *Malika* just in time to see Eve wielding an impact wrench to close up the access to the IS drive. The tool whirred a few times as she tightened the last few bolts on one end of the floor panel under the watchful eye of Bellig.

"Are we all set?" Tenik called out.

"The ship's all yours," Bellig answered as she led Eve out.

The other Trenthan led Tanner through the empty cargo hold into the main corridor. Ahead, he could see into the cockpit, where Neekol sat at the controls, fiddling with the computer and entering commands on his tablet, connected by cables to a pair of ports inside an access panel. The bird-like pirate glanced back behind him as they approached, his head pivoting on his neck without turning his body, before resuming his work.

"Your quarters," Tenik said, gesturing to Tanner's usual room on the right. He stuck his head inside and saw that it had been thoroughly tossed, and stripped of almost all his possessions. All that remained was the simple cot, sloppily made, a stool and small table, and a dresser. Of course, those were built into the wall, so they would have been difficult to remove. For the same reason, he presumed the toilet was still folded up into the wall. "You've got all your study materials?"

"Right here," Tanner said, waggling his borrowed tablet in the air.

"Good," Tenik said. "You'll be confined to quarters for most of the trip, for safety reasons. We'll bring you food at mealtime. Make sure you study up, because once we get back, you'd better be ready to work."

Tanner sighed. "Of course." He stepped inside, and Tenik shut the door behind him. He heard the scrape of a lock on the outside. The trip would take the rest of the day and part of the night, and he'd need some sleep in there at some point, so had to make the most of it. He examined the dresser, pulled out the drawers, and found a change of clothes, along with the heavy Bible he kept there. He said a quick prayer of thanks that it hadn't been confiscated, then sat on the bed with it and began to read.

Ghenni worked until his fingers ached, crudely stitching wounds with thread made from some local fiber he didn't recognize. The aliens seemed strange on the outside, but stitches and tourniquets worked the same to keep the bleeding under control. His hands dripped with blood, with little time and no facilities to clean between patients. But given the situation, infection seemed to be the least of their problems. Andrew worked alongside him, but several of the Badasal succumbed to their wounds while they struggled to get to everyone. Jun-Ha listened at the door periodically, and reported the sounds of enemy warriors still congregated around the bunker.

Cries of pain and anguish filled the room, along with the stench of blood, feces, and death. He had seen violence before, but not savagery like this. Even his people had adopted the use of guns, which made kills relatively clean. The occasional shelling or landmine brought more serious injuries, but these were in another league. Flesh ripped from bones, and limbs severed from brute force rather than any cutting edge. Intestines spilling out from open cavities in their torsos, with nothing to do except scream until the mercy of death.

Finally, after what seemed like hours, everything that could be done had been done. Many were beyond help, but after surveying the wounded, Andrew told him that there were a few who would have died if not for their treatment, and others who would have lost limbs. It wouldn't remove the memories of the screams from his ears, but it did offer some solace.

After Ghenni had a few minutes to catch his breath, Jun-Ha came up from the lower level, his electric lantern lighting the way in one hand, and rifle slung over his back.

"What now?" Ghenni asked.

"We have a couple of options. We can wait and hope they lose interest, but I don't like our odds with that. They can live off the land quite comfortably while we have limited supplies. I can always lift the lock-down, and fight them off. Or we can try the escape tunnel."

"Escape tunnel?" Andrew said. "You're telling us this *now*?"

"Hey, don't get too excited. It collapsed years ago. We'd have to dig it out."

"Where does it lead?" Ghenni asked.

Jun-Ha shrugged. "About a quarter mile into the jungle. The soil's too loose to go much farther, but we didn't exactly have time for a geological survey, so that's what we got."

"How far in is the collapse?"

"About halfway. If we tried to tunnel up from there, we'd be past the treeline, but not far. Hopefully the blockage isn't too big, so we can get through it quick."

"There's not many left in good enough condition for that kind of work," Andrew said.

"All the better that we get started soon then, yes?"

Andrew heaved a heavy sigh, then stood up slowly. Ghenni followed, his body aching as he pushed himself to his feet from the cold concrete floor. Jun-Ha assigned a few of the injured men to stand watch in the main lobby, then rounded up the men, women, and children who were in good shape and took them down to the lowest level. They raided one of the supply rooms for lanterns and tools, but the tools were ill-suited for the task: a couple of brooms and mops with rolling buckets, along with plastic bowls from the kitchen.

Ghenni set to work, ignoring the aches and scrapes on his hands. The progress was slow and backbreaking; they used the bowls to scoop the loose, sandy soil into bags and boxes, then carried it out of the tunnel and dumped it into the conference room. When they came across larger stones, they used the broom handles to pry them loose. Airborne dust streamed through the light of the lanterns, and every so often the soil shifted above them. When it did, everyone held their breath, waiting to see if the tunnel would collapse over them.

Littered in the fallen soil were about a dozen plastic beams that must have been used to shore up the tunnel. Ghenni didn't recognize the material, so it must have been some kind of advanced plastic. From what he understood of how his own planet was colonized, it wasn't efficient to ship materials through space, and they were instead fabricated in place from local feedstock. Maybe the materials here weren't as sturdy as they should have been, because a couple of the beams had snapped, indicating where the collapse had occurred. Jun-Ha helped to replace a couple of them into the wall, but they didn't seem very reliable.

Finally, after what felt like several hours, they broke through to a hole on the other side. A pair of the support beams had collapsed into a triangle, which managed to preserve a bottleneck just large enough for a man to crawl through. Shining a lamp through showed the tunnel on the other side relatively clear.

"Good, good," Jun-Ha said, slumping against the wall and drinking from a plastic cup. "That was the easy part."

"What is the hard part?" Ghenni asked.

"Next, we exit the tunnel, hoping of course that the tunnel hasn't been discovered and guarded, and try to get the jump on the warriors around the bunker."

"So much blood has been spilled today already," Ghenni said. "We can't just flee?"

"What, you would have the Badasal flee their home rather than fight for it?"

Ghenni flushed with embarrassment at the question. "It may be better to flee than to fight hopelessly against an overwhelming force and die."

Jun-Ha studied Ghenni's face. "I sense I've struck a nerve there. I suppose I've stuck my foot in my mouth, and you fled some kind of fighting on your home planet?"

Ghenni didn't know what that had to do with him eating his own foot, but he nodded. "The Brotherhood took our planet with overwhelming force. We had no hope of fighting them off. Some resisted, but I didn't join them because I wanted a quiet life. Unfortunately, the doctors from the mission made some enemies, and I had to leave my home with them."

Jun-Ha chuckled. "People like us, trouble finds us, no matter where we go. But today we don't run. This isn't a hopeless battle yet; we just need some proper tactics."

"We only have a handful of fighting men left. Will that be enough?"

"All warfare is deception, yes? They think we are trapped, and we use that to our advantage." Jun-Ha grew more animated as he explained his plan in detail. "We scout the battlefield to ensure we have the best information about the situation, then we attack from stealth. I figure if we open with just the lasers, we can conceal our location for longer, and score more kills while they try to figure out what's happening. Then when they attack, we bring in the bows and spears for a surprise attack again."

"Your plan relies on the laser rifles, which means it relies on myself and Andrew," Ghenni said.

"True." Jun-Ha shrugged his shoulders. "I hate to ask you to get more involved, but, well, I'm not sure you *can* get more involved than what you are right now."

"Shooting people shooting at me is one thing," Andrew said, "but I don't know if I can fire on people who don't know I'm there."

"If it helps," Jun-Ha said, "you know they absolutely would kill you without a thought if they did know you were there."

Ghenni shrugged and offered a silent prayer to Mennas. "So when do we move out?"

Chapter Thirteen

The sand whipped at Damien's face as he watched the *Malika* take off into the afternoon sky. Landing thrusters blasted the beach with a roaring force as it rose ponderously into the air. Somber as he was, Damien noted a distinct whine from one of the thrusters that sounded like the beginning of a mechanical problem; he'd have to make sure Eve checked it out when they got back. *If* they got back.

He stared at the ship as it shrank into an almost imperceptible dot against the sky, until he finally lost it in the bright yellow sun. He sighed, then brushed the sand from his shirt and trudged back inside. Damien told himself he'd see her again, but the practical side of his brain wasn't too sure.

The concealable holster with the plastic holdout pistol burned against his thigh. It was two against three now. He could probably get the jump on one of them, but then they'd be evenly matched, assuming he could grab the rifle from Bellig or Carter before the other showed up. Eve wasn't a trained fighter, but she could handle a gun well enough, although he figured Amber was at about the same level if he read her right, and he wanted better than 50-50 odds. That meant either getting the jump on *both* of the heavies, either together or doing the first secretly, or switching Amber to his side.

Or maybe a third option. If Ghenni and Andrew were still out there, maybe hiding, trapped, or injured, that could be a huge boon to get them back. Over and above getting his friends back, that is. He hadn't been equipped to do it before, but he had a few shots with that gun. It might be enough to keep the monsters at bay, although if he fired it before he got deep enough into the jungle, it might give him away. It was a serious gamble of his limited resources, but on the other hand, they might not have the time to wait until he gained control of the ship.

Damien strode purposefully into the ship, past Amber and Eve playing cards on top of a crate in the cargo hold, and knocked on the door to Bellig's quarters. She opened the door a moment later, hand on the hilt of her combat knife. Behind her, he spied one of his boxes of cargo cracked open, the luxurious fabrics inside tossed haphazardly about the floor. "You need something?" she sneered.

"Just wanted to let you know that I'm going out into the jungle to look for my shipmates."

Bellig looked him over from head to toe before speaking. "Well, I admire your loyalty. Won't do you much good when one of those things has your throat in its teeth, but that's your call. You taking your mechanic with you?"

"No. No sense in risking both our lives. I need her to collect on our deal once the Father has gotten your captain back on his feet. Or tentacles or whatever."

Bellig snorted. "Well, have fun." She moved to close the door, but Damien blocked it with his foot.

"No chance you'd let me borrow at least a knife or something to go out there?"

"Nice try," she replied, then she drew back the door and slammed it hard into his foot. He pulled back and let her finish closing the door.

"Pleasant lady," he muttered.

He passed back by the two women playing cards and cleared his throat to catch their attention.

"Eve, just so you know, I'm going to go out and see if I can find any trace of Ghenni and Andrew."

"Is that safe?" Eve asked, dropping her cards. "You're unarmed."

"I'll be careful," Damien said, winking at her. "I've got my wits, and my disarming smile."

"He's dead meat," Eve said to Amber with a chuckle. Then her face dropped and her voice took on a somber tone. "Seriously though, make sure you come back. I can't lose anybody else."

"You won't," Damien said.

Sand, leaves, and sunlight poured into the opening as Jun-Ha slowly opened the hatch above him at the end of the tunnel. Andrew clutched the laser rifle to his chest to protect the mechanisms from the particles filling the air. After a few moments of peering through the gap, Jun-Ha turned back to address the others.

"Looks like the coast is clear," he said to Andrew. Turning to Goom, he continued, "Ready to deploy as discussed. Fan out and wait for my signal."

Jun-Ha opened the hatch fully, letting the late afternoon sunlight stream in, then crawled out cautiously and raised his rifle to scan the immediate area. Andrew slung his rifle over his shoulder and followed up the ladder after him. The sunlight hurt his eyes for a moment, but they adjusted quickly. When he breached the surface, he stood up as quickly as he could to get his bearings. They'd emerged somewhere in the jungle, but Andrew could spot motion far off in the trees back the way they'd come. It looked like some of the enemy tribe were patrolling a little way into the woods. The trees around them were thick with vegetation, dead leaves forming a thick layer on the sandy soil, but Andrew could see the edge of the clearing where the plant life thinned out.

Ghenni, Goom, and a dozen Badasal tribesmen followed, keeping low and spreading out through the trees and underbrush. Ghenni had the third laser rifle, while the Badasal carried their spears, clubs, and bows.

"Are those the, uh, targets?" Andrew asked in a low voice, gesturing with his head toward the other tribe in the distance.

"Roger," Jun-Ha said. "We'll need to get closer though; the range on these rifles has deteriorated. Not too close, though. You don't want to tangle with them hand-to-hand."

Andrew gulped and wiped his sweaty palms on his pants. Even for the heat, he was sweating quite a bit. He was a doctor, not a killer, although he had to admit the cause seemed more or less righteous. Thinking back to his theological training, there had been some discussion on the concept of Just War, but it had focused on more civilized, political conflicts, especially the war between the Brotherhood and Consortium. Here, he had witnessed the savagery when they attacked the village, not discriminating between men, women, and children. So his hang-ups weren't moral, just ones of inclination.

Goom directed eight of the Badasal warriors to climb into trees with their bows and throwing spears, taking positions high up to attack from above. The lieutenant along with the other four fanned out, crouching behind bushes and larger trees to hide from the enemy. Andrew, Ghenni, and Jun-Ha darted from tree to tree to draw nearer to the rival tribesmen. Andrew hadn't had any military training, and he couldn't help but feel it was obvious to anyone watching. He tried to make up for it by closely following Jun-Ha's steps, but the old soldier gestured for him to stop suddenly a couple of times. Evidently, he was missing something that Jun-Ha noticed in watching the enemy troops to let him know when it was safe to advance. Or maybe he was just making too much noise in the underbrush.

Finally they had approached to perhaps sixty or seventy meters away when Jun-Ha held up his hand to call for a full halt. He crouched behind a tree to the left, while Andrew and Ghenni hid behind a pair of trees to the right of him. Jun-Ha gestured for them to get their rifles ready, and Andrew raised his to his shoulder, but didn't lean out from behind cover yet.

Jun-Ha pointed to his eye, then toward the enemies, then held up five fingers. Andrew took that to mean that he spotted five of the Badasal ahead. He risked a glance out from around the tree and only saw four. Maybe he just had a worse angle. Jun-Ha signaled again, gesturing with his rifle toward the left side, then pointing at Andrew and Ghenni and gesturing to the right side. Were they both supposed to focus on targets on the right? That's what he decided to go with, anyway.

Jun-Ha nodded at them and began aiming, so Andrew followed suit. He swore he could hear his heart beating above the buzz of insects. Jun-Ha rested his rifle on a branch, then used his free hand to start counting down from five. Andrew focused on one of the warriors ahead of him. He was a burly man, swiping at bushes with one of the jagged clubs, looking for stragglers hiding in the brush. Andrew's throat went dry; he was staring now at the man he was supposed to kill, and that man had no idea who he was or even that he was there. It just didn't seem fair, although the rational part of his brain, buried somewhere deep under the adrenaline, told him that man wouldn't hesitate if the situation were reversed.

Jun-Ha's fingers ticked down one by one, taking what seemed like minutes, until his fist closed and he pointed it toward the enemy.

"Fire!"

The command coincided with the whine of Jun-Ha's rifle, and a barely visible beam lanced out at one of the enemy soldiers, who cried out briefly in pain. Andrew hesitated, then aimed his rifle a hair lower, targeting the legs. His target toppled to the ground, clutching at his calf where it had blackened with withering, focused heat. Ghenni must not have had a good shot, because his blast hit a tree nearby with a puff of flame.

The remaining two warriors, and a third that Andrew hadn't clocked, raised a cry and barreled toward them. Another went down to Jun-Ha's rifle before they scattered into cover, moving from tree to tree as they closed the distance.

"Run!" Jun-Ha shouted, turning and sprinting full speed back the way they came. Andrew and Ghenni followed suit, although the two of them were slowed down by their leg wounds. Jun-Ha turned around and fired some more shots as he ran backward, but didn't seem to have any luck.

They were still about twenty meters away from the ambush site when Jun-Ha tackled Andrew to the ground. He didn't have time to be confused about it before the enemy spear landed in the ground right where he had been, sending up a puff of sand with the force of impact. His rib slammed into something on the ground, knocking his breath out with a sharp pain, but he maintained the momentum to roll onto his back and raise his rifle up. One of the tribesmen had another spear ready to throw, but Andrew fired three quick shots with his rifle, and the energy blew the man's arm clean off at the elbow, sending the spear clattering to the ground as he crumpled with screams of pain.

An arrow came sailing over their heads from one of the trees, striking the last charging warrior in the chest. Two more soon joined it, and he fell dead.

"Thank you, Goom," Jun-Ha said. "Good work, everyone. But that was one patrol. More will be here soon. Get into position."

Father Tanner woke to the sound of the door scraping open, and a clatter as a tray slid onto the floor just inside.

"Dinner," Tenik said.

Tanner checked the small clock on the wall. It was late evening according to ship time, but his body disagreed strongly. All this space travel messed up his internal clock.

"Thank you," he said, as Tenik began to close the door. He halted, hesitating, and Tanner saw him only in silhouette against the light from the corridor outside.

"We'll arrive in a couple of hours," he said. "I hope you have been praying."

"Without ceasing," Tanner remarked.

"Do you think it will work? The surgery, I mean."

"Yes, I think it will," Father Tanner said. "Although as always with surgery, I can't offer certainty. In the end, it's all in God's hands."

His eyes having adjusted to the light a bit, Tanner thought he saw Tenik pursing his lips. "Please pray before the surgery as well. He is a good man."

"I'm sure he is. And I always do."

Tenik nodded, then slipped out and closed the door quietly. Tanner turned on the light and got off the bed to retrieve the tray and eat his daily bread.

Chapter Fourteen

Damien made sure he was over the sand dune, out of the sight of the ship, before reaching into his pants and retrieving the holdout pistol. He didn't want to have to fire it unless absolutely necessary, but just holding it certainly made him braver. He wasn't really an outdoorsy kinda guy, but firepower made up for a lot of that in his experience.

By now, the bits of carapace left over from the blasting of the crab creatures had been scraped clean of any meat, with long grooves of claw and tooth marks indicating where they had been feasted on. The stink of rotten meat wasn't nearly as bad as he'd expected. The scavengers must have been *very* thorough.

Damien picked through some of the smaller pieces, looking for something that might serve as a weapon. The natural edges of the shell seemed to be jagged, and would have made a wicked cutting edge, but he had nothing to fashion a handle out of. The best he could come up with was a small trapezoidal piece with a fibrous scrap of tendon dangling from it. He wrapped the connective tissue around one hand and wielded it as a sort of buckler. The long edge bore some serration, so it had some offensive potential, but it was rather lacking in the ergonomics department. He took a couple of practice swings, and the tissue snapped, sending the shell fragment hurtling into the sand. Oh well, the pistol it was then.

He trudged into the trees, carefully stepping over craters and shattered trees, walking as quietly as possible to avoid giving himself away. Those things probably hunted by smell though. Or at least he assumed, based on all of the science shows he'd seen as a kid.

The destruction stopped several yards in, and the jungle swallowed him up. As Damien crept forward, he heard sudden, furtive rustles of leaves that spun him around, searching for the source. It was just a bird or rodent scurrying away, at least so far, but in the thick leafy cover of the woods, every animal sounded bigger than it was. He hated to think what a *really* big animal would sound like sneaking up on him. Probably like nothing.

Damien didn't really know what he was looking for. By the looks of that carapace, his friends would be nothing but skeletons by now if they'd been eaten. He didn't see anything like that, but they may have been dragged back to a nest or something. The jungle floor was covered in sand and detritus, and seemed like it should have left footprints or drag marks behind. He didn't see any though, so Damien looked over the trees instead. He remembered people sometimes left scratches on tree trunks to mark their trail, so he studied the patterns in the bark for anything like that.

Peering closer at one tree, surrounded by a low, thorny bush, he saw what looked like vertical claw marks, like some large animal had tried to climb up. Had it been chasing something up the tree? Then Damien spotted the blood. Streaks and drips of faded red, soaked into the bark. It looked like it had dripped down from above and been smeared by something. That had to have been them, climbing the tree to get away from the animals.

Damien wasn't much of a tree climber, but this one didn't look too hard. He tucked the pistol in his waistband and jumped up to the lowest branch. He climbed several yards higher, until the thicker foliage threatened to obscure the view. He spotted more blood splotches on the way up, so if it was them, they managed to climb up out of reach. But looking down, he didn't see any indication of where they went from there. No remains, and no shelters.

Did they go tree-to-tree? It seemed possible, but there was no telling which way they would have gone. It would be impossible for him to track, and he'd just be wandering aimlessly in a jungle full of man-eating beasts.

"Where did you go?" Damien muttered to himself. If they could move safely from here, why didn't they try to come back? Maybe they thought they could regroup and somehow get the jump on the pirates or something. No way of knowing now, though. Damien sighed, then climbed back down.

"Godspeed," he whispered.

Ghenni fired the laser at another of the attackers, part of the third group that had advanced on them once they'd ambushed the first. This time, instead of the whine of the optics, a red light flashed on an electronic screen. There was some kind of text, in a language he didn't recognize, but it a smear of sand that had intruded into the display made it even more unintelligible.

The Badasal warrior he had been targeting didn't seem to care that Ghenni's weapon had malfunctioned, leaving him unarmed. Instead he charged with furious rage, swinging his jagged club in a great arc above his head, ready to crash into Ghenni's skull. With no other tool at his disposal, he braced the gun in both hands, holding it in the path of the weapon to block the blow. It struck, and cracked the laser rifle in two pieces easily, sending Ghenni staggering back with carried over momentum. He tripped on something and went toppling over backward.

The warrior didn't let up. He swung again before Ghenni had even hit the ground, but missed by a hair's breadth, miscalculating the path of his fall. Ghenni threw one of the halves of the gun at the man's chest, but he blocked it easily with the club before advancing again. Ghenni shuffled backward along the ground, clutching the broken gun as his only remaining weapon; the broken plastic was jagged, at least, and might actually do some damage if he weren't so disadvantaged in terms of positioning and reach.

The tribesman swung in a low swipe at Ghenni's leg, apparently aiming to disable him before approaching closer. Ghenni pulled his leg up out of reach, but the club still made contact with his boot. Luckily it didn't penetrate the thick leather, but the force wrenched his leg painfully to the side and sent him twisting sideways. With another mighty overhand swing, the Badasal prepared to deliver the killing blow. Ghenni closed his eyes, praying to Mennas for safe passage for his soul, but the attack never came.

He risked opening his eyes, and saw the man collapsed to the ground, a spear penetrating his scaly torso and lodged between his ribs. The friendly Badasal called Goom approached and held out a hand to help him to his feet. Ghenni took it, then surveyed the battlefield. Jun-Ha still fired at the retreating warriors, while some from their own side searched the battlefield for survivors, mercilessly slashing the throats of any enemies left breathing. Such savagery turned his stomach, but these were not his people. He turned away.

"Andrew?" he called out. He saw no sign of his friend, and set to searching. He'd been right beside him until only a minute or two ago. Ghenni swatted at bushes nearby, looking for signs of him in the brush.

"Here," Andrew groaned. Ghenni turned and spotted him coming out from behind a tree that he had been sitting against. He staggered to his feet, looking woozy, and possibly concussed.

"Are you OK?" Ghenni asked.

"I jumped out of the way of a spear," Andrew said, rubbing at the side of his head. His hand came away with a little bit of blood. "I guess I slammed my head into that tree. I think I'll be alright."

"Sit. Let me look." Andrew complied, his face dull with fatigue, and plopped down on the ground. He sifted though Andrew's hair, full of blood, dirt, and bits of plant matter from the ground. It didn't look too bad: just a slight scratch on the scalp that was already almost stopped bleeding. He didn't flinch when Ghenni felt around the wound, which was a good sign that it wasn't bruised.

"Feeling dizzy or nauseous?" he asked.

"No, no. Well, maybe a little dizzy."

"It might just be from adrenaline," Ghenni said. His own hands shook slightly, and he was physically and mentally exhausted, even from only a few minutes of combat.

Jun-Ha jogged over, wiping sweat from his brow. His eyes still scanned the trees as he addressed them, but night had fallen quickly. The dark put a severe limit on visibility in the brush.

"Good work," he said. "I think they're on the run for good this time. If no one else shows up in the next ten minutes or so, I'm going to tell them to lift the lockdown in the bunker, and we can start assessing damage.

"When can we go deal with the pirates?" Ghenni asked. After

what they'd been through, he surely would not forget why they had agreed to help in the first place.

Jun-Ha took a deep breath and sighed. "We took a lot of casualties. I have maybe five men who are in any shape for further battle, and I see we're down one laser rifle. And we *all* need rest."

"We risked our lives for you and your tribe," Andrew said.

"I know, I know," Jun-Ha replied, throwing up his hands. "Listen, let's take the night to sleep. But I hope you're not expecting a large expeditionary force. I need to leave some to defend the village, so I don't see taking more than two men with me. I gave my word, so of course I'll come personally. We'll have to assess the tactical situation when we get there, so I can't promise anything."

Ghenni ground his teeth in frustration, but he kept it to himself. All that work, all that risk, all that killing. And they'd gotten back a 3-man team and vague half-assurances.

"Very well," he finally said after a few deep breaths. "Tomorrow, bright and early."

Tenik let Father Tanner watch the approach to Tiluug, on the condition that he be handcuffed. It was part of the ruse anyway, so they went ahead and put Tanner in the prisoner clothes, which consisted of a simple shirt and slacks in a bland khaki color, made from an uncomfortable synthetic fabric. He'd once worn a hairshirt in one of his history classes at seminary, and the experience wasn't completely dissimilar.

The planet on the viewscreen was a deep blue sphere swathed in dark clouds, heavy with moisture. Tanner didn't spot any brown, but as they approached, small globs of dark green resolved in the oceans. The few islands visible appeared in clusters, none very large. Any standard terrestrial species would have passed it over for settlement, but such a biosphere represented vast open space for the Tuudolian race.

"This is the *BCS Kinthar*," Tenik said into the comms microphone. "Requesting permission to land for supply pickup." He and Neekol were both dressed in Brotherhood uniforms, neatly pressed and pinned with meager designations of rank.

"*BCS Kinthar* does not apply on resupply schedule," came back the reply in synthetic tones. "Please explain."

"Transmitting clearance code. Supply list is classified as security level 2. Requesting level 2 for all further communications."

The conversation stalled there for several moments as the computer screen lit up with automatic clearances and code checks. Messages and graphics flashed red, flickered, then turned green as ciphers and passcodes passed between the computers to verify their identity. Tanner could only guess what it took to fake even a low-level security clearance, but then again, that's why they were the professionals.

"Landing codes transmitted," a voice finally said over the radio. Despite being synthetically translated, Tanner detected a change in the voice. He guessed the case had been handed off to a superior due to the security classification. "You will submit for inspection and interview upon arrival."

"Understood." Tenik hung up the radio. "Everyone ready?" Neekol bobbed his head in agreement.

"Secured for transport," Tanner said, holding up his cuffed hands and tugging on the chain.

The viewscreen went black as they approached, replacing the camera view of the landing area with a security override message. As a military outpost, the details of the facility were secret, so the camera feeds were evidently jammed as a safety precaution. With nothing but instruments to navigate by, which he didn't know how to read properly, Tanner could only guess how close they were to landing.

After just a couple of minutes, however, he realized he could feel the ship slowing down, followed by the lurch of the artificial gravity turning off in favor of the local gravity. The walls vibrated as directional thrusters kicked in, fine-tuning their trajectory toward the designated landing spot.

A bright red alarm lit up on the control panel, and Tenik scrambled to check it. "Flaming Mennas," he muttered. "And I thought *our* ship was in bad shape…"

Tanner chuckled as the two pirates struggled to land the borrowed ship. Damien had always said it took a personal touch to pilot the ship. Only he knew the hundred little jury-rigged systems and idiosyncrasies that had accumulated over the years. Finally, with a shudder, the ship touched down and went still, and the whine of the engines began to wind down.

Tenik flipped the switch to unseal the doors, and the atmospheres equalized with a hiss. "Don't you have a mechanic on board?" he asked, turning around in his chair.

"Mechanic? Yes. Maintenance *budget*? Not so much."

Tenik growled under his breath, then got up. "Let's go then. They'll want to meet with us in the cargo bay. Don't do anything to get us arrested."

"Of course," Tanner said. "Out of the frying pan and into the fire." Tenik looked at him quizzically, but didn't ask for an explanation of the idiom.

The three of them gathered in the cargo hold and awaited inspection. They stood for a few minutes, while, Tanner presumed, the outside was inspected. The Brotherhood was nothing if not conscientious, and a surprise visit from a ship with secret orders was sure to raise some red flags. Tanner fidgeted behind the two pirates, trying to look more dejected and downtrodden. The ill-fitted and uncomfortable clothing helped, but he was used to being in charge, not subservient. He hunched his back and stared at his shoes intently. Hopefully that would sell it.

After several more minutes, the doors opened with a *ka-thunk*, then slowly lowered to the landing pad. Two figures stood on the other side. One was a tall, thin bipedal creature wearing a broad-brimmed hat, despite the dismal overcast sky outside. He stood at least seven feet tall, but with long, spindly limbs that looked like they would snap in a light breeze. As he drew near, Tanner saw the face and finally recognized the species. He was a Kikkilak, an amphibious PN_{OP} type that frequently coexisted with Tuudolians, despite coming from opposite ends of the galaxy. Its exposed skin was translucent, but actually extremely hard and resilient, almost a type of exoskeleton, with only cartilage underneath. Tanner could see the muscles move beneath the surface as it walked. Back in his boxing days, he had watched some bouts between Kikkilak; their muscles were highly specialized to short bursts of incredible strength, but they lacked the power to sustain effort for long. That made them great boxers, but terrible grapplers. Their translucent skin also made them vulnerable to the UV rays of most stars, which explained the hat. Underneath it, mandibles and bulging eyes gave it a horrific face that could easily haunt a man's nightmares. The creature wore the uniform of a

Lieutenant, and carried an electronic tablet.

The other figure was not a person at all, but a robot, about five feet tall, rolling up the ramp on two sets of treads. The top third of it was taken up with a screen, on which was carried the broadcast image of a Tuudolian. While not wearing a uniform, his rank marking and service awards were displayed in the corner of the screen, designating him as a Commander. The robot carried no manipulator appendages, evidently relying on the other officer to carry out its commands.

The two of them strolled in silently, casting long, probing glances at every corner. The robot wheeled around the group, ignoring them in favor of examining the walls. Tanner could only guess what he was looking for. The Kikkilak snapped his attention to the three newcomers, examining their uniforms and giving Tanner a once-over. He tapped on his tablet a few times before speaking.

"Orders please," he said. His words were relayed in Trenthan through a translation program on the tablet, but the crisp military discipline behind them was clear.

Tenik handed him a folded sheet of paper, sealed with a large piece of tape, embossed with a digital code of some kind. The officer took it from his hand, and angled his tablet to scan it. He studied the readout for a moment before replying.

"This code is out of date. Explain."

"Apologies, sir," Tenik said. "The ship we were dispatched from has been out of radio contact for some months, for security reasons. This is the code I was given by my superiors."

The Kikkilak's mouth chittered in annoyance, but it opened the paper and read the contents. Finally, it turned its attention back to Tenik.

"Your prisoner, he is a doctor then?"

"Yes, sir. A specialist in treating Tuudolians."

Tanner winced internally when he said that. He was no expert, with only the barest grasp of the species' internal medicine. If anyone with medical training interrogated him, it wouldn't take long to expose him as a mere dilettante.

The lieutenant spoke in his native, clicking language over their shoulders to the robot, which wheeled around and joined him in looking the three over.

"Please come with us," the Tuudolian on the screen said through its translator. "The supplies you requested will be loaded for you. We will continue with the inspection while we discuss your needs in more depth."

Chapter Fifteen

"So you think they're still alive?" Eve asked.

Damien shrugged as they spoke in low voices in their room in the pirates' ship. Somehow, even after two days of baking in the tropical sun, the metal floor was still cold on his butt where he sat. "It's possible. Maybe just wishful thinking, but I definitely didn't see any bodies or anything."

"That's good, I guess. But if we do get released, I don't think we'll have a chance to scour the island for them."

"Yeah. Too bad we don't have Pops here to pray for them to make it back."

"You could pray too, you know," Eve said.

"Well, maybe I already did a little bit," Damien said sheepishly. "But don't spread it around or you'll ruin my reputation."

The half-open door swung fully open as Amber leaned through the doorway.

"Spot check," she said in a sing-song voice with a playful smile. "Carter's battening down for the night." Amber seemed to already be dressed down for bed, with a baggy flannel shirt buttoned daringly low over a pair of tight shorts.

"Isn't that my shirt?" Damien asked.

"Is it?' Amber asked. "I took the liberty of going through some of the things we took from your ship. I haven't been able to go shopping in a while, you know."

"I was told I'd get to keep my personal belongings when you let us go."

"You can't spare one little shirt? It's just *so* comfortable."

"Of course it's comfortable; it's my puttering-around-the-ship shirt. I got it from-" He stopped himself. If he had any hope of swaying her, he needed to take a softer approach than the last time she came on to him. "Well, I've just had it for a long time."

Amber gave Damien and Eve a once-over. "Well, if you want to come over to my quarters in a minute, I can give you the shirt back. And anything else I wasn't supposed to take." She flashed another smile and slid out of the doorway.

"Wow," Eve said when she'd left. "Someone is on the *hunt*."

"Ugh. I'm gonna have to go through with it, aren't I?"

"If you don't, she'll be pissed. And she'll probably never side with us when you make your move."

"I don't like the idea of using sex to manipulate a woman," Damien said. "Now, manipulating a woman to *get* sex, that's something else entirely."

"You're disgusting," Eve said, rolling her eyes.

Damien sighed and heaved himself up to his feet. "Just you wait."

He stepped out the door and glanced up and down the passageway. Bellig was nowhere to be seen, but Carter was staked out at the end of the passage, just inside the cargo hold, sitting on a crate and cleaning his rifle. He glanced up when Damien came out, keeping his eye on him until Damien nodded at him and slipped across the hallway to Amber's quarters.

Amber was sitting on the bed when he entered, leaning back and propped up on her elbows, with her legs crossed to show off a whole lot of leg.

"Glad you finally came around," she said with an impish grin.

"I just came for my shirt," Damien said, shutting the door behind him.

"Then come and get it."

Damien gave her what he hoped was a rakish grin, then sat on the bed next to Amber. If he had to go through with it, hopefully she'd at least let him sleep on the bed afterward instead of the bare floor. She swung her legs over his lap, laying back on the bed with a sigh. He leaned down alongside her, resting on one elbow and brushing a lock of blond hair from her face.

"You really are persistent," he said.

"I never had to be before."

"You know, I told you that I haven't really been with anyone since my wife died, but-" He cut himself off with a chuckle. "No, forget it."

"Come on, tell me."

"I dunno, maybe it's the Stockholm Syndrome talking, but there's something about you that I can't get out of my head."

"Well," Amber said, "I'm glad to know I'm putting ideas in your head. Care to share any of them?"

"Look, I'm not the type to have a girl in every spaceport. And not to get ahead of myself, but I'd hate to fall for you and then have to go our separate ways. Or get killed, for that matter."

Amber sighed and closed her eyes. "But that's the life, isn't it? We're both out here trying to get by on the fringes of civilization in the middle of a war. You're gonna what, whisk me away to settle down in the suburbs?"

"I'm more of a downtown loft apartment kind of guy," Damien said. "But I don't know. You ever think about joining another crew?"

"Leaving with you guys?" Amber asked. "I mean, the lifestyle might suit me a little better, and they did lie and manipulate me, but Lopuul and the others are the only family I have anymore. I don't know if I could go through losing another one."

"I could promote you to first officer," Damien said with a grin. "We'll get business cards printed up and everything."

"Oh, please," Amber chuckled. "And have everyone know I slept my way to the top? No thanks. Besides, I don't think my crew would let me go even if I wanted to."

"Who says they get a say in it?"

The smile sank on her face. "You're saying I should just run away? Isn't that mutiny or something?"

"It's only mutiny if you take the ship with you." He screwed up his face in mock contemplation. "Technically, this would be desertion,

I guess."

Amber sat up, pushing Damien off of her. "Look, I'm not going to risk turning against my crew just for a lay."

"But I'm not talking about just a lay. I'm talking about a chance at a new life. On *your* terms. No matter what happens with us."

"So what, *exactly*, are you asking me to do?"

"For now, just think. Think about where you want to be when this is all over, and how bad you want to be there."

Amber pulled the shirt tighter around her, clutching it closed. "I think you should just go."

Damien got up and paused at the door. "Just think about it, OK?" He left without waiting on an answer.

Broad steel bunker doors opened up before Father Tanner as he followed the robot and its *aide-de-camp* inside the complex to meet in person. On the left side was a plain steel wall, with doors to various rooms labeled in an unfamiliar alien script. However the right wall was glass, looking into a sort of aquarium that mirrored the terrestrial corridor they passed through. A handful of Tuudolian personnel in uniform flitted about, going into and out of offices whose doors ran along the far aquarium wall in two levels.

As they penetrated deeper into the facility, the aquatic portion of the building criss-crossed to the other side of the hallway a few times, bridging the gap in tunnels overhead. The air around them stank of sea water and a faint whiff of acid, though the floor was remarkably clean of any spills or leaks. Evidently, they ran a tight ship, so to speak.

Other Kikkilak watched them warily as they passed by in the hallway, and a few Tuudolians lingered as well, eying them through the glass. Tanner kept his head low, doing his best to play the part of a downtrodden prisoner; it wasn't far off from true, anyway. After a few more turns, they finally arrived at a non-descript door in an obscure side passage. The aide swiped an access card, then swiftly opened the door to usher the others in.

On the inside, a rich wooden conference table sat bifurcated by the aquarium glass. Spartan-looking chairs circled the dry half, while the underwater side was surrounded instead by horizontal bars raised about a foot above table level by a series of poles. A single Tuudolian hung from one such bar, his tentacles wrapped around it for support. In front of him on the table was a computer tablet, and Tanner quickly surmised from his interactions with it that this was the officer controlling the robot. About the room were a few tastefully planted bits of decorative plants, and a door leading out of the room.

The Kikkilak gestured for the rest of them to sit. Tenik nodded an acknowledgment to him, snapped a sharp salute through the glass to the Tuudolian, then took the seat at the end of the table. Tanner sat unceremoniously next to him, and Neekol settled uncomfortably on the other side after an awkward salute of his own. The robot trundled into a corner and powered down, as the Tuudolian officer looked up from his tablet at the three of them directly.

"I am Commander Puulok," he said through the speaker set in the middle of the table. "As you are the ranking officer of your ship, is the Trenthan translation sufficient?"

"Yes sir, we all speak it," Tenik said.

"Very well," Puulok said. "I see the military discipline among Trenthans is as sloppy as ever. I thought we had beat that laziness out of you troglodytes years ago. I count seven deficiencies in the appearance of your uniform."

Tenik stiffened his back and sat up straighter in his chair. "I- I apologize sir. My first officer and I have been alone in transit for the last several days, and I regret to say that I let discipline slip. It will not happen on our return."

The squid creature gurgled something that wasn't translated, but it sounded an awful lot like a *harumph*. It regarded its tablet again for a few silent moments, then turned its attention back to the group.

"Your orders are rather vague. What is the nature of your mission?"

"We are to acquire the artificial respirator and other supplies necessary for invasive brain surgery," Tenik said, "as well as basic supplies for Tuudolian personnel."

"Yes, yes, I see that," Puulok snapped. "I mean the nature of your greater mission, to which you intend to return with our equipment." Tanner noted the subtle distinction in the grammar of the word "our"; the officer had used a declension that excluded their own crew, seemingly claiming exclusive ownership of the equipment in question. A significant faux pas among the communalist hierarchy of the

Brotherhood.

"I'm sorry sir, but the details are classified as Security Level 2. I was given strict instructions not to divulge them unless it was mission critical."

"But I am your superior officer," Puulok said, "and I have determined that it is mission critical."

Tanner glanced up from where his head drooped to look at Tenik. Beads of sweat glistened on his brow as he sat ramrod straight in his chair. They had expected scrutiny, yes, but not a megalomaniac.

"Apologies, Commander. But I was given a briefing on the security classification before departure, and the conditions for disclosure have not been met."

The Tuudolian regarded them coolly for a moment before responding. "Very well. Your OpSec discipline is better than your uniform maintenance. Hikak!"

The aide snapped to attention beside Neekol, and responded in an alien language. The two Brotherhood officers conversed for a brief moment, before the aide turned on his heel and hustled out of the room.

"I'm having the requested supplies loaded onto your ship," Puulok said. "In the meantime, tell me more about this prisoner of yours. Unless that is classified secret as well?"

"I can tell you that he was captured in an attack on a Consortium outpost. He had been employed in the torture and interrogation of Tuudolian prisoners." Tanner winced again. He didn't really like the idea of being called a torturer, even if it was just a temporary ruse.

"I would like to speak to him directly, if I can."

Tanner glanced over at Tenik, his heart pounding. Was he suspicious? Had they made a slip?

"Approach the glass, please."

The doctor got up from his chair and shuffled toward the glass wall. On the other side, Puulok unraveled his tentacles from his perch and moved closer to the glass, resting on the table. One penetrating squid eye looked over Tanner from head to foot, studying him with an eerie intensity. Tanner's palms grew sweaty as he waited for the Commander to speak. Finally, he lifted a tentacle and addressed him.

"I have a rash here," he said, gesturing with a second tentacle to the base of the one he'd lifted up. "The nurse on base says it's nothing, but it hasn't cleared up after several days. What do you think?"

Tanner stifled a chuckle; people always want free medical advice. Unfortunately, his knowledge of skin disorders was lacking. He thought it over for a moment, examining the reddish patch closely, and decided the more vague, the better.

"I'd put some ointment on it, and see if it's better in the morning."

The first rays of the morning sun found Andrew already awake, fiddling with the settings on his borrowed laser gun, nervously waiting for the others to finish their preparations to scout out the pirates. Two of the Badasal women had stoked the fire, and already had vegetables and fresh fish roasting on a spit. Jun-Ha spoke in a low voice with Goom, chuckling over some private joke. Andrew bounced his leg nervously as he waited.

Ghenni plopped down on a log next to him. "Did you get any sleep last night?" the Trenthan asked.

"Not much," Andrew said. "Too anxious to get back."

"Do you think there have been any developments since we left?" Ghenni asked.

"It's been what, a whole day? We didn't even have a diagnosis yet, let alone a treatment plan. I can't imagine they've wrapped everything up by now."

"Things could have gotten worse somehow."

Andrew sighed. "That's what I'm afraid of. If something happened to... well, to anyone, because we were delayed here..." He trailed off for a moment, then saw Jun-Ha approaching.

"We'll leave right after breakfast," Jun-Ha said. "An army marches on its stomach, you know."

"Hardly an army," Andrew shot back. "It's just five of us."

"And only three of us trained fighters," Jun-Ha said. He raised a finger pedagogically. "But we have the element of surprise."

"They have a plasma cannon," Andrew said.

"Someone's in a cheery mood, yes?" Jun-Ha asked, nudging Ghenni with his elbow. "Grousing won't do us any good. We'll see what the situation is when we get there, then make a plan."

It took about half an hour, by Andrew's estimation anyway, for

Jun-Ha and his men to eat and prepare their weapons. Ghenni ate tentatively, but Andrew couldn't stomach food at the moment, even if it did smell fantastic.

Finally, the small crew assembled, with Andrew and Ghenni carrying the two surviving laser rifles, the Goom and the other Badasal warrior with javelins and coral daggers, and Jun-Ha wielding a smaller version of one of the jagged clubs, along with a combat knife in his belt. They set off, but Andrew and Ghenni didn't really know the path through the jungle to go back the way they'd come. Instead, they chose to skirt the edge of the jungle along the shoreline. Jun-Ha explained that the shore was a longer route, full of bays and peninsulas, but it was faster and safer than travel through the jungle. At least by a little bit.

Of course it wouldn't be just a casual stroll along the beach. Andrew knew he wasn't that lucky. After a bit, the land started to flatten, and the pristine sandy shoreline transitioned to silty wetlands. There was no dry land to walk on here, unless they penetrated much deeper into the jungle and risked losing their way, so they resorted to trudging through waist-deep, brackish water instead. Sucking mud threatened to keep Andrew's shoes forever, and he made sure to keep one hand on one of the broad tree roots that jutted from the water, in case the ground gave way completely under him.

Tall grasses protruded from the water here, bearing pods of seeds that burst when he so much as brushed against them. The fluff that erupted sent Andrew into sneezing fits, so he did his best to avoid it entirely. The others didn't seem to suffer that problem. Thick trees rose from the muddy water, with roots that arched out ten feet above the water's surface, almost forming tunnels through the swamp. Red, shriveled fungus grew in sheets along the roots, crusted with sea salt where they were washed by the tides. The scent of the vegetation hung heavy and musky, even amidst the sharpness of the salt air.

Goom raised his hand to call a halt and everyone froze, listening to the subtle sounds of the swamp around them. Leaves rustled deeper in the jungle, as if something dropped through the branches after being knocked loose by passing wildlife. Something else sloshed to Andrew's left, and he whipped his head around to look. He started to bring his laser rifle to bear, but Jun-Ha shook his head. Of course, it wouldn't do much to anything underwater, especially not as dirty as this.

The Badasal both had their javelins raised, ready to strike, while Jun-Ha slowly drew his combat knife, passing his club to his left hand. Something darted through the water, leaving ripples in its wake, passing through a patch of the grass, whose seed pods erupted above the water, marking its movement. Goom hurled his javelin into the water in its path, and something thrashed under the water. With a snap, the back half of the javelin bobbed up, the end severed almost cleanly. Goom dove under the brackish water and struggled with something for a moment, while the other Badasal ducked down and swam toward him under the surface. After a few moments of thrashing, the two emerged, holding a strange creature, impaled on the sharp end of the broken javelin.

"Kopah," Goom said, shaking the corpse and gesturing to it. Andrew couldn't tell if that's what it was called, or some word in the native Badasal language. It was no wonder the javelin had snapped; the thing was almost pure mouth. Its jaw, ringed with small, regular teeth, was perhaps three feet wide fully open, with a body the size of a small dog. Its skin was a deep brown, matching the color of the mud, and it had only the tiniest eyes at the base of the jaw.

"Muck snapper," Jun-Ha said. "They lie in wait beneath the water, waiting for a careless animal to step in its mouth. Those things'll take a grown man's leg off without a second thought."

"Fantastic," Andrew muttered. "Do they hunt in packs?"

Jun-Ha shook his head. "Solitary. Good thing he was on the move, or we might not have spotted him. But you might want to find a stick to feel out your path until we get back on dry land."

"Great," Andrew said, ripping a limb from a nearby tree. He glanced up at the sky. "God, I'm sorry I ever complained about med school."

The group continued on for a few hours, eventually emerging from the swamp and back onto sandy ground that gradually got drier as they went. The gap between the jungle and the water steadily grew, and not just from the falling tide. Andrew jogged up to the front of the group.

"We may be getting close," he said to Jun-Ha. "The geography looks about the same."

"We'll hug the trees then," Jun-Ha said, signaling to his men.

"Don't want to be out in the open and get spotted."

They moved to follow right along the treeline, with Andrew and Ghenni leading now, while the natives kept their eye on the jungle to their right for signs of dangerous wildlife. It still took another hour or so, but eventually they turned a corner and saw a single ship in the distance. Jun-Ha signaled for everyone to get down low. Andrew dropped to his stomach and crawled the rest of the way to a dune in the sand, peeking up over the crest.

"I thought you said there were two ships, yours and the pirates," Jun-Ha said.

"There were. Looks like that's the pirate ship that's still there."

"So what happened?" Ghenni asked.

"I don't know," Andrew said. "I don't think they would have just taken the *Malika* and left their old ship behind. Ours was definitely a downgrade."

"Could be island hopping," Jun-Ha said. "Looking for supplies. Or looking for you."

"Do you think they would see your village if they did?" Ghenni asked.

"The bunker is camouflaged, visually and from sensors. But if someone's already looking, they're likely to spot it."

"If that didn't happen," Ghenni asked. "What is your tactical assessment?"

Jun-Ha stroked his beard, considering. "The approach on land is too open. We'd need to get closer to use the lasers in their condition, but that plasma cannon is the problem. Dunes can protect us from small arms fire, but not that thing. If we catch them at the right time, and it's high tide, I think a Badasal strike force could surprise them from the water, and maybe rush the turret. Is there exterior access?"

"Yeah," Andrew said. "There's a ladder on the far side from here."

"Good. I think three of my men should be plenty for that. Once that cannon's out of play, we can advance dune to dune and engage them on two fronts."

"I like it. When do we start?"

Jun-Ha spoke to the second Badasal in Korean, ordering him back to the village. He nodded, then slunk back the way they'd come and dove into the water.

"If they are looking for you, they almost certainly would have found the village by now. I sent him back to check. Now that we know where we're going, they can swim there and back must faster. If no one has visited, they must have gone somewhere else. In that case, I think we can spare another man or two. Tide will be at its peak just before dawn. That's when we strike."

Chapter Sixteen

It wasn't long into Tanner's meeting with the Tuudolian officer that Puulok excused himself and left the room. The Kikkilak lieutenant remained with them for several minutes, standing silently in the corner, until he received some message in his earpiece and left after a curt nod to the three visitors.

"How long do you think this will take?" Tenik eventually asked, leaning back in his chair and stretching.

Father Tanner tapped at his ear and gestured with his head at the door. They were probably listening in. He dared not speak while playing the part of the prisoner. Tenik stood and paced the room for a bit, drumming his hands on his pant legs.

"Gone long time," Neekol said. "Problem?"

"That's what I'm afraid of," Tenik said. He crept over to the exit and gently tried the handle. "It's locked," he hissed. He pressed his ear up against the door and listened intently for a few seconds. "I hear voices out there. Can't understand anything. Do you think they're talking about us?"

"I think you're being paranoid," Tanner muttered under his breath.

"Why would they lock us in then?"

"To keep us from wandering around, maybe?"

"I don't like it. I think we're compromised. Can we break down the door and make a run for it?"

"Where, exactly?" Tanner asked. "If they *have* turned against us, surely we'd never be able to fly out. You want to go hide out in the swamps the rest of your life?"

Tenik scanned the room, and his eyes landed on the robot that Puulok had used to interact with them on the ship. "That thing's hooked up into the computer systems, right? It's gotta be. Can you do anything with that, Neekol?"

"Can try," the bird creature said. He got up from his chair and examined the robot, eventually reaching up to the front panel and pulling down a retractable keyboard. The display screen which Puulok had spoken through lit up with alien script and a basic visual interface. Neekol typed furiously at the keyboard, tilting his head from side to side as he considered whatever he saw on the small display screen.

"Security alert," he finally said, turning back to the other two. "We're made."

Tenik launched into a stream of swear words, while Tanner jumped to his feet and ran over to Neekol. "What can you do about it?"

"No good to override. Can unlock door."

"Can you keep the ship clear for us to take off?" Tenik asked. "That's got to be the priority."

"Take time," Neekol said. He launched into another furious burst of typing as he navigated the Brotherhood computer interface.

"Father, help me with the door," Tenik said.

"Help you what?" Tanner asked.

"Break it down!" Tenik pulled his sidearm from its holster and aimed it at the door lock, but the priest pushed his arm down to stop him.

"We can't throw that door open now," he said. "We need to buy time until the ship is clear."

"What's our timeline, Neekol?" Tenik shouted over his shoulder.

"Two minutes," Neekol said.

Father Tanner grabbed one of the plastic chairs and hefted it in his hands, testing its balance as a potential weapon. It didn't have the mass to do any damage, but it might deflect a bullet or a punch. Maybe. Tenik kept listening at the door.

"I think they're forming a perimeter just outside," he said. "How do we look?"

Neekol hit one last keystroke with a flourish, then shouted, "Done! Had the-"

His explanation was interrupted by the sound of gunfire as Tenik blasted three rounds at the door lock. A single solid kick sent the door flying open, and he fired at a trio of Kikkilak soldiers who had only just begun reacting to the initial gunshots. One of them went down hard, but the other two quickly split to the side and raised their own rifles in response.

Father Tanner charged out the door right behind Tenik and hurled the flimsy chair at one of the soldiers in the hallway. He flinched enough for an opening, and Tanner lunged at the man, grabbing for his rifle. A carapace fist launched at Tanner's face at impossible speed, unleashing tremendous force stored in the alien's specialized muscle fibers. The priest turned away, but not quite soon enough. The fist landed a glancing blow, sending Tanner's face twisting to the side and opening up a wound that blossomed with warm blood. Tanner grabbed the arm and twisted it, taking advantage of the Kikkilak's physiology to keep it from cranking up another rocket punch. They dropped to the floor and tussled there until Tanner ended up on top, slamming the soldier's head against the floor until he went still. He said a quick prayer that the soldier was merely unconscious, then grabbed the rifle and looked up to assess the situation.

Tenik had already gotten the best of the third soldier, picking up his rifle and firing a few rounds for good measure into the fallen Kikkilak's chest. The creature thrashed, but no wounds opened up.

"These things sure have tough skin," he remarked.

"Non-lethal rounds," Neekol said, picking up the third rifle. He gestured at the aquarium walls around them. "Don't break glass."

Red warning lights on both sides of the aquarium wall lit up, and klaxons blared down the hallways.

"We need to get going," Tenik said. He took off running the way they'd come down the passage. "No telling what kind of security personnel they have here."

The three of them jogged through the twists and turns of the passages toward the bunker doors leading outside, their footsteps and heavy breathing drowned out by the blare of the alarms. A few isolated soldiers rushed out of side rooms to try to stop them, but they were put down quickly with a few short bursts of fire. Evidently, the Brotherhood didn't station their best soldiers to guard a third-rate supply dump.

Finally, they reached the last hallway, with the large doors in front of them. The large *closed* doors. The flashing red light above them didn't bode well for their chances of getting them open.

"Neekol, can you get us out of here?" Tenik asked.

"On it." Neekol ran for the control panel next to the door and started working the software, trying to lift the lockdown. Just as he did, a pair of Kikkilak soldiers came from one of the side passages. Tanner raised his rifle, but it clicked when he pulled the trigger. Empty. Tenik for his part tried to get off a shot, but a burst of fire from one of the enemies made contact, and Tenik's rifle went flying as he cradled his injured hand.

Tanner charged and dove low this time. He took the soldier's legs out from under him, while the Kikkilak slammed on his back. Luckily, he didn't have the right angle to use his powerful punch, and Tanner was able to weather the blows somewhat. Out of the corner of his eye, he saw the other soldier fire a few more rounds at Tenik straight into the gut, sending him doubling over in pain and, potentially, internal bleeding.

As Tenik fought for his breath, Tanner's foe struggled back up to his feet, pulling Tanner with him and pushing him up against the glass. This one wasn't such a slouch when it came to wrestling. The other soldier raised his rifle at the two of them, but gave up at getting a clean shot with the two of them struggling in close combat. He approached the pair as Tanner struggled to get out of the other man's pin, rearing back his fist, which packed enough power to crush Tanner's skull in a single blow.

The doctor waited until the last possible moment. When he saw the tell that the punch was coming, he threw himself down with all the power he could muster. It was enough to drop his head eight inches, and the fist whistled past his hair, colliding with the glass behind him. The man screamed in pain and clutched at his hand, while ominous pinging sounds behind him told Tanner that the glass had been cracked. The soldier grappling him pulled him back up and then threw him to the floor and went for the rifle on the ground.

Tanner made a lunge for the rifle, but he was too far away, and the Kikkilak got his hands on it first. A hiss off to his left grabbed Tanner's attention, and he saw the bunker doors open, with the *Malika* perhaps a hundred yards away with her cargo bay door hanging open. Standing next to the door was Neekol, his rifle ready.

Neekol fired. He was a terrible shot. The recoil sent his rounds spraying wildly up the wall and onto the ceiling. But it distracted the soldier enough for Tanner to jump to his feet and go for the gun. The two of them wrestled over it, straining with more or less equal strength to gain control of the weapon. Tanner could feel his grip slipping, and knew he wouldn't be able to hold on much longer.

"The glass!" he shouted through clenched teeth.

"What?" Neekol said.

"Shoot the glass!"

Neekol looked, then unleashed an unfocused burst of fire at the spider-webbed cracks in the glass. In its weakened state, the force of even the non-lethal rounds compounded the damage, sending bigger cracks spreading further almost instantly. For a brief second, the shattered portion bowed out from the pressure of the water behind it, then it suddenly gave way. The force of rushing water slammed Tanner to the ground and sent the gun clattering from both of their hands. The doctor picked himself up and grabbed Tenik, who struggled to his feet.

"Let's go!" he shouted, leading Tenik to the outside.

The three of them ran as fast as they could given Tenik's condition, out into the open air and toward the waiting refuge of their ship. Tanner risked a glance behind them, and saw the deluge of water and a few unlucky Tuudolians tumbling through the hole in the glass, their tentacles thrashing in the open air. The few Kikkilaks who had rushed to help seemed focused on damage control rather than the escaping saboteurs.

They reached the ship, and saw a couple of pallets of supplies still sitting on the landing pad just outside the door, with some more already loaded inside. Tenik ran directly into the ship, but Tanner stopped to check the supplies outside.

"Is the respirator in there?" Tanner called out.

"That's what this box says," Tenik called back from inside. "Leave the rest. Come on!"

Tanner got into the ship and slammed the button to close the cargo bay door. Tenik was already down the hall and in the pilot's seat, and he flipped the switches on the controls to start up the engines, favoring his injured hand.

"When you were in the computers," Tanner said to Neekol as he checked the respirator that had been loaded on the ship, "did you see anything about surface-to-air weapons?"

"Started diagnostic routine," Neekol said. "Down few minutes. Must hurry."

"Splendid," Tanner said. The respirator checked out, though most of the general supplies were still sitting on the landing pad just outside. The ship slowly rose out of the atmosphere, and the flashing red alert faded into the pale gray of the cloud cover.

Eve woke to pounding on the door outside of her crew's room. She rubbed the sleep from her eyes and heaved herself unwillingly to her feet as the noise continued without slacking. She finally cracked open the door and squinted against the flood of bright light from the hallway. Carter stood on the other side, rifle over his shoulder but dressed in a threadbare undershirt and sweatpants.

"What is it?" Eve asked.

"Just got a message from the *Malika*. They're back with the equipment. Get the captain ready for surgery."

Eve nodded, then closed the door and threw on some more presentable clothes. It had been more than a full day since they'd left, and she and Amber had been on babysitting duty with Lopuul for that whole time. The two of them had been so paranoid of something going wrong that they didn't even leave the room until she couldn't keep her eyes open. Thankfully nothing of note had happened, but it was a bit exhausting wondering if he might take a turn for the worse with no real doctors around to do anything about it.

"They're doing the surgery immediately?" Damien asked, slapping his face lightly to wake himself up.

"Sounds like it."

"This is it then. Either it works, and they let us go, or things go south and we have to make a move."

"So can we count on Amber or not?" Eve asked. "You came back from her quarters pretty quick. Are you sure you made an impression?"

Damien sneered at her. "I always do. But I don't think I got through to her. The devil you know, and all that."

"You've got your weapon?"

"Right here," Damien said, patting his thigh. "Let's hope it's enough."

Eve huffed, then left and headed to the captain's quarters. Amber was already inside, with a tumbler that smelled of cheap instant coffee. She nodded in acknowledgment when Eve entered.

"How's the patient?" Eve asked.

"Same as usual. Little bit of movement, but mostly sleeping. Or just lying around at least. He doesn't seem to get as riled up without the priest around."

"If we hadn't seen those tumors on the brain scan," Eve said, "I'd almost believe the whole demon idea. When are they landing?"

"They dropped out of hyperspace about half an hour ago. They should be lining up an approach vector as we speak."

Amber went about arranging the surgical instruments and preparing the sedative, disinfectant, and other medicines they'd need. Eve did her best to help, but since she wasn't very familiar with the set-up, she was in the way more often than not. After about ten minutes, they had everything as ready as possible until Father Tanner arrived with the respirator.

Bellig's voice came in on the intercom. "Ship incoming. All hands stand by."

Eve and Amber went outside through the cargo hold to watch the *Malika* approach. By the time they got there, they could see a pair of signal lights blinking up in the dark, night sky. Eve pulled her shirt tighter around her as the salt wind blew in off the sea, carrying a chill with it. After a few minutes Bellig joined them on the beach, crossing her arms sternly as she watched.

The *Malika* grew steadily larger in her view until the shape resolved into something familiar, if indistinct, in the moonlight. The wind whipped up with more fury as her landing thrusters started pushing off against the sand, sending particles swirling so that Eve had to shield her eyes. The tell-tale whine of the well-worn drive grew louder, until the ship hovered right above the beach, about thirty yards away from the pirates' ship. It set down gently, landing struts sinking deep into the sand, and settled nearly on its belly. The tone of the engines wound down, and with a hiss, the atmospheres equalized, and the cargo hold door swung open onto the beach.

Tanner and Tenik emerged almost immediately, carrying a crate between them, marked in alien script.

"Father," Eve said, rushing over to him. "Good to see you made it."

"Good to see you're still safe here," Tanner replied. "How's the patient?"

"Pretty sedate since you left," she replied. "You bring out the worst in him, I guess."

"It's a talent. I want to get into surgery as soon as possible."

The whole crew followed along as Tanner and Tenik carried the respirator into the captain's quarters. Tanner began unpacking it and getting it ready, while Tenik ran to retrieve the rest of the miscellaneous supplies they'd managed to get.

"Any trouble?" Eve asked quietly, as only Bellig watched from a several feet away.

"God protected us," Tanner said with a sigh. "But you know what they say about plans and first contact with the enemy."

After several more minutes, the respirator was reassembled in the captain's quarters and powered up. Eve helped Father Tanner fill the reservoir with water from Lopuul's tank, and the aerator hummed as it frothed the liquid to infuse it with oxygen. The circulation system was equipped with nozzles intended to press close to the gills, or whatever it was that these things used to breath underwater, hosing the captain down with oxygenated water, then collected the runoff to recirculate it. It seemed a little unsanitary to her, but what did she know?

Father Tanner looked up at her when the preparations were complete. "It's time," he said. There was a nervous edge in his voice, and palpable tension in the room. Everyone from both crews, or at least everyone still with them, was crowded into the hallway outside. Eve's eyes met Damien's, and he pursed his lips. Father Tanner grabbed the sedative and started up the ladder.

Chapter Seventeen

The roar of an engine overhead woke Ghenni from restless sleep, and his eyes slammed open. Andrew had been on watch, and he was already ducking low to hide from the approach of whatever had made the sound. A ship. It had to be the *Malika*, right? The small camp had hidden around the corner of the treeline from the parked pirate ship, but he would have to pray they hadn't been spotted from the air by the approaching vessel.

"Is it ours?" Ghenni asked, belly-crawling through the sand to where Andrew watched.

"I think so, but I can't be positive," Andrew said. "I'm not an aficionado when it comes to ships, especially in the dark."

Jun-Ha sidled up to the two of them, rubbing sleep from his eyes. "This changes things, you know."

"How?" Andrew asked. "I mean, tactically speaking."

"The first approach should be the same," Ghenni said. "Sneaking up from high tide."

"True," Jun-Ha said. "But now we have two positions to take and hold. They could fortify one while we take the other, and we end up in a stalemate."

The distant hum of the engine suddenly cut off, and its mechanical whine began to wind down. "I think they've landed," Ghenni said.

"See if you can get eyes on them," Jun-Ha said. "Figure out what they're doing and where they went."

"It must have been some kind of supply run, right?" Andrew asked. "That's the only reason they would have left and come back."

"Maybe," Jun-Ha said. "They could have gone to get something. Or they might have gone to drop something off."

"What do you mean?" Ghenni asked.

"Classic pirate move," Jun-Ha said with a chuckle. "They might have been marooning troublemakers on another island."

"I hope not," Andrew said. "We'll need some troublemakers when we attack."

Ghenni left the two of them and crept down the beach, more and more of it sweeping into view as he rounded the edge of the treeline. He kept his ears alert for noises from the jungle to his right, in case any wild beasts intended to attack, but he heard nothing. After a few moments, he caught sight of the landed ship. It certainly looked like the *Malika* from where he watched, and the cargo bay door was already open, spilling artificial light onto the moonlit beach.

From that distance, Ghenni couldn't make out faces, but he saw three figures unloading crates from the interior of the ship. One was definitely Neekol, the bird-creature, just based on the shape. And he thought he recognized the confident gait of Father Tanner. Evidently it was a supply run, a successful one at that, and if the Father had been part of it, it was for medical supplies. Ghenni felt a wave of relief at that; if they'd been out for medical supplies, that meant they were still working on the captain, and his friends hadn't been cut loose. It looked like there might be more people watching from beside the pirate ship, but they were shielded from view. Ghenni carefully sneaked back to where the others waited and reported what he saw.

"Encouraging," Jun-Ha agreed, nodding his head. "Did they split up after?"

"Everyone I saw went into the pirate ship," Ghenni said.

"That's where everyone was staying for the most part," Andrew said. "They really only went to the *Malika* to deal with the cargo."

"Then I'll have my warriors take the *Malika*," Jun-Ha said. "They can secure it and make sure there are no surprises waiting for us, while we take the pirate ship.

"Should we attack sooner?" Ghenni asked. "If they just returned with supplies, they're probably treating the captain now. They may be distracted. And if it fails, things may go bad before we can strike."

Jun-Ha shook his head. "I wish we could, but we're waiting on the tide. The attack's no good without the element of surprise. Besides, if your doctor's busy with treatment, we know for sure he's not in a position to join in the attack. Better to wait until after anyway."

Ghenni nodded at the soldier's reasoning. He wasn't happy about it, but he saw the logic of waiting. He wished he had his soulstone to do some prayers before battle, but it was still back on the ship. Ghenni tried to pray without it, but found his thoughts and words unfocused. Jun-Ha placed a hand on his shoulder.

"There's nothing we can do now, friend. Except get sleep to be ready for our time of action."

Ghenni gave him a weak smile. "Very well. I will be ready."

The last of the sensors on the respirator had been connected, and all vital signs read normal for a sedated Tuudolian, at least as far as Father Tanner's meager knowledge of the species went. The squid-like alien lay still, a steady spray of oxygenated water keeping its skin moist around the respiratory membranes on the side. A plastic screen shielded the area of the operation from overspray, to give Tanner a somewhat dry area to work in. Of course, Tuudolians typically operated on each other completely underwater, so it wasn't as if some water in the opening would do any damage, but proper visibility and a good grip on his instruments were crucial for a surgeon.

Only Amber was allowed in the operating theater, that is, the temporarily renamed sick bay, to assist him, while Bellig watched from across the room, her arms crossed and a pistol prominently displayed in a holster on her hip. As if Tanner needed another reminder of the stakes.

He took a deep breath behind his surgical mask. "Ready to open," he said. "Scalpel."

Amber handed him the instrument, and he hesitated only a moment before beginning the incision. The skin was tough, requiring more pressure than he was used to in order to cut through, but with a little effort, it gave way. Thick red blood oozed around the wound, and Amber followed with a suction tool to keep the area clear.

The skin peeled back to reveal a pale yellow cartilage, tough and rubbery. It was sturdy enough to still require a saw to penetrate, but compared to bone, he didn't have to worry so much about the heat generated by the cutting process. Amber handed him the small, circular saw, and he fired it up with the whine of the tiny motor. If he were in a properly-equipped facility, he'd be using a computer-guided laser, tuned to cut in just the right place, with safeguards in place to keep the heat from building up beyond acceptable limits. He also wouldn't have a heavily-armed pirate breathing down his neck, ready to kill him if he made one wrong move. Instead he had Amber with a squirt bottle to rinse and cool the incision, and God to guide him. He said one more silent prayer as the saw began its work.

Flecks of hardened tissue flew from the saw as the channel opened deeper into the cartilage. Amber squirted water every few seconds, washing away the particles and keeping the area cool, where it heated up due to the friction of the blade. Slowly, Father Tanner carved a rectangular section right above where he'd detected the tumor. About half a centimeter in, he felt the cartilage give way as he penetrated all the way through, and he carefully traced the entire circuit at the same depth until the square of tissue came loose, exposing the last major covering of the brain.

Unlike the cartilage, the dura was heavily vascularized, with a spider-web of blood vessels carrying dark red fluid across the brain. Father Tanner gently brought his scalpel to bear on the thin membrane, while Amber followed with the squirt bottle and the suction tool to keep the area clear of blood. As he slowly cut into it, the dura pulled back under tension, revealing the brain itself.

The brain. Not a tumor.

He turned back to the tablet, propped up on the counter behind him, with the relevant information at the ready. He held his hands in the open air, careful not to touch anything that could cause contamination, and issued a voice command to the tablet.

"Display example of tumor, contrasted with brain tissue." Maybe he just didn't know what he was looking at; brain surgery wasn't his specialty, especially not on Tuudolians. But the picture was clear: a typical tumor should have been pale yellow, almost white, against the pinkish brain tissue. It would be difficult to miss.

"Something wrong?" Bellig asked. She shifted on her feet into a less relaxed stance, her hand drifting toward her holster.

"No, nothing's wrong," Tanner said. Technically not a lie; a tumor would have been something wrong, but he saw nothing. "Just being careful."

He turned back to the patient and examined the area again, looking for something he'd missed. This was definitely the right area, although he would have preferred using computer-guided surgery for something like this. Then he glanced down at the section of cartilage he'd removed. There, on the back side of it, was what looked like a large mass. Was this an epidural tumor, growing out of the cartilage? If so, that would make his job immensely easier. Removing a tumor from cartilage didn't carry nearly the risk of mistakes as separating it from the brain tissue itself.

He prodded at the mass, and it gave way easily under his finger. There was fluid inside it. This was no tumor. He lanced with the scalpel, and dark yellow pus flowed out as the pocket deflated. A blister? That's what he saw on the scan? It gave way under his finger so easily, he wasn't sure that could have caused the neurological effects he had seen. The pressure needed to induce a behavioral change would probably be enough to rupture the blister. But he didn't know that for sure. He'd have to do some more research once they were out of surgery.

"Let's stitch it up," he said.

"Already?" Amber asked. "That was it?"

"We won't know until the recovery."

Damien jolted awake when the door to their quarters opened, and a ragged-looking Father Tanner stumbled in and collapsed in a chair with a weary sigh. He plopped his tablet on the floor, its screen still glowing with the medical program he'd been using.

"How did it go?" Damien asked, his voice a whisper to avoid waking up Eve.

"He's stitched up and recovering," Tanner said. "We won't know anything for sure until he wakes up."

"Any complications?"

Tanner leaned forward in the chair and cast a glance back at the closed door. "It wasn't a tumor. It was a blister inside the skull."

"So that wasn't the cause of the craziness?"

"I don't know, I don't know," Tanner said, taking his head in his hands. "Like I said, we'll have to see when he wakes up."

"And if he's not any better?" Damien asked.

"The only diagnosis I have left is demonic possession. I'll have to attempt an exorcism."

Damien shook his head. He'd seen a lot of things in his time, but *this* was a bit much for him. "How exactly do you see this going down? Bellig doesn't really seem very open-minded about that kind of thing."

"Well, you talked about taking the ship by force. I think we'll need to do that first. We'll do the exorcism whether they like it or not."

"OK, OK, I see where you're going with this, but, counterpoint: if we've already taken the ship back, why exactly are we still helping their captain?"

"I am a minister *and* a doctor, you know. I have a higher calling than mere survival."

Damien shrugged. "Fair enough. I guess if you want to play with your toys once we're safe, I can humor you."

"You're very generous."

"So when does Lopuul come out of anesthesia? If he's still stark raving mad, things might go down the second he opens his mouth."

"A couple of hours, probably. About dawn, by my reckoning."

"Then you'd better get some sleep," Damien said. "It's gonna be a big day."

Chapter Eighteen

As the first golden rays of sunrise peeked over the gentle ocean, Jun-Ha muttered some orders to the three Badasal warriors that had rejoined them. They acknowledged in their alien tongue, then slipped into the water with hardly a splash.

"Do we have a signal?" Andrew asked.

"Hopefully, the signal is when their man on the gun up top dies," Jun-Ha said. "Let's make sure we're in position."

Andrew, Ghenni, and Jun-Ha crawled across the sand, back into sight of the pirate ship, and kept down low behind a small sand dune. The sun wasn't quite in their eyes yet, but if the attack didn't happen soon, the visibility was going to be working against them. Andrew's palms dripped with sweat despite the chill of the early morning, and he fidgeted with the laser rifle in his hands. His heart pounded, adrenaline surging in anticipation of going into battle again. He was a doctor, not a soldier, but somehow he continually found himself tossed into violent encounters. He closed his eyes and prayed.

God, protect us in battle as we fight to rescue and protect our friends. Spare us in Your mercy, and guide us in Your will.

Andrew watched the distant figure on top of the ship. From this distance, silhouetted by the sunrise, it was difficult to tell which way he was facing. After what seemed like hours of interminable waiting,

Carter snapped his attention toward the ocean. A spear thrust up from behind the ship, out of view of Andrew, catching the pirate somewhere in his upper body. It must not have been a fatal blow, because he brought his rifle to bear, firing down toward the waterline. The gunfire cracked in the open air, ringing out clear and strong.

"Go!" shouted Jun-Ha. He sprang to his feet and charged across the sand, club at the ready. Andrew and Ghenni followed close behind, carrying their laser rifles at a low ready as they sought to close the distance as quickly as possible. It was a couple hundred yards to the ship, with nothing but wide open beach in between them. Even a tactical novice like Andrew recognized how vulnerable that made them.

Before they'd cleared another twenty yards, the gunfire stopped. Up on the ship, Carter tumbled into the ocean and out of view. A few moments later, one of the Badasal appeared on top, his torso and head visible above the protective metal barrier surrounding the plasma cannon.

"They'll be coming out to check on the gunfire any second," Jun-Ha panted as he ran.

As he said that, among the last of the fading stars in the morning sky, a blinding white flash erupted in a monumental explosion.

Damien watched Lopuul intently, as his tentacles began to twitch in his pool. The whole crew had gathered around the doorway to the captain's quarters, waiting to see the results of the surgery. He and Tanner, along with Amber, stood inside the room, and he had maneuvered himself to stand near the door controls. Just in case things went bad and he needed to slam the door shut. All of the pirate crew except Carter, as well as Eve, had bunched up outside. He shot her the most intense glances he could without giving himself away, but there was no casual way she could push through the crowd to get in the room with him.

"I thought you said he was waking up," Bellig said, her arms crossed as she leaned against the opposite door outside.

"It's a process," Tanner said. "We gave him an extra large dose of the tranquilizer to make sure he didn't wake up during surgery. He's already moving, but it will take some time for the effects to wear off enough for him to be lucid."

"Rebooting takes time," Neekol remarked, extending his neck to look over the crowd.

Lopuul's limp body twitched a little more, and he began to dart back and forth a few inches as he got his bearings within the tank. Faint murmurs sounded through the glass, too incomprehensible to be picked up by the microphone translator.

"Heads up," Damien said. "Looks like he's starting to move." His hand went to his waistband, and he thumbed at the fabric, testing how easily it would accommodate his hand if he needed to go for the small pistol he still had strapped to his thigh.

Tanner approached the intercom on the wall. "I know one way we can get a reaction if it didn't work," he said. He pressed the button and began to speak. "Our Father, who art in Heaven, hallowed by Thy name..."

The half-closed eyelids on the squid creature snapped open. It thrashed about, weakly slamming its tentacles against the glass, its force hindered by the anesthetic. Blasphemous curses came back through the intercom as Tanner released the button.

"You said this would work!" Bellig shouted as she reached for her pistol. To her side, Tenik raised his rifle, and Neekol and Eve darted to opposite sides of the doorway to get out of the line of fire. Damien pressed himself up against the wall on the inside, face first, and his hand dove down to grab the grip of the pistol.

"I have one last thing to try!" Tanner shouted back. He strode into the middle of the doorway, right into the path of Tenik's rifle, and stared down Bellig. Damien froze, leaving the gun in its holster. He wanted to see how this played out.

"You said the brain tumor was the problem," Tenik said. "What happened?"

"I'm not sure," Tanner said. "I've exhausted every physical ailment I know how to diagnose or treat."

"You said you had something else to try, though," Bellig said.

"I wanted to eliminate any possible medical issue first," Tanner replied. "Having done that, I believe the problem is spiritual."

"What do you mean?"

"I think we're dealing with a case of demonic possession," Father Tanner said. "I want to try an exorcism."

Bellig snorted. "Demons? I think you've just been stringing us along, trying to stall. You've got nothing."

"At this point," Tanner said, "what do you have to lose? He's getting worse; he won't survive much longer. Let me try this."

Bellig opened her mouth to reply, but she was interrupted by the sound of gunfire from outside.

"Carter," Tenik said. His eyes darted toward the ladder to the gunnery hatch. "Is it more of those crab things?"

"He'd be using the cannon," Bellig said, her eyes and pistol locked on Tanner. "Is this one of your tricks? Maybe your friends came back? I've had enough of this. Amber, Tenik, grab them."

Damien slammed his hand on the door controls while his other hand pulled the hidden pistol from its holster. The doors slid closed from either side, but Tenik ran forward and blocked them with the barrel of his rifle. The doors automatically recoiled from the obstruction, sliding back into the wall. Damien leaned out from the wall and fired a shot at Tenik outside, but it missed and ricocheted down the hallway.

In the meantime, Amber had frozen, not even moving for cover. Tanner ran in front of her and grabbed for Tenik's rifle, struggling to point the barrel at the ceiling.

Out in the hallway, Neekol ran down the hallway, away from the action. Bellig grabbed Eve with one hand and put the gun to her head. "Fire at them, dammit!" she shouted.

Tenik slid to the side, wresting his rifle from Tanner's grasp while getting out of Damien's line of fire. "I might hit the Captain's tank," he said.

"Damn the Captain!" Bellig snarled. "Take them out!"

"Not if you want her to live!" Damien shouted, grabbing Amber and putting his own pistol to her head.

"This isn't how we do things," Tanner hissed. He pressed himself up against the inside wall on the other side of the doorway.

"Normally, no," Damien said. "But right now, I'm feeling *very* flexible."

The sound of the gunnery hatch opening caught everyone's attention. "Carter?" Bellig called out. "Is that you?"

In answer, a scaled, blue humanoid figure dropped down from the hatch, bypassing the ladder entirely, and landed with a thud. He carried a primitive wooden spear with a jagged coral head. A bright red drop of blood fell audibly to the floor in the stunned silence.

"What the hell?" Damien muttered. He slammed the controls again, and the doors slid closed as Neekol, Tenik, and Bellig ran away from the creature toward the cargo hold, dragging Eve with them.

Ghenni skidded to a stop in the sand, gawking at the explosion in the sky. The flash had passed, and a small cloud of light gray smoke hung almost frozen in the air far above them. What could that have been?

Jun-Ha and Andrew slowed down, looking up alongside him. "That was a ship," Jun-Ha muttered. "There's a battle going on up there. We'd better turn back."

"Why?" Ghenni asked. "They may not even know we're here."

"Your ship just returned hours ago. Smart money is that they tracked you here."

"Who?" Andrew asked. "The guys who just exploded, or the ones who exploded them?"

"Beats me. But the winner probably has his sights on these ships, and they could get blasted from orbit any second."

"Then we must get our friends out first," Ghenni said.

Jun-Ha sighed, barely detectable amidst his panting. "You're right. Let's go."

The three of them took to running again, covering another hundred yards or so before a piercing shriek erupted, and three plumes of white smoke streaked across the sky at a mind bending speed. They touched down in the jungle to the right with deafening thuds that sent a flock of birds scattering to the wind.

Sharp ringing sounded in Ghenni's ears, and he just barely heard Jun-Ha shouting to the left of him, "They're landing troops! Make for the open cargo bay!" Ghenni ran with renewed energy toward the *Malika* on the right, into the welcoming cover of the ship. After a few moments, he glanced to the left and saw Andrew running leftward, toward the backside of the pirate ship. He must not have heard Jun-Ha's instruction over the deafening noise of the impacts, and he was too far to shout at now.

Ghenni and Jun-Ha finally arrived at the cargo bay, but it was stripped bare of any cargo that could have served as cover. He glanced back, and in the distance at the treeline, he saw humanoid figures advancing in barely-discernable combat stances. Ghenni had heard stories of soldiers dropping from the sky, protected by advanced technology to absorb the impact, when foot soldiers needed to be deployed quickly. But which side were these soldiers on? It was better not to risk it. Jun-Ha hit the button to close the door, and their view of the advancing marines was cut off. They'd bought themselves some time, but now what?

Chapter Nineteen

Bellig's surprisingly meaty hand had a good grip on Eve's shoulder, and the first officer dragged her bodily down the passage toward the cargo hold and away from the blue alien creatures. The Trenthan woman tossed her behind a pile of metal containers, and Eve managed only a glance down the hallway on the way down to her knees. The aliens weren't in a rush to close the distance, but they had their spears ready to throw. Where in the world did they come from, and why were they attacking now?

"What those?" Neekol asked, craning his neck out from behind a box to get a better look.

"How did they call reinforcements?" Tenik asked.

"They're not with the captives," Bellig replied. "They closed the door on them too. Must be natives or something. I didn't think this planet had any."

"They killed Carter with a home-made spear," Tenik said. "They're primitive, so how did they know how to open that hatch?"

"Doesn't matter," Bellig said. "Just waste them from here."

"Wait-" Neekol began, but Tenik was already leaning out with his rifle to take a shot. Before he had the gun to his shoulder, something whistled through the air, and the next thing Eve knew, Tenik stumbled back with an arrow in his upper arm. He swore in Trenthan and grabbed at the wound, blood seeping through his fingers. Bellig grunted in frustration and peeked out from behind the boxes herself, firing off her pistol before she could even see what was down the hallway. Only then did she venture a glance.

"They ducked into my quarters across the hall. Knew I should have locked it."

"What plan?" Neekol asked. He crouched down behind a wooden crate, his neck turned at a right angle to keep his head down, while he tore a strip from Tenik's shirt to tie around the wound. It didn't look critical to her untrained eye, but Eve knew enough not to remove the arrow if they didn't have to.

Bellig tapped her foot as she thought. "We send her down there to see what they want."

"But, how do they know I'm not with you?" Eve stammered. "They could just kill me."

"So, what do we care?" Bellig asked. "Then we'll know where we stand. But if you refuse, we kill you anyway."

Eve's mouth went dry in an instant, and her throat closed up. She wasn't ready to die, especially not stabbed through the heart with a spear or arrow by some weirdo alien she'd never seen before.

"No leverage," Neekol said.

"What?" Bellig snapped.

"She dies, no hostage. No trade Amber."

Bellig grunted and sneered. She checked the ammunition in her gun, as if by unconscious reflex. "We got any more weapons stashed here?" she asked.

"Nothing of ours," Tenik said through gritted teeth.

"What about you?" Bellig said, turning to Eve. "We haven't sorted everything here. Any weapons on your manifest?"

"I-I don't think so," Eve said.

Bellig grunted even louder, practically a roar at this point. "Then we wait. These blue things want something, so we wait for them to come to us for it."

A trio of thuds sounded outside, like artillery fire.

"What now?!" shouted Bellig. "Are we being fired on? Neekol, get to the terminal."

The bird creature ran low to the ground, darting from box to box, until he reached the computer terminal on the edge of the room. With a few keystrokes, he pulled up a sensor display and studied it for a moment. "Drop capsules," he finally said, cocking his head in confusion.

"Allegiance?"

"Can't tell."

"How many damn people are after us?" Bellig asked.

"Don't know," Neekol said. "But other ship just closed up. Someone on board."

"For the love of Mennas," Bellig muttered. "Tenik, Neekol, start tossing the crates we haven't inventoried. We may need some heavier weapons before this is over. Until then, we sit tight and wait for more information. Or for some of these people to kill each other."

When Andrew glanced back over to his right, he realized the others weren't with him anymore. Had they changed plans? He couldn't hear a thing on his right side after those drop capsules landed, so maybe he'd just missed it. Had they gone into the *Malika*? He looked over, and saw the cargo bay door closing. Guess he wasn't following them, then. In the distance, a trio of figures ran toward the ships, closing fast. Andrew guessed they were wearing some kind of powered armor or exoskeleton that let them survive the drop, and it seemed to be letting them cross the sand at an impressive speed. He wasn't sure what side they were on, but he was nothing if not hopeful. Andrew turned to face them and waved his arms to catch their attention.

"Hello there!"

A quick barrage of automatic weapons fire served as answer to his greeting, skittering through the sand about a foot to the right of him. So much for that.

He dove around the corner of the pirate's ship, shielding himself from the bullets and making his way around to the exterior ladder. The front end of the ship was partially underwater now that it was high tide, and he splashed his way to the bottom of the ladder and started climbing up.

Andrew kept his head low as he reached the top. When he could see the gun emplacement, he also spotted Carter's body. The spear was gone, but the savage hole it had left behind spoke to the violence of their fight. Blood stained his light blue shirt across the front, and gashes cut into his forearms where he'd tried to defend himself against the jagged clubs. His eyes stared emptily at the sky above him as he lay on his back. Andrew gulped, and grabbed the rifle from his body. His laser rifle was nearly done for anyway, and he was a little more familiar with the old-fashioned kinetic weapon.

He did his best to slide onto the roof with the lowest profile possible, shielding himself behind the bulk of the cannon and the barricade around it. The hatch hung open where the Badasal hadn't bothered to close it, and he shimmied inside. His last glance up showed the soldiers only about fifty yards away, but in their suits he couldn't determine which force they were aligned with. He dropped through the hatch and into the ship.

He swept the hallway with his pilfered rifle, even though his eyes were still adjusting to the interior light. To his left, the Badasal hunkered in Bellig's bedroom with the door open. They quickly waved him inside. As he followed them in, the crack of weapon fire sounded from down the hall in the cargo bay, followed immediately by the ping of bullets hitting the closed cockpit door. Above it all, he thought he heard the sound of Eve yelling at them not to shoot. Was that friendly fire, or was she a hostage? His stomach twisted at the thought.

"Thank you," he said to the Badasal in Korean. "What news?"

"Friends through door," Goom said, pointing across the hall at the captain's quarters. Andrew's eyes instinctively gravitated to the bloody tip of the spear he carried. More blood decorated a smaller club that hung on his hip. "Enemies in storeroom."

"Y-Yeah, I got that much," he stammered. "I need to get over there."

"Door locked."

Andrew scanned the room, and his eyes set on the intercom in the wall. He didn't see a way to send a private message to the captain's quarters, so if he asked for an opening, the pirates would hear it too. Risky, maybe, but he needed to see them.

He pressed the button. "Uh, Father, you read me? I'm coming over. Open the door please."

"Covering fire?" the Badasal warrior asked, gesturing around the corner down the hallway.

"No, don't shoot. I think they have my friend."

The door across the hall slid open, and Andrew spotted Damien, Father Tanner, and Amber standing around the captain's tank. No sign of Eve. That must have really been her that he heard earlier.

"What the hell, man?" Damien asked. "The blue guys are with you?"

"Long story," Andrew said. "I'm coming over."

"Go fast, then."

Andrew crouched down into a sprinting stance, then waited a beat or two to throw off the pirates' timing in case they decided to take a shot. With a quick silent prayer, he bolted across the gap, stumbling into the side of the tank before he could slow himself down. No bullet holes yet.

"Good to see you," Father Tanner said, grabbing him into a hug.

"You too, Father. And Damien." He looked over to where Amber sat slumped on the floor, her arms crossed. "And, uh, you too Amber, I guess. Is she on our side?"

"I'm a hostage, apparently," Amber said, rolling her eyes. "He put a gun to my head."

"Hey, I'm not proud of it," Damien said. "But desperate times, and all that."

"Fair enough," Andrew said.

"What about Ghenni?" Tanner asked.

"He's here. He's safe. I guess. I think he went into the *Malika* to get away from the soldiers."

"The *what* now?" Damien asked, cocking his head.

"The soldiers from the drop capsules. A ship got blasted out of the sky when we were charging in. I was hoping you could tell me who they were."

"I heard the booms, but I didn't know what it was," Damien said. "Who are the new guys?" He waved at the trio of Badasal warriors.

"The Badasal. They're native to the planet, and they've got a village on the other side of the island. The tall one is Goom, but their leader is a Korean human soldier. He's with Ghenni."

"OK, great, it *aaall* makes sense now," Damien said, rolling his eyes.

"I'll give you the long version later," Andrew said. "Anyway, what's the plan?"

"We've exhausted all medical diagnoses," Father Tanner said. "I was about to try an exorcism. Thank God you've arrived just in time to help me."

"Even *if* that's the problem with this guy," Damien said. "That does nothing to solve the whole hostage crisis. Or whatever crisis is happening outside."

"One problem at a time," Tanner said through gritted teeth. "I'm not going to surrender this soul to the enemy if I can avoid it."

"Right now," Damien said, "I'm more worried about our souls."

"I'm worried about everyone's souls!" Tanner shouted, slamming his fist on the wall. He froze and took a few deep breaths before continuing, while Damien raised his eyebrows and turned away. Tanner continued in deliberately measured tones. "I'm doing what I know to do, and trusting in God for the rest. Are you willing to assist me, Andrew?"

"If that's what you think is best," Andrew said, his voice wavering. "But these are... less than ideal conditions."

"Probably the worst conditions imaginable," Tanner said. "But with God, all things are possible."

"OK, you work on that," Damien said. "Give me that rifle, and I'll figure out something to get Eve back."

It was a relief, at least a little bit, for Ghenni to be back in the *Malika*, even if they were under attack by an unknown force.

"This is your ship, right?" Jun-Ha asked.

"Yes," said Ghenni.

"You've got to have weapons hidden around, or other defenses, yes?"

"I think it was all taken by the pirates. Can you fly it away? I know a little bit to help in the cockpit."

"No good," Jun-Ha said, shaking his head. "They'll blast us out of the sky, no problem. The only reason they haven't bombarded us from space already is they want something from us."

"What is it?"

"I don't know. If we can figure it out, maybe we can bargain."

They sank into thought, but in the silence, as Ghenni finally had a chance to catch his breath, he heard a beeping noise coming from the cockpit.

"What's that?" he asked.

"They're probably hailing us on comms," Jun-Ha said. "But we need a game plan before we answer. Who even knows you're here?"

"I don't know," Ghenni said. "As far as I know, no one. But this ship only recently returned from somewhere. Perhaps they made an enemy?"

"No doubt whoever they raided for supplies," Jun-Ha said, nodding in agreement. "But they were all off-loaded, so we can't offer them from here. They'd have to go to the other ship."

"Where all my friends are," Ghenni pointed out.

"True. And we can't negotiate anything until we know who's got control over the other ship. The last thing we want is the pirates cutting a deal with these guys, and tossing us to the wolves."

"We could hail the pirate ship, then."

Their conversation was interrupted by a series of metallic thuds from the cargo bay door. Sparks flew into the cavernous room as the familiar sound of a cutting torch began to crackle and hiss like a lit fuse.

"And let's hope they answer quick."

Chapter Twenty

"Bellig, being hailed." Neekol tapped away at the computer terminal and twisted his head around to check in with the first mate. "Should answer?"

"Who is it?" Bellig snarled.

"Says Consortium ship. Maybe trick."

"Did you have any run-ins with the Cons when you were out on the supply run?" Bellig asked, turning to Tenik.

"No, nothing," he replied.

"Then how would they know we were here?"

Tenik's eyes went wide with panic. "I have no idea."

Before she could issue any more commands, Neekol spoke up again. "Second hail," he said. "From *Malika*."

Eve perked up. Andrew had come back; she'd seen him come through the gunnery hatch. Was Ghenni in the other ship? Or was that whoever was in the drop capsules?

"Looks like you're surrounded," Eve said, steeling her voice as much as possible. "But you can use me as leverage. Make a deal for safe passage out of here by trading me."

"Even if those really are Consortium soldiers," Bellig said, "do you really think they know or care about you? You're nobody."

"But you don't have any other options."

Bellig grunted. "Answer the hail from the *Malika*."

Neekol tapped out a command, and an unfamiliar voice came over the intercom. "Ahoy, pirates!" it called out. "This is Park Jun-Ha of the Joseon Colonies Defense Force. With whom am I speaking?"

He sounded human, and spoke fairly fluent English, which was encouraging, but if those soldiers had taken over the *Malika*, that meant Ghenni was nowhere to be found. Eve's throat caught, and she struggled to force back a tear.

"This is Bellig of the freighter ship *Kuupon Luk*. You should know that I'm currently holding multiple hostages. I'm open to negotiating a deal."

"What is it you propose?"

"I want safe passage for myself and my crew to leave here unmolested. In exchange, I offer to free several Consortium citizens I'm holding as hostage, as well as turning over the notorious pirate captain Lopuul, who has a sizable bounty on his head, last I heard."

Tenik gritted his teeth, strode over to the terminal, and muted the channel. "This is mutiny!" he said. "You would bargain away our own captain?"

"He's dying," Bellig spat. "The doctor wasn't able to save him. He can get us out of one last scrape this way. And regardless, *I'm* first mate, and therefore acting commander. It's *my* call, not yours, and not *his* anymore."

Tenik pursed his lips and glared at Bellig for a moment. Neekol's head turned back and forth between the two a few times, watching the standoff unfold. Finally, Tenik slammed the mute button again and stepped away.

"What do you say?" Bellig asked.

"An interesting proposal," the man said. "I'll have to run it by my superiors. Stand by."

"That sounds like a good deal," Ghenni said.

"It would be a great deal," Jun-Ha replied, "*if* we could collect on it. We don't control shit outside this ship, and we won't even have that for long."

Ghenni looked back at where the cutting torch slowly traced its way down the door. The ship's allow was strong and thick, so they'd only made a few inches of progress, but within half an hour they'd be breaching the door with ease.

"But we know Andrew and your warriors were not able to take the ship. Though at least they're alive."

"Allegedly," Jun-Ha said. "Could be a ruse."

"What do we do now?"

"If Andrew and the Badasal couldn't take the ship, we won't either. The only way we're going to rescue them is to ally ourselves with the new soldiers."

"But we have nothing to bargain with."

"Bargaining time's over," Jun-Ha said, glancing back at the sparks from the torch. "We'll just have to surrender and hope we can reason with them." He reached out his hand, and Ghenni clasped it in a firm handshake.

"It has been good working with you."

"You as well," Jun-Ha said with a smile. "Time to run up the white flag."

"Are you ready?" Father Tanner asked.

Andrew shrugged. Tanner had his crucifix necklace outside his shirt, and Andrew held a crude cross he had cobbled together from a couple of surgical instruments tied together with tape. It wasn't much, but it was the closest to holy relics they were going to get while under siege on a pirate ship. "Ready as I'll ever be."

"Confidence, Andrew. We're ministers of the almighty creator God of the universe. His Spirit has the power to do this and much more."

"Right, yes. Of course."

Out of the corner of his eye, Tanner saw Damien back across the hall with the Badasal, trying to mime to them.

"Anything for me to do?" Amber asked sheepishly. She looked up from the corner near the ladder, her hands tied behind her back. Just a precaution, according to Damien.

"It's best that you not be seen crossing the hallway," Tanner said. "It might destroy their perception of you as a hostage. Please, just keep your distance and don't listen to anything he might say. The devil has a way of pushing your buttons, bringing out your guilt and shame to undermine you. That goes for you as well, Andrew."

"Can't we turn off the translation system?" Amber asked. "Or does he need to understand what you're saying?"

"She's got a point," Andrew said.

Father Tanner nodded, and tapped some buttons on the control panel to turn off the microphones. "That should do it."

Tanner said a silent prayer for protection before beginning. *O merciful Father, our only hope is in You. Protect us as we do battle against foes both spiritual and earthly. Grant us the grace and power to do Your will as it needs to be done. Amen.*

With a heavy sigh, Father Tanner held out his crucifix necklace and began to recite the exorcistic prayer. Immediately, Lopuul thrashed about in his tank with renewed force. The water inside almost seemed to be boiling, as the squid creature worked it up into a froth. Specks of water flew out of the tank and onto Tanner, but he ignored them as he continued the recitation.

"God arises; His enemies are scattered and those who hate Him flee before Him. As smoke is driven away, so are they driven; as wax melts before the fire, so the wicked perish at the presence of God."

The captain convulsed harder as Tanner continued with the prayer; he'd never seen him with such fury. Presumably blasphemous gurgles sounded from the water, hardly deadened by the glass in between them. Tentacles began to slam into the tank wall with an almost frightening force, blurring the images within from the vibrations.

"We drive you from us, whoever you may be, unclean spirits, all satanic powers, all infernal invaders, all wicked legions, assemblies and sects."

Crack.

A spider-web fracture appeared in the glass where Lopuul struck it with a tentacle. As Father Tanner continued his prayer, more blows rained on the glass in its weak point, and the cracks slowly expanded and thickened.

"Father..." Andrew muttered.

Before the priest could answer, water sprayed from the center of the damage, hitting Tanner square in the chest. The glass wall collapsed, the opening cascading into a torrent of broken glass and fetid water.

Father Tanner staggered back under the assault, and Lopuul leaped from the wave into his face. The alien's tentacles wrapped around his chest and arms, squeezing him with an inhuman force. Andrew ran to him and grabbed at the captain, pulling at the tentacles to wrest Tanner from its grasp.

He felt as if his bones were going to snap, and he struggled to get any air into his lungs. The creature's bizarre alien eyes were mere inches from his face as it sneered in demonic derision and tried to curse God in the open air. As blackness encroached on his peripheral vision, it focused his attention on Lopuul's face. And a strange mark that hadn't been there before. Right in the middle of the area Tanner had stitched up after the surgery, he saw a small, perfectly round puncture mark.

Tanner gasped for air as he felt the creature's grip slackening. Amber and Andrew struggled to pull the weakening tentacles from around him.

"Are you OK, Father?" Andrew asked.

"Yes, I think so," he choked out. "He's getting weaker. He's suffocating."

"We can't let him die!" Amber cried. "We need to get him into water!"

"Is there another tank anywhere?" Andrew asked.

"The ocean," Tanner said, as he pulled the last of the tentacles from him. "We have to get him into the ocean."

"Through the shooting gallery and past the hostile space marines?" Andrew asked.

"God has gotten us this far."

Andrew ran to the doorway and called out across the hallway. "Damien! We need covering fire. We're going out the gunner hatch."

"Are you insane?" he asked.

"It's debatable," Father Tanner replied.

"Just don't hit Eve, OK?" Andrew asked.

Damien shook his head and shouldered the rifle. "Give me a countdown."

Father Tanner picked up the now-limp figure out of the shards of broken glass, heaving him up on his shoulders. The creature had to weigh well over 100 pounds. It was going to be a struggle getting him up the ladder. Andrew silently counted down on his fingers, and when he dropped the last one, he darted out toward the ladder. Damien leaned out in the hallway and fired a series of three-round bursts down the passage.

Tanner followed close behind Andrew, doing his best to keep his grip on the captain with one hand while he held onto the ladder with the other. His legs burned with effort as he lifted the weight of two people up, rung by rung. As gunfire continued to erupt down the hallway, two of the Badasal saw what was happening and moved to help, pushing the two of them higher up while Andrew pulled them from above.

More gunfire responded from the cargo hold, and bullets pinged against the cockpit door past the ladder. Tanner felt the searing hot pain of a graze tearing open the flesh of his calf, but he pushed through. Finally, Andrew took the full weight of Lopuul onto the top of the ship and Tanner pushed himself out of the hole, into the bright morning sun and fresh salt air.

"Grab the head end," Tanner said, reaching for a bundle of tentacles. They swung the captain back and forth, counting down from three, and on the third swing, let the limp body go, splashing into the ocean. Lopuul was still for a moment, then stirred to life and darted off into deeper water.

"Is he just going to run off?" Andrew asked.

"I think he'll be back," Tanner replied.

"What's going on up there?" A voice called out behind them. Tanner turned around and saw a ragged-looking Asian man waving at the two of them. Surrounding him was Ghenni, along with three soldiers in 7-foot-tall combat exoskeletons. Heavy-duty ballistic armor plates and a tinted full-face helmet obscured their species from view, but Tanner recognized the triple-globe insignia on the chest: Consortium forces.

"Are they with you?" Tanner asked.

"I know Jun-Ha there, but not the soldiers," Andrew said.

They hurried down the exterior ladder, Tanner's feet landing in the soft, wet sand with a squish. "I'd be happy to explain it to you," Tanner said, "but we've got people in there who need rescuing. Can you help us?"

As he approached, one of the figures stepped forward, with an obscenely large caliber bolt rifle slung on his shoulder. His face-plate retracted into the suit with a click, revealing a dark-skinned human man squinting into the sun with a mischievous grin.

"Master Sergeant Sinha, at your service. Just give us the layout."

Chapter Twenty-One

"Where in the hells are they taking our bargaining chip?" Bellig roared. "They're cutting a deal without us!" Eve flinched instinctively from the anger that practically radiated from the first officer as she paced briskly back and forth behind their cover. Bellig looked ready to punch someone, and Eve hoped it wouldn't be her.

"He's not a bargaining chip," Tenik said. "He's our captain."

"Priest doctor," Neekol pitched in. "Maybe helping. Somehow."

"We're losing ground just sitting here," Bellig said. "We need more hostages."

"Amber's still down there," Eve said. "You're going to risk her life?"

Bellig leaned down and stared Eve directly in the eyes, studying her expression. "I think your people are soft. You travel with a preacher. Your captain isn't going to hurt her."

Eve steeled herself, trying hard not to give anything away with a twitch of her face. The Trenthan's gaze bored into her, demanding that she slip, and even against her better judgment, she couldn't help but fill the silence with something.

"The last patient the doctor treated? Damien planted a bomb inside him, hooked to a dead man's switch." She wasn't sure if her voice trembled, or she just imagined it.

Bellig smirked. "But he didn't set it off, did he?" The woman's pupils flicked back and forth, studying Eve's face. Her *glia* dangled close to Eve's lips, and her breath smelled like stale rations. Finally, with a satisfied smirk, she stepped back and adjusted the holster on her belt. "Like I said, he's soft. We're going in."

"What about those blue things?" Tenik asked.

"Neekol, can you lock down that room from here?"

"Need access cockpit," Neekol replied. "Or five minutes."

"Then we go fast and hard," Bellig said. "The blue things, I don't care about. Gun them down. The human captain gets kneecapped; he's the one we need. Got it?"

"Aye-aye, captain," Tenik said, hoisting his rifle up to his shoulder. Eve caught a hint of resignation to his tone.

Bellig reached down and took a smaller pistol from her boot. "Neekol, you bring up the rear with the hostage, and keep her in line with this." She handed it to the bird creature, and Neekol wrapped the three fingers on the end of his wing around it.

"We go on three. I'll cover left, Tenik you cover the blues on the right." She began to count.

"One."

"Two."

"Three."

The two Trenthans surged forward out from behind the boxes, guns at the ready. They stepped forward quietly, low to the ground, but moving fast. Eve shuffled along behind them, keeping up against the wall. Halfway down the hallway, a cry rose up from the room where the blue creatures holed up. The three aliens ran out toward them, wielding spears and clubs as they let out an ear-piercing battlecry of "Ah-ah-ah-ah-ah!" Tenik and Bellig fired as soon as they appeared, and the one furthest back threw himself back into the room before he loosed his spear, grazing Bellig's arm as she spun away. Another threw his spear, sending it sailing just over Tenik's head and into the cargo hold, before dropping to several rounds from Tenik's rifle. The biggest of the aliens just charged forward, swinging a large club studded with jagged rocks. It came down in an arc toward Tenik, and he blocked the first blow with his rifle. Tenik pushed back, trying to angle his rifle barrel toward the blue man's chest, but it swept his legs out from under him. As the club came down at his head, Bellig fired three times, catching him in the thigh and shoulder, and sending him down with a thud.

Damien leaned out of the door on the other side with Carter's stolen rifle and took a split second to survey the scene, making eye contact with Eve. "Stay down!" he yelled, and Eve dropped to the floor. Damien fired a volley down the hallway at waist height, but Bellig dropped to her stomach as well, bringing her pistol up in front of her. A pair of hands reached out from behind Damien, bound with rope, and slipped over his head, sending his gun swinging toward the ceiling as his neck was pulled forcefully back.

"I told you not to shoot at them!" Amber's voice cried from inside the room. Damien tried to wrestle free of her, but she wrenched him to the side. As soon as Damien's gun pointed the other way, Eve dove across the hallway onto Bellig's back. She landed hard, and the Trenthan woman grunted at the impact.

Eve reached forward, clawing at her arms for the pistol. She couldn't get a good grip, but it was distracting enough that Damien had time to duck back into the room before she got off another shot, throwing himself and Amber back through the doorway.

"Neekol!" Bellig shouted. Eve didn't dare look back at what he was doing, and focused on grabbing at the gun. Bellig rolled over onto her side, then threw an elbow back at Eve, catching her in the face. Warm blood gushed from her nose and into her mouth with a coppery taste, and she felt a feathery hand grab at her collar from behind. A gunshot rang out next to her head, setting her ears ringing, and the fighting stopped.

"Drop weapons, or else," Neekol said. "Not playing."

"Alright, alright," Damien said from around the corner. His rifle clattered to the ground in the doorway then slid farther in. Damien stepped out, his hands above his head and the rope cinched around his neck.

Bellig slowly stood up, along with Tenik. He kicked the downed aliens, confirming that one was dead and the big one out of commission, then gestured with his rifle for the other three survivors to bunch up.

"Get over there with them," he said to Eve.

She pulled herself to her feet, then wiped the blood from her face. "Well," she said, "it was a nice try."

"Sorry, kid," Damien said.

"You alright, Amber?" Bellig asked. She undid the ropes at her wrists, freeing her hands, while Tenik kept his rifle trained on Damien.

"Yeah," Amber said, rubbing at the rope marks. "I'll be fine." She reached up to her busted lip and gingerly felt the wound.

"So what's your plan with us?" Damien asked. He put his arm around Eve, and even though they were at the end of the road, it was a little comfort to be back together.

"I'm gonna barter you with your friends out there," Bellig said.

"What friends?" Damien asked.

Before she could answer, the gunnery hatch above creaked. Bellig swung her weapon up to intercept whoever was coming down, but all that came through the opening was a small object, clattering along the floor.

"Flashb-" Tenik started to shout, until he was drowned out by the blinding light and deafening boom of an explosion in the hallway. Eve couldn't see or hear, but she felt Damien's arm wrap tight around her, and she buried her head in his shoulder. The high-pitched ringing of her ears was cut through by a few quick, deep thuds of gunfire, and she shut her eyes tight, seeing only the afterimage of the initial explosion.

After a few moments, she felt another hand touch her arm. She opened her eyes, and could just make out Andrew in her peripheral vision.

"Are you OK?" he asked, his voice muffled by the ringing in her ears. She nodded her head.

"Yeah, yeah, I think so."

As her vision cleared, she looked around and saw three strangers in heavy combat armor securing the rest of the pirate crew with restraints. The leader, a dark-skinned man with a heavy rifle, turned to the group.

"Situation is under control. Now, does someone want to tell me what in hell is going on here?"

"And I *believe* that's where you came in," Andrew said. He glanced around at the others for confirmation, and Jun-Ha and the rest of the crew of the *Malika* all nodded their heads. "So can you fill us in on how you guys fit into the picture?"

The leader of the soldiers, Master Sergeant Sinha, leaned back on the crate he'd dragged into the sand for a seat, and took a drag from his cigar. Nearby, a shuttle had joined the two larger ships on the beach, and a squad of space marines was busily engaged with inspecting all of the cargo. A ship doctor treated the injuries of Goom and the captured pirates, while a couple of the soldiers kept a close eye on them.

Sinha blew out a puff of smoke before speaking. "We're with the Bharat Corporate Space Defense. I don't know if you all keep up with the state of the war, but things are heating back up, and the battle lines have shifted recently. This planet is recently in Consortium control, and we're on mission to patrol the border space. Our scanners picked up a pair of Brotherhood ships, one in pursuit of the other. Didn't make sense, so we investigated. Caught up with the pursuing ship in orbit here, and took it out when it powered weapons. They dropped us in to investigate the landing zone. As you know," he said, pointing to Jun-Ha, "there used to be a Consortium outpost on this island."

"And can be again!" Jun-Ha said, jumping to his feet and saluting. "First Sergeant Park Jun-Ha, reporting for duty!"

Captain Sinha sighed and took another drag. "There may be a problem with reactivating your commission," he finally said.

"What's that?"

"You've been living behind enemy lines for years. The brass isn't going to buy your story, and even if they did, they could still nail you for violating regulations in a hundred different ways. Passing out military-grade weapons to civilians, inviting un-contacted natives into a secure Consortium facility, getting us involved in a *war* between their factions. I could go on."

Jun-Ha's face fell, and his saluting hand dropped limp to his side.

"That's ridiculous," Andrew said. "He should be treated as a hero."

"I agree," Sinha said. "He *is* a hero. But the fact that he was left behind is egg on the face of whichever commander signed off that this place was successfully evacuated. Why face embarrassment when they can just grind you in the system instead?"

"Let him come with us then," Damien said. "We could use a solid fighter in our completely legitimate independent shipping business."

"Right, of course," Sinha said with an exaggerated wink.

"I appreciate the offer," Jun-Ha said, straightening back up. "But I'm a military man, through-and-through. I'd rather face the court martial and get back to fighting the enemy."

"Maybe there's a way to split the difference," Sinha said. "I could issue you a letter of marque."

"What's that?" Andrew asked.

"Think of it as an official pirate license. You promise to only target Brotherhood ships, and you can operate as privateers, with the full faith of the Consortium government behind you."

"But I'm not a pirate," Damien said. The rest of the crew nodded along.

"But *they* are," Sinha said, pointing at the captive pirate crew with his cigar. "Seems like they need some new leadership."

"I don't know if they'll go for it," Andrew said. "We did just attack their ship."

"Well, they committed a lot of crimes against you in Consortium space. The alternative for them is to face a quick military court before we leave, followed by the appropriate sentence. I bet between the two of us, we could talk them into it."

"An intriguing offer," Jun-Ha said. "Come to think of it, the military might be a bit too strict for me after living here for so long."

"What about Lopuul?" Andrew asked. "Father, you said he'd be back."

"Once the drugs are out of his system, I think he'll be back to normal," Father Tanner said.

"Drugs? What about the possession hypothesis?"

"Well, while he was trying to strangle me, I noticed a fresh puncture mark. Combine that with that missing syringe, and the sedative being used up faster than I could account for, and it seems someone was injecting him with something."

"Who would do that?" Andrew asked. "They all seemed to love him."

"Not Bellig," Eve said, shaking her head. "She was ready to sell him out to negotiate."

"And of course, she would take over as captain if he died," Damien pitched in.

"But what about the aversion to your crucifix? And the religious mania?"

"You know," Captain Sinha said, "I looked up this Lopuul in our database. He's known to the Consortium, with a pretty big price on his head. He was actually held captive for a while, and interrogated, very, uh, *vigorously*, by a human military chaplain. The guy got court martialed for it. Nasty stuff."

"So nothing supernatural there," Damien said. "He just hates priests, and recognized the symbols."

"You said there's a price on his head," Andrew said. "So are you going to hunt him down?"

"As much as I'd love to spend a week fishing on the beach," Sinha said, "I don't have the time or equipment for that. I'm more inclined to leave him marooned here. That's a fitting punishment for a pirate, right? Unless our new privateer wants to take a crack at the bounty, that is."

"Maybe for the sake of morale, I'd better pass," Jun-Ha said, stroking his beard.

"By the way," Sinha said, turning to Damien. "Just how legitimate is this shipping business of yours?"

"As legitimate as, say, two cases of Caloovian malt whiskey?"

"Sounds pretty legitimate," Sinha said, smiling and nodding. "Now, Captain Park, what do you say we talk to your new crew, see if we can come to some kind of arrangement?"

Sinha stood up and tossed his cigar into the ocean, and the two of them strode over to where the captive pirates sat in handcuffs in a circle.

"I guess we'll be taking off soon, then," Andrew said.

"Just as soon as we get my cargo loaded and door repaired," Damien said.

"Sinha said he'd help us out with that," Eve said.

"Something wrong?" Tanner asked.

"I guess I just feel a little bad for the Badasal here," Andrew said. "They fought for us, and now we're just abandoning them."

"I know what you mean," Father Tanner said.

"We *are* missionaries, you know," Andrew said. "Should we, you know, start a new mission here?"

Tanner sank into thought for a moment before replying. "We are missionaries, yes, but we're also doctors. I believe that's part of our calling that we can't fulfill here."

"I just feel like we should do something to help them," Andrew said.

A commotion rose up back where the pirates were, and Andrew looked over just in time to see Bellig rise from the ground, hands still cuffed behind her back, and charge at Sinha and Jun-Ha. Sinha effortlessly redirected her charge, sending her sprawling to the sand face-first. Jun-Ha followed up with a kick to the head, which collapsed her into unconsciousness.

"Looks like she's been relieved of command," Damien said.

Jun-Ha jogged back over to the rest of them. "Well, they've agreed to the terms, in light of the alternative. Bellig has graciously offered to stay behind to be with the captain."

"It was a pleasure serving with you," Andrew said, sticking out his hand.

"You as well," Jun-Ha said, shaking it. He offered his hand to Ghenni as well. "You also. Now I'd better check out my new ship."

As the day wore on, the soldiers helped both crews load their respective cargo, minus the whiskey and a few weapons that Sinha simply couldn't look the other way on. They had a repair crew down to patch up the door and run through some checks, and by nightfall, they were ready to take off. Andrew entered the cockpit with Damien as he ran pre-flight checks, and sat in the chair next to him.

"You need something?" Damien asked.

"Actually yes," Andrew said. "Just a quick stop on the way out."

Epilogue

As the big sky-box flew away, Goom studied the book he'd been handed by the man they'd found in the jungle. He had seen such things in the hands of Jun-Ha many times, and the old man had taught him what the strange shapes meant, and the sounds that went with them. He pulled back the front panel, and began to read.

"In the beginning, God created the Heavens and the Earth..."

If you enjoyed this story, please consider leaving a 5-star rating and review at Amazon, Goodreads, or wherever you like to find new books.

For more of my work, visit my website at JosephLKellogg.com.

www.ingramcontent.com/pod-product-compliance
Lightning Source LLC
Chambersburg PA
CBHW021531250626
47154CB00006BA/2071